W9-AWA-298

Praise for

THE NINTH DAUGHTER

"An exciting new mystery series set in revolutionary Boston. Abigail Adams could become my favorite historical sleuth."

—Sharon Kay Penman, author of *Devil's Brood*

"Barbara Hamilton plunges us into colonial Boston, where we walk beside the legendary Abigail Adams as she tries to find justice for a murdered young woman while also helping with the birthing pangs of a new nation."

—Victoria Thompson, author of *Murder on Lexington Avenue*

"[An] exceptional debut . . . While bringing to life such historical figures as Sam Adams and Paul Revere, Hamilton transports the reader to another time and place with close attention to matters like dress, menus, and the monumental task of doing laundry. Historical fans will eagerly look forward to the next in this promising series." —*Publishers Weekly*

"Hamilton . . . has just the right touch to guide the intelligent Abigail through the dangerous shoals of being a patriot while seeing the good side of the colonies' English rulers. There are no missteps here in what should prove to be a captivating series for all historical fans." —*Library Journal*

"The wry repartee between Abigail and John, together with the fact that this clandestine investigation of the murder of loose women would never have made the official record, make Hamilton's debut believable and gripping." —*Kirkus Reviews*

"A deep historical mystery. Based on true activities of that time, Ms. Hamilton weaves a tale that could have actually taken place . . . A finely written first in a new series story with a surprise ending. I am eager to see what comes next."

—*The Romance Readers Connection*

"The story line provides a deep look at Boston as rebellion is in the air. Fans will want to join the tea party hosted by Ms. Hamilton with guests being a who's who of colonial Massachusetts." —*The Mystery Gazette*

Berkley Prime Crime titles by Barbara Hamilton

THE NINTH DAUGHTER

A MARKED MAN

A Marked Man

Barbara Hamilton

BERKLEY PRIME CRIME, NEW YORK

THE BERKLEY PUBLISHING GROUP
Published by the Penguin Group
Penguin Group (USA) Inc.
375 Hudson Street, New York, New York 10014, USA
Penguin Group (Canada), 90 Eglinton Avenue East, Suite 700, Toronto, Ontario M4P 2Y3, Canada
(a division of Pearson Penguin Canada Inc.)
Penguin Books Ltd., 80 Strand, London WC2R 0RL, England
Penguin Group Ireland, 25 St. Stephen's Green, Dublin 2, Ireland (a division of Penguin Books Ltd.)
Penguin Group (Australia), 250 Camberwell Road, Camberwell, Victoria 3124, Australia
(a division of Pearson Australia Group Pty. Ltd.)
Penguin Books India Pvt. Ltd., 11 Community Centre, Panchsheel Park, New Delhi—110 017, India
Penguin Group (NZ), 67 Apollo Drive, Rosedale, North Shore 0632, New Zealand
(a division of Pearson New Zealand Ltd.)
Penguin Books (South Africa) (Pty.) Ltd., 24 Sturdee Avenue, Rosebank, Johannesburg 2196, South Africa

Penguin Books Ltd., Registered Offices: 80 Strand, London WC2R 0RL, England

This book is an original publication of The Berkley Publishing Group.

This is a work of fiction. Names, characters, places, and incidents either are the product of the author's imagination or are used fictitiously, and any resemblance to actual persons, living or dead, business establishments, events, or locales is entirely coincidental. The publisher does not have any control over and does not assume any responsibility for author or third-party websites or their content.

Copyright © 2010 by Moon Horse, Inc.
Cover illustration by Griesbach & Martucci.
Cover design by Judith Lagerman.
Interior text design by Laura K. Corless.

All rights reserved.
No part of this book may be reproduced, scanned, or distributed in any printed or electronic form without permission. Please do not participate in or encourage piracy of copyrighted materials in violation of the author's rights. Purchase only authorized editions.
BERKLEY® PRIME CRIME and the PRIME CRIME logo are trademarks of Penguin Group (USA) Inc.

FIRST EDITION: October 2010

Library of Congress Cataloging-in-Publication Data

Hamilton, Barbara, 1951–
A marked man : an Abigail Adams mystery / Barbara Hamilton. — 1st ed.
p. cm.
ISBN 978-0-425-23708-3
1. Adams, Abigail, 1744–1818—Fiction. 2. Lawyers' spouses—Fiction. 3. Sons of Liberty—Fiction. 4. Murder—Investigation—Fiction. 5. Massachusetts—History—Colonial period, ca. 1600–1775—Fiction. I. Title.
PS3558.A4215M37 2010
813'.54—dc22

2010014888

PRINTED IN THE UNITED STATES OF AMERICA

10 9 8 7 6 5 4 3 2 1

For Hazel

Special thanks to Peggy Wu

A Marked Man

One

"She's dead," said Abigail softly, and knew it to be true.

Her husband looked up from a cold Sabbath breakfast of bread, salt butter, and cider, the cows having only that week come into the new spring's milk. "Who's dead?"

"I don't know her name." Abigail slid last Monday's *Boston Gazette* across the table to him, profane reading that her parson father would never have permitted on the Lord's Day, no matter what retaliation the colony was expecting from an outraged Crown.

RAN AWAY

Upon the 26th of Feb. 1774 in the Morning. A Negro Woman, from the house of Thomas Fluckner, in Milk Street. She is twenty-three years of age, of Medium height and complexion, rather freckled, with prominent front teeth. She is well-spoken and reads well. She left

behind her a Child of two years, and a Babe of 3 months.
A Reward will be given for information leading to her capture.

"I fail to notice"—John peered at Abigail over the oval rims of his spectacles—"the passage in this advertisement announcing this poor young woman's decease. Or do you infer her demise from the circumstance that any sane person would prefer slavery to death?"

"I infer her demise from the fact that no woman will desert her children for her freedom. Certainly not an infant at breast."

"My dearest Portia." John Adams folded the newspaper, glanced a trifle guiltily across at his son and namesake—six years old and consuming his bread-and-butter with the studied appearance of total deafness. Young John Quincy Adams was already aware that if he showed undue attention to this un-Sabbath-like discussion, the interesting topic would cease. John lowered his voice. "My dearest wife, sometime you must accompany me to the magistrate's court. There I can introduce you to any number of perfectly free women in this city who would cheerfully desert their children for the price of a bottle of gin."

Abigail was obliged to admit that her husband had a point. As the daughter of a country parson, and the wife of a Boston lawyer, she had seen maternal misconduct that would have made Medea gasp.

But something about the way John tucked the newspaper away into his coat pocket, with the implied admonition that circumstances that would lead a young woman to abandon children so helpless were matters that could be put off until Monday, roused her contentious side. "In the morning?" she asked. "In broad daylight, when she could as easily walk out of her master's house carrying her babe as not? 'Twould be understandable, if she and her owners were on a journey, and the surety of her freedom were thrown against the fact that her children were back in some place where retrieving them would cost her her chance. But that isn't the case."

John opened his mouth to expound some precedent from either his own experience in the Colony Courts of Massachusetts or from the collected decisions of British judges that made up his legal library—*or from the annals of ancient Rome, belike, knowing John*—then closed it again. His blue eyes—rather protuberant in a round, short-nosed face—narrowed suddenly in thought.

Abigail reiterated, more to herself than to John, "The woman has come to harm."

She rose from the table, folded her napkin and ringed it, and went to help Charley dispose of the last of his bread-and-butter. At three, her middle son was a fussy eater, far likelier to experiment with how many times he could dunk bread into his cider before its inevitable dissolution, than to actually consume much. "Time to finish," she informed him. "You shall be a hungry boy by dinnertime."

He regarded her with enormous blue eyes, clearly without the slightest idea of how long that was going to be and with only the dimmest recollection of his previous experience with this kind of improvident starvation. "I shall eat it, if you won't," offered Johnny, not out of greediness, Abigail was certain, but because he knew the suggestion would have its effect: Charley quickly wolfed down his soggy breakfast. Johnny and Nabby—a few months short of her ninth birthday and quiet as a little barn-fairy—cleared away the dishes and folded their own and their brother's napkins, rinsing the plates but leaving them stacked on the sideboard for a more thorough washing tomorrow. Abigail knew houses in Boston where not even that much work was performed on the Sabbath, but she drew the line at it. A God who spent so many verses of Leviticus discussing the purification of any vessel that has so much as touched mice, moles, tortoises, or chameleons would *not* consider it an honor to have dishes left unrinsed overnight in His name.

As the children went upstairs to ready themselves for church, John unfolded the *Gazette* and reconsidered the advertisement by the strengthening gray light of the kitchen's wide windows.

"I think you may be right, Portia."

Abigail smiled at her old nickname, which he'd called her during their courtship: Shakespeare's intrepid lady lawyer. Even ten years ago, they'd both known that were it possible for a girl to obtain the education to do so, Abigail would have made a fine lawyer herself.

He went on, "'Twere another man I'd think, the girl was driven by desperation. But though Fluckner's an ass, and he's toad-eaten for the governor so that it's a wonder he doesn't have warts from his lips to his hairline . . ." He shook his head. "He has no name for being a cruel master, nor for meddling with the women in his household."

"But he would sell children left behind. The mother would know this."

"Curious." He drank the rest of his cider, which was growing cold. The bells of Boston's earlier-assembling congregations—the French Meeting-House on School Street and the Anabaptists over by the Mill-Pond—had not yet begun to sound, but Abigail's ear was cocked for them as she cleared her own plate and John's. Once the early bells started up, it was time to go upstairs for the children and herd her family toward the door. "Why should anyone do harm to a slave-woman? Unless she's returned or been found"—he checked the date on the paper—"in the course of this week. Here, let me do that—"

As he sprang up to forestall her putting another log on the kitchen hearth a tremendous thump sounded upstairs, followed by a furious confusion of treble voices. John's face crimsoned, and he hurled the wood into the fire. "Drat those children, can they not respect the Sabbath?"

"Not when they were born with your temper, dearest," replied Abigail, fetching the tongs to straighten the log.

As she did so, she made out Nabby shouting, "'Tisn't true! You're a liar!"

"So are you!"

And Pattie, the fourteen-year-old hired girl, cried, "Such words on a Sunday—!"

Small feet rattled in the boxed-in spiral of the stairwell, and a small body caromed off its corners. The next moment Nabby flung herself through the kitchen door and skidded to a stop before Abigail. Had she been a year younger, Abigail reflected, her daughter would have grabbed her around her waist.

"Mama, you wouldn't run away, if you were a slave, and leave us, would you?"

"She would." Johnny almost fell through the doorway behind her, pale hair tousled and neckcloth pulled awry. He could never bear to have his older sister get to anything before he did.

"Wouldn't!"

"Would!"

"Liar!"

The boy stepped back as Nabby's hand jerked, as if she would hit him, but she remembered the holy day and stayed herself. He made sure all was safe before turning to Abigail again. "You'd value freedom more than *anything*." Johnny looked up at his mother with those disconcerting light blue eyes. "And *anything* means *us*."

Abigail was spared the answer to this conundrum by Pattie's voice calling out upstairs, "Charley—!" and the wild clatter of descending feet, followed by the inevitable crash and series of thumps, then, comfortingly, Charley's wails, which indicated that the boy had not knocked himself senseless. Still, John and Abigail were both across the kitchen and at the door to the hallway when Pattie came down the stairs with eighteen-month-old Tommy in her arms, and knelt beside the stairwell door where Charley sat clutching his head and howling.

"There!" Abigail was on her knees beside the child in the next second, moving aside the round pink hand and the silky light brown hair to ascertain that the damage was, in fact, no more than a bruise above the bridge of his snub nose. "And how did you come by that, sir?"

"Fell down!"

"And were you walking slowly?"

Charley only sobbed and held out his arms; Abigail gathered him in and kissed the brow above the injury.

"A gentleman walks in the house, sir," she said sternly, and brushed—very gently—the baby-soft quiff of hair aside. "*And* on the Sabbath! What must the Lord think of you?"

"He's always running," pointed out Nabby righteously. "Mama, you wouldn't leave us, if you were a slave and leaving us was the only way you could be free? Johnny says you would."

"*I* wouldn't mind," declared Johnny, who already showed signs of wanting to grow up to be an ancient Roman. "I would rejoice that Mother valued liberty above all things."

"You wouldn't!" Nabby took Charley's hand and led the boy back toward the kitchen, throwing a glance over her shoulder at Johnny. "You'd cry."

"Would not!" He lunged at her and Abigail caught his arm with the deftness of long practice.

Why don't my children ever argue over normal things? "What I do not value," stated Abigail, "nor does God either, is children who quarrel on the Lord's Day. And there's the meeting-bell," she added, as John—who had preceded them all back into the kitchen—put into her hand the clean washrag, wrapped around a handful of the snow that still lay inches deep and iron-hard in the yard.

"Nabby started it—"

"Don't contradict your mother, sir," said John.

Johnny—who contradicted everybody these days and heard this admonition a great deal—looked instantly abashed. "I'm sorry, Mama."

At least he no longer protests that he's only telling the truth.

"I'll do that, Mrs. Adams." Pattie had set Tommy down at a safe distance from the hearth—not that anywhere in the kitchen was a safe distance from the hearth, as quickly as the boy moved—and took the washrag from Abigail's hand. "Though we should by rights have a piece of fresh meat for it—There's my brave boy," she added encouragingly, as Charley glanced from her to his mother, clearly wondering if renewed protestations of mortal injury would serve to keep her at his side with the meeting-house bell ringing around the corner on Brattle Street.

He evidently concluded that they would not, and held out

his arms for Pattie. The girl—the daughter of neighbors of the family's farm in Braintree across the bay—had practically grown up in the kitchen of the Adams farm herself and was much more an older sister to the children than a servant. She was friendly and pretty and much taken with the bustle and busyness of Boston. With the first notes of the Anabaptists' off-key bell, Nabby had gone to gather everyone's cloaks and scarves from the cupboard by the back door, and Johnny to dump a shovelful of hearth-coals into the fire-box that it was his duty to carry to their pew. Charley, at three, and little Tommy were too young to attend the meeting-house with their parents yet, so it was Pattie who stayed with them during the first service. At eight, almost nine, Abigail deemed Nabby old enough to look after the three boys when she, John, and Pattie returned to church for the afternoon service after dinner.

When John laid the folded *Gazette* on the sideboard, Pattie glanced at it, asked hesitantly, "Is there word about England yet, Mr. Adams?" and despite the bell that tolled like a nagging conscience, John turned back. "About the King, I mean," continued Pattie, "and what he means to do about the tea?" She sounded as apprehensive as if she, and not a gang of *unknown persons* disguised as Indians, had dumped three hundred and forty-two chests of East India Company tea into Boston Harbor.

"Nothing yet." John smiled encouragingly at the girl. "Best we not worry over what we don't know."

Pattie bit her underlip and nodded, clearly trying to look as if she hadn't heard the rumors that had begun to fly around the town in the ten weeks since John's wily cousin Sam had led the Sons of Liberty in this act of protest, about what the Crown's reaction would be. Damage was estimated at some

$90,000. Given Boston's history of riots, protests, and stubborn disobedience to every effort of the King to establish royal control over the town and the Colony of Massachusetts, only the most delusional optimists could believe that retribution would not be crushing.

"They wouldn't send to arrest you, would they, Mr. Adams?"

Abigail paused in the act of taking off her day-cap, tucking up the heavy coil of her sable hair, conscious of the swift glance that passed between her two older children.

"Arrest me?" John widened his eyes at the girl. "For remaining peacefully at home on the night of the ruckus? As any of my good neighbors will attest."

This made Nabby giggle. Even at the age of eight, she knew perfectly well that no member of the mysterious Sons of Liberty was ever without a dozen witnesses to his spotless conduct, whatever he'd been doing. Johnny, ever the stickler, asked, "Then it's all right, Father, to lie to the King's officers?"

Another man—*Cousin Sam, for instance*, reflected Abigail—would have answered the question with a broad wink that said, *Well, what do YOU think, my boy?* But John replied soberly, "'Tis never 'all right' to lie, Johnny. But men, when they are grown to the age of judgment, are sometimes forced to it by the threat of greater evil that would come upon others should the whole of the truth be told. Only God knows whether this is 'all right' or not. And we are now," he added, scooping his Bible and hat from the sideboard, "well and truly late—"

Johnny picked up his own small hat, pulled his scarf over his fine blond hair, and jammed the hat on top for warmth, as Abigail put on a fresh cap and tied the strings of Nabby's hood. *And now the whole of the congregation will see us troop in during the opening reading . . .*

John picked up the little metal fire-box of hot coals and they turned toward the door into the yard—nobody in Boston went in and out their own front doors except on the most formal of occasions—and stopped with a sort of shock at the sight of looming shadows beyond the misted windows. Two men . . . Nabby caught Abigail's hand, as if all this talk of treason, liberty, and arrest had conjured the redcoat troops from their camp. A sharp knock sounded on the panels and a voice called, "John? Are you there?"

Cousin Sam.

Who should, Abigail reflected, *be in church—which is where WE should be—*

John opened the door. It was wily Cousin Sam, all right, wrapped up in his gray greatcoat and a dozen scarves, knocking the snow off his boots on the scraper. The muffled shape at his heels was the street-level organizer of the Sons of Liberty's information network, silversmith Paul Revere.

Revere pulled the door to behind them as they stepped inside, for the morning was like frozen iron.

Sam said, "The British have arrested Harry Knox."

Harry Knox, aged twenty-four, bookseller, was responsible for printing and distributing any number of seditious broadsides penned by the Sons of Liberty . . . and, under a variety of pseudonyms, by John. One of which, Abigail knew, was to have been printed in the cellar of his Cornhill Street shop last night. "The British—"

John asked, quite calmly, "Did they find his press? Or the pamphlets?"

Sam shook his head. "Not that I've heard. They took him on his way to church. He's being charged with murder."

Two

Abigail was accustomed to the sensation she periodically experienced of wanting to smite the husband of her bosom over the head with a stick of firewood.

She knew, when John looked at her following Cousin Sam's announcement, that the next words out of his mouth were going to be the request that she take the children on to church while he and Sam consulted on the matter, leaving her to speculate, through the two and a half hours of the Reverend Cooper's sermon, upon who young Harry—whose youth had been surprisingly rowdy for a scholarly bookseller—was supposed to have murdered and why it was the British Army authorities who had come for him rather than the Boston constabulary.

And she knew, too, that if she was going to set a good example to the children about refraining from quarrels on the Sabbath, she could not protest.

Feeling blackmailed, she said brightly, "Come now Johnny,

Nabby, we are woefully late," and took each child by the hand. John handed his Bible to Nabby, and Sam—whom Abigail would cheerfully have brained with a skillet—opened the door for them.

As she had anticipated, the entire congregation of the Brattle Street Meeting-House turned in its pews and stared as she led her children—fatherless—down the aisle in the middle of the first reading of the service, to the little white-washed cubicle of the Adams family pew.

Devoting the whole of her mind and heart to the Reverend Cooper's argument, "The State of the Soul Laid Bare before the Eyes of God," was as difficult for her, she realized, as it was for Nabby and Johnny under ordinary circumstances: a reminder to herself, she reflected wryly, to be mindful that her adult concentration was only a matter of practice and degree, and not any special quality of adulthood. Given sufficient distraction—the possibility that the Provost Marshal of the King's Sixty-Fourth Regiment might be even now on his way to arrest John for sedition, for instance—she was no more capable than her six-year-old son of focusing her thoughts.

"For behold, God did not set his mark upon Cain in the spirit of vengefulness, but in the spirit of forgiveness, that any that slew Cain should be avenged sevenfold; even Cain who had slain his brother and brought murder into the world."

Murder. Harry Knox?

Five years ago, one might have believed it possible. Today—

Tall, fat, and scholarly, Harry had spent the years of his early teens running with the South End street-gangs and had been acknowledged as the best fistfighter in many a Pope's Night brawl. He had helped found the Boston Grenadiers, one of the patriot militia companies, and in his position as second-in-command he'd had no trouble trouncing whoever he needed to among the ranks. But with the acquisition of his own bookshop, he had consciously and firmly put his rough-and-tumble youth behind him.

Nabby's eyes were closed. Abigail nudged her sharply. Johnny, on the far side of the little girl with the fire-box on the floor between their feet, was reading his father's Bible. As a Christian, Abigail knew she shouldn't countenance such inattention to the sermon, but at least it would improve his command of the language. Not every six-year-old could manage those archaic phrases.

"When Cain in his sin cried out before God, *My punishment is greater than I can bear,* God's punishment of Cain was not death, even though he had murdered his brother, but exile, that he might learn of his punishment what it was like to have no brother forever and to be afraid . . ."

Who would Harry have had the opportunity—or the desire—to harm? He was a loyal friend, but his only family was his younger brother; and these days, Harry was far more likely to talk his way out of trouble than to resort to violence. Besides, if he'd cracked a thief or burglar over the head with a poker, the charge would be manslaughter, and his captors, the local Watch, not the Provost Marshal.

For the British military to be involved, the crime had to be one that touched the Crown. And in these times—given that Harry and his Grenadiers had been among the men who'd stood guard at Griffin's Wharf in December to keep the British tea-ships from unloading their cargoes—the only crime Abigail could think of that would involve arrest by the Provost Marshal would be treason.

That being the case, was Harry's arrest only the first, with more to come?

Abigail shivered, and not simply because yesterday's snow lay thick in Brattle Street outside.

"We bear the stain of our deeds on our foreheads, or on our right hands, as the Book of Revelation teaches us: *Though thou wash thee with nitre, and take thee much soap, yet thine iniquity is marked before me, saith the Lord God.* Think you, before you accomplish any deed for your own willfulness or pleasure, *What mark will this leave upon me?* Some there are, for whom the mark obscures the whole of their faces, so that those who behold them see only that mark, and could not say, *This man is dark or fair, or comely or otherwise*, but only, *This man bears a mark . . .*"

Last night, thought Abigail. Last night Harry was supposed to be printing pamphlets in the basement of his shop on Cornhill, leaflets concerning the assault of a girl in Dorchester by two British soldiers who had crossed to that little village from their island camp to buy wood. These pamphlets, leaflets, and broadsheets appeared in taverns from Philadelphia to Maine, and westward deep into the backcountry, carried by the Sons of Liberty and trumpeting to all that the King's efforts to tighten his hold on the colony were not merely a matter that concerned a few merchants in Boston or which townsmen would run for office. In many cases, Abigail was quite well aware, these incidents of violence between civilians and soldiers were either wholly fictitious or blown wildly out of proportion, though this assault had at least actually happened. John had written the original broadside, and by the time Sam had edited it and turned it over to Harry for printing, it was guaranteed to put men in a frame of mind to fight—

Was the murder charge simply a screen? Did the British really suspect that Harry had a printing press hidden in his cellar, one that they weren't keeping an eye on the way they kept an eye on the *Gazette* and the *Spy* and the various other printers in town?

LISTEN to what the Reverend Cooper is saying . . . You cannot chide Johnny for reading John's Bible, or even poor Nabby for sleeping, if your own mind is straying like a cow in a meadow. Discipline your mind, woman . . .

"For each deed leaves its mark, and God can read all of them upon our faces and in our right hands. And we cannot know which of these marks is the sign of the Cross, and which the number of the beast . . . Which, the Evangelist tells us, is the number of a man, and of the deeds of a man and not a beast. How can we know that what seems right to us, what seems natural, is not natural at all in the eyes of God? How can we know that what we seek will not mark us before those all-seeing eyes as those who have turned away from God, and from man, and from our own families, in pursuit of fleshy shadow?"

You wouldn't leave us, if you were a slave, Nabby had asked that morning, *and leaving us was the only way you could be free?*

Was that in fact what that Negro Woman, twenty-three years old, well-spoken and rather freckled, had done?

Abandoned a two-year-old child and a baby at breast—tiny orphans who would be sold off for a dollar or two to spare Thomas Fluckner the cost of raising them—to seek her own liberty? What mark would *she* bear before the eyes of God who knew everything?

And what mark would Sam and John and Revere and all those others bear for putting the affairs of politics and rebellion before the commandment that the Sabbath should be kept holy?

The case is entirely different—

Any trace of heat had long ago faded from the fire-box at their feet. Vainly, Abigail wiggled her frozen toes. In the next pew, despite the discreet muffling of several layers of quilted petticoat, Abigail heard the thin tinkling of Mrs. Hitchbourne using what the French called a *bourdaloue*: a small, portable chamber pot named after a French bishop given to notoriously long sermons. Such devices were frowned upon in New England—Abigail had long disciplined herself to drink nothing at Sunday breakfast and had taught Nabby likewise—but in a fashionable church like Brattle Street, there were always those less fastidious in their observances than they should be.

She saw Johnny catch Nabby's eye and giggle, and Abigail reached across to pinch the boy's arm.

"How many seek out the Mark of the Beast for themselves, without which *no man might buy or sell, save that he had the mark, or the name of the beast, or the number of his name*? So consider your desires and whether they are worth the consequence. Is anything worth God's punishment of exile, and vagabondage, and living as Cain lived on through the rest of his mortal span, *out from the presence of the Lord*? A man may say that it is permitted to do ill that good may come of it—but consider what mark that ill might leave upon our foreheads and our right hands. How can we do good in the sight of the Lord God, if the doing of it will transform us into the Servants of Ill? Will mark us, ourselves, with the Mark of the Beast that considers naught but the urgency of his own desires and claims them as good only because they seem good to him?

"*I had planted thee a noble vine*, saith the Lord, *wholly a right seed: how then art thou turned into the degenerate plant of a strange vine unto me?*"

"Mama," asked Johnny, as they retreated up the aisle at

last, "if the Lord put the Israelites into the hand of the Midianites because they sinned, why did the Lord then help the Israelites slaughter the Midianites later? Weren't the Midianites doing just what the Lord told them to do?"

"We can't know what the Lord asked the Midianites to do," explained Abigail, who had never been quite comfortable with this particular aspect of Predestination herself, "or how to do it." She tucked Johnny's scarf more tightly around his throat and over his head, thankful that both her children took after John in their sturdy strength. Poor Arabella Butler next door had just lost her three-year-old son, a fragile child she had vainly nursed through measles, fevers, sweats, and croup, and whose loss had left her desolate. "Perhaps the Midianites overstepped their instructions." That's what came of letting a critical, too-intelligent six-year-old get his hands on the Holy Writ.

"Yes, but if God knows everything from the beginning of Time, wouldn't He have known the Midianites would oppress the Children of Israel that cruelly—?"

"Mrs. Adams—"

Abigail turned gratefully to meet the three women silhouetted against the queer snow-light of the doors that led from the vestibule to Brattle Street outside. The one who had spoken stepped forward, pushing back her cardinal red hood to reveal herself not a woman but a girl of sixteen: black-haired, blue-eyed, stout, and dressed in a vivid and stylish polonaise of mustard-colored silk that made her stand out among the sober dark garments of the congregation like a macaw in a chicken-run. "You may not remember me, m'am, but I'm Lucy Fluckner—"

"Of course I remember you." Abigail smiled at the girl and held out her hand. "And Philomela—?"

Miss Fluckner's maidservant curtseyed: slender as Miss Fluckner was buxom, quiet as Miss Fluckner was bossy, she had been, some three months before, the target of a religious madman whom Abigail had been instrumental in trapping. The third woman, older than either of the others, was still gazing about her with the precise expression of a schoolgirl at a raree-show, as if she couldn't quite believe the Spartan plainness of the church vestibule or the somber garb of its inhabitants. When Lucy Fluckner introduced her—"Mrs. Sandhayes, Mrs. Adams"—she propped one of her canes against her wide, whaleboned panniers and extended two fingers only, in the manner of English ladies. "*Well*, I wouldn't have believed it, m'am! Do this many people *really* come out on a morning like this to be told they're all going to *Hell*?"

Abigail opened her mouth to snap a retort, but recalled that that was the deserved destination predicted by the Reverend Cooper for at least seven-eighths of the world's population, past and present, if not more. So she merely gestured about her, at her neighbors crowding to shake the pastor's hand, and replied, "As you see, m'am. I understand that in England, those who aren't destined for Heaven don't wish to know it," and Mrs. Sandhayes laughed, a light, cheerful sound like shaken silver bells, which caused the grimmer stalwarts of the congregation like Fearful Perkins and old Mr. Gilbert to turn their heads and glare.

"Mrs. Adams, I came to beg your help." Lucy drew back from the group around the outer door and back into the sanctuary, where the minimal heat from the small fire-boxes of coals brought by each family on so bitter a morning had managed to raise the temperature a degree or two during the course of the service. "And Papa would *flay* me if he knew

I'd come to you, and throw poor Margaret"—she nodded toward her chaperone—"out in the street for letting me do it, because she's supposed to keep me out of trouble, but you were so brilliant in helping Philomela . . . Really she was, Margaret. She can help us if anyone can." She turned back to Abigail. "There's been a murder."

Several things seemed to click into place in Abigail's mind, filling her with a sense of shock and dismay. "The slave-woman?"

Great Heavens, what had Harry to do with—?

Lucy stared at her, taken aback.

"Your father's slave-woman. The one who disappeared—"

"Bathsheba? Has she been found?" Her dark brows puckered in swift consternation. "Why do you say she's dead?"

"I'm sorry," said Abigail quickly. "I thought—" She shook her head, trying to collect her thoughts. "Forgive me. Who is it who was killed?"

"Sir Jonathan Cottrell. The King's Special Commissioner—"

"And your fiancé." Mrs. Sandhayes, who had been leaning on her canes and gazing around the sanctuary with the bemused expression of an explorer contemplating a grass temple on Otaheite, gave her an arch wink.

Lucy flushed a dark pink, not with maiden modesty, but with anger. "He was *not* my fiancé," she snapped.

"'Tis not what your father thought, my dear."

"My father could marry him, then." The girl turned back to Abigail with a little flounce. "Sir Jonathan was sent last year by the King to collect evidence about where the Sons of Liberty—'Rebels and Traitors,' he called them, but that's who he meant—were getting their money from. He'd been staying with Governor Hutchinson all last month, which was where he met Papa, and he was found dead in the alley behind the Governor's house early this morning: horrible! And they've arrested . . ."

Again she colored, and this time there was no mistaking the blush. She turned her head aside, a startling display of timidity in a girl Abigail knew was ordinarily as straightforward as a runaway goods-wagon.

"They've arrested a—a friend of mine for it," she finished shyly, in a voice that Abigail had never before heard her use. "And you've got to help us, Mrs. Adams. Help me, I mean—Help *him*. Help Harry."

"Harry Knox."

Lucy raised her eyes, brimming with the transformation of a bossy girl's first love. "Harry Knox."

Three

Since even the presence of a maidservant and a chaperone would not have protected the marriageable daughter of the wealthiest merchant in Boston from gossip for long—at least not from the gossip of the wives of other wealthy merchants—to say nothing of consideration for the Fourth Commandment and her family's dinner, it was agreed that Abigail would present herself at the Fluckner mansion on the following morning to hear all the details. She found John at home, but Sam and Revere both gone. Sam's wife Bess shared Abigail's attitude about Sabbath dinner and attendance at *both* church services on Sundays: it was all very well to pull an ox out of a pit on the Sabbath, as the Lord had said, but one needn't take the whole day at it. Sam, to do him credit, was not one to put even the Sons of Liberty before God's Law unless he really had to. And though Paul Revere might have inherited a greater carelessness about Sabbath-keeping with his French blood, Abigail knew him well enough to know that having missed the first service at the New Brick Meeting-House, he would not miss the second.

"'Tis a bad business, Portia," said John quietly, when after helping his children disengage themselves from scarves and cloaks, pattens and overshoes, he drew Abigail aside into the corner of the kitchen near the hearth. "The man who was killed—"

"Was the King's Commissioner, Sir Jonathan Cottrell." Had she been a Papist, Abigail reflected, she would have owed her confessor a few Paternosters for the smug relish she felt at the look on John's face. She supposed she could only throw herself on the mercy of the Lord, if sin there was in her enjoyment of her husband's realization that he wasn't the *only* member of the Adams family who could pull oxen out of that particular pit. "Which would account for the Provost Marshal's interest in the matter. Thomas Fluckner's daughter sought me out to ask my help with finding the killer. She and her chaperone were apparently at a ball at the Governor's last night when the man was killed—"

"Did Miss Fluckner mention that it was her engagement to Cottrell, which was to have been announced at the ball?"

Abigail raised her brows. No wonder Mrs. Sandhayes had looked coy. "I should dearly like to have been there to see them try it. The girl appears to have an understanding with Harry Knox."

"Ah," said John. He helped her off with her cloak and spread its heavy folds over one of the wooden settles that flanked the kitchen fire. "Well, that explains a great deal." On the opposite settle, Nabby and Johnny had already spread their cloaks, and the thick wool steamed gently in the heat. The advancing morning had not lessened in the slightest degree the previous night's cold; as Abigail dumped the fire-box's coals back onto the hearth and set the box ready for that afternoon's ration after dinner, she shivered at the thought of another three hours in the freezing sanctuary. Rail thin and unhealthy as a girl, Abigail had never, in her thirty years of New England winters and long sermons, grown used to the discipline of attending to the Lord's Word in the bitter season.

Charley and Tommy, who had spent the morning in their usual Sabbath pastime of listening to Pattie read to them from the Bible while they fidgeted, scurried at the heels of their older brother and sister to set the table: anything being preferable to "playing quietly" and refraining from the "profane" toys of the rest of the week. John followed Abigail into the pantry to help her bring in the cold roast pork cooked yesterday, mush, sweet potatoes and molasses, and the minute quantity of milk that Semiramis and Cleopatra had only just begun to provide again as they freshened after the winter's drought. "They'll have taken Harry out to Castle Island, won't they?" she added quietly, and John nodded.

For a moment they regarded one another in apprehensive silence.

After the Governor's request for troops to "keep order" some three years ago had resulted in those troops opening fire into a crowd of civilians, it had been agreed upon that, though Boston would remain garrisoned by a regiment of the King's forces, it would probably be better if those forces were not brought into daily contact with mobs stirred up by the Sons of Liberty. As a compromise, the Sixty-Fourth Regiment now occupied Castle Island, a brick fortress in the bay that had been built during the most recent French War. Since the dumping of the tea into the harbor in December, contact between the Bostonians and the much-outnumbered redcoats had been very limited indeed.

But Abigail—and every man, woman, and child over the age of five in Boston—was aware that Colonel Leslie was only biding his time. A man taken up for the murder of the King's Commissioner would not only be imprisoned on the island: there was every likelihood he would not be tried in Boston at all. Like a smuggler, he would be taken before an Admiralty Court of three Crown judges and no jury at the British naval base in Halifax, three hundred miles from the sort of inflammatory pamphlets that Harry had spent most of the night printing up.

And despite John's having defended the troopers who fired into the mob at the so-called Boston Massacre back in '70, with his involvement in the Sons of Liberty an open secret, there was a very good chance that if he went out to the island to speak with Harry Knox, he would not be permitted to return.

She asked worriedly, "Will you send Thaxter to see him?"

Thaxter was John's clerk.

"I suppose I must."

Abigail nodded, understanding John's tone rather than his words. Young John Thaxter was steady, intelligent, and cool-headed in such emergencies as were likely to arise in either the courtroom or in the Adams' kitchen where he'd taken so many of his meals over the past year or two: he would, John often said, make a fine lawyer. He was observant, articulate, and assiduous about double-checking facts. Neither John nor Abigail had ever been able to quite put their fingers on what he lacked, but they both knew it was something. Perhaps only the cynicism that comes from a decade of riding Massachusetts court circuits in the backwoods.

Whatever it was, it was in John's eyes as he looked at her.

"Might I go?"

"What, disguised as a boy?" His chuckle was affectionate, admiring, but a chuckle nonetheless. *"A young doctor of Rome; his name is Balthazar,"* he quoted Shakespeare's description of Portia's alter ego from *The Merchant of Venice. "I never knew so young a body with so old a head . . ."*

"And Balthazar won her case," pointed out Abigail.

"You can't be serious."

"Not serious?" Abigail drew herself up in burlesque indignation. "*Not serious* about visiting my poor, wretched cousin in that horrible jail and taking him a few paltry comforts? After Mr. Thaxter's kindliness in offering to escort me?"

"The Provost Marshal is never going to believe that *my wife* or any person named Adams is making a call on a man suspected of seditious activities solely for the purpose of giving him clean stockings."

"I'm surprised at you, John Adams, making assumptions about what another man might be persuaded to believe." She spooned butter from the little crock that had been brought up from the cellar—nearly rock-hard in the cold despite the fact that she'd set it near the door into the kitchen—and collected the milk-jug from the warmest corner of the pantry. The thin skin of ice would melt off it after only minutes in the kitchen's warmth.

"The most they can do is forbid me to see him and make me sit on a bench for an hour in the cold while Thaxter asks his questions. They're certainly not going to clap me in a dungeon and send you a note demanding you come alone and unarmed to some deserted spot, you know."

"I suppose not." John grinned, and followed her back into the kitchen, platter of pork in his hands. "I should dearly love to see them try, though. If they forbid you to visit Mr. Knox, dearest Portia, I daresay you might improve the idle hour by paying a call on your friend Lieutenant Coldstone."

Abigail's smile widened in return. "My thought precisely, dearest Lysander."

He set down his prosaic burden and kissed her hand at the old courting nickname. Lieutenant Jeremy Coldstone of the Provost Marshal's guard was the officer charged, last November, with arresting John for the murder of Colonel Leslie's mistress, and from that inauspicious beginning, respect and liking had grown up between Abigail and that stiff-backed young servant of the Crown. Sternly, Abigail disciplined her thoughts against a twinge of regret as she poured warmed cider from the hearth-kettle to a pitcher, and John gathered the children to table. It would be the Sabbath until bedtime tonight, so she would be unable to bake fresh bread to carry across to Castle Island as a gift for Coldstone, whom she knew was at the mercy of Army food-contractors: a pity. The goodwill was cheap at the price. And Harry, of course, would appreciate it, too.

She gave herself a mental shake, and turned her thoughts resolutely back to the morning's sermon and the questions the Reverend Cooper had raised about the Mark of the Beast, and conversation over dinner reverted to Sabbath thoughtfulness. *If keeping the Sabbath holy were easy, God would not have needed to enshrine it in Eternal Law.* When John sent a note to Cousin Sam, however, requesting that transportation to the island be arranged in the morning with one of the smugglers who worked for fellow-Son John Hancock, Abigail scribbled a quick message for Lucy Fluckner, postponing their own meeting until Tuesday, when at least the delay would result in some information to impart. Officially there was no post in Boston on Sundays, but there was no harm in asking the next-door neighbor's prentice-boy if he would happen to be walking that way this evening on his return from Meeting.

She, John, and Pattie returned to the meeting-house that afternoon with righteous hearts and proper attitudes.

The short spring evening, however, brought a knock on the front door and a resumption of Abigail's career as a Sabbath-breaker.

She had at least the comfort of knowing that she wasn't the only one in the household engaged in violating the Lord's Commandment—if comfort one could take in such a reflection—because on their return from the afternoon service John had been greeted by a note from wily Cousin Sam, followed closely by the man himself: was John agreeable to conceal two boxes of the pamphlets Harry had been printing last night and several pieces of the frame of the press itself, which Paul Revere, indefatigable Sabbath-bender and *bricoleur*, was going to dismantle that night?

"So far as anyone can tell, they've got no one watching the bookshop," Sam said, as he guided John out of the kitchen and down the short hall to John's study at the front of the house. By *anyone*, Abigail assumed he meant any of the prentice-boys, layabouts, and stevedores out of work who constituted the eyes and ears of the Sons of Liberty in Boston's narrow streets. *And men pride themselves on not being "gossipy" like women!* "We'll have the pamphlets out of there and the press broken down by midnight, and if it *does* occur to the Provost Marshal to get a man in to search the cellar, he'll find nothing but *Caesar's Commentaries* and quires of stationery for his trouble—"

Presumably, thought Abigail as she returned to the kitchen to pour cider and lay out a plate of yesterday's gingerbread for the men, *Sam has decided to take the Sabbath as ending at sunset . . .*

What mark—she could not keep herself from wondering—

would this decision about where the boundaries of the Lord's Day lay leave on Sam's head and hand and heart, once the goal of political representation for the colonies in Parliament was achieved? Would the Sons of Liberty disband then? Or would they begin to turn on one another, as the ancient Romans did? Or on anyone they perceived as an enemy to whatever the new order was?

And in that case—

"Mrs. Adams?" Pattie, who was standing at the front door even as Abigail stepped out of the study into the hall again, turned, and beyond her Abigail saw a cloaked form on the threshold in the dusk. "A lady here to see you."

Miss Fluckner? Thank goodness there was a fire in the parlor fireplace this afternoon . . .

"My *dear* Mrs. Adams!" As Pattie stepped aside, Mrs. Margaret Sandhayes limped into the hallway, paused to prop one of her gold-headed canes against her pannier, and this time—second encounter being obviously ground for a promotion—extended her entire hand instead of the cool two fingers as before. "I am *desolated* to interrupt you at this hour, but *dear* Lucy warned me—at the same time that she *begged* me to bring you this—that you Puritans spend the *entire day* in Church on Sundays. Is that *true*? Doing *nothing* but listening to the minister prose on about God and holiness? How very extraordinary—but very morally uplifting and good for the character, I'm sure."

She smiled and held out a thick-folded packet of paper, crusted everywhere with blots of sealing wax into which a seal of a flying bird had been hastily squished. An equally impatient hand had scrawled *Mrs. Adams* across the front.

"Won't you come in?" Abigail nodded to Pattie and stepped back to open the parlor door.

"Well, just for a moment, thank you so much." In a vast rustle of petticoats Mrs. Sandhayes shed her cloak into Pattie's hands and preceded Abigail into the parlor, her panniered skirts—a style worn by only the wives of the wealthiest merchants in the colonies—swaying uneasily with her lurching stride. "Of course I should attend more regularly—*Dear* Hannah Fluckner tells me that the minister at King's Chapel is *dazzling*, and so handsome, too, for a man of his years, and with a beautiful voice. I always think a Man of the Cloth *must* have a beautiful voice, don't you? *So* much more important than all that dusty Bible-quoting! Yet vestries over here *never* seem to think of that when choosing them, or even offer training in elocution or rhetoric at seminaries, which makes it such a *bore* for the poor parishioners."

She settled in the chair beside the fire and propped her canes beside her, her movements suddenly graceful: as she removed her gloves, Abigail noticed the length and pale beauty of her well-cared-for hands. "And God forbid if there's some perfectly simple word that he habitually mispronounces, like *concupiscence*, which dear Dr. Ellenbrough at St. Onesimus's always pronounced *con-cuppy-since*, and I'm afraid we girls would start giggling and could not stop ourselves—Why, thank you," she added, as Pattie came into the parlor with a tray: softly steaming teapot, small plates of bread, marmalade, fig-paste, and soft cheese. "How very kind of you, m'am! Such a freezing night as it promises—" Mrs. Sandhayes broke off, started back for a moment as Abigail poured out the un-Sabbatical tea: "*Chamomile*?"

"Would you prefer mint?" Abigail inquired serenely. "I know some people think mint is rather everyday."

"Oh, dear me, I *completely* forgot." She laughed, the silvery sweetness accompanied by a dismissive wave. "The *notorious* tea *fracas*! Don't tell me you subscribe to the boycott, Mrs. Adams? La, such a to-do dear Lucy makes of it, and all just to annoy her Papa, as girls will—especially girls whose Papas insist they marry dreadful little snirps like Sir Jonathan, *nihil nisi bonum* and all that, of course . . . Please do read Miss Lucy's letter."

The outer note enclosed a thicker inner packet, sealed but unaddressed. A blotted scribble implored:

Mrs. Adams,

Got your note! What luck that you'll see Harry! I beg you, put this into his hand! Philomela and I will go walking on the Common Tuesday 10 o'clock . . . I beg of you, meet us there, away from prying ears! I am consumed with envy—will you go disguised as a boy?

Lucy

William Shakespeare, Abigail reflected, had a great deal to answer for.

"The poor child." Mrs. Sandhayes heaved a deep sigh. "I positively weep for her, but of course one understands one can't have one's daughter marrying a bookseller. But I'll swear the boy is no fortune hunter."

"Of course he isn't!"

"No *of course* about it, my dear Mrs. Adams." Mrs. Sandhayes took a sip of the chamomile tea, politely suppressed a grimace, and set the cup aside. "Mr. Fluckner's ships, cargoes, and property in Boston are worth a hundred and twenty thousand pounds if they're worth thruppence, not to speak of proprietary rights to over a million acres in Maine, wherever

Maine is"—she laughed again, dismissively—"once the title is confirmed. It has a very *French* sound, don't you think? And say what you will about the French, they may be our enemies and Catholics and all that, but they cut a dress in a way that no Englishwoman ever could, not if she lived to be a hundred. I had a mantua-maker in London—"

"And I'll swear"—Abigail returned to the subject under consideration—"that Lucy hasn't formed an attachment to Mr. Knox simply to disoblige her father."

"What? Oh, dear, no." Mrs. Sandhayes folded her lovely hands. "I think that's why dear Lucy was so taken with Mr. Knox: because they'd met half a dozen times, and talked of books and battles and horses and dogs, before Harry ever knew who she was or that the man who won her should be rich for life. That he was taken with *her*, she said, and not with her dowry, which is a great deal more than could be said about Sir Jonathan Cottrell. It was really very sweet."

"'Twill be a good deal less sweet if Harry is taken for a military trial in Halifax and hanged for it," replied Abigail grimly. "Was Sir Jonathan wealthy?"

"My dear Mrs. Adams, the King does not have penniless friends." Disconcertingly after her babble of mantua-makers and fashionable preachers, a flash of worldly wisdom glinted from the Englishwoman's green eyes. Even with the last of the evening light fading from the windows, and the gentler glow of candles and the parlor hearth concealing the details of the day, Abigail could see that however fashionable the cut of Mrs. Sandhayes's clothing, the fabric itself was faded, and the lace and ribbons that decked her bony bosom either clumsily refurbished or repaired. At the meeting-house that morning Lucy had spoken of her chaperone as her social equal, her mother's "friend who is staying with us," but now it occurred to Abigail to wonder if this were not simply a polite fiction. Had Mrs. Sandhayes delayed borrowing her hostess's carriage to deliver Lucy's message until a time when she knew that the light would be kinder to a gown that had seen better days? The pearl earrings and the Medusa-head cameo at her throat were old and probably valuable—this was a woman who wouldn't wear trash. But they were also the jewelry she'd had on earlier in the day.

"It's surprising," the woman went on, "the number of people who subscribe to the belief that just because a man has a respectable fortune, he isn't going to pursue a woman with a larger one. I use the word *pursue* advisedly," she added drily. "Sir Jonathan adhered to the Kiss-Me-Kate School of wooing and seemed to think that a girl of Lucy's boisterous temperament would find violence of conduct as well as sentiment appealing."

Abigail's thoughts snapped back from consideration about who it was who might have left Margaret Sandhayes penniless, and said, "Toad."

"Well, to be perfectly accurate, my *dear* Mrs. Adams, *weasel* would be *le mot plus bon*—though it is not a terribly nice thing to be saying about either toads or weasels, poor things. A little spindle-shanked fellow with a voice like a mouse at the bottom of a barrel and a nose like one, too, always aquiver for what would benefit him. Or for a well-turned ankle, I'm afraid, though he managed to convince Mr. Fluckner of his respectability. Do you make this marmalade yourself? You colonials are positively *astonishing*! *Please* tell me the oranges were smuggled from Spain! I *must* be able to write my friends in Bath and tell them I've supped on smuggled goods with a patriot who refuses tea on political principle! La, I shall be the *envy* of Abbey Crescent!"

"Was Miss Fluckner aware that her father was going to announce her engagement to Cottrell at the Governor's ball?"

"Dear, me, yes, and such an uproar as there was over it! With Miss Lucy vowing one moment she wouldn't go at all, and the next, that she'd slap Sir Jonathan's face before all Boston and spring up on a chair and denounce him for a blackguard, and Mr. Fluckner bawling at the top of his lungs he'd throw her into the street for a disobedient trull, and her poor little sisters crying! Like a bear-garden, it was! I suggested that the best thing she could do would be to speak to her host about the matter when they arrived, for the dear Governor would know better how to get 'round Mr. Fluckner than poor Lucy, and he'd never have permitted the announcement in his house against her will, you know. *Such* a gentlemanly man—not at *all* what one expects in the colonies—and *perfectly* good *ton*! Shocking, how the lower orders here have treated him!"

"Perhaps they don't care for the spectacle of every paying position in the colony being handed to members of His Excellency's family."

"I don't see what business it is of theirs." Mrs. Sandhayes frowned. "Though come to think of it, that's just what Lucy is always saying." She considered the matter for all of about a second and a half with the expression of one trying to make out an inscription in Chinese, then shrugged. "Well, however it was, the Governor, I understand, agreed to intercept Sir Jonathan the moment he stepped into the house and speak to him—"

"I thought Sir Jonathan was the Governor's guest?"

"And so he was." The tall woman's hand strayed toward the teacup, then she glanced at its despised contents and returned the hand to her lap. Because of the boycott on British tea— and the truly shocking expense of the Dutch tea that Mr. John Hancock and others smuggled in defiance of the King's efforts to control colonial trade—Abigail had poured out warmed cider for John and Sam rather than break the Sabbath by the making of coffee, but with water kept hot in the kitchen boiler, a tisane was also possible. Peppermint and chamomile were poor substitutes for bohea and oolong, as far as Abigail was concerned, yet annoyance flashed through her at her guest's politely veiled contempt. "But Sir Jonathan had been gone for ten days in Maine—Where *is* Maine?"

"'Tis the northern district of the colony that borders on Canada," Abigail explained. "'Tis where we get most of our ship timber from. There's very little there beyond that. Why Sir Jonathan would go there to search for 'rebels and traitors,' as Lucy said, and not return 'til the very eve of his own engagement-party—"

"But without Sir Jonathan's journey to Maine, there would be no engagement-party, you see." The chaperone cocked her head, beaky as an absurdly crested bird's in the elaborate rolls and poufs of her heavily powdered hair. "Apparently there's some sort of question about title to part of the lands, and Sir Jonathan had agreed, when he returned to England, to speak to the King about settling it in Mr. Fluckner's favor, if Mr. Fluckner agreed to the match with Lucy. But Sir Jonathan insisted upon seeing the lands—since a portion of them will comprise the bulk of dear Lucy's marriage-portion—to see what he'd be up against, I daresay. It seems there are tenants living on them that nobody wants there, what are they called? Oh, I know—*squatters*! Such names you people do come up with!" She laughed again delightedly, but Abigail settled back in her chair, cradling the creamy queens-ware teacup and thinking.

She'd heard all her life about the Maine squatters, and the cat's cradle of lawsuits, chicanery, and looking-the-other-way that entangled the relationships of the dozen or so Great Proprietors who'd managed to get claim to those cold inhospitable forests to the north. Various Proprietors had brought in tenants to settle the land—mostly the Protestant Irish who'd originated in Scotland—and treated them, as far as Abigail could ascertain, like medieval peasants, to be robbed both of their rental and their lands depending on where negotiations were among the Proprietors themselves, and nobody outside the charmed circle of the very rich Boston merchants really had any clear idea of who had legal title to which portions of Maine's broken coast.

So Thomas Fluckner wanted to beat the other Proprietors to the post with a clear title newly granted by the King, did he?

And was willing to trade his eldest daughter's happiness to get it.

She poured herself a little more tisane. "And *did* His Excellency manage to intercept Sir Jonathan before the engagement was announced?"

"Good Heavens, no!" Mrs. Sandhayes regarded her in surprise, as if she suspected Mrs. Adams hadn't been properly keeping up with the affair. "Sir Jonathan never arrived at all! He got off the boat from Maine that morning, and the next time anyone saw him, he was lying facedown in the mud of the alley behind the Governor's mansion, frozen through."

"Frozen?" Abigail frowned. "The Provost Marshal finds a man *frozen* in an alley and concludes that Harry Knox must have had something to do with it?"

"Of course!" exclaimed her guest. "Because of the quarrel, you know. Last Thursday week, the day Sir Jonathan left for

Maine, Sir Jonathan went riding with Lucy on the Common and offered her intolerable insult! Fleeing him she encountered Mr. Knox, and Mr. Knox—after quite properly escorting her home—repaired at once to lie in wait for Sir Jonathan in the lane behind the Governor's stables, in the very place where the body was found this morning! When Sir Jonathan came riding in, Mr. Knox pulled him off his horse practically in the stable gateway and shouted at him in front of the entire stable staff that if he—Sir Jonathan—dared speak to Miss Fluckner again, he—Mr. Knox—would 'kill him like a dog.' Oh, dear, look at the time!"

Mrs. Sandhayes groped for her canes, and laboriously—with the first expression on her face that Abigail had seen of anything besides a vapid and condescending cheer—got herself to her feet. "I absolutely swore upon the Testament that I wouldn't be late to Caroline Hartnell's loo-party, and here I am forsworn and my immortal soul is in peril—I daresay the City Fathers would tell me, as much from playing loo on the Sabbath as for broken vows . . . Well, never mind. I have kept you"—she propped her cane against her pannier, extended her hand to grasp Abigail's with strong warmth—"away from your family for an unconscienceable time, not to speak of making those poor lovely horses stand all this time in the cold street . . ."

She hobbled with surprising swiftness along the hall, Pattie springing out of the kitchen to wrap her in the heavy velvet layers of her worn cloak. "Thank you so very much for the marmalade, Mrs. Adams—delicious! I dare swear I couldn't make a marmalade myself if you held a gun on me! Well, I'm off to endanger my immortal soul at loo—*Is* it still the Sabbath? Or does it end at sunset here?"

As she swayed and lurched out into Queen Street, with the

Fluckner coachman—for whose frozen feet, Abigail reflected, she hadn't spared a thought—springing down from his box to help her, Abigail glimpsed, at the edge of the lamplight, a couple of the young men whom she recognized as Sons of Liberty, waiting until the carriage pulled away. One carried a big box of seditious pamphlets, the other, a couple of pieces of what was clearly Harry Knox's printing press.

Paul Revere—and wily Cousin Sam—had evidently taken sunset as the definition of the Sabbath, for today, anyway. *And that done, wherein lies the difference between defense of one's country, and silver-loo?*

Four

Are you sure you wish to do this?" John handed Abigail's marketing basket—crammed to bursting with bread, butter, candles, cheese, apples, and clean linen that fifteen-year-old Billy Knox had brought for his brother that morning—to Thaxter and helped Abigail down into the skiff *Katrina*, which bobbed gently among the clots of ice at the end of Wentworth's Wharf.

Abigail wasn't at all sure she wanted to do it. The granddaughter of one of the oldest merchant clans in the colony, she knew everything about tonnage, bills of lading, and where to hide cargoes from the excise men, but being on the water made her joints ache within minutes and even the shortest voyage rendered her queasy. Nevertheless, she clasped John's gloved hands in her own and said, "All will be well, Mr. Adams."

"If we gets back by afternoon, all'll be well." Ezra Logan, who brought in firewood and butter from the north side of the bay in the *Katrina* three market-days per week and smuggled illegal cargoes of French molasses on the other three nights, shaded his eyes to consider the clouds that barred the morning sky. "Squally weather comin' in."

He took the basket from Thaxter, then the larger bundle of two striped woolen blankets, of the sort the British fur companies traded with the Indians. "Don't you worry, Mr. Adams. I'll have her back safe, 'fore the first sign of chop." He cast loose the lines, and poled the *Katrina*'s nose from the end of the dock; the deck-boy swung the foresail yard around to catch what light wind there was. Thaxter, who wasn't a much better sailor than Abigail, unfolded one of the blankets and laid it around her shoulders, then settled himself on the bench at her side to stay out of the way of Logan and the boy, shivering in the icy spray. Much as Abigail detested the British troops that for five years now had been stationed in Boston, as they approached the low gray shape of Castle Island—two and a half miles out in the iron waters—she felt a throb of sympathy for them. The Crown may have dispatched them to suppress the colonists' demands for their rights as Englishmen, but that didn't make the damp, freezing brick barracks they had to live in any more endurable in the bitter season.

The camp was quieter than it had been the last time she'd come ashore here, in early December. During the confused days after the tea-ships had first docked, when Boston's bells had tolled day and night to summon in from the countryside the armed mob whose presence had made the so-called Boston Tea-Party possible, many Loyalists, including the Fluckners, had come out to the camp for protection. Most had returned to Boston, but a number of the Crown's clerks and officers, Abigail was well aware, had chosen to remain.

Coming ashore she observed that the grubby village of tents, sheep pens, horse-lines, and makeshift shelters occupied by soldiers and camp followers that had sprung up around the fort's walls in those days had shrunk almost to nothing, smaller even than its summer and autumn dimensions. When Abigail and Thaxter were admitted through the fortress gate, smoke clawed her eyes from campfires and Spanish-style braziers set up even in the corridors, where soldiers, camp-servants, and laundresses huddled for warmth. The central parade-ground, glimpsed through the windows, had acquired a ring of lean-tos around its walls, clinging to the brick as if for warmth. Everywhere wood was stacked; in the corridors, shirts and drawers hung to dry, frozen hard. The smell of cooking, of dirty wool, of men and women too cold and too crowded to bathe, nearly choked her.

Lieutenant Coldstone, Assistant to the Provost Marshal, rose when they were shown into the cubbyhole that he shared with two other military clerks; the fireplace there was the size of Abigail's breadbox back on Queen Street and the so-called blaze there wouldn't have melted the ink in the standish. "It happens that Mr. Knox is a cousin of mine," Abigail replied to his lifted eyebrows, after Thaxter had requested an interview with the prisoner. "I've brought him some things from his poor dear mother."

"Have you, m'am?" Coldstone bowed. The wintry pallor of his face and the marble white of his wig turned his dark eyes even darker, in features as delicate as a girl's. "She must be most concerned for her son."

"Dreadfully," said Abigail. "'Tis only her age and illness that have kept her from bringing them herself."

"Those, and the fact that the lady has been dead since 1772. I am afraid, m'am, that there is no facility at present where you might speak to Mr. Knox, save in his cell. The late cold weather has driven even the hardiest of the men indoors, and we are severely crowded at the moment."

"'Tis quite all right."

The Lieutenant drew off the writing-mitts he had been wearing, donned stouter gloves, and took a cloak from the peg on the wall. He opened the room's other door, to admit men's voices and a renewed fug of smoke from the cubbyhole beyond, and called, "Sergeant Muldoon? Please take Mrs. Adams's things. This way, m'am, Mr. Thaxter."

"Might I ask the Provost Marshal's reasoning, in treating this matter as a military one?" Thaxter's breath puffed white as they passed a window, turned a corner down a hall that seemed to have been converted into a laundry-room, wood-store, and nursery for the ragged little camp children who ran to and fro underfoot like cocky rats. "As I understand the accusation, it rests upon the presumption that the crime was a crime of passion: a young man in love shouting threats at the older man who offered insult to a girl."

"That is one way of looking at it," agreed Coldstone. "But one seldom finds that passion retaining its heat for ten days, then lying in wait to do murder once the object of its ire came back into range again."

"I suppose that depends on the degree of passion," remarked Abigail, "and the magnitude of the ire."

"As you say, m'am." They turned down another corridor, and Coldstone returned the salute of the guard who stood at attention next to a tiny brazier and stingy fire just beyond the corner of a short corridor. "But if the young man is a member of an organization whose stated purpose is to encourage disobedience to the Crown and the victim a servant of the Crown in lawful pursuit of information about that organization, then the crime becomes not passion but treason. And as such, it enters the domain of military law."

They descended a few steps to a sort of anteroom, stacked in its corners with trunks and barrels: Flour? Apples? It was impossible to tell by the smell because even in the cold, the room stank like a privy, and from the door at one side came the desultory murmur of men's voices, and now and then, the soft clank of chain.

"I had no idea the Boston Grenadiers encouraged disobedience to the Crown," said Abigail. "And here I thought their stated purpose was to wear handsome uniforms and foregather in the Bunch of Grapes on Saturday afternoons!" She stepped back as Coldstone took the torch from one of the wall-brackets that burned close to the other locked door, trying to keep from shivering not only with the cold, but with the smell of hopelessness in this place, the sense of trapped despair. "And whatever the criminal's intent, if Sir Jonathan's body was found first thing Sunday morning by the Governor's stable hands, it would follow that he was killed sometime late Saturday night. While Mr. Knox may not be able to prove himself *Alibi* at that time, I doubt that you or I or indeed the working half of the population of Boston could do so, either."

"No, indeed, Mrs. Adams." Coldstone held the torch aloft for the guard, who had followed them in from the corridor, to shift the heavy bar that closed the second, nearer door, and to find and turn the iron key. "But though Mr. Knox was arrested on the presumption of a crime of passion alone, yesterday afternoon an eyewitness came forward who saw him emerging from Governor's Alley at shortly after three o'clock that morning, only hours before the body was found. Please excuse me, m'am."

He stepped through the door; Abigail heard him say, "Mr.

Knox?" within, and saw the flare of the torchlight on the unplastered brick walls. The room had not, to judge by the judas in the door, been completely dark before. Both it and the common cell across the vestibule appeared to have windows, for which she thanked Heaven even as she glanced in alarm at Thaxter, then in startled enquiry at Sergeant Muldoon. That young man—whom John had once described as a mountain walking about on legs—returned her look with a grimace—*I haven't the faintest idea, Mrs. A*—and shook his head, even as Coldstone reemerged from the cell, and signed them with a bow to precede him inside.

Henry Knox was sitting on the low cot that was the cell's single item of furniture—the single object that the tiny chamber was capable of containing, in fact. There wasn't even a latrine-bucket, only a hole in the brickwork of the floor from which noxious vapors emerged to make the whole room reek of sewage. Harry rose at once and held out his hands to Abigail, saying, "My dear Mrs. Adams, please forgive me for getting myself into a situation that obliges you to come here—and thank you, from the bottom of my heart."

As his plump, powerful hands gripped hers he glanced across at the three red-coated soldiers still grouped in the cell door, and went on, "And I swear to you, m'am, I didn't actually *get myself into this situation* at all! I don't know what witness this officer is talking about. I was in bed and asleep, *as I've told these gentlemen any number of times*." His blue gray eyes met Abigail's urgently as he said this, and she nodded, congratulating him silently on his good sense. Though any number of the Sons of Liberty would be perfectly happy to corroborate any tale Harry wished to concoct, Abigail could only shudder at the thought of the logistics necessary to coordinate a convincing story.

Much better to follow Aristotle and stick with the plausible that could not be proven, rather than come to ruin pursuing firmer proof that ultimately wouldn't hold up.

"Never mind that for the moment, *Cousin* Harry."

He started a little at the claim of kinship but nodded in his turn.

"We've brought you food—please don't tell me they're feeding you what the troopers get, knowing some of the contractors for it—and blankets—"

Muldoon brought the basket forward, and Harry gathered the blankets to his bosom with the fervor of a mother reunited with her child. Harry Knox was a young man comfortably padded by nature, like a somewhat rotund whale, but the cold in the cell was fearful. Had he not been taken on his way to church, as Sam had said, and thus wearing his greatcoat and gloves, Abigail reflected with an uneasy glance at the single filthy blanket on the insalubrious cot, he probably would have frozen in the night as surely as his purported victim.

"I've also brought you a book," she added, turning the basket a little so that her own body, and Thaxter's, interposed for a moment between its contents and Coldstone. As she opened the volume of Herodotus that she'd brought, she slipped the unaddressed note from Lucy between its pages. Harry met her eyes again, startled, then colored slightly in the torchlight.

"Thank you, m'am—Cousin Abigail," he remembered to add. "That is of more worth to me than all the rest put together." His gloved hands closed briefly around hers again. Then he straightened and turned back to Coldstone. "But as to this man who says he saw me, it is simply not true. I despise the Governor and his friends and wouldn't go near his house on a wager, much less at three o'clock in the morning. Who was this man?"

Coldstone's voice was dry as withered grass. "His name is Millward Wingate; he lives in Lindal's Lane. Last night was clear, though extremely cold as it has been these two weeks, and the moon set late. Mr. Wingate claims that he was passing the lane called Governor's Alley at three, having been sent to the Governor's house by his master to claim a wallet that his master had left there at the ball. He says he recognized you clearly—"

"That isn't true!"

"Moreover," Coldstone went on, "he says that he found on the ground when you had passed a red and yellow scarf, knit of silk and wool—"

Harry's mouth fell open with shock.

"Have you such a scarf?"

"I—Yes. But—"

Into his silence, Abigail inquired, "And who is Mr. Wingate's master?"

Without change of expression, the Lieutenant replied, "Thomas Fluckner. I will add," he added, "that I personally attach less significance to this evidence than does Colonel Leslie, who considers it damning."

"Oh, that's good!" said Abigail hotly. "That's very good! You establish Admiralty Courts in Halifax because you claim not to trust Massachusetts witnesses, yet when a Massachusetts man speaks against someone you wish to convict, then you're perfectly ready to believe him!"

"Let us begin our discussion by defining precisely who is meant by 'you,' Mrs. Adams." Coldstone bowed. "*I* have established no courts because it lies beyond my jurisdiction, as Assistant Provost Marshal of the Regiment, to do so, whether I wanted them or not. And if *I*, as Assistant Provost Marshal, have a crisis of trust concerning the testimony of Massachusetts witnesses, perhaps it comes from hearing so very many of them swearing to events that I personally know to be untrue. May I?" He gestured toward the blanket. "I'm sure Mrs. Adams will be more comfortable sitting down, and I will not answer for the state of her dress once she sits on that bed—"

"Oh, of course! Absolutely!" Harry unfolded one of the blankets, and together he and the officer spread it over the cot.

As he conducted Abigail to sit, Coldstone continued, "*Personally*, I consider Mr. Knox as likely, or as unlikely, to have murdered Sir Jonathan as I did before this helpful employee of Mr. Fluckner's was—ah—moved to come forward. I have little data for any suppositions at the moment, but I prefer to begin any line of enquiry with evidence untainted by lies. Mr. Knox, perhaps you would like to tell Mrs. Adams—I mean, of course, *Mr. Thaxter*—of the events of last Thursday week, and of Saturday night. That will be all, Farquhar, Muldoon," he added, glancing back at the two men still in the doorway. "I shall be quite safe here. Muldoon, perhaps you'd like to prepare some coffee for Mrs. Adams and Mr. Thaxter, when we return to my office?"

"Yes, sorr. Thank you, sorr."

The door clanged shut.

Abigail folded her hands. "Thank you, Lieutenant," she said. "I apologize for my outburst. I deeply appreciate your confidence—and your commitment to the truth, which is rare in any place, at any time. Mr. Knox, before you go into what happened Thursday night, would you tell me about yourself and Miss Fluckner? I mean," she added guiltily, "tell Mr. Thaxter—"

Thaxter grinned. "And I'll just take notes, shall I, m'am?"

Harry's story was a simple one. In the fall of the previous year he had become friends with Miss Lucy Fluckner. She would come into his bookshop on Cornhill, and sometimes they would talk there—about ancient Roman battles and Harry's personal passion for artillery—for as much as an hour, while her mother and schoolgirl sisters shopped among the various emporia along Hancock's Wharf. It was all perfectly innocent. There was never a time his visitor was without her maid, by which he guessed she was a well-off merchant's daughter.

"She told me her name was Lucy Andrews," said Harry. "From *Pamela*, you know. I didn't guess it at the time, of course—lots of people really *are* named Andrews—and you know, I just didn't think about it. We'd play chess, though we never could finish a game all at one go. Sometimes she'd send me little notes during the week, about what her next move would be, and I'd give Philomela notes in reply." By the time he'd guessed "Lucy Andrews" was in fact the daughter of one of the richest merchants in New England, they were well and truly on the way to being in love.

They would meet on the Common. Lucy loved to watch Harry's militia company, the Boston Grenadiers, drilling on Saturdays, and unlike many gently bred maidens of her class, she was perfectly capable of saddling her own horse. Sometimes she came with a groom, sometimes without one: in any case she'd generally send him off to a nearby tavern. "I daresay it's why old Fluckner finally got the Sandhayes woman to stay with them as chaperone. That was right after Cottrell came to town and began to hobnob with Mr. F. I think they wanted someone more than a servant to keep an eye on her. The woman rides like a Cossack, you know, if you but get her into one of those English sideways ladies' saddles and a horse that's been properly trained. I think, myself, they were afraid Lucy would elope."

"Would you have?" asked Abigail, curious.

Harry stood silent for a moment, wrapped in the second blanket, his head a little bowed in thought. His hard upbringing, Abigail knew, had left this young man with a strong sense of propriety, not from any innate punctiliousness but from cruel experience of what happened to those who violated society's rules. He had grown up in poverty—in his silence she read his knowledge of what would be Lucy's lot if she defied her father too far.

At length he said softly, "M'am, I simply don't know."

Lucy had spoken to Harry a number of times of Sir Jonathan's high-handed assumption that she could not keep herself from falling in love with him, an assumption that had progressed from knowing glances and unwanted touches on shoulder, back, arm to cornering her here and there in her father's house, when her parents would archly leave them together alone.

"And it wasn't only Miss Fluckner," he added grimly. "He was one of those men who seem to believe that servant-girls choose to be so because they're lusty, not because they're poor—even those who never chose their condition at all. Lucy told me that when he called, he would accost the maids in the halls or in empty parlors and kiss them, or worse, the randy little brute. He'd told her father she was already halfway in love with him but wouldn't admit it, at least not to her father—which unfortunately Mr. F. could readily believe, since he already thought her political views were adopted just to vex him. She and I were to meet on the Common on that Thursday morning—the twenty-second—out beyond the

Powder-Store—that round stone tower on top of the hill," he added, with a glance at Lieutenant Coldstone. "It's nearly a quarter mile from the nearest house, and there's a sort of copse of brush at the foot of the hill. At that hour of the morning and as cold as it was that day, we knew there would be no one about."

"Was Mrs. Sandhayes with her?" asked Abigail. "Or Philomela?"

Harry shook his head. "She said in her note that she had to meet me alone. She'd just learned about the Maine scheme, she told me later, and that her father was expecting Sir Jonathan to arrange things with the King in exchange for a share of the land as Lucy's dowry. Well, Sir Jonathan got wind of it and was at the meeting-place before either of us, waiting in the brush at the foot of the hill. He seized Lucy—Miss Fluckner—and—well—" Harry glanced aside, his mouth suddenly tight. "Attempted to caress her," he finished in a stifled voice. "I'm pleased to say she blacked the fellow's eye for him. I suppose I should have waited for her to tell her father of it. Fluckner may be a Tory and a cheat, but I shouldn't like to think he'd have pushed the match on his daughter in the face of—of behavior like that. I didn't think of it at the time, though."

He folded his heavy arms and looked aside once more.

Softly, Abigail said, "And there was always the chance that if she'd told her father, Sir Jonathan would simply say she was lying. How serious was this *caress*?"

Harry kept his gaze fixed resolutely on the window, a heavily barred slit set high in the wall with nothing visible beyond it but indistinct gray sky. "Very serious."

"You believe in other words he intended to dishonor her, as a means of forcing her consent?"

"I think so, yes. I wouldn't put it past him."

"And in this frame of mind," said Thaxter, after short silence, "you went to the Governor's house and intercepted Sir Jonathan when he returned?"

"I did, yes. I thought he'd have come in already. Lucy—Miss Fluckner—fled from him on horseback and met me on my way to our meeting-place and told me the whole, much more in anger than in sorrow—" His mouth quirked in sudden grim amusement at the remembrance of that big-boned, bossy, black-haired girl fizzling over with wrath at the seducer whose eye she'd just blacked rather than melting in tears of shock and shame. "I'm afraid I lost my head a bit. Mr. Thrisk—the Governor's butler—told me Cottrell hadn't come in yet, so I went to the end of the alley there behind the mews and waited for him."

"And pulled him off his horse," said Abigail softly. "And told him that if he ever touched or spoke to Miss Fluckner again, you would kill him like a dog. Was that where you lost your scarf?"

Harry shook his head. "That was later," he said. "Lucy—Miss Fluckner—got away to meet me a few mornings later. It was bitterly cold. God knows what old Fluckner said to poor Mrs. Sandhayes when he found out Lucy'd given her the slip again, but since that time she's stuck to Miss Fluckner like a burr."

"And Saturday night?" asked Thaxter.

Harry sighed. "I was home, asleep, in bed, by myself. Good God, am I to be hanged because I wasn't with a mistress? My brother had ridden across to Cambridge with a delivery; I closed up the shop early, for there was no one in all afternoon, and I was not feeling quite well. I do take cold easily and felt the rest would do me good."

If he'd been up all night Saturday night working his printing press, reflected Abigail, and concealing the boxes of pamphlets about the shop and his rooms above it, he had probably looked suitably haggard when he'd emerged on Sunday morning and walked straight into the arms of the Provost Marshal's men. "I will attest to his taking cold easily, Lieutenant," she affirmed in her most motherly tones.

Coldstone eyed the stout six-footer with understandable skepticism.

"They go straight to his chest," she admonished in a tone of reproach. "His brother and I had a fearful time with him last winter." Harry nodded and did his best to look frail.

Coldstone said politely, "Indeed? Then your gift of blankets is doubly appreciated, to be sure. If you have finished, Mrs. Adams—I mean, Mr. Thaxter—perhaps it would be well if we did not promote yourself taking cold. Sergeant Muldoon will have prepared coffee, and with luck lieutenants Stevenson and Barclay will be about their business elsewhere in the camp, and we can have the office to ourselves long enough for me to inform you of my own findings concerning Sir Jonathan's activities between his return from Maine on Saturday morning and being found dead in an alley twenty hours later. I am sorry Mr. Adams was not able to cross here himself."

I'll wager Colonel Leslie was even sorrier. "He has a case to prepare for the Assizes in Haverhill next week that demanded his attention," replied Abigail, more or less truthfully—John did have a case and would undoubtedly burn a great deal of whale-oil tonight in making up for the time he was spending this morning stowing boxes of seditious pamphlets and fragments of Harry's printing press behind the trunks in the attic. "Mr. Knox—"

"Harry."

"Harry. Don't worry." She extended her hands, took his in hers. Though he was only six or seven years her junior, she felt toward him a sudden protectiveness, as if he were a son or a nephew. "We'll see justice is done."

"For justice to be done," replied Coldstone drily, "it must first be defined, m'am."

"And you think officers in service to the Crown are capable of that?" She turned back to the young bookseller. "One more question. You say Cottrell would ill-use the servants in Mr. Fluckner's house. Did he ever attempt liberties with a woman named Bathsheba? A young woman, light-skinned, with two children—"

Harry made a face. "Lord, poor Sheba! At least Philomela could stick close to Lucy. The man could scarcely steal kisses from the maid with her mistress looking on. Bathsheba is a sewing maid, m'am, and often by herself—has anything been heard of her?"

"Not to my knowledge," said Abigail. "I find it odd that she would leave her children behind her—odder still, that she would choose to disappear *after* Sir Jonathan left for Maine. I'm rather curious to know why."

Five

I take it," remarked Abigail, as Lieutenant Coldstone poured out coffee for herself and Thaxter in the cramped cubby-hole of his office, "you think as little as I do of this business of, *I happened to find his scarf in the lane*?" The office wasn't appreciably warmer than it had been an hour ago, and neither Lieutenant Stevenson nor Lieutenant Barclay appeared to have refilled the wood-basket before departing, but after Harry's cell, the dank little chamber seemed a paradise of comfort. Abigail perched on Lieutenant Barclay's high desk-stool, and set her cup among the account-books he had left behind him.

"Regrettably," returned Coldstone, "what I think has no bearing on the matter. My apologies that I have no milk to offer you, m'am, and only muscovado sugar. Sugar of any sort is most difficult to obtain."

"I can recommend you a very good smuggler to obtain as much of it as you'd care to use, straight from the West Indies," offered Abigail, and tonged a small lump of the sticky brown substance into her cup. "I've always considered it a shocking waste of energy, to ship it to England and then trans-ship it back here, only so that the King's friends can make money off transport fees and import duties."

"I have, of course, no opinion on the subject," responded Coldstone politely. "Yet I would be pleased to have your sugar-purveyor's name."

"Frederick North, wasn't it, Thaxter?" Abigail named the Chancellor of the King's Exchequer who was responsible for the tea-tax and much of the Crown's fiscal policy toward the colonies. "Something like that. Surely Colonel Leslie can't believe that a clerk who owes the whole of his living to a wealthy merchant isn't going to tell whatever lie his master instructs him to? Or is there some other reason that Colonel Leslie would like to send Mr. Knox to Halifax and put a rope around his neck?"

Her glance crossed the young officer's, and he nodded, not pretending that he didn't understand what she meant. "Naturally, should Mr. Knox feel moved to turn King's Evidence against whomever he can think of in Boston who might be connected with the Sons of Liberty—or with John Hancock's smuggling operation, which in Colonel Leslie's eyes amounts to the same thing—it would affect the verdict of the Tribunal. Colonel Leslie is not being arbitrary in this matter, m'am. Mr. Knox is a known associate of men believed to be involved with traitors; information concerning traitors is what Sir Jonathan came to the colony to obtain."

"Why don't you just arrest my husband, then, or Sam Adams, or Mr. Hancock, and put a pistol to their heads, if you think you'll get information under threat of death?"

"Because neither your husband, nor Sam Adams, nor John

Hancock was so unwise as to shout *I will kill you like a dog* to a man who subsequently was found dead. Would you like to hear details of Sir Jonathan's arrival Saturday morning, insofar as we have been able to ascertain them? I fear that the day is turning blustery, and would not wish to detain you longer than is necessary."

As if on cue, wind snarled in the chimney, and Abigail, glancing swiftly at the chamber's small window, saw to her dismay that the bars of cloud visible that morning in the eastern sky were changing rapidly to scudding fragments of gray racing in from the east and north. At the same moment the chimney sneezed out a quantity of gritty smoke. Abigail coughed and managed to say, "Yes, thank you, Lieutenant—I apologize for my ill temper. But Mr. Knox is a friend of mine, and I promise you, he would not harm a fly. I presume you've obtained Mr. Fluckner's version of what Sir Jonathan was doing in Maine?"

"Speaking with Mr. Fluckner's agent in Boothbay, I understand—a Mr. Bingham, who handles the timber shipping for several of the Great Proprietors. Bingham was the owner of a schooner called the *Hetty*, on which Sir Jonathan took passage from Boothbay Friday night, arriving at Hancock's Wharf between ten thirty and eleven Saturday morning. When he came ashore, Sir Jonathan repaired immediately to the livery stable of a man named Brainert Howell, in Prince's Street, and rented a saddle horse—"

"Rented?" Abigail's eyebrows drew sharply together. "The Governor's mansion lies less than a mile from Hancock's Wharf. Had he not free use of his host's stables?"

"He had indeed. Yet a man of his description was seen walking up Prince's Street, and it was certainly the name of the man who rented Brainert Howell's horse—an animal that was found, saddled and bridled, in the open fields of the Marlborough Street ward on Sunday morning, not long after the discovery of Sir Jonathan's body. Sir Jonathan further arranged with Howell to have his trunk and portmanteau transported from the wharf to the Governor's house, Sir Jonathan's manservant not having gone to Maine with him on account of illness."

"So in fact," said Abigail, "we have no evidence as to what Sir Jonathan actually *did* in Maine or who he might have offended or enraged in the ten days preceding his murder. He could have attempted the virtue of every damsel in the Maritimes and run onto the *Hetty* between a gauntlet of outraged Mainers all shaking their fists at him and crying, *I shall kill you like a dog—*"

"'Tis not a conviction *I'd* like to try to get in court," mused Thaxter, scribbling away in his memorandum-book.

"Possibly not," Coldstone agreed. "Yet until you produce an eyewitness of the scene described who has provably no connection with either the Sons of Liberty or any of Boston's less political smuggling rings, I fear that we are left with the facts as they stand and with no alternative to Mr. Wingate's story. Mr. Knox's young brother, I understand, has been in Cambridge this past week, only returning on Sunday—not that his testimony would serve to acquit Mr. Knox, unless they slept in the same room, and even then might not be believed."

"Surely," said Thaxter after a pause, "if Cottrell were assaulted and murdered a dozen yards from the Governor's stables, someone would have heard an outcry? Or seen him lying there? How far from the stable gate was the body discovered?"

"About twenty feet from where Governor's Alley ends in Rawson's Lane," said Coldstone. "Sir Jonathan lay facedown in frozen mud and had clearly been dead for many hours. His flesh was quite cold. Myself, I would have said that he died of the cold rather than of the beating. His extremities were nearly purple with it despite gloves and boots, and the abrasions on his face did not suggest blows hard enough to be fatal. Yet he had clearly been thrashed: a fate often incurred by men who attempt the virtue of other men's sweethearts."

"Thrashed, yes," said Abigail softly. "Murdered—not so often. Even what could be construed as an attempt at rape is more likely to result in a man's cork being drawn than his life ended—and it seems to me that Miss Fluckner herself took a hand in that."

Coldstone's seraph lips twitched in something perilously like a grin. "It's true that I've seldom seen so comprehensive a 'mouse,' as the street-urchins call it. Yet a man may set out to thrash another and leave him lying alive in the mud, and his victim may still be dead of cold in the morning."

"Who found him?" asked Thaxter.

"Governor Hutchinson's stable boys, when they opened the mews gates. They thought he might have been a late-departing guest from the previous night, ran to him and turned him over, and recognized him at once. The coachman, Mr. Sellon, ordered him brought into the coach-house, hoping against hope that he might be revived with brandy by the tack-room fire. He had, of course, been long dead, though owing to the extreme cold he was not stiff. Sellon sent for Governor Hutchinson, who immediately sent for us."

"And you just as immediately arrested Mr. Knox?" concluded Abigail.

"When a man is killed," replied Coldstone primly, "it is difficult to keep one's mind from leaping back to the phrase, *I will kill you like a dog*. The stablemen all informed me of

Mr. Knox's threat the moment I arrived, and seemed to take Knox's guilt as a given, particularly as Miss Fluckner had been at the ball the previous night, and word had gone around that the engagement was to have been announced."

Abigail said, "Hmmm," and Lieutenant Coldstone poured her out another cup of coffee. In the hall outside the doorway, the voices of the cubbyhole's two other occupants, Stevenson and Barclay, could be heard, protesting Sergeant Muldoon's dogged insistence that himself was after talking with a couple of mainland folks over Sir Jonathan's murder—

"Rot, Sergeant, I'll bet he's got a woman in there."

"Is she pretty?"

"Bet you he's snabbled all the tea and the sugar, too—"

Thaxter asked, "When did the last guests leave?"

"Shortly after two. The alley is a narrow one, but Rawson's Lane is barely wider, unpaved, and in nasty condition this time of year. When sent for, the carriages went around by School Street to the mansion's front door, so the body could have been lying where it was found as early as nine or ten, when the latest arrivals came in. At that time the lanterns around the gate were taken in and the alley would have thenceforth been quite dark."

"And I take it the tavern frequented by the footmen and grooms is in School Street rather than Rawson's Lane?"

The corner of Coldstone's mouth twitched again at her deduction that such a thing existed, and he replied, "The Spancel, yes. I have made arrangements to question the coachmen and footmen of all the guests over the next few days, but I assume that had any encountered Sir Jonathan's body that night they would have notified Mr. Sellon, if no one else. Sir Jonathan was clothed as he had been that morning at the wharves, and his watch, his silver penknife, and

English coin to the value of nearly ten pounds were found on his person. The only things missing were his gold signet ring and the memorandum-book that he usually carried . . . a book that contained his findings here in Boston regarding smuggling and the Sons of Liberty, and whatever notes he may have taken while in Maine."

Abigail glanced up again at that, and the dark gaze that met hers was impassive, watching her take in the implications of this fact. But after turning the whole of what she had heard over in her mind, she said, "It began to get light at five. *Is* seven hours sufficient for a man's body to turn quite cold? When my Grandpa Quincy died, I recall he was laid down on the cooling-bench for quite twenty-four hours. And at slaughtering-time on the farm, the pigs and calves are hung up for many hours before the heat goes out of the meat."

Thaxter—a city boy—looked a trifle disconcerted at these matter-of-fact speculations on the logistics of mortality, but Coldstone nodded. "A small man like Sir Jonathan would cool more swiftly, I think, particularly on such a night. He cannot have encountered his killer much sooner than nine, or even in darkness the commotion of the beating would surely have been glimpsed at the far end of the lane by the latecomers."

"Could he have been killed elsewhere?" suggested Thaxter hesitantly.

"The thought occurred to me," said Coldstone. "But why? Why take the trouble to bring a beaten corpse, obviously murdered, to a place where it will be discovered, when with very little trouble it can be disposed of in the river or the harbor? In fact it did cross my mind that he might have been moved, because I saw no sign of postmortem lividity in the face or chest, but quite frankly, as cold as it was, I'm not sure there would have been any."

Abigail turned her coffee-cup round in its saucer, seeing in her mind the towering, bulky shape of Thomas Fluckner, as she had seen him here and there about the streets of Boston during the few years that she and John had lived in the town. A bosom-bow of the Governor's and the recipient of any number of favors from the Crown; a King's Commissioner himself and a member of that elect, golden circle of merchants and Great Proprietors, who twenty years ago had induced the then-royal governor to give them all those acres of land in Maine and build forts against the Indians on it at public expense, in trade for a share in the profits. It was expected that any of Fluckner's daughters would marry a Hutchinson or an Oliver, a Bowdoin or an Apthorp, and keep the lands that would be theirs within that privileged group.

Nobody would welcome a bookseller who read too many of his own books and printed up broadsheets decrying Crown monopolies in his basement.

"And nothing of where Sir Jonathan went after he rented this horse of Mr. Howell's? If he rented a mount to ride to the ferry, which lies in that direction, he must surely have returned by sunset, when the town gates close, and after that he must have been in town somewhere, between sunset—say, six o'clock—and ten, which I think must be the latest he could have died. Where could he have ridden, if he took the Charles Town Ferry, in order to be back before the ferry ceased to operate?"

She glanced at Thaxter, who had relatives in Lynn. Her own knowledge of the territory north of Boston ended five or six feet on either side of the Salem Road.

The young man frowned doubtfully. "At this season, he might reach Cambridge." He didn't sound as if he thought it a likely possibility. "Horse and man would tire very quickly in cold like Saturday's. Of course, the countryside is thickly settled up, you know. He may just have gone visiting—er—Well, he could have had a sweetheart in any of a hundred farms . . ."

Coldstone moved his head a little, and for a moment, Abigail had the impression that he was about to crack his self-imposed calm and make some remark about the victim.

"Has he been in these parts before?" she asked. "Miss Fluckner indicated that he came down from Halifax late in December, but is this the first time he's been in the colony? How would he have known how long to give himself, or where to go, if he took the ferry to the mainland Saturday?"

"Before Halifax, Sir Jonathan spent two years in Barbados," replied Coldstone, in tones chillingly correct. "Prior to that he was about five years in Spain, upon the King's business. Yet had he thought it worth his while, he would have learnt the ways of the countryside hereabouts quickly enough. And so might others have learnt where he was likely to go, so that they could close up their shops in good time and wait close to the ferry for his return."

Abigail set down her coffee-cup with a clink. "To be sure, what does a man need to do to witness that he sought his bed at an honest hour because he felt poorly?"

"Cough now and then." Coldstone folded his long-fingered hands upon his knee. "Which the guards assure me Mr. Knox has not once done in the thirty-some hours he has been in his cell."

"I'm pleased to hear he's feeling so much better," responded Abigail promptly. *Drat the man . . .* "So to the regiment of problematical Mainers whose wives and sweethearts Sir Jonathan has spent the past ten days debauching, we might add any farmer or villager between here and Lynn, wives and sweethearts ditto—without coming anywhere near Sir Jonathan's missing memorandum-book *or* Harry Knox's unfortunate decision to get an unobserved night's sleep." She stepped down from the tall stool on which she'd sat and readjusted her scarves—the only outer garments of full-out protection against the weather that she'd been even slightly tempted to loosen the entire time she had been in the fort. "If you would be so good as to tell me, Lieutenant Coldstone, what it is that I and my husband and Harry's friends need to discover in order to convince Colonel Leslie of Harry's innocence, I would very much appreciate it. Because as it is, we're put in the position of proving a negative, difficult even without the Colonel's hopes that Mr. Knox may accuse others of sedition—in which he is *not* involved—in an effort to save his own skin, or Mr. Fluckner's objections to seeing his daughter marry a man who is of no social use to *him*."

Coldstone, who had risen when she did, stood before her for a moment without replying, without giving the slightest indication that he heard his two office-mates arguing with and harassing Sergeant Muldoon in the corridor, or the sharp clatter of weapons-drill in the parade-ground. Abigail wondered whether Harry could hear these camp-noises in his cell, and how long it would take him to read *The Persian Wars*, and whether this would distract his mind from the thought of the twenty minutes or so that it took a man to strangle, once he had been hoisted on the gallows.

She looked up at Coldstone's face, cold as a marble angel's. The servant of the King, whose job was defined by the crimson uniform he wore: first serve the King, then seek Justice . . .

Provided, as he had said, one could define the word.

What did *he* hear, or think about, as he lay at night in

this dank brick fortress set in the midst of the ocean, waiting for word to come from his master about how to punish rebel colonists for defying the King's commands?

At length he said, "If you would be so kind, m'am—What you can discover is who else might have seen Sir Jonathan after his debarking from the *Hetty* on Saturday morning, and who in Boston might also have wished to do him harm. Mr. Knox's defense is based upon the proof of a negative and I cannot do anything about that, and for that I am sorry. However much I am dissatisfied with the case against Mr. Knox, Colonel Leslie finds little amiss in it. My superior officer, Major Salisbury, has instructed me to draw up an accusation. When the *Incitatus* arrives here from Jamaica next week, unless some new evidence is found, Mr. Knox will be taken to Halifax and tried before an Admiralty Court for conspiracy and treason."

Six

John said, "That's ridiculous!" and slammed his hand down on the top of his desk, making the standish jump. "To convict a man on the perjured evidence of a clerk frightened for his position and the word of rich man who'll do anything to keep his daughter from wedding a poor one—"

"I suspect Lieutenant Coldstone would remark that you're making a bit free with the burden of proof as to Mr. Fluckner's motives—"

"Damn the burden of proof!" John pulled off his wig and hurled it against the opposite wall of his study. "You know, and I know—"

"And the Provost Marshall does not know."

"Does not wish to know, you mean!" Red-faced with wrath, John looked around him, as if seeking something else small enough to fling that wouldn't leave the books in the shelf splattered with ink or sand. Abigail fished in her pocket and handed him her pocket memorandum-book. He flung it with a satisfying smack. "Damn the man!"

In the hallway behind her, Abigail heard the faint creak of the kitchen's door-hinge: Johnny, Nabby, and Charley pressing close to hear their father in his wrath. Young Mr. Thaxter, standing by his own small desk in the corner of the study, looked far less sanguine, despite nearly two years of dealing with his employer's rages.

"Lieutenant Coldstone says he will try to wangle the appointment as Harry's defender himself, but he may not succeed." She crossed the little study, retrieved John's wig and the faded little Morocco-leather notebook, and placed both on the corner of the high desk at John's elbow. "If the Tribunal appoints an officer from the garrison at Halifax, he will almost certainly share the prevalent opinion that any Bostonian will lie about the whereabouts of any other Bostonian—"

John swept the wig up and hurled it again, followed at once by the memorandum-book.

"—so whatever evidence we manage to locate about the actual killer had best be of a solid rather than a verbal nature." Early in their married life John had sometimes been moved to hurl teacups, but Abigail's practice of gluing them back together and serving him his tea in them had gradually broken him of this practice: in any case the boycott against tea had made the entire point moot.

"Is there any chance you might put off your journey to Haverhill? Even a day—"

John hesitated, looking at the notes on his desk with an uncertainty that told her this wasn't the first time he'd considered doing exactly that. "I had rather not, Portia," he said after a time. "The husband of my client there has cast her and her children out of his house, claiming her to be a whore, and the children not his own; if her suit against him fails, she will have nothing to live by. She seems to me an honest woman, and there are rumors that 'tis the husband who wishes to put her away and marry a neighbor lately widowed: an ugly story. If the weather holds cold like this, I should be home on Monday."

"That will do." Abigail laid her palm to his cheek. "Any woman bringing suit about a man's misdeeds before a jury of men needs all the help she can get. Mr. Thaxter and I will do what we can. Still, if on your way north you hear word of"—she unfolded Coldstone's description of Cottrell—"*A fair, well-looking gentleman, of small stature, with a long nose and a cleft to his chin. Blue eyes and a fair pigeon-wing tie-wig; a stone-gray greatcoat of four capes, top boots, and a gray- or snuff-colored coat and breeches beneath. Yellow waistcoat, silver basket-weave buttons, gold signet ring on his left little finger.* Possibly last seen in pursuit of a woman," she added drily, and went to retrieve notebook and wig once again.

"I shall make a note of it." John fetched back his wig, brushed it off, and set it on the corner of the desk again. It was the same color as his close-cropped hair, and dressed simply, yet when he wore it—to Meeting or to visit friends and family—Abigail always felt him to be slightly in disguise. A lawyer, a writer, an arguer of politics and the rights of Englishmen . . . but not the husband and father, lover and friend she had loved since the age of fifteen.

"And I," said Abigail, preceding him down the hall to the kitchen where Pattie was checking the contents of the Dutch-oven dinner, "shall see what Miss Fluckner and Mrs. Sandhayes can tell me about who was at the Governor's ball who might have made the occasion to slip out and intercept Sir Jonathan upon his arrival . . . provided Miss Fluckner can steal away from her father's house tomorrow." She put on a clean apron, opened the door of the oven beside the hearth, and held her hand just inside for a count of two or three; the fire she'd begun that morning before leaving for Castle Island had settled to darkly throbbing coals, and the oven felt right for bread. "If nothing else," she went on, closing it and turning to the warm corner of the hearth where the covered loaves were rising, "I may learn more about the woman Bathsheba."

"Who? Oh, the young Negress who disappeared." John perched on a corner of the big worktable. "You think she knew something of it?"

"I haven't the smallest idea." Abigail fetched the shovel, opened the oven again, and moving swiftly, transferred the coals back to the hearth. "It could be happenstance that she walked out of her master's house—leaving behind her two children too young to do without a mother's care—two days after the departure of a man who made attempts on her virtue . . . a man who was beaten to death upon his return to town." She caught up the whisk, swept the ashes from the bricks. "But I should like to learn more of the matter if I can."

"I daresay." She turned to get the loaves from the table, found John just behind her, the risen, rounded dough ready on the peel in his hands. She smiled at him, stepped back—for a lawyer and a scholar, John had a wide streak of farmer in him . . . and a little element of housewife, too. He shuffled the loaves deftly off the peel and into the oven, where they would bake slowly for the remainder of the evening, filling the kitchen with an incomparable scent.

"But ask Miss Fluckner as well where her suitor went in Maine and whatever she can recall of her father's dealings with the tenants on the land. I've heard it said that the chief reason Fluckner needs clear title is so that he can put the tenants off the land—men who've been farming there for two generations—and bring in German settlers who'll pay more for the privilege of freezing while being robbed." With a neat gesture, he dropped the peel back into its place on its pegs, turned back to her with a grave wariness in his eyes. "My experience has always been that of all the things a man will kill for, land is ever close to the top of the list."

Abigail had expected Lucy Fluckner to be accompanied only by Philomela on her walk to the Common the following morning. But when she caught sight of the girl's bright red walking-cloak among the elms of the Mall that bounded the Common's eastern side, she was surprised to make out the tall, swaying form of Mrs. Sandhayes at Lucy's side. "My dear Mrs. Adams, I wouldn't have missed the opportunity to assist at a romance for a thousand pounds!" replied that lady, smiling, when Abigail tactfully inquired whether the icy wind was not too bitter for her. And, reading Abigail's true concern, which had little to do with the weather, she added, "My physicians insisted that exercise will eventually strengthen my limbs—and indeed, I get about much more handily than I did! So I welcome every step. Did you convince the authorities to let you visit Mr. Knox?"

"How is he?" demanded Lucy. "Did you give him my message? He isn't—they didn't"—her face suddenly changed as she fought a shiver of dread from her voice—"they didn't put him in *irons* or anything, did they?"

"They did not," said Abigail briskly. "Nor is he in a common cell with the camp drunkards and troublemakers, but in a little room—a *very* little room, rather dank and cold, but he has blankets and his greatcoat—by himself. I took him food and a book—"

"Oh, *thank* you! *Bless* you!"

"—and slipped your note between its pages, and I shall see Mr. Thaxter goes across tomorrow with more. But," she added, cutting short the girl's next rapturous exclamations, "matters are worse than we knew. Did Mr. Knox lend you a scarf of his recently? Red and yellow—"

"The one I knit for him." Lucy nodded, black curls bouncing in the frame of her scarlet hood. "Saturday a week ago, when I sneaked away and got poor Margaret into such trouble with Papa . . ." She threw an apologetic glance at her chaperone. "We met at the burying-ground, and I'd slipped out so quickly I forgot to bring a scarf of my own, and he lent me his, because I was nearly freezing. Does he want it back? I think it's in my drawer, or maybe I left it in the pocket of the cloak I had on that day—"

"He has it," said Abigail grimly. "Or, rather, the Provost Marshal has it. A Mr. Wingate made a special journey out to Castle Island with it on Sunday afternoon, with the information that he saw Harry emerge from Governor's Alley at three o'clock Sunday morning—your father having sent him back to collect a forgotten wallet from the Governor's after the ball—"

"The liar!" Lucy stopped in her tracks, mouth momentarily ajar with shock. "Oh, the *blackguard*!" She made a move as if she were about to run all the way to her father's countinghouse, cloak flying, and throw herself at him in rage, then whirled back to face her companions with her face twisted with disillusion, betrayal, and dread. "Oh, how *could* he!"

"Dearest—" Mrs. Sandhayes laid a hand on her young charge's shoulder. "Now, you know he must have done so at your father's behest—"

"Well, of course he did! Because he's a cheat, that's why . . . About five years ago he borrowed a little money out of my father's strongbox without telling him about it—" She pursed her lips, pulling herself back from her rage, and her blue eyes filled with sudden tears. "I shouldn't speak badly of him, because it was when his wife had their last child, and both she and the baby were so sick . . . But Papa caught him putting the money back, you see. So if he were to dismiss him, you know it would be without a character—"

"La, child, your Papa wouldn't do such a thing!"

"He would." Lucy sighed, and wiped at her eyes with the back of her wrist, like a child. "Just as he'd think to send Harry's scarf over to the Provost Marshal, with that ridiculous story about a wallet, only to get Harry into trouble."

"And so we must get him out of trouble," said Abigail stoutly. "Come, shall we walk? And you must tell me all about Saturday night, in as much detail as you can recall. There must have been a great deal of comment when he did not appear at a ball to announce his own engagement."

"My dear Mrs. Adams, like hurling a grenado into a dovecot!"

"Well, it was supposed to be announced at dinner," said Lucy. "And *of course* Papa had arranged to have me seated next to Sir Jonathan, or where Sir Jonathan would have been sitting had he been there. I caught Governor Hutchinson first thing, as he received us in the hall, and begged him for a word, and told him that whatever Papa had said, I *would not* marry the man, and he arranged to have my place changed at the table. *That* set everyone talking, and Papa looked ready to have an apoplexy, but at least I didn't have to sit next to his empty chair. And of course, no one would say things in front of me—"

"They did before *me*," reported Mrs. Sandhayes, limping gamely along the frozen gravel of the walk on Lucy's other side. "La, the rumors that flew about the cardroom! That Sir Jonathan had heard you'd jilted him and had walked out of the Governor's house—that you'd told His Excellency some terrible tale about that *charming* Sir Jonathan and had *obliged* the Governor to eject him—that Sir Jonathan had discovered that your Papa was about to cheat him over the Maine lands, which really belonged to Mr. Gardiner—"

"They do not!" Lucy protested.

"That's not what Felicity Gardiner says."

"Felicity Gardiner's a—Well," said Lucy. "Anyway, His Excellency kept sending servants to ask in the stables, had Sir Jonathan arrived yet? He even sent a footman down to the wharf to see if Mr. Bingham's boat had come in from Maine as it was supposed to, and he brought word back that yes, Sir Jonathan had debarked that morning and gone off no one knew where, without sending word or anything. *That* set the cat among the pigeons! And everyone kept staring at me and whispering behind their fans—"

"They weren't whispering about *you* at that point, my dear." Mrs. Sandhayes raised her kohl black eyebrows. "I suppose you're aware by this time, Mrs. Adams, that Sir Jonathan's appetites would have shamed a rabbit in the brambles. I don't doubt—and neither did anyone at the Governor's that night, I assure you—that he had a sweetheart somewhere in town, for whom he'd been pining all those days in Maine. Not that he wasn't perfectly capable of trying to get up an intrigue or two in the Penobscot or the Kennebec—lud, what names you Americans think up! But then I understand the women of the province tend to be of the granitey, Gog and Magog variety—"

"But no one you know of?"

Margaret Sandhayes considered the matter, forehead puckering in a manner that threatened the thick pink and white maquillage that habitually plastered her rather horsey face, then shook her head. The whaleboned stays in the hood of her cloak creaked alarmingly—it was of the variety boned out to accommodate a much-curled and decorated coiffure, and the sharp gusts of wind that slashed across Boston from the bay gave Abigail the impression every minute that the whole structure was going to be whipped away like a kite, carrying the gawky chaperone with it.

"Would Mr. Fenton know?" asked Lucy. "Sir Jonathan's man. He came down with *la grippe* the night before Sir Jonathan left for Maine. He was going to follow when he got better, but I think he's still at the Governor's."

"La, child, one doesn't go about questioning a man's servants!"

"Not even to save an innocent man's life?"

"It is shockingly bad *ton*, child, and your reputation would never recover if it got about! As well have it said that you pay peoples' maids for copies of their letters!"

"Margaret—" Lucy looked almost as if she wanted to shake the older woman. "This is Harry's life we're talking about!"

"Oh, pooh." Mrs. Sandhayes looked aside uneasily. "I daresay they won't hang him on a clerk's tittle-tattle—"

"They will," said Abigail quietly. "Mr. Knox has been—er—*outspoken* in his objection to some of the Crown's policies regarding the colonies, and yes, he stands in grave and immediate danger of being hanged. Whatever Mr. Fenton might be able to tell us truly could save Mr. Knox's life."

Mrs. Sandhayes made a face expressive of her opinion as to how much any servant could be useful for anything besides fetching her another tea-cake, but Lucy exclaimed, "Mr. Barnaby will know. Our butler, you remember, Mrs. Adams. His sister's husband is Governor Hutchinson's steward—Mr. Buttrick. Do you mind walking back with us to ask? It isn't far."

They had come opposite the writing-school by this time, so it was, in fact, something more than a half mile to the handsome house on Milk Street that Thomas Fluckner had purchased with his wife's money, many years ago. This part of Boston lay west of the original town that huddled around the waterfront, and the streets were far less crowded, with open spaces of fields and gardens lying behind the houses of timber and brick. As they passed along Marlborough Street, Abigail slowed her steps before the Governor's house itself and stood for a moment considering the mansion through the bare branches of the oak trees on its snow-covered lawn. On the cupola, the copper Indian weather vane swung in the cutting wind, and had the day not been so cold—and Mrs. Sandhayes lagging farther and farther behind—Abigail would have suggested a detour down the frozen muck of Rawson's Lane, to have a look at the scene of the crime.

First things first.

"Did Sir Jonathan write your father while he was in Maine?" she asked as they walked. "I understand he was to stay with your father's agent in Boothbay."

"Mr. Bingham," affirmed the girl. "He's in charge of collecting the rents for that whole section of the coast, from Moscongus Bay down to the Kennebec, but half the time he doesn't send much. The whole section's in a state of revolt against the Proprietors, and only a month ago Mr. Bowdoin's agent was beaten up and sent back to Boston in a load of bad herring." She laughed her schoolgirl laugh, and Mrs. Sandhayes looked shocked.

"No, he didn't write—neither to Papa nor to Governor Hutchinson, which I thought pretty high-handed of him, considering he was going to be guest of honor at a dinner and a ball, and I don't think he would have written to Mr. Fenton, either. From what Mr. Barnaby told me, he treated Mr. Fenton worse than any dog."

"There," declared Mrs. Sandhayes gloomily, catching up with the other three. "*Now* tell me servants can be trusted to keep their mouths shut about anything."

Philomela, carrying extra scarves and shawls for the others, turned her head as if to admire the tall steeple of Old South Church on the corner and pretended she had not heard this remark.

Mr. Barnaby, who opened the door to the four women and clucked over the coldness of the weather, confirmed all of Lucy's information about Sir Jonathan's manservant. "It's not unusual for a gentleman to have so little regard for his man, and I'm sorry to say some of the gentlemen from the home country are the worst I've seen in that regard." A stout, genial, middle-aged man with a deeply pockmarked face and the accent of London to his voice, he bowed and signed a liveried footman to collect their wraps. "Most vexed he was that poor Mr. Fenton should have been taken sick the night before their departure, leaving him no time to replace him before he left. He said if Mr. Fenton didn't follow him within two days, he could consider himself discharged and find his own way back to England or wherever he wished to go, but I wouldn't have wanted to think he meant it."

Mrs. Sandhayes, emerging from the chrysalis of whaleboned hood and two woolen cloaks, looked surprised at this view of the matter. "Whyever not? One can't let people of that order start believing that claiming a bellyache will excuse them from their duties. The man should have taken better care of himself."

Lucy ignored this remark. "So what will Mr. Fenton do now?"

"That I don't know, Miss. It's the worst case of the grippe I've seen; the Governor's had a surgeon in twice to bleed him, and he's worse, if anything."

Abigail sniffed. "You astonish me, sir." She had a deep mistrust of physicians other than her friend Joseph Warren, having seen too many at work. "Is he well enough to speak to, do you think?"

"Oh, yes, m'am. He's never had a fever, nor lost track of his senses, or anything like that. Would you like me to arrange it?"

"What on earth for?" inquired Mrs. Sandhayes, from the pier glass where she'd gone to readjust the high-piled edifice of her coiffure with an ivory comb. "The man's not been out of his bed. It sounds to me as though some of these Maine ruffians followed Sir Jonathan back from his journey and lay in wait for him on his return to the Governor's house. I daresay they're safely back home in Obseybobscott or Pennywayback or whatever outlandish place they come from, and so the Admiralty Court will see, once they've heard the whole story."

"Will they?" said Abigail drily. Despite aching gratitude

for the warmth of the parlor after the morning's bone-breaking cold, she could not keep from her mind John's descriptions of the houses he had seen in Maine—two-roomed, primitive, buried beneath snow for months at a time—as she considered the curtains of pea green velvet, the printed Chinese wall-papers, and the delftware bowls displayed in the mahogany cabinets. "I am not, myself, quite so sanguine about what three Crown servants in Halifax are going to see."

On the opposite wall, a portrait of Lucy's mother—whose father had talked then-governor Dunbar and the Board of Trade into granting him the Maine land—smiled stiffly into middle distance. Her pink and silver gown was rendered with such meticulous attention that Abigail could recognize that the lace was Dutch rather than French, but her face might have been a whittled doll's.

"Was there anyone at the Governor's ball Saturday night, who might have wished Sir Jonathan ill?" she asked, interrupting Mrs. Sandhayes's raptures over the entrance of her hostess's overfed lapdog Hercules. "Anyone who disappeared for a period of time—"

"My dear Mrs. Adams, you are not suggesting that one of the *Governor's guests* might have been responsible for this—this outrage?"

"Does social standing exempt a man from vengeance, or greed?" demanded Lucy indignantly. She added wryly, "Sir Jonathan himself is proof that it doesn't exempt one from lust."

"Lucy!"

Lucy turned eagerly back to Abigail. "People were coming and going all the time, m'am, but I think I can remember who I danced with, and the order of the dances. And Margaret was in and out of the cardroom—she plays like a Greek bandit! We can surely come up with some idea of it, if someone was absent for any period of time, especially if I gossip about among Mama's friends. They all tear up characters like Harpies! I'll ask if anyone knew anything to Sir Jonathan's discredit or if he had a mistress—"

"You had best let me do that, dear," said Mrs. Sandhayes firmly. "Your mother would expire of horror if she thought you even knew what a mistress *was*, and I would certainly be blamed for not giving you a more elevated tone of mind. Ah, Mr. Barnaby! *À la bonne heure!* What ambrosial delights has dear Mrs. Prawle prepared for us? Not her wonderful molasses tarts! There now, Mrs. Adams, I told you Barnaby was a genius: he's even thought to prepare you some of that nasty tisane that dear Lucy has taken to drinking in preference to tea—"

"It's rose hips and licorice-root," said Lucy, with shy pride. "I tried getting coffee, but it's Dutch, and Papa wouldn't have it under his roof, and it's a terrible nuisance to roast and grind the beans, and you can smell it all over the house. Philomela went down to the market and got me this, and I keep it hidden in my dresser-drawer. Thank you, Barnaby."

"Think nothing of it, miss."

"Mr. Barnaby." Abigail lifted a finger to stay him. "Before you leave—what was Bathsheba's reaction to Sir Jonathan's departure? Was she relieved, as you'd expect, or was she troubled?"

"There now!"

Abigail was conscious again of a twinge of un-Christian pride, at the expressions of astonishment on the faces of both the butler and Mrs. Sandhayes.

It was Mr. Barnaby who spoke first. "How the—? M'am, I don't know how you'd know of it, but you're dead right. Poor

Sheba . . . Well, he pestered her, as he did all the women of the house—"

"*Pestered* nothing!" exclaimed Lucy hotly. "He broke into her room one night, after he was supposed to have left here, and got into bed with her—"

"Lucy, *really*!"

"Well, he did. He told her if she didn't shut up he'd buy her from Papa and use her how he pleased! Papa claimed he 'took care of' the matter," she added mutinously, "but of course Sir Jonathan denied he'd done any such thing—"

"Dear child," protested Mrs. Sandhayes, "your Papa could scarcely take the word of a *servant* over that of a King's Commissioner, and a *Negress* at that—Dear Philomela, run and take Hercules outside, I see him contemplating his favorite corner of Mrs. Fluckner's carpet in a way that I mistrust. Mind you"—she turned back to Abigail—"I wouldn't put anything past the man."

"Bathsheba's as truthful as you or I," protested Lucy. "*Far* more truthful than me, in fact . . ."

"Be that as it may, m'am, miss," Barnaby interposed tactfully. "It's true, as you'd expect, the day he left, poor Sheba went about like she'd just been let off a whipping, knowing he wouldn't be coming to the house for a week and more. But Friday evening, it was like she'd seen a ghost on the stair: not able to settle to her work and barely did a third of what she'd usually accomplish with her needle. Mrs. Barnaby spoke of it—my good wife has the charge of the maids and the sewing," he added almost shyly. "Showed me some of it, too—as badly mended and clumsy as if she were a girl in love with her mind a thousand miles away, and Sheba generally so neat and particular. There was something weighing on her mind, I'll swear to that."

"'Tis true." Philomela, coming back in with the relieved Hercules in her arms, spoke for the first time in the morning. "Begging your pardon for speaking, Mrs. Adams, Mrs. Sandhayes. But the Friday evening, after she returned from being out, Sheba was not herself."

"She didn't say why, did she?" asked Mrs. Sandhayes, and Philomela shook her head. "Because now that you speak of it, I do recall how distracted the poor girl was, when she was shopping with me that morning—and I must say, it is *such* a nuisance, not knowing what new colors of ribbons they're wearing in Town until they're the *old* colors—"

Abigail guessed that by Town she meant London.

"At first I thought it was only that her baby had the croup or something—brats forever ailing with one thing or another, in winter—but after she'd missed the way twice—and *what* a tangle those streets are, by Hancock's Wharf!—I asked her, what on earth was the matter with her, and she begged my pardon and then burst into tears, right there on the street! She said, 'Something terrible has happened, and I don't know what to do!' I asked her what, but she would say nothing of it, only that there was nothing to be done, and begged my pardon again for having troubled me. Well, she was in such a state that one couldn't get any sense out of her then, so I made up my mind to speak to her again on Saturday, when she was a bit calmer. Frankly, it crossed my mind that as wan as she looked, and in view of Sir Jonathan's *disgraceful* behavior, she might have found herself *enceinte*. But before I even came downstairs on Saturday, she walked out of the house and has not been seen since."

Seven

What will become of her children?" John asked, when Abigail returned to the house, full of tea-cakes and speculation. "So far as I know, not even a dealer will pay as much as two shillings for a two-year-old that will only be underfoot and a burden 'til he's seven or eight—"

"She," corrected Abigail. "Marcellina, and the babe is Stephen. Mrs. Barnaby is looking after them. No woman in the household has given birth recently, so she's spoon-feeding the poor mite on gruel and cow's milk, and getting no thanks for it from Mrs. Fluckner." As she returned with him to the kitchen—where Pattie, contrary to Abigail's express instructions when she'd left for the Common that morning, was doing the ironing beside the warm Hell-mouth of the hearth—she saw in her mind again the servants' hall of the Fluckner residence, to which Mr. Barnaby had escorted herself, Lucy, and the protesting but incurably inquisitive Mrs. Sandhayes to see the orphans.

Someone had tied little Marcellina by the leading-strings of her dress to a table-leg, to keep her from interfering with the work of the sewing-women and the maid, who there, too, had been doing ironing. Only at the Fluckner house, this involved the full panoply of goffering-tools, three different grades of starch, and irons narrow and wide, laid out on a rack above the hearth-coals, tempting to tiny fingers. Mrs. Barnaby—half her husband's age and pretty as a kitten—had been mending one of Mrs. Fluckner's lace-trimmed chemises, with tiny Stephen laid on a pillow at her side.

Children who, as John said, were worth nothing to anyone—except, by all accounts of everyone in the household, to their mother. "Spent every spare moment she had making dresses for them," Mrs. Barnaby had said, reaching a careful finger to touch the sleeping infant's cheek. "And Miss Lucy so kind, as to give her worn-out chemises and such to be made over into dresses for them—and talking her mother into doing the same. She'd never have gone away from them. Never."

"I told Lucy I'd write to my father," Abigail said to John, kneeling by the big kitchen sideboard where Tommy—also affixed by the leading-strings—raised joyful arms to be liberated and lifted. "He can surely find a family in Braintree or Weymouth who can be trusted to care for them, if they can be bought from Fluckner—"

"You speak as if you're certain their mother is dead." John opened the drawer of the sideboard, drew out a folded note. "There are other reasons that a woman could be 'distrait' or 'beside herself'—fear is the one that springs to my mind the quickest—that would drive her from her home and her children, always supposing your Mrs. Sandhayes isn't correct and the woman wasn't simply in a state of sickened horror to find herself with child by a man who'd raped her. This came for you just after you'd left. You're right," he added thoughtfully. "It is odd."

"Well, I'll take oath she wasn't pregnant, with a baby still at breast." Abigail straightened with her son in her arms, and unfolded the note. "The idiot," she added dispassionately, after a quick perusal of that lovely Italianate script.

Seth Balfour—age 45—coachman for Mr. Apthorp—last to arrive at the Governor's, between ten and ten thirty (heard the clock at the French Meeting-House strike as he let the family off at the front door)—says he is certain there was no body in the lane when he turned his team into the yard. Roughly twenty minutes to unharness, rug the team, then sat with Sellon, Havisham, Lane, Cover in the tack-room next to the gate. Cards, quiet talk. Thinks he would have heard men quarrelling in alley.

Grant Sellon—age 30—His Excel'cy the Gov's coachman—remained on the premises to supervise—says card-players in tack-room those who have little taste for noise, smells at Spancel. Has known other four for years. Jug of beer from kitchen, Cover had flask of brandy but none of the players became drunk or loud. Heard dogs bark in alley near midnight, went out with lantern, saw nothing but says lantern-light carries only five feet. Attests Balfour could not possibly have seen by light of carriage-lanterns, from carriage-seat to the place where the body was found. Agrees that after Apthorp team unharnessed, rugged, yard was quiet until two a.m. when first guests (Mr. Bowdoin) called for carriages.

Wm Havisham—age 19—His Excel'cy the Gov's head stable boy—sent by Sellon to fetch in lantern from the gate at 11 p.m.—says saw nothing in alley, but gate-lanterns illuminate only immediate area of the gate, radius ten feet at most. Walked about the yard at quarter past midnight, again at quarter of two, all quiet. Did not go into alley.

Arthur Cover—age 52—head footman for Mr. Bowdoin, Sr.—arrived immediately before Apthorps—while Bowdoin and Apthorp teams being unharnessed, caught short and retreated to alley to relieve himself some twenty feet from yard gate toward Rawson's Lane. Took a lantern, noticed nothing amiss in direction of Rawson's Lane. Somewhat nearsighted. Attests barking dog in the alley near midnight, thinks they would have heard men quarreling.

Nicholas Lane—age 22—under-footman for Mr. Vassall—corroborates barking dog, sounds from alley would carry. Walked about the yard at quarter of one, twenty past one, all quiet. Did not go into alley. Attests Spancel tavern favored by stablemen, footmen, does not think anyone would have walked from yard gate southwest to Rawson's Lane.

Walter Clegg—age 28—ferryman, Winissimet Ferry—no one of Cottrell's description crossed from Boston to Winissimet morning of Saturday, March 5.

Obed Hussey—age 20—ferryman, Charles Town Ferry—no one of Cottrell's description crossed from Boston to Charles Town morning of Saturday, March 5.

"As if anyone in Boston would tell a British officer anything about anyone's movements, if he came asking." Abigail folded up the sheet, set Tommy down, and took out her pastry-board. "And now of course if I go inquiring for a slender little fair-haired fellow with a cleft chin and the remains of a black eye on Saturday morning, both ferrymen will leap to the astute conclusion that I'm hand in glove with the British and give me a second helping of what he got. Drat the man!" She edged past John into the pantry, scooped out flour from the barrel there into a bowl, and gathered the lard-crock from the kitchen's chilliest corner. "Perhaps if I inquire after Mr. Howell's horse and ask the men who'd be on duty late in the afternoon when he'd have been coming back—"

"If he went," pointed out John, and caught her for a firm kiss before turning back to the hall and his study. "The man could as easily have had a lady-friend in the North End as across the river."

"Then why rent a horse?"

"Perhaps his toenail had become ingrown while he was in Maine, and he didn't feel able for walking."

Abigail threw a dishrag at him as he ducked through the hall door, to Charley and Tommy's crows of delight.

But after she'd got the vegetables chopped for a rabbit pie, and the dried herbs that her mother-in-law sent her every autumn from her garden in Braintree pounded up, and caught Tommy twice as he attempted to toddle out the back door and freeze to death in the yard—Abigail took coarse paper from the sideboard drawer and wrote neatly in kitchen-pencil,

Sam,

Can you inquire if men from Boothby in Maine or its vicinity came to town on Saturday morning, and if so, the name of their vessel and their ostensible business? There is a good chance they know aught of Cottrell's true killers.

A.A.

Sam's reply came on Thursday afternoon.

As one of Boston's busiest lawyers, John was one of the few who rode the circuit of all the colony's courts: from New

Bedford up to Newburyport, west into the backcountry as far as Worcester, and on up into Maine. Unlike many of Boston's lawyers, he came from a relatively poor family. Though his younger brothers still in Braintree sent the produce of the family farm—barrels of flour and apples, cider, corn, and potatoes—with three sons (so far) to educate and a daughter to whom he hoped one day to make a suitable marriage-portion, John would take whatever work was offered, wherever it might be.

Abigail sometimes wondered whether the success of her marriage with this driven, vain, overly erudite man owed something to the width of her own interests. While she missed him sorely while he was away—both in bed and around the kitchen table in the evenings—she was never bored. There were too many books in the world, too many newspapers, too many interesting friends . . . completely aside from the fact that nobody could be bored who had four such enterprising children as Nabby, Johnny, Charley, and Tommy.

She occupied herself on Wednesday with enquiries between Prince's Street and the Winissimet Ferry after *a fair, well-looking gentleman, of small stature, with a long nose and a cleft to his chin . . . etc.* and learned what she had always suspected, that most people were far more preoccupied with making shoes or sewing shirts or chasing after their own errant children at ten thirty on a Saturday morning than they were with passersby. In the afternoon, after taking another basket of bread, cheese, cider, and clean shirts to Harry's brother Billy for dispatch to Castle Island, she wrote letters to her mother and sisters—busy, gossipy Mary and the lovely and studious Betsy—and, when Nabby and Johnny returned from school, with sorting the household laundry preparatory to the gargantuan nuisance of boiling and soaking that night, before washing on the morrow.

Fitful squalls had flickered over Boston on Wednesday, rain freezing to sleet, but Thursday dawned clear, windy, and brutally cold. By the time the last of the rinsed and wrung-out sheets had been hung over the lines in the yard, the first shirts and shifts and baby-clouts had frozen solid. She, Pattie, and Nabby had just cleared up after dinner, and she was settling with the mending when the children came dashing in from the yard in a skirl of mud, and Johnny gasped in passing, "Ma, something's going on!" as they pelted through the kitchen to the hall that led to the street door.

Abigail called, "*Don't* go out!" as she sprang up to stride after them. Four years ago, at nearly this hour of the spring evening with the snow still on the ground, she'd heard the shouting of men in the street, even as she heard it now when her son yanked open the door. She'd heard shots fired, had run from the house they'd had in those days in Brattle Street and around the corner, to see blood black on the snow in the twilight, bodies lying where they'd fallen under a haze of powder-smoke—

Even with lingering daylight still in the sky, the jeering voices of a mob caught her with a twinge of dread.

She caught Charley by one shoulder, Tommy by his trailing leading-strings, and looking down Queen Street saw the men: jostling, shouting, throwing ice-balls and rocks.

Coming toward the house.

DRAT the man! Has he NO sense?

She drew her children into the house, shut the front door, and unhurriedly returned along the passage to the kitchen to collect her cloak and pattens. At the same time Pattie hurried in from the yard: "Mrs. Adams, 'tis Lieutenant Coldstone, I think—"

She wrapped a scarf around her neck. "Yes, I know. Keep the children inside, please." At the market that morning she'd heard all manner of rumors about what vengeance the King was going to take on the rebellious Massachusers for dumping his precious tea, and violence hung in the air like the whiff of powder-smoke. It would be too easy for someone to start shooting. Johnny and Nabby were sensible children, but they were still terribly young.

She stepped into the street.

Lieutenant Coldstone was indeed walking up Queen Street from the direction of the customhouse, with the burly Sergeant Muldoon at his heels. A dozen men followed them, layabouts from the wharves, mostly—Abigail judged by their rough coats and ragged breeches—and prentice-boys who should have been at their work. One man hurled a snowball at Coldstone, which shattered in a way that told Abigail that there'd been a rock inside it. By the state of his long military cloak, she surmised it was far from the first. Sergeant Muldoon had a musket—shouldered—and was glancing about him, ready for an attack but with no evidence of panic. Somebody shouted "Lobsterback!" and somebody else yelled something a great deal worse.

Abigail strode quickly toward them and held out her hands. "Lieutenant Coldstone, what a pleasant surprise! Were you coming to see me?"

A man yelled, "Tory whore!" and Abigail was gratified to see another of the ragged group grab him by the shoulder and explain to him who exactly she was. The others were already falling back to a respectful—but still visible—distance.

"I wanted a word with you, m'am, yes." Though his voice was impassive, Coldstone bore himself as if he'd just swallowed his own ramrod.

"I do apologize for my townsmen." Abigail led the way back up Queen Street toward her door, where she could see Pattie looking out and holding the children back. "I fear that as sailing-weather improves, everyone is counting the days until the King's message—whatever it is going to be—arrives. Some of the most shocking things are being said and believed."

"Your countrymen are well to be anxious, m'am. I know not what Parliament's reaction will be to such wanton defiance and destruction of property, but I suspect—and you must know also—that the actions of the Sons of Liberty will be regarded as a test case in dealing with rebellion in the colonies. And I am sorry to say," he added, as he bowed Abigail across her own threshold, "that the issue serves only to cloud what might or might not have happened in Governor's Alley Saturday night."

"Sergeant Muldoon." Abigail turned back on the doorsill. "You shall simply freeze to death if you stay here on the doorstep. Might he be permitted to go around the back to the kitchen, Lieutenant? There's no need for him to remain on the street, is there?"

Coldstone glanced at the men who had now taken up loitering stances all along Queen Street, and said stiffly, "None, m'am."

Muldoon saluted her as he disappeared down the passageway between the Adams' house and the Butlers' next door.

"Thank you again for keeping me apprised of your interviews with the coachmen," added Abigail, leading him into the parlor. Pattie, God bless her, had kindled the fire there and entered a few moments later with a tray bearing two cups and a pitcher of hot cider, and bread-and-butter for Abigail's guest. "Did you come to town to do more of them? I appreciate your visiting, but you needn't have. 'Twould be silly of either of us to deny how risky it is."

"I came across principally to arrange for Sir Jonathan's

trunk and portmanteau to be taken out to Castle Island, and to speak to Mr. Fenton, who still lies sick at the Governor's house. I also wished to have another look at the alley behind the mews in daylight and return to you this."

He set on the small parlor table the covered basket he had been carrying, and Abigail saw it was the bundle of food, linen, and *Don Quixote* that she'd handed Billy Knox that morning. "Colonel Leslie has forbidden the prisoner to receive further gifts, fearing—he says—clandestine communications."

"About what, for Heaven's sake?"

"If we could anticipate all schemes devised by those who seek to foment rebellion," Coldstone replied stiffly, "we would have little need for a regiment here, m'am. I regret to say that none of today's enquiries yielded information, and it occurred to me that you may have learned something from Miss Fluckner or her chaperone about events at the Governor's ball that might have escaped the host."

"Not yet." Abigail settled back again in her chair. "Though Miss Fluckner and Mrs. Sandhayes assure me that they will gossip their way through the parlors of every other guest that evening and learn what they can of who might have absented themselves from the ball at ten or eleven in the evening—I doubt we can place Sir Jonathan's death much later than that, on account of the heat of the body—or whether anyone in Boston hated the man enough to kill him."

"Other than the Sons of Liberty?" enquired Coldstone politely. "Or the man whose sweetheart he attempted to ravish the morning of his departure?"

"Possibly a friend of the maidservant he attempted to ravish in her own room in the Fluckner house?" returned Abigail. "The one who disappeared? He seems to have made a habit of that sort of behavior."

"He did." Coldstone's voice was suddenly dry and flat. "He was known for it. My mother would not have him in our house."

"You knew him?" Abigail regarded him in startled surprise. And yet, she thought, Lieutenant Coldstone came from the same class of society that Sir Jonathan Cottrell did, the English gentry whose landed wealth and sense of social responsibility formed the backbone of government and society in the home country. They were the men who were elected to the House of Commons, the magistrates who enforced its laws in thousands of England's villages from Land's End to Hadrian's Wall, the officers who commanded her armies, and the churchmen who were given livings whether they deserved them or not. They knew one another, married one another's daughters to their sons, attended the same plays and salons, patronized the same modistes and bootmakers. Rich or poor, they sent their sons to the same schools, where they learned to write with Coldstone's elegant hand, to speak with his clear diction, to wear clothes with a certain style—even if they were refurbished like Margaret Sandhayes's gowns, or put on, as Coldstone had put on his crimson uniform, because the family had not the money or the influence for him to do otherwise.

Of course their families had moved in the same circles.

"I did not know him personally, as I was at school when he was obliged to leave the country."

"Was there a scandal?"

"Of sorts. A girl hanged herself." The savagery in his voice was all the more shocking because it was not raised above his usual soft conversational tone. "It would have raised no eyebrows, except that she wasn't a servant. A number of people cut him after that and he went to the Continent for some years, but of course such things do get forgotten, particularly if the man in question is a friend of the King's. My mother knew him. If you will pardon me, the recollection played a part in the immediacy of my suspicion of Mr. Knox. But it is equally likely that another outraged husband or brother or sweetheart did the office, or that the crime was connected with the absence of the memorandum-book from his pocket."

"It was not in his luggage, I suppose?"

"No. Nor in his room at the Governor's."

"Did his luggage contain a journal or daybook of any sort, recording where he went in Maine?"

"Nothing. Not even notes. His regular daybook of expenses he left at the Governor's. Mr. Fenton says that his master's memory for such things was quite good, and he would frequently go for a week without making any notation, then tally up all the preceding expenses at once. His luggage did contain letters of introduction to Mr. Bingham at Boothbay, and to another agent of Mr. Fluckner's on Georgetown Island, further along the coast. Both letters bore the appearance of having been unfolded, handed about, and read, as is to have been expected."

"Please don't tell me," sighed Abigail, "that we're going to have to pursue enquiries into Maine at this season."

The afternoon was darkening, and as she genuinely liked Lieutenant Coldstone, when he rose to go, Abigail went to the kitchen and donned cloak, scarves, shawls, and pattens to accompany him as far as the wharf. The mob that had followed him from the Governor's would still, despite the cold, be waiting in Queen Street, and while they might have orders from Paul Revere not to lay a hand on the two British soldiers, she wouldn't have wanted to wager on the chance that they'd protect them if others tried.

Sergeant Muldoon, his red coat off and his musket placed carefully in the pantry where none of the children could get at it, was helping Pattie fill the lamps at the big worktable in the kitchen, while Johnny and Nabby, instead of doing their lessons, were listening to the sergeant's tales of camp and transport and fighting the French. At Abigail's appearance in the doorway the children dived back into their books and slates; Pattie and Muldoon scrambled to their feet. "I trust you're not corrupting my son?" Abigail inquired.

"No, m'am. I doubt I could," he added with a grin, "with all his da's already havin' him read of what the Romans got up to! Lord, think of a boy that age, able to write Latin and all."

"Young Mr. Adams brought you a note from Mr. Sam." Pattie produced a folded paper from her apron pocket.

> *The* Magpie, *out of Boothbay, sloop of 94 tons. Master: The Heavens Rejoice Miller. Put in at Scarlett's Wharf Saturday, March 5, cargo butter, potash, skins. Still there. Ship's boy Eli Putnam sleeping aboard, Miller and Matthias Brown, also of Boothbay, went ashore morning of March 5 shortly before arrival of Cottrell on the* Hetty, *not seen since.*

Eight

The *Magpie* was a thirty-five-foot sloop, Jamaica-rigged, that badly needed a coat of paint. Among the tall oceangoing vessels of the harbor it blended in, like a shabby idler in a crowd, but Abigail picked it out at once as she crossed the icy black planks that joined Scarlett's Wharf with the higher ground along Ship Street. Somebody on board had built a fire in the little galley. Smoke trickled from the cabin's half-open door, snagged and whipped away by the wind that tore at Abigail's cloak and cut through the quilted jacket, skirt, and petticoats beneath.

"You know a man's poor, when he's living on water in weather like this." Paul Revere hunched his shoulders and kept one steadying hand on Abigail's elbow against the force of the squalls, the other hand being engaged in holding on to his hat.

Abigail could only nod agreement, so tightly were her teeth clenched to keep them from chattering.

One truly knew one's friends, she reflected, on evenings like this: after escorting Coldstone and Muldoon to Rowe's Wharf, she'd walked along the waterfront to North Square in the fading twilight and knocked at the door of the tall, narrow Revere house. The silversmith, God bless him, had not inquired why she wanted an escort to Scarlett's Wharf, which lay only a few yards beyond. He'd only laid aside his pipe, kissed his wife and his numerous offspring, and gotten his coat.

He called out now, "Ahoy the *Magpie*!" as he held out his hand to help Abigail up the gangplank. The boy who appeared in the low cabin doorway was well in keeping with the vessel and with everything Abigail had heard about the inhabitants of Maine: unwashed, glum, his shaggy hair drooping in his eyes, he was dressed in castoffs that would have embarrassed a scarecrow.

"You'd be Eli Putnam?" Revere enquired briskly. "We're looking for Mr. Miller or Mr. Brown."

The boy's eyes widened with alarm and he whirled like a hare seeking its burrow. Only Revere's quickness kept the boy from slamming the cabin door behind him. Revere got a shoulder and a thigh into the aperture and leaned his weight on the door as the youth struggled to shut it. "Don't know nobody by that name," the boy shouted out of the smoky murk below.

"Are you the master of this vessel, then?" demanded Revere.

The boy, confused, said, "Yes."

"Don't be daft, son." Revere leaned his weight on the door and heaved it open, leaned in to catch the youth by the arm before he could disappear down the hatchway. "You've no more beard than my baby daughter and a vessel this size needs a crew of two at least. Did Miller follow Cottrell down from Boothbay?"

"Matt Brown made him!" blurted the boy. "You ain't magistrates, are you?"

"Don't be a dunce," said Revere good-naturedly. "Do we look like magistrates? My name's Revere. This is Mrs. Adams."

The boy's dark eyes got bigger still. "Like Sam Adams?" he whispered.

Abigail nodded, since this was technically true. John and Sam shared a great-grandfather, who had doubtless spent the past decade rolling over in his grave at the thought of Sam's politics. "We need to speak to Mr. Miller or Mr. Brown," she said.

"That's just it, m'am—mister," said the boy. "I dunno where they be. Come down," he added belatedly, and gestured down the nearly pitch-black gangway. "There's a bit of a fire. You'll be froze up here, stiff as a pig in the shed. I got tea," he added. "I mean smuggler tea, not Crown tea. And rum."

"What did your friends want with Cottrell?" asked Revere, once the three of them were crowded knee-to-knee in a cabin barely the size of Abigail's pantry. "What did he get up to in Maine?"

"He were lookin' about, sir. Everybody down east said they'd teach him not to fool with Maine men. But he kept cautious. Kept indoors at night and got old Bingham to send a man with him when he went about. Quimby, that owns the public house, said we's not to harm him, though the boys was all for showin' them Proprietors here in Boston they can't pull us about and put us off our land. But it's hard to put Matt off a plan when he's got one. Matt took it in his head that if every man the Proprietors send up got his head broke, pretty soon they'd decide not to send any more men, and he says Quimby's a coward that's read too many books and newspapers."

"And is that what Cottrell said he'd do?" asked Abigail. "Turn you off your land?" Someone had clearly been cheated on the tea—about a soupspoon's worth of crumbles and dust at the bottom of a decades-old box. The brew it yielded was grayish and utterly flavorless, and judging by the cautious way her companion sipped his rum, the contents of his cup was either just as bad or murderously strong or both.

"They been sayin' it at the public house for months," said the boy Putnam. "How after we fought the Indians and cleared the land, it wasn't really that Dunbar feller's to let in the first place, and Mr. Fluckner or Mr. Bowdoin or Mr. Apthorp or one of them others, they're going to clear us all off." He pushed back the hair from his eyes for the tenth time: a thin boy, the skin of his face reddened and darkened from a short lifetime at sea, his fingers—where they showed beyond roughly knitted mitts—calloused and knotted already with work. Some of John's strangest tales of his legal journeying involved men and women he'd encountered in that cruel and stony land, Scots and Germans clinging to unyielding acres, fighting Indians or trading with them until many of them were very like the savages themselves, barely knowing God's name and with only the sketchiest notion of His Commandments. The hard work broke men without giving them enough to feed their families; the sea from which they took the bulk of their living was a cold and greedy creditor who demanded from every family a son or a husband or a brother every few years.

It isn't just about tea, Abigail thought, *and it isn't just about taxes*. Looking into the boy's eyes in the near-dark of the little cabin, she saw again Mrs. Fluckner's smiling lace-decked portrait on the wall and the liveried footman bringing in a tray of cakes for Mrs. Sandhayes to slip to the lapdog. And suddenly, she understood Sam. *It's about the fact that men who're friends with the King can do this to men who're not friends with the King.*

"So what did Mr. Brown plan to do?" she asked, and set her teacup aside.

"Only beat the shite out'n him—Only hammer him good," the boy corrected himself, when Revere kicked him hard on the ankle. "He was for goin' on the *Hetty* himself if Hev wouldn't take him down in the *Magpie* . . . Hev Miller," he provided, when Abigail looked puzzled. "That owns the *Magpie*. He's my cousin and Matt's, too, and he only agreed because Matt loses his temper like he does and he thought he'd better be along to keep an eye on him. Only somethin's gone wrong, and I'm feared they come to harm, and I've been here waiting for 'em six days now, and if they've killed him, the magistrates'll come for me, too. But I don't like to ask, in case there's somebody askin' about for me. I'm scared even to steal food. I can't just leave 'em, but I can't let myself be took. I've got my ma to look after and my sisters, and I don't know what to do."

He looked from one to the other of them, pleading for guidance. Abigail had guessed his age at fourteen or fifteen, but now she wondered if he were younger than that. Or did he only seem so, because she had grown used to the sharp town prentices of Boston and had forgotten how much at sea these backwoods boys were, when they came to one of the biggest cities in all of America?

"Would you tell Mr. Adams how I'm fixed, m'am?" asked

the boy timidly. "Mr. Quimby—that owns the Blue Ox in Boothbay—he'll read us from what Mr. Sam Adams writes, about Freedom and the King and no taxes, and nobody to throw us off our land. He says, Sam Adams is a friend to us, though he's never seen us." His smile, suddenly shy, was like a ray of sunlight; a flash of hope in a life unremittingly bleak. "He says he's a friend to all those that don't hold by bein' pushed about by the King's rich friends. *Would* Mr. Adams stand a friend to me?"

Abigail's glance crossed Revere's in the murky darkness of the cabin. "To be sure he will," she said. *Sam, I shall strangle you myself if this boy comes to harm.* "If nothing else, I'll send someone over with something for you to eat—what *have* you been eating all this time?" And she clucked her tongue sharply at the boy's mumbled recital of barter for the remnants of the cargo. "But you must tell us the truth. Did Mr. Brown and Mr. Miller wait for Cottrell when he came ashore?"

"Oh, yes, m'am. We all three was on Hancock's Wharf when the *Hetty* put in, and saw him come off, in that fine gray coat with all the capes to it that he wore and a French cocked hat like Mr. Bingham wears. Hev says, *You stand to and be ready to take the* Magpie *out the second we come on board, and I mean the second.* Then Matt tells me to cut along back here, and cut I did. I seen him and Hev follow Mr. Cottrell off round the corner and up the street that leads away from the wharf—Lord, there was so many people about, and carts and things, they didn't even need to take care not to be seen or anythin'! And that's the last I saw them."

"How were they dressed?" asked Revere, and young Putnam's brow furrowed.

"I dunno. Just regular clothes."

"Boots or shoes?"

"Moccasins," said the boy, astonished that his questioner hadn't known that.

"Is Hev's coat brown or blue?"

"Green," said the boy. "Matt's used to be blue but it's mostly all faded out sort of gray." Then, as if it finally dawned on him that neither Revere nor Abigail would have the slightest idea what his friends looked like, he added, "Matt's got a cocked hat, Hev's has got a brim on it like a preacher, except he's got a couple bear claws and some feathers hangin' off it, 'cause he'll go sometimes into the woods and trade with the Abenakis. His mother just hates it when he does that. Hev's tall and thin, Matt's about your height, sir, or maybe shorter, dark like you, and built like you but fatter. Matt brought his rifle and a pistol," added the boy, "but Hev took 'em away from him. He left the rifle here"—the boy nodded at it, lying across two pegs driven into the wall—"but he took the pistol with 'em. And Matt had a club."

Softly, Abigail said, "Did he, indeed?"

"Is Mr. Cottrell killed, m'am?" asked the boy. "Would you know how to find that out?"

"I'm afraid he is dead," replied Revere quietly. "He was killed—apparently beaten to death—sometime Saturday night."

If Abigail had Jesuitically neglected to mention which Mr. Adams she was married to, her companion, she noticed, had likewise been less than ingenuous in answering the question of whether they were magistrates or not. In fact, Paul Revere was active in the politics of his ward, and had served as clerk of the North Square Market on a number of occasions, and knew most of the selectmen of the town. "Something the boy didn't need to know just now," he remarked, as he steadied Abigail in her unwieldy iron pattens up the slippery planks of the wharf once more. "I'll call on the Chief Constable in the morning and see if my suspicion is correct about where our two friends have been this past week."

"I think jail's the only place they could be, don't you?" Abigail glanced back at the feeble glimmer of the *Magpie*'s porthole in the frozen stillness of the new-fallen dark. Even in the harbor, sitting in the little sloop's damp cabin had left her aching and slightly sick. "If they were looking to flee the town, they hadn't far to run to get on a ship. Going inland across the Neck would only get them to Cambridge, where it doesn't sound as if they had friends. They could take the ferry to Charles Town or Winissimet, but why? Thank you," she added, when they turned along Ship Street, toward her home and the much-belated supper that poor Pattie would have been obliged to prepare. "I beg you extend my apologies to Rachel for taking you away like this—"

Revere waved a hand good-naturedly and then grabbed for his hat again. "Lord, Thursday is Rachel's night to have her sisters over," he said. "They'll be clustered around the fire, stitching and talking like a tree-full of finches in the spring." He grinned. "You've only made me a trifle late for my pint at the Salutation—" He named one of the North End's most notoriously Whig taverns. "And I know for a fact that that's never killed a man, because Rachel's told me so a thousand times. I'll send you a note in the morning, to let you know if anything turns up at the jail."

But the note that arrived the next morning, as Abigail was scalding the churn and the dasher preparatory to starting (*Heavens be praised*!) the first butter of the year, was borne, not by Paul Revere, Junior, but by the young black footman who had served her tea and cakes at the Fluckners'. He emerged from the passway from the street, grinned with relief as he recognized her, and hurried up to her, shivering a little and wrapped to his cheekbones in scarves and a coat. "Mrs. Adams, m'am." He held out a note. "This from Miss Fluckner. She say it's important."

"Come inside." She left the bucket standing on the icy bricks, deposited the butter-making equipment in the shed as they passed its door, and took a silver bit out of the box on the sideboard to pay the youth. Though she heartily disapproved of tipping the servants of rich people who probably ate better than did her own children, Abigail knew also that the small pleasures of freedom would be few for a slave. "Does she need a reply?" she asked as she broke the seal, and the young man, who was holding out mittened hands gratefully to the fire, shook his head.

"She didn't say, m'am. Just that it was important that you get this right away."

Mrs. Adams—

Can you come at once? I don't know what to do about what I've found, or what it means, but everyone will come home before dinner and I'd like you to see this before that happens. Mr. Barnaby has instructions to let you in.

L.

Nine

What on earth—?" Abigail knelt in a whisper of petticoats to peer behind the narrow bed that Lucy had pulled away from the wall of the little attic room.

"I put it back exactly where I found it," provided the girl. "Bathsheba had a piece of planking over the hole, braced in place with the end of the bed. I know a lot of the servants hide their tips, because there's always somebody in any house who steals. You couldn't see this, unless you moved the bed and lay down on the floor."

"I see." Abigail brought her own cheek close to the worn planks, tried to angle the candle to the hole that had been gouged straight through the thick layer of plaster and broken-off lathe, without burning down Mr. Fluckner's very expensive residence.

"This whole attic used to be one huge room," explained Lucy. "This"—she slapped the wall—"covers a truss-beam about twelve inches square, and there's another partition wall there on the other side, with a hollow in between where the beam goes. You can reach in," she added, when Abigail hesitated. "There's nothing awful in there."

Abigail obeyed, bringing out first an old teapot, half full of something that made it weigh several pounds, and then an apron, rolled together around what felt like coins. Quite a number of coins.

"I wanted you to see them exactly how they were."

She spread the apron out on the bed. "Good heavens!"

"I counted," said Lucy in an awed voice. "There's twenty-three pounds in there."

Abigail picked up one of the coins. Silver—English. On its face, King George stared superciliously off into space. She sorted the rest of the coins with swift fingers, while Lucy held the candle above her shoulder, for the window in the little dormer was small and faced west, away from the fitful morning sun. "All English," she murmured, still trying to adjust her mind to the fact that a slave-woman would have that much hard cash.

She opened the broken-spouted teapot, and from it dipped out more coins. These were more typical of the little hoards of hard money collected and saved by all of her friends: quarters and bits of Mexican doubloons, French deniers, Dutch rix-thalers. As a girl, she'd scarcely ever seen currency. Most business in Weymouth and the surrounding farms had been done by barter: *I'll fix your shoes if you give me some butter.* John still had a great many clients who paid him in potatoes. When he did get paid in cash money, it was always like this, minted in the name of a dozen European kings because Parliament would not give any colony the power to hold silver or strike coins of its own.

She didn't think she had ever seen twenty pounds in English coin all together at the same time.

She let the bits and coppers slither through her fingers, touched the hem of the apron, clean and still stiff with starch. "That apron hasn't been in there long. Nor has the silver tarnished."

"And Papa isn't missing any money," added Lucy. "Believe me, the whole house would know it if even a penny went missing out of his desk. Sir Jonathan's the only person—maybe even counting Governor Hutchinson—who would *have* that much English coin. But why would he give it to her? He could get fifty harlots for it—couldn't he?"

"At least," agreed Abigail absentmindedly, her thoughts on other things than her companion's moral upbringing. "Depending on how fastidious he was. And what were *you* doing, young lady, searching your servant's room?" She looked around her at the bare and icy little chamber. Besides the bed there was only a low bench that appeared to do service as both table and cupboard. There were two stools tucked beneath it, and along its back edge a neat line of folded petticoats, caps, and stockings, piles of clean baby-clouts and tiny garments. Both children must have shared their mother's bed, a desperate necessity in the unheated room. Something in the stale air of the place made her think that the room had been closed up for the almost two weeks since Bathsheba's disappearance, and Abigail breathed a prayer of relief. At least they weren't making poor little Marcellina stay up here alone.

"I remembered what you said," said Lucy slowly, "about Sheba maybe being dead. I hope she isn't—Papa's still offering a reward for her—but if she doesn't come back soon, I *know* he's going to sell the children, or even just *give* them away just to get them out of the house!" There was real distress in her voice. "I know it isn't my business, but I thought . . . I know some of the servants keep their tips. When Sheba was my maid, men were *always* paying her off to carry love-notes to me. I don't mean that to sound like it does," she apologized. "But it's true. For three years now, I've been . . . It makes me sick, Mrs. Adams. Sick and mad. That's why Harry—"

She stopped herself, her jaw tightened at the thought of Harry Knox. Abigail laid a hand on the girl's shoulder, and Lucy shook her head, pushing the thought aside.

"Anyway, I knew Bathsheba was saving her tips, to buy Marcie free, and then Stephen when he was born. And I thought, she might have saved enough that if I gave it to you, *you* could buy at least one of them. Mama's already spoken to Mrs. Barnaby about the time she spends changing Stephen's clouts and feeding him and Marcie. I honestly don't know where they can go. I don't even think the orphanage would take Negro children, and that only leaves the poorhouse . . ."

"I won't let that happen," said Abigail firmly, seeing the tears start in Lucy's eyes. "And who told you it wasn't your business, what becomes of the children of a woman whom you've known since you were Marcie's age I daresay? This"—she scooped up a handful of the heavy silver coins—"will vastly help matters, if it comes to that. But as you say," she added shrewdly, "'tis a great deal of money for a man to give a slave-woman when there are others who can be bought for less . . . If that's what he was buying."

Lucy frowned, puzzled. "What else would he have wanted to buy from a woman?"

"Silence."

"About what?"

"About whatever was worth twenty-three pounds to him—maybe. And twenty-three pounds may not be the whole sum of what he gave her, if she took some with her when she left."

Lucy knelt beside the bed and ran the coins through her fingers, listening to their heavy, musical clink. "Why would she leave any?"

"We can't know that until we know why she left."

"Could that be what she meant, when she said to Margaret, *Something terrible has happened, and I don't know what to do? Could* she have been pregnant?"

"I've been told a woman *can* become pregnant while she's still nursing," said Abigail, "but I've never known it to happen. And I've never known a white man who considered impregnating some other man's servant-girl—by seduction or by force—sufficiently shameful to pay twenty-three *pence* to the girl to keep quiet about it, much less twenty-three pounds. *Something terrible has happened*," she repeated slowly, "*and I don't know what to do*." She replaced the lid on the teapot, folded the silver together in the apron again, and tied its bands into a loose bundle. "And this on the Friday, *after* Sir Jonathan had departed but nine days before his death. May I keep these?" she asked, rising to her feet. "I'm sorry," she added, as Lucy preceded her out the door into the main attic. "I didn't mean it to sound—"

"No, it's all right." The girl laughed. "I know what you mean, and yes. I mean, if I left them here, or even in my room . . . I know at least one of the footmen steals. Mama's like Margaret and says all servants always steal, but your girl doesn't, does she? Neither does Sheba, nor Philomela, nor Mr. Barnaby, though I actually wouldn't put anything past Mr. Barnaby if he was protecting his wife. He dotes on her. I think it's sweet, really," she added, as they crossed through the upper hall toward the main stair. "Let me get you something to carry those in, so if Papa comes home for his dinner early, he won't accuse you of stealing a teapot." She dodged into her room, emerging a moment later with a hatbox, into which teapot, apron, and coins were tucked and tied. "Will you stay for some tea?" she asked, when they were in the downstairs drawing room again.

"Thank you," said Abigail, "but I honestly can't. With John away there's always more to be done. Really, Miss Fluckner, if you don't stop beating and starving this poor dog"—she stooped to scratch Hercules behind the ears as the obese pug waddled up to her, its curled tail wagging so that his whole backside threshed—"your reputation will never recover. I'm sorry, sirrah, my hands are empty. No food. See? There is nothing edible in that hatbox, either—" She turned her head at the sound of the outer door opening, and a moment later, Hannah Fluckner's rich, slightly overloud tones.

"Good Heavens, Barnaby, company before *noon*? What on *Earth* was the girl thinking?"

"Just in time," Lucy whispered.

"My dear Hannah," laughed Mrs. Sandhayes, "they all go to bed at sundown here! Of course they're all up and doing at the crack of dawn—"

"Should I tell Margaret about this?" Lucy nodded toward the hatbox. "She blithers like a perfect nincompoop, but she's really very clever. You should see the list she's putting together, of people who were in the ballroom that I didn't even remember, and when people came and went out of the cardroom."

"Caroline Hartnell?" Mrs. Sandhayes's voice lifted in reply to some remark of her hostess. "Dear m'am, there's no sense expecting *her* to contribute a penny. She lost *five hundred guineas* at silver-loo Wednesday night . . ."

"Great Heavens!"

"I almost fancied myself in London again. And playing so

badly! I wanted to go around the table and shake her, except that I was winning at the time—"

"I don't think so," murmured Abigail. "And she complains of *servants* gossiping!" She stroked Hercules's little round head, and though she did not approve of lapdogs, smiled as her fingers were thoroughly licked. "As we're going on the assumption that Harry *didn't* murder Sir Jonathan, it follows that someone else *did* . . . and that someone might just as easily be a member of the Governor's circle of friends, as some poor disgruntled ruffian from Maine."

"—La, my dearest Hannah, *surely* you know about her and that *dashing* Major Usselby . . . *such* a name, Usselby . . . ! The one who always seems to win, when she plays across from him . . ."

"Until we know more about who might have done it and where they were just after full dark fell on Saturday night, I had rather we keep whatever we might learn between ourselves. My dear Mrs. Sandhayes," she smiled, turning from Lucy's protesting headshake to greet the chaperone as she appeared in the doorway.

Lucy sprang to her feet: "How went your shopping, Margaret?"

"Astonishing—I positively *made* your mother purchase the most *exquisite* yellow silk for you—"

In the hall beyond Mr. Barnaby's shoulder, Abigail could see a parade of footmen bearing parcels and hatboxes up the stairs, sufficient to have furnished an expedition to China.

"I'll take oath it was French, for all that pirate who was selling it claimed it was Indian and *perfectly* within the regulations of the Board of Trade. It should make up divinely into one of the new polonaise gowns—*le dernier cri*, my dear: *nobody* but dowdies like me are wearing panniers anymore.

Has Mrs. Adams seen young Mr. Knox again?" she asked more softly, drawing close. "Is he well? They're not *really* going to be such imbeciles as to ship him off to Halifax . . ."

"Well, they'll need a ship to do it on, first," said Abigail, shaking hands. "And given the weather, I doubt that will appear any time soon. The fact is, I came to ask about Mr. Fluckner's plans regarding that poor girl Bathsheba's children, if their mother does not return."

"Poor little mites," sighed Mrs. Sandhayes. "Worse of course that the older one's a girl, because one *can* sell boys as young as five for pages, if they're pretty enough." She shook her head. "I cannot even *imagine* what sort of despair a woman would have to be in, to walk away from them like that . . ."

"Do you think it was what she intended to do?" asked Abigail, as a footman—the same young African who had brought Lucy's letter earlier that morning—relieved the Englishwoman of her half-dozen shawls and scarves, and of her faded cloak with its elaborate whaleboned hood.

"I wish I could say yes or no. But honestly, Mrs. Adams, I don't know." She drew off her gloves, resettled the Medusa cameo on its ribbon at her throat, tucked and patted and twitched the powdered mass of hair—genuine and false—into order again. "She loved her children, and I know she would never have gone away from them in her right mind . . . But had you seen her, weeping, and shivering, and . . . and turning about as she did, at any noise or movement nearby . . . I should have spoken to her then. I should have taken her aside . . ." She limped to the nearest chair, sank carefully down into it, and propped her canes against its arms. "I should have done *something*. But I did not."

Lucy walked Abigail to the door, carrying the hatbox for her carefully, so that the coin inside neither jingled nor shifted its weight. Mr. Barnaby brought Abigail's wraps to the hall, and as she donned them one by one, Abigail asked quietly, "Mr. Barnaby, the last time I was here you spoke of the chance that I might see Mr. Fenton, at the Governor's house. Can that still be arranged?"

"I'll ask my sister about it," said the butler. "But I can't see why not. I can't imagine His Excellency would deny the poor man a little company in his illness. He's barely able to eat, Mattie says—my Emma's sister—and weak as a babe."

"Then I shall make him a blancmange," said Abigail.

By which form of bribery, she reflected, she might very well be able to find out whether Sir Jonathan Cottrell had indeed handed over the cost of a good horse to a slave-girl . . . and possibly, why.

Two notes lay on the sideboard when Abigail came into her own kitchen again, to find Pattie telling Charley and Tommy the story of the Three Billy Goats Gruff while she chopped up yesterday's chicken into a stew for today's dinner . . . a task which Abigail knew she herself should have been doing. Yesterday's laundry, like a maze of whitewashed planks, swung awkwardly on the lines that crisscrossed the yard, and a glance into the shed told her that Pattie had not yet had the time to churn the small amount of cream into butter.

Good. There were still three crocks of last fall's butter in the cellar—tired as everyone was of the salt taste of it. Even this modest contribution from that morning should suffice for a blancmange.

She turned her attention to the notes. The one from Lieutenant Coldstone contained a neatly drafted plan of the mews behind the Governor's house, the alley, and the mews gate, with the location of Sir Jonathan's body, of the lanterns on the gate, and of the farthest range (ascertained by experiment by the Governor's head-coachman Mr. Sellon) at which a hundred-pound sack of corn could be distinguished on the ground once full dark had fallen. There was also a list of the names of all footmen, coachmen, and stable hands present in the yard that night.

The other message was from Paul Revere.

Matthias Brown, The Heavens Rejoice Miller taken up for brawling at The Dressed Ship 8 o'clock Saturday night. Will be there after dinner, to take you to see them at the gaol.

Ten

The city jail of Boston stood on Queen Street, not a hundred feet from Abigail's front door. Because Hoyle—the dour and rum-breathing jail keeper—knew John of old, there was only cursory bargaining for the use of a penitential cubicle that had been built to one side of the grim brick structure, rather than obliging them to conduct the meeting through the judas of the cell door. Because John knew Hoyle of old, Abigail knew enough to bring her own firewood to warm the interview chamber.

"Two Maine men, eh?" grumbled the jail keeper. "Fat one and tall one. Sometimes the one calls himself Smith, sometimes Jones. Magistrate'll sort 'em out."

"When will they be up?" Revere asked over his shoulder as he clacked flint to steel over the kindling in the disused and spidery fireplace. "I'm surprised they're still here." He paused, used a billet of the kindling to shovel aside what looked like several weeks' accumulation of ashes, and rearranged the sticks to try again.

"Won't give names like honest men." John always said Hoyle gave him the impression of charging for his own conversation by the word. "Monday, he'll sort 'em out."

Abigail and Revere traded a glance as the jailer retreated in a clanking of long iron keys. Though the jail was barely five years old, already this room was acquiring the old jail's lingering stink: of mold, of dirt, of old vomit and filthy garments. Abigail was only grateful to be in a position to pay for the use of this room. Both John—who had interviewed clients there—and Abigail's younger brother William—who had fetched up in the place himself upon occasion—had described to her the single long chamber, freezing as an icehouse in this season and reeking like a cesspit in the summer. *Hell on earth*, one journalist had described it when he'd had the misfortune to learn that fact firsthand.

She settled herself on one of the benches that flanked the little hearth, pulled her cloak closer around her slender shoulders, and watched as Revere coaxed the fire into being. Abigail prided herself on her judgment of cooking-fire and coals, but as a silversmith, Paul Revere was an artist with flame. With air-draft, too, she reflected, coughing, and retreated as her companion adjusted damper and flue. Though it was far colder near the window, it was out of the smoke—through the wavery and unwashed glass she had an impression of a yard blotted with dirty snow, of the brick jail building itself and a window shuttered tight.

Because the opening was unglazed, behind those shutters?

What had "Smith" and "Jones" used to pay Hoyle for food,

she wondered. The only person they knew in town—poor little Eli Putnam back on the *Magpie*—didn't even know they were there. Her brother had told her, and John had confirmed it, that Hoyle and his wife routinely sold half the foodstuffs the city allotted them for the prisoners. A man who had no family to bring him extra rations—as she had tried to do for Harry—went hungry indeed.

Under two layers of stockings, her toes were growing numb.

Fetters clanked on the bricks of the hall.

"Whoever they be, they got the wrong folk," growled a deep voice. "We got nobody here in this stink-pit town."

"Well, they think they know you," retorted Hoyle's voice. "*Smith.*"

"I'm Smith," corrected another, lighter voice. "He's Jones."

They entered the room, one tall and one short, one fairish—his hair the color of the lowest grade of molasses sugar—the other swart. Yet something in their eyes and the shape of their unshaven chins whispered of cousinry. Abigail remarked mildly, "Well, the heavens rejoice," at which the tall so-called Smith started like a spooked deer. Smiling, she continued, "Mr. Smith—Mr. Jones—permit me to introduce *Mr. Eli Putnam*, master of the sloop *Magpie*," and gestured to Paul Revere. "And I am Mrs. Adams."

The two men stared at her with widened eyes. "Jones," the shorter, darker man in the much-fouled and faded once-blue coat, whispered reverently, "That wouldn't be—*Sam* Adams?" and Abigail's smile widened.

"Let's just say Mrs. Adams for now." She glanced significantly toward the door, through which Hoyle had disappeared. "And as my mother always says, *First things first.*" And she unpacked the basket she had brought, and set out two loaves of bread, half a crock of butter, a chunk of cheese the size of her two fists, and two bottles of cider. The men fell on these like starving dogs, without a wasted word.

"M'am," said "Smith," after an appropriate time, "Mrs. Adams, we owe you whatever you care to name for that."

"I'm pleased you feel that way, Mr. Miller," responded Abigail. "Because we really do need to know what happened last Saturday night."

"It wasn't us," blurted Matt Brown. "I swear on my mother's grave it wasn't us!"

"Your ma's not dead," pointed out Miller. "Ow!" he added as Brown punched him in the arm.

"What wasn't you, Mr. Brown?"

The two men traded a glance. Miller lowered his voice, leaned toward her, though he kept a polite distance owing to the reek—and the infested condition—of his clothing: a consideration Abigail found surprisingly fastidious, after seeing him eat. "In the jail they're saying how the King's man was killed that night," he said softly. "It wasn't us. We never saw him after he went into that house beyond the Common, and that's God's truth, strike us both dead for our sins."

"What house?"

Brown and Miller traded a glance.

"We know you followed Sir Jonathan Cottrell back from Maine," said Abigail.

"We wasn't going to hurt him," said Brown earnestly. "Just beat the innards out of him, to show them psalm-singing stinkard Proprietors they can't mess with us in Maine."

Abigail said, "I see."

"Bingham's man always put the *Hetty* in at Hancock's Wharf," explained Miller, "so we knew where to wait for him when we came in, since the *Hetty's* the slowest thing on the water between Philadelphia and the Bay of Fundy. We loafed around the wharf for maybe two hours, 'fore they arrived. Cottrell got off the boat and left his luggage, and went up the hill to rent a horse from a feller at a livery—"

"A little bay Narragansett," said Revere. "White star, white stockings on the near fore and off hind—"

"That's the one!" said Brown, impressed. The single bar of his black eyebrow quirked down in the middle, over the short, ugly curve of his nose. "You wan't there, was you?"

Revere looked wise and tapped the side of his nose.

"We thought we'd be left in the mud, us not havin' two shillings for our dinner, let alone the price of a horse," said Miller, leaning forward on the bench with his manacled hands folded on his knees. "But he rode along at a walk, in no hurry, down the main streets of the town and out west of town near the Common, where they got a couple of streets cut but not so many houses to speak of, and cows and gardens and maybe a house or two. Cottrell rides straight up to one of the houses that is there, a good-size brick place with what looks to be an orchard at one side of it, that nobody's taking care of, and puts his horse up in the stable like he owned the place and goes inside. We couldn't get close, on account of him knowin' us and us not wantin' to be seen."

"How did he know you?" asked Revere, and Matthias Brown looked puzzled, as if there were some self-evident portion of the story inscribed in the air above his head that Revere had neglected to examine.

"Because I'd laid hold of him in the ordinary-room of the Blue Ox and told him I'd beat the innards out of him for the festerin' English Tory psalm-singin' bastard he was."

Revere echoed Abigail, "I see."

"Only after that the festerin' psalm-singin' English Tory bastard kept indoors, or had two of Bingham's men go about with him, so I never got the chance in Maine, y'see. I followed him all the way down to Georgetown Island and back, too. And that witch-friggin' coward Quimby that owns the Blue Ox kept close to him, like they'd got engaged, as if there's any harm in poundin' the Proprietors' agents, the festerin'—"

"Quite so," said Abigail. "So you threatened Cottrell with a beating in front of witnesses." No wonder Miller—who seemed in charge of what brains the duo possessed—had exhibited anxiety over the magistrates learning their right names.

"Ain't I just told you that? But like Hev was sayin', we never got the chance." Brown's deep voice was tinged with regret.

"Did you wait for him outside the house?"

"Oh, yes, m'am," said Miller. "The house stands on a rise of ground, some two–three hundred yards off from the meeting-house that looks out over the Mill-Pond. I had my glass with me, so we stayed by the corner of the meeting-house and watched the place, turn and turn about, all the afternoon. Just before dinnertime a man rode up on a dapple gray horse and went inside, and stayed maybe an hour. Bar that, there was nothing, though just after Cottrell got there, smoke came out the chimney, white and clotty-looking the way it is when the chimney's cold. We didn't see no servants, no stableman, nothing."

"When it grew dark," asked Abigail, "did you see lights in the house?"

Both culprits looked abashed and scratched in silence.

"It was mighty cold there by the meeting-house, m'am," said Miller at length. "As bad as back home, or nearly."

"And we hadn't had but a heel of bread and some cheese we brought from the boat," added Brown. "And no rum for hours and hours."

Abigail said again, "I see." The Lynd Street Meeting-House stood largely isolated in that hilly, thinly built district north of the Common, but along the Mill-Pond nearby stood little clumps of habitation, which included at least two distilleries and several of Boston's less salubrious taverns.

"We weren't going to be gone from our post but for a few minutes," added Miller earnestly. "Either of the pair of 'em would have been in sight when we came out, if they'd left, and if those festerin' Massachuser scoundrels at the Dressed Ship had been able to hold their rum like real men."

"It wasn't the rum," insisted Brown. "'Twas the damn butter."

"When you show witch-friggin' Massachusers how to make hot buttered rum," explained Miller to Abigail, "you've got to watch out for the butter. Lot of men can't take it. Renders 'em quarrelsome."

"Ignorant festerin' bastards," added Brown.

Abigail sighed. She'd heard all about hot buttered rum from her brother William, and how it was indeed all the fault of the butter. "And did it," she asked, "render the other customers of the Dressed Ship quarrelsome?"

"It has to be good butter," insisted Brown. "This slime they had at the Dressed Ship wasn't hardly butter at all, so we wasn't to be blamed really for what happened. If they'd had decent butter there, all would have been well, and so we told 'em."

Miller nodded agreement.

"What time did the fight start?" asked Abigail resignedly. "Was there still daylight in the sky?"

"Oh, yes, m'am," said Miller. "But only just."

"The sun was down," agreed Brown. "But when they throwed me through the window, there was plenty light in the sky for me to find a good stick of firewood to go back in with." He made a gesture indicative of brandishing a club. "Those table-legs, they just break first thing you hit with 'em."

"I'll remember that," said Abigail. "Was it still light when they brought you here?"

"Yes, m'am," said Miller promptly, though his friend looked a bit puzzled, possibly because he had not been completely conscious at the time. "Fight didn't last but a minute or two, before the Watch came in. Probably drinkin' just down the street, festerin' Puritans. Dusk it was, when we come in here, and that scoundrel Hoyle took my glass in trade for just enough wood so we didn't freeze to death in the night, the witch-friggin' Massachuser bastard. The magistrate had already gone home, and next day was Sunday, so nobody asked us our names. And by Monday everyone in the jail was talkin' that Cottrell had been found beat to death. So we figured, better we not give our names nor nuthin', and take our whippin' at the stocks, and be on our way. Only *someone*"—he glared pointedly at his friend—"got mixed up whether he was supposed to be Smith or Jones, and the magistrate said, we's to stay in the jail 'til they figured who we really was and if we'd done some other crime like robbery, and he wouldn't pay no mind when we swore on the Bible an' everythin' that we'd been with each other the whole of the day and neither of us had done anythin' barrin' defend ourselves from a bunch of witch-festerin' Massachuser scoundrels who can't handle hot buttered rum on account of the butter bein' unfit."

"Your time's up." Hoyle reappeared in the doorway,

possibly brought back in by the incautious raising of Hev Miller's voice. Paul Revere got to his feet and crossed to meet Hoyle. Abigail heard the clink of a coin, followed by the discreet closing of the door again. *Money may be the root of all evil, but it can certainly make the affairs of the world more convenient.*

"He says we're going before the magistrate Monday," murmured Miller, lowering his voice again. "Then we're going to get shut of this town, quick as ever we can. Eli's all right, isn't he?" he added. "You seen him? The *Magpie*'s all right?"

"It is," said Abigail. "But—"

"I'm afraid getting out of town isn't in it for you yet." Revere came quietly back to the remains of the fire, to which Abigail and the two prisoners had been huddling with greater and greater intimacy as the sticks were consumed. "They're searching for you—not the Watch, but the Provost Marshal of the Sixty-Fourth Regiment—and they've got a man keeping an eye on the *Magpie* at the wharf." This was news to Abigail, but he laid a hand, very gently, on her shoulder to suppress her start, and she nodded quickly and made her face grave.

"'Tis true. We were afraid we wouldn't find you in time."

"But don't worry, men," Revere went on bracingly. "And hold yourselves ready. I'll talk to Mr. Adams tonight." He winked at them. "We'll find a place to keep you, 'til we can find another way to take you out. In the meantime I've given that brute Hoyle the price of a half-decent meal and a blanket for the two of you, and we'll get word to Eli that all's well." He clasped Miller, then Brown by the hands. "You boys stay sharp. And not a word to anyone. Someone will see you tomorrow."

"Yes, sir—Thank you, sir—"

"Mr. Revere!" Abigail stopped herself from scratching as

they followed Hoyle back through the cold little vestibule and grudgingly handed the man a tip as he bowed them out the door. "You aren't going to have Sam arrange a jail deliverance for those two ruffians, are you?"

"The way I see it, we have little choice, m'am." They crossed Queen Street, then turned down the little passway that led to the Adams yard, Abigail reflecting in annoyance that her dress, both her cloaks, and every petticoat she had on would have to be hung up outside overnight in the freezing cold to rid them of the livestock they'd picked up. *And* she would be obliged to wash her hair . . .

"For one thing," Revere went on, "we're going to need them to point out the house. There's probably half a dozen within that distance of the Lynd Street Meeting-House, and at least two I know of have the remains of orchards or gardens attached. For another, it may take us some time to locate Cottrell's mysterious visitor—the last man to see him alive. The last thing we need is to have to send to Maine for them—and get them sobered up and back down here to testify in court that it was indeed he whom they saw enter the house."

Always provided they haven't done something else in the meantime . . .

"What about the boy Putnam?" asked Abigail, surrendering to the inevitable. "You can't oblige that poor child to stay living on the water like that—"

"Heavens, no! We'll have to tell him some tale that will get him out of town altogether—Lynn or Salem should do. One of our boys there will see to him, so we can send for him quickly if need arises."

"I suppose now our only problem will be," she sighed, and maneuvered her arm beneath her cloak so that she might scratch without being obvious about it, "whether when we find Cottrell's visitor, the Provost Marshall will believe our witnesses about a mysterious visitor to an unknown house . . . or whether he'll find a more complicated explanation too much bother to pursue."

Eleven

The jail deliverance took place the following night.

In the cozy pitch-black box of her curtained bed, Abigail heard dimly the crack of shots from Queen Street and the clatter of hooves on the cobblestones. Then, more muffled, the trample of fleeing feet. *Two minutes for the Watch? Five? Ten . . . ?*

She had almost slipped into sleep again when the constabulary finally arrived, muffled voices shouting from the door of the jailhouse: Hoyle's and those of his wife, mother, and the crippled sister who shared bleak quarters on an upper floor of the jail itself. The elder Mrs. Hoyle especially had a voice that could shatter a cannonball, and even through the thick walls of her house and the curtains of her bed, Abigail could make out a word or two: *rogues*, *ruffians*, *pistols, outrage* . . .

And let's hope Sam and his friends didn't deliver the entire population of the jail while they were about it, to pick pockets and steal washing off the line . . .

Which was what had happened, she recalled, sliding back toward sleep, when her brother William's friends broke him out of the jail the year before last. Like Hev Miller and Matthias Brown, William had sworn on his honor—an item Abigail regretfully reflected was as fictitious as the grave of Matthias Brown's mother—that he'd had nothing to do with the fraudulent removal of three horses and an anvil from a local blacksmith's shop, for which he'd been scheduled to answer to the local magistrates on the morrow of his arrest. Like the two Mainers, he had declined to give his name to the constables who'd taken him up, though being brighter than Miller and Brown—a distinction he shared with seven-eighths of the population of Boston and the kitchen cat—he'd cheerfully provided an invented one. "I wouldn't have cared, for myself," he'd told their parents—in her dream Abigail could see him, filthy and beaming on the family doorstep, fair hair falling into bright brown eyes. "I knew my innocence would be my shield. But I could not bear that your names would be spoken in open court."

And Mother, Abigail reflected—still tasting the bitterness that flavored her resignation—*Mother believed his tale of mistaken identities and lying witnesses, as she will always believe . . .*

Annoyed as she'd been with her brother, she'd been sufficiently curious about how one went about breaking out of the Boston town jail to put aside her rancor for her parents' sake and ask him, and had learned that jail deliverance was, in fact, laughably easy. "Oh, they'll search a visitor for something like a pistol or a cutlass," William grinned. "But anyone can slip you a chisel or a file, and the bars aren't set into the bricks, only into the wood of the framing. People come in and out of the place all day, selling food and wood and visiting the prisoners. There's always someone there who can arrange for things."

No wonder Colonel Leslie had placed an embargo on clean shirts for Harry.

"You are incorrigible," she said, and hugged him, smelling even in her dreams the stink of his unwashed clothing, of tobacco and ale. Though she knew he was wrong, she could not help her gladness that he'd been spared the lash and the stocks.

In William's case, she'd gathered that his friends had broken open the jail-yard gate, and used a horse and a wagon-chain to pull out one of the barred windows . . . an indiscriminate method that had resulted in most of her current neighbors (she and John had been living in Braintree at the time) being subjected to a brief rash of petty thefts and burglaries by the other occupants of the jail. The Sons of Liberty, she gathered when Revere appeared at her side as she shopped in the market Monday morning, had exercised greater finesse.

"I saw the Hoyles in Meeting yesterday, so I assume those shots I heard Saturday night didn't hit anyone," she remarked, as she selected fat, shining mackerel from the baskets set along the Town Dock. This time of the year, when it would be months before anything fresh appeared in any garden in Massachusetts, was in some ways one of the most discouraging in the markets, but at least one could get fresh fish to eat with one's corn-mush and potatoes.

"Good Lord, no!" Revere put on an expression of shock. "That was Mrs. Hoyle, and without her spectacles she can't hit the side of a barn. No, two of Sam's smugglers broke into Hoyle's rooms and took the keys. We—*they*"—he corrected himself quickly—"shoved a bench in front of the door and ran downstairs to get our birds out, and Hoyle himself only got off a couple of shots at us—*them*—as they were on their way out down the street. At least, so I've been told."

"Hmph." Abigail eyed him up and down cynically. She agreed wholeheartedly with John that the colonies could not win their rights before King and Parliament if those rights were championed by a law-breaking mob of smugglers and hooligans. Most members of Parliament would have looked askance even at this brilliant and quick-minded artisan and be damned to the fact that he made the most beautiful silver pieces in the colony. *One doesn't want one's daughter marrying a bookseller*, Margaret Sandhayes had said, as if the matter were self-evident.

Revere himself seemed to see no problem in giving political power to illiterates whose vote—and fists—could be bought for a quart of rum and a friendly handshake.

Like her mother—and herself—with the ne'er-do-well William, Abigail found herself accepting the situation, because without the help of Sam's tame ruffians, Harry Knox would undoubtedly hang. But her heart told her that trouble would one day come of their violence, as it would come—*was coming*—from the mob's violent defiance of the King's orders concerning tea.

"And where are our friends staying now that they've ceased to be Mr. Hoyle's guests?"

"The storeroom at Christ's Church," replied Revere cheerfully. "Young Rob Newman's the sexton there, and his brother looks after the organ. Between them they're able to keep our friends fed and happy and out of everyone's way for the time being. With baths and different clothes, and a wig or maybe an eyepatch, they should be quite well able to meet us at the foot of Beacon Hill in an hour and show us where it is that Sir Jonathan Cottrell went—on a rented horse though the distance could be walked in a quarter hour—instead of returning to his host's house and the party given in his honor on the day that he died."

With only an hour before the rendezvous, Abigail scarcely had time to change Tommy's clout, measure out potatoes, cabbage, and onions for dinner, and order Pattie *not* to do her mistress's work as well as her own while her mistress went and played sleuth-hound with the Sons of Liberty: "'Tis my own punishment if I'm to be making beds after dinner instead of calling on my friends," she told her servant firmly. "I'll not have you loading yourself with an extra burden because of my sloth."

"No, m'am." But as Abigail set out with Revere again—he had obligingly cleaned the fish while she was dealing with Tommy and chopped a hunk of the frozen pork in the pantry to thaw for tomorrow—she had the suspicion that she'd come home to find her chores done for her, something against which her Puritan soul revolted. Pattie was very fond—and a little in awe—of both Harry Knox and Paul Revere, and she took a vicarious delight in doing extra work so that Abigail might engage in her investigations. Abigail, who hated housework like the mouth of Hell, felt that there was something profoundly wrong with this arrangement: a yielding to her worser nature against which she had been warned all her inquisitive and disobedient life. There was too much chaos in the world, she reflected, her pattens slithering on the uneven, icy earth of the Common, for citizens to leave their children to come home to no one but the servants while they rushed off and did as they pleased, even if the goal was to save a man wrongly accused of murder . . .

. . . or to learn the fate of another woman who had abandoned *her* children.

The north side of the Common was empty at this hour of the morning, the frozen ground still patched with last week's snow. In the distance she could see the town herd-boys moving the cattle along the slope of Fox Hill, near the river. Further out on the slatey waters, a couple of men were crossing the mudflats in a punt. After dinner, despite the steel-colored roof of scudding cloud and the taste of sleet in the air, those muddy spaces would be dotted with boys released from their lessons and shouting madly as they flew their kites in the ice gray sky, or rolled hoops, or ran footraces, or risked their lives skating on ponds whose ice was, at last, beginning to thin.

Perhaps it was the memory of William and his good-for-nothing friends—stealing back horses that one of them had lost at cards to the blacksmith, and the man's anvil to "teach him a lesson"—but Abigail found herself remembering wistfully the open countryside around Weymouth, where her father had been parson now for forty years. About her and Mary and Betsy, walking those snow-covered lanes arm in arm or running races themselves, all bundled in their quilted petticoats and the bright red cloaks considered suitable for young girls, in the confidence that anyone they might meet would be a neighbor and a friend.

Here in Boston, crammed into this stony little peninsula surrounded by salt marshes, one had to come here to the Common to run, or to play, or to ride at a gallop . . . and not even then, if one was a little girl. She guessed her daughter Nabby missed the countryside—and her cousins in Braintree—as much as Abigail herself did, and as a child,

Nabby did not have the social and intellectual compensations of living in town. In town, Abigail was aware that she kept her daughter much more circumscribed, as if she still wore a toddler's leading-strings on her clothing. There was more that could befall a child—a girl—in town.

And girls always paid a higher price for carelessness or ill-luck than did boys.

The chilly precision of Lieutenant Coldstone's soft voice came back to her, when he spoke of the man who'd been murdered. A boy who'd been "led astray" by "evil companions" was seldom reduced to such desperation as to seek the razor or the noose. His evil companions would break him out of the local lockup, and he'd show up dirty and beaming on his parents' doorstep, and even his disapproving sister would take him in her arms.

For a girl, it wasn't like that. Not only would she be cast out by her friends, but her sisters would find their chances of marriage halved, or worse: *If the one girl was loose, who's to say the rest are honest . . . ?* They would be forced to turn their backs on her in sheerest defense of their own futures.

No wonder Hannah Fluckner had leaped upon the chance to enlist her shabby but genteel houseguest as a chaperone for the adventurous Lucy.

They skirted the grim brick Almshouse, the crumbling stone wall of the old burying-ground, and moved through the orchards on the footslope of Beacon Hill into the fields beyond. Here, as Hev Miller had said, streets had been laid out, in what had once all been the common land of a smaller Boston years ago. Now speculators bought up what they hoped would one day become valuable town lots.

At the moment it was only these ice-slicked tracks that distinguished much of the land here from the Common itself. Here and there, houses had been built, and occasional gardens enclosed or orchards planted. But these were few and far between, and the place had a forlorn air. Downslope toward the town, a string of dwellings fringed Treamount Street, the wind from the bay raveling smoke from their chimneys like dirty wool. Just beyond where the land leveled toward the frozen slab of the Mill-Pond, the Lynd Street Meeting-House reared its red-brick steeple, and across the street from it, a little group of men stood talking, watching in their direction as they came.

Even at a distance of fifty yards, Abigail picked out the black coat and sturdy form of the young sexton of Christ's Church, and the burly figure of Matthias Brown. When she and Revere came closer, she recognized Hev Miller despite a respectable-looking gray wig, somewhat more civilized footgear, and one of Sam's hats. The fourth man was Ezra Logan, the master of the *Katrina* who'd taken her across to Castle Island a week ago. He'd probably been included, Abigail guessed, to keep an eye on Miller and Brown in case they decided they didn't want to stay in Boston after all.

"There's the place." Miller pointed almost due southwest of where they stood. The house he indicated was almost new and stood back from the road. Abigail was familiar with it, in that she'd passed it dozens of times, on summer afternoons when she and John would come walking on the Common and up and down these rough-cut, unpaved streets. She'd had the impression on those occasions that the place was uninhabited, and on this blustery morning she could see no trace of smoke from its chimneys.

"Who owns it?"

Revere shook his head. "Should be easy enough to find out."

She glanced up at Miller. Abigail herself was reckoned tall for a woman, but the young Mainer stood a good six feet. "Did Cottrell knock at the door, or did he have a key?"

"I didn't see." Miller produced a spyglass from his pocket, unfolded it, and handed it to her. Evidently, the jail key wasn't the only thing that had been extracted from Hoyle's apartments. "He rode round behind, so there might have been someone in the stables, though I didn't see smoke. He'd been out of our sight for some little time, before smoke came from the house chimney."

Revere capped the horn flask of rum that Logan had handed him, and gave it back to the boatman. "Let's have a look."

"Won't they be watching the place?" asked Miller uneasily. "The Provost Marshall? It *is* your bird's house."

"That's just it," said Abigail. "It isn't. Nor was he staying there, that anyone knew of. Of course there's been nothing to tell us," she added, as the little party set off up the steep grade of the hill, "that he *wasn't* staying there. But I'll take oath that the Provost Marshall doesn't know."

"Ground's frozen hard." Paul Revere hacked at the surface of the driveway with his bootheel as they approached from the lane, which maps optimistically designated as George Street. "I doubt it's taken a track in the past two weeks."

"The heavens be praised for small favors," remarked Abigail. "I should hate to try to approach the house if the mud *wasn't* frozen. This drive doesn't look as if it's been graveled in years. Yet there's a knocker on the door," she added, as they reached the shallow granite steps. "Curious."

"A cheat and a come-on," declared Revere, after several

minutes' hammering with the ornamental brass hand—unpolished, Abigail noted, and beginning to tarnish. The steps beneath their feet were muddied with tracks, coming and going; a slatternly note on so elegant a façade. "A lure for the unsuspecting and a snare for the foot of the curious."

"Yet the house itself is well maintained," she observed. "The shutters have been painted recently. So has the door." She moved to the edge of the step, studied the first of the ground-floor windows on that side, all shuttered tight. "Were the windows shuttered when Cottrell came here, Mr. Miller?"

"They were, m'am."

"So you would not have been able to see it, had there been a light on inside or not? Had you not," she added, "been otherwise occupied after it grew dark."

He grinned a little shyly. "No, m'am. Matt—!" he added, as his comrade stepped forward, jerked hard on the handle of the door, and dealt the green-painted panels a brutal kick.

Matt Brown shrugged, as if breaking and entering were something one did every day to the houses of witch-festering Tory bastards. "Just thought I'd try."

Further evidence of occasional usage rather than habitation was forthcoming when they circled the house. A small heap of soiled straw, frozen solid, lay outside the locked stables. "In this cold it's hard to tell whether someone was here Monday or Tuesday," remarked Revere, cracking at one of the rock-hard balls of dung with his heel. "Neither this nor the straw looks to be much older than last week, that's for certain. None of it's fresh."

"So it could be from Cottrell's horse on Saturday."

"Easily."

Abigail turned and looked back at the rear of the house. Closed as tightly as the front, it nevertheless had not the appearance of a place long deserted. There was a small woodpile beside the kitchen door, nothing like the cords of logs stacked in the shed at home. She asked Miller, "Did you get a look at Cottrell's visitor?"

"Not well, m'am. He moved brisk, like a young man. Dark cloak—dark gray or maybe dark blue—gray scarf, and bundled up good. Leaped off the horse rather than eased off, if you take me, and led him into the yard like he owned the place."

"Led him *himself*?"

"Cold as 'twas, you couldn't let a horse stand."

"So you didn't see who let him in?"

Miller shook his head.

Revere muttered, "I'll wager it was Cottrell himself who opened the back door. It doesn't sound like there was a servant in the place."

"Fenton being sick, of course," Abigail replied thoughtfully. "I wonder, though—Mr. Miller, Mr. Brown, I thank you more than I can say for your observations. As it happens, I'm acquainted with the Provost Marshal's assistant—"

Both culprits looked startled and awed, and as Revere had done, Abigail put on her wisest face and tapped the side of her nose, as if to say, *I would tell an' if I could . . .*

"Mr. Adams has eyes and ears everywhere," she said. "On our next meeting, I'll find out for certain what they know. Until then, gentlemen . . ."

Shortly before dinner, Young Paul Revere—at thirteen turning into a sturdy, dark, second edition of his father—arrived panting with a note in the silversmith's neat hand: *No word in any livery stable of a dapple horse rented to a young man in a gray scarf Saturday 5th inst. Pear Tree House (as it is called) owned by Thurlow Apthorp.*

This information Abigail copied onto a square of note-paper, together with the statement: *I understand from reliable witness that this is where Sir Jonathan Cottrell went between his arrival Saturday morning and at least sunset of the day of his death.* From the little money-box on the sideboard, she took two silver pieces of eight and gave them to Young Paul, to take the message to Apthorp's Wharf and make sure it was sent across to Lieutenant Coldstone on Castle Island.

Twelve

When Paul Revere had brought Abigail home from the Common that Monday morning, it was to find that firstly, Pattie had completely disobeyed her orders and had made the beds, and was in the process of fixing bubble and squeak for the family dinner, and secondly, a note had arrived from Lucy Fluckner, enclosing one from her father's butler Mr. Barnaby.

> *Permission has been obtained from His Excellency Governor Hutchinson, for you to visit Mr. Fenton this evening, when dinner is done. Mr. Buttrick will be waiting for you in the servants' room at seven.*

The late hour at which the fashionable ate their dinners gave Abigail sufficient time to make a blancmange—assisted by Nabby, when the girl and her brother had returned from school—and to let it cool sufficiently in the icy pantry to be of a proper consistency at half past six, to be carried to the invalid. "I think it would be horrid," Nabby said as they took turns stirring the steaming mix of slowly thickening sugar and cream, "to be sick in a foreign country, and not know anyone, and have to accept charity from someone else's servants."

And Charley, watching from the other side of the table with the expression of a starved orphan stamped on his round-cheeked rosy face, added hopefully, "I'd thank God and pray, if someone brought *me* a blancmange."

Though it took all the little cream that Cleopatra and Semiramis were producing these days, Abigail made four small extra portions of the tender white dessert, to be ready for the children's supper that night. Bad enough, she reflected, viewing the cat scratches on the boy's nose, which had recently been added to the faded remains of last Sunday's black eye, that John was forever riding off to Salem or Worcester or Haverhill, without them having a mother, too, who put her self-perceived "duties" ahead of listening to their lessons and being there to put them to bed.

Thaxter walked with her to the Governor's. Abigail had met the King's representative in the colony briefly, upon exactly two very formal occasions, and since her business was with Cottrell's servant and the brother-in-law of Thomas Fluckner's butler, she and the clerk entered the property through the mews gate rather than the porter's lodges and front door. As they picked their way along Governor's Alley, she could not help looking for the spot where, according to Coldstone's chart, Sir Jonathan Cottrell's body had lain. There was very little to see by the light of Thaxter's lantern: the muddy ground had been cut to pieces with hooves and carriage wheels, ruts and marks refrozen by half a dozen nights. Yet Abigail could not keep herself from turning, as she and Thaxter passed between the orange blobs of light shed by the gate lanterns, to see for herself how far their light *would* carry.

And was forced to conclude that a mountain of slaughtered rhinosceri could have lain in that spot, at any hour after full darkness, without detection, let alone the mere dark little bump of a small and slender man.

A German maidservant let her and Thaxter in through the back door, and led them downstairs to the half-basement servants' hall. It was as large as the one at the Fluckner mansion, whitewashed, blessedly warm from an ample fireplace and redolent of cooking-smells and the tallowy odor of work candles. As they entered, two men rose from the long central table to greet them

One—small and trim except for a round little paunch—Abigail assumed to be Mr. Buttrick, the governor's steward and husband of Emma Barnaby's sister.

The other, tall and slender and quietly dressed, was—Abigail realized with a start as she drew near enough to make out his proud, scholarly face in the candlelight—His Excellency the Governor himself. "Mrs. Adams." He made a graceful leg exactly as if she were not related to one of the men who'd encouraged a mob to sack his previous dwelling a few years before. "Welcome to my house. Mr. Buttrick tells me you're here to visit poor Sir Jonathan's manservant—a blancmange?" he added, his eye falling on the pewter dish she carried, and he smiled, with great and genuine charm. "How extremely Christian of you, m'am."

"If I'm here to put the poor man on a gridiron about his late master," returned Abigail, drawn in spite of herself to the Governor's serene ease of manner, "the least I can do is bring him something, poor soul. This is Mr. Thaxter, my husband's clerk." The two men shook hands, and the little gentleman in the striped waistcoat was introduced, as Abigail had suspected, as Barnaby's brother-in-law Mr. Buttrick.

"I fear poor Fenton may not yet be in a condition to appreciate the work you put into your offering," the Governor continued, as he led his guests toward the servants' stair, which ascended, like a secret spine, through the whole height of the building. "Dr. Rowe has bled him almost daily, and though he claims to see improvement, poor Fenton is still extremely weak."

As the German cook took the blancmange from Abigail's hands to set aside in the cold pantry, Abigail saw the woman glance at Hutchinson's face with a sidelong look—*What? Anger? Disapproval?* As if words unsaid were tightening those heavy lips. But she only curtsied and backed away. Buttrick fetched a branch of candles from the table and bore it ahead of them up what felt like a thousand cramped, wedge-shaped little stairs.

David Fenton occupied a room among the neat little cubicles in the Governor's attic, allotted to his servants and those of his guests: stifling in the summertime, Abigail guessed, and freezing tonight. Like the room at Fluckner's in which Bathsheba had shared her narrow cot with her children, its walls consisted of lath and plaster slapped up between the struts and queen-posts of the roof, and its illumination by day would have come from the single dormer now shuttered against the cold. A candle on a mended table provided a modicum of light and a tremendous amount of smoke as the wind that moaned outside whispered and tugged at the flame. By the look of the wick, nobody had been up here for hours. It would smell, too, were the cold and stuffy air not thick with stenches worse by far. She wondered if the sick man could hear rats scratching among the rafters, if he woke in the night.

He didn't turn his head when the door opened, but she saw the gleam of his moving eyes.

"Mr. Fenton?"

As Buttrick brought the other candles closer, Abigail caught her breath, shocked at the appearance of the patient on the bed. Dr. Rowe, whoever he was—and by his name he was a member of one of that elite circle of merchant families that ruled Boston—deserved to be horsewhipped, if he had continued to bleed a man in this state.

"Mr. Fenton, my name is Mrs. Adams. This is Mr. Thaxter, my husband's law clerk. Mr. Buttrick said you were willing to speak with us, but if you're tired now, we can return another time."

"Quite all right, m'am." It was almost surprising to hear the soft words coming out of those cracked, unshaven lips. "Don't know what I can tell you, but if it'll save some poor bloke a scragging, I'll let you know what I can. Is there water in that pitcher, m'am?"

There was only a spoonful. Buttrick took the vessel, and he and Governor Hutchinson bowed themselves from the tiny room. Abigail made a silent vow, as Thaxter brought her up the single rush-bottomed chair, to have a few words with His Excellency on the subject of Dr. Rowe when she was finished here.

"We will all be most grateful for whatever you can tell us." Abigail pulled her cloak tight around her. "And I apologize for troubling you like this. But yes, young Mr. Knox—who is accused of killing your master—is likely to be tried by an Admiralty Court in Halifax for the murder, and he had no more to do with killing Sir Jonathan than I did."

"I dunno, m'am." A ghost of a smile flickered at the corner of the man's mouth. "You look as if you'd do a fair job of murder yourself if you had to, beggin' your pardon."

She said, "Go along with you, sir," but smiled in return. "The trouble is that Mr. Knox cannot *prove* he was in bed and asleep like a decent workingman, and so we are obliged to find the true culprit, if we are to keep his head out of the noose. I shall try to be as brief as I can."

Mr. Fenton moved his fingers a little, as if to say, *It's all one, m'am.* But his brow tweaked for a moment, and she heard his breath catch as if at the pinch of some inner pain.

"Did your master ever visit a house on the far side of Beacon Hill while you've been here? It stands by itself, beyond the edge of the settled buildings of town, near the Common? Do you know who lives there?"

"No, m'am, that I never knew." He glanced past her, to where Thaxter sat on the floor with the branch of candles at his side, scribbling in his commonplace-book. "'Course, he was often out and about without me. Often he'd ride out from town into the countryside. It was his job, after all, to learn what he could of where the troublemakers in town was gettin' their money from, for paper an' print an' rum for the mob."

Abigail opened her lips to snap, *What makes you think men need to be drunk or paid to express disgust with the King's rich friends?* but stopped herself. Politics were all beside the way, and the man who lay before her, she knew, would tire very quickly. "Did he tell you whom he met on these rides, or where he went?"

"No, m'am. I don't think it ever crossed his mind, to say where he was goin' nor when he'd be back, and I'd served Sir Jonathan twenty years. Just I knew to have a clean shirt ready, an' his coat brushed an' his wig powdered for him to go to dinner. There's gentlemen like that, m'am." He made a movement that might have been a shrug. "All part of bein' a gentleman's gentleman, like gettin' boots chucked at you. My uncle that brought me up did for a baronet in Hampshire that used to thrash him with his ridin' whip. Wouldn't even get angry." He shook his head again, wonderingly. "When I come down sick, if he could have found a man to take my place that short a time before we sailed, he'd have sacked me without thinkin' twice about it. Thank God decent servants is thin on the ground in this daft land, beggin' your pardon, m'am."

"Would he truly have sacked you when he got back?" It had nothing to do with Harry Knox getting hanged or where Sir Jonathan Cottrell had spent Saturday afternoon, but Abigail could not keep herself from asking. "As ill as you are?"

"Lord love you, m'am, it's kind of you to ask. 'Course he would. What use is a sick man to him? Specially if he was to be goin' back to England once good sailin' weather comes."

Abigail's lips tightened. "Was there any who hated your master?"

The servant tilted his head again to look toward Thaxter. "You down there with the cocked hat . . . How many pages has that little book of yours got?"

Thaxter, taken by surprise, ran a swift thumb over the corner. "Thirty still blank."

"Not near enough, m'am. The way he treated me—treated the chaps in the stables—the boots in any inn we stayed in . . . It was all one. You, an' me, m'am, an' your good husband, too, I'll wager, if here you are out doin' a good turn for your fellow-man without no fuss raised at home—we look at other folks an' we think, *Well, she or he has his troubles, too, an' if I don't like bein' treated like that chair you're sittin' on there, probably t'other chap doesn't like it, either.* But I swear to you, m'am, Sir Jonathan Cottrell was . . . It was like he didn't think about other people *at all*. Like they was no more real to him than faces in a painting. Not just servants an' beggars in the street, but everyone."

He grimaced and turned his face aside, his breath suddenly swift, and the door opened again to admit a very young scullery maid carrying the water-pitcher. Abigail filled the spouted invalids-cup that sat on the table at the bed's side, beside the wavering candle, and helped the sick man to drink. "It's like I got a fire in me," he whispered, when she refilled it and he drained it again. "I drink enough to drown a horse, an' it's like I've had nuthin' at all. I had the dysentery when first we got to Barbados, if you'll pardon me mentionin' such a thing, m'am, and before that was sick from bad water in Spain, an' it was never like this."

"Your master sounds," opined Thaxter quietly, "like a man walking about the world asking for someone to lie in wait for him with a club."

"He could be charmin', though." Fenton sketched another weak small gesture. "When he wanted somethin'—I've seen it. He had a nice voice, Sir Jonathan, and a way of listening like you were his dearest friend. It was somethin' he'd learned off, like a piece of music, to get what he had his eye on. It's like the lads in the stables say of His Excellency the Governor, not meanin' no disrespect of him: that he's a good man, a kind man, an' a brilliant one, and I'm here to say that's true . . . But they say, too, that folks all over this colony hate him, 'cause he gives all the plum jobs to his relatives and can see only the one side of any problem, an' that side his own. Like those magistrates that *can't see* that a man might steal 'cause he's hungry and can't get no work, not 'cause he's a thief in his heart. He was as he was."

"I suppose the question is not, who hated your master," murmured Abigail. "But who hated him enough to kill him. Not to *want* to kill him, but to actually go through with it. And who, of those people, was in Boston last Saturday, when Sir Jonathan came off the boat from Maine. How long were you in Barbados?"

"Two years," said Fenton. "Two years and four months."

"What was Sir Jonathan there to do?"

"Same as here. To report back to Lord North about smugglin', which is worse there than it is here, if you can believe it, the French and Spanish bein' so close. We stayed with Sir Damien Purcell, that's on the Governor's council in Bridgetown—" He winced again, and his breath caught as his hand pressed momentarily to his belly.

"Was there any trouble down there? Over women, or cards, or politics?"

Fenton's breath whispered in a laugh. "Lord, Sir Jonathan didn't care one way or t'other about politics, m'am. He'd follow whoever was strongest and make 'em think he'd believed what he said all his life. And women . . . beggin' your pardon for speakin' of such a thing, m'am, but Sir Damien, and about ten of the other big planters that was involved in the smugglin', they bought him the prettiest slave-women they could find. The men he reported, it wasn't that they didn't bribe him, but whether they could help him get on with the King or not. Up here, there's fewer that can do that for him.

"As for the women, he tired of 'em pretty quick. There was a little trouble over a white girl that was the daughter of Sir Damien's wife's mantua-maker, but he paid her parents twenty pounds and that was the end of that. There was no one about her to follow him up to Boston, even if they had had the money."

"What was her name?" asked Abigail, in spite of the fact that she knew he was probably right.

"Fanny Gill."

Thaxter wrote it down.

"Since you've been in Boston," she asked, "have you seen anyone Sir Jonathan knew in Barbados?"

Fenton shook his head.

"Anyone from Barbados at all?"

"A couple of the actors that was tourin' in Bridgetown while we was there, but no one that my gentleman would have spoke to."

"None of the servants from Sir Damien's house, for instance? Or from any of the houses of his friends?"

"No, m'am. Servants in Barbados, they're all black. Even had he done one of 'em wrong, and a bad wrong, they can't come and go the way folks can here. They can't just take a ship after him. Nor none from Spain, either, though he did have trouble there over a girl, a maidservant in the house of the Marques de Tallegas: bad trouble. Could I bother you for another cup of water, m'am? Thank you. Does me no good, it doesn't feel like—" He sighed. "The girl's sweetheart ended up killed. It wasn't ever proved who'd done it, but I always wondered if the Marques had had it done, to stay on Sir Jonathan's good side. That was a sorry business."

He stretched his hand feebly toward the cup as Abigail filled it again—she made a mental note to take the pitcher down to the kitchen with her to be refilled when she left. When he had drunk, Fenton's head dropped back onto the thin pillow, his face twisting in the dim candlelight; the filthy smell of sickness grew stronger in the room and mixed with the trace of fresh blood.

"A last thing," said Abigail softly, "and then we'll go. Did your master ever speak of the maidservant at the Flucknerses'? A black woman named Bathsheba?"

"In passin'," murmured Fenton. "Laughed about her, like it was a lark." His eyes had slipped closed. "Like a kid pissin' on the schoolmaster's doorstep."

"Did he give her money?"

"Him?" The servant's breath puffed out in a whispered laugh, a tiny cloud of gold in the icy dark. "A black girl?"

Abigail drew the blankets—ample, she was glad to see—up over the man's shoulders, tucking them gently in. Even in the thrashing light of the single candle at the bedside, she could see how sunken his eyes were, and when Thaxter stood and picked up the branch of lights that had been at his side, she started back, appalled at the dusky lividity of jaundice that the stronger glow made clear.

When she and the clerk returned to the servants' hall and thanked Buttrick for his kindness in arranging the interview, she asked, "Is Governor Hutchinson still at home, Mr. Buttrick? Could he spare me a moment of his time?" and in a very few minutes was shown into the front part of the house, where the Governor rose to greet her from beside the fire in his study. *John would expire with envy*, she reflected: books lined the walls, some new and imported from England, others old, clasped in clumsy bindings—the remains of the early records of the colony, whose history His Excellency had made his lifelong study. Despite the man's pigheaded intransigence about the tea last December—despite the letter that he'd written the King urging His Majesty to deal with the discontented colonists in the harshest possible fashion—still Abigail's hair prickled on her nape at the thought of the irreplaceable colony records that had been lost, trampled in the mud, and burned when one of Sam's mobs had looted the Hutchinson family home in the North End.

And yet, as Fenton had said of his master, the Governor had great charm, warmth, and intelligence shining from his gentle eyes. Abigail curtseyed and thanked His Excellency for his hospitality, "And for your willingness to help us gather evidence to be used in favor of Mr. Knox. What I wish to say now has little to do with that matter, sir, and is perhaps none of my business—except insofar as it is every Christian's business to do one's best to help a man who is suffering. Has any doctor other than Dr. Rowe seen Mr. Fenton?"

The Governor's fine brows drew together over his nose. "Dr. Rowe is my personal physician, Mrs. Adams, and the nephew of one of my closest friends."

"And I'm sure he is quite a fine one," replied Abigail. "Yet I'm sure you have observed how each physician has his own methods of going about a cure, and it appears to me—Sir, do you think, from your own observations, that Mr. Fenton is improving, simply by being bled?" When Hutchinson was silent, considering this, she went on, "I have had some experience of illness, Your Excellency, and Mr. Fenton appears to me to be jaundiced—and to be suffering from symptoms far beyond those of *la grippe*. Dr. Joseph Warren—"

He reacted like a horse suddenly enraged by a fly. "Dr. Joseph Warren is a fomenter of sedition and a professional troublemaker."

"And is a very good physician, with experience in this type of disorder." She comforted herself with the reflection that this might well be actually true, since it was clear neither of them had the slightest idea what type of disorder had Jonathan Cottrell's servant in its grip. "This is not a matter of politics, sir. I honestly believe this to be a case in which a misdiagnosis could mean a man's life. The man is a stranger in a strange land," she went on quietly. "His very life has been left in the hands of strangers. Could you not at least permit Dr. Warren to see him?"

The Governor's flat, square shoulders relaxed a little. He said a trifle grudgingly, "I could do that."

"Thank you, sir." She rose and curtseyed again. "Thank you from the bottom of my heart. May I write to Dr. Warren, asking him to attend on Mr. Fenton tomorrow?"

Hutchinson smiled wryly, and again, Abigail felt the warmth of his charm. "Would it do me the slightest bit of good, Mrs. Adams, if I said, 'No?' "

'Tis all well to say no one whom Sir Jonathan wronged in Bridgetown has followed him here, nor from Spain, either," remarked Thaxter, as he and Abigail made their way along Marlborough Street in the windy dark of early evening. Spits of sleet struck their faces, and Abigail shivered, thinking of the sick man, lying between waking and sleep in the dark of a stranger's attic, feeling his life leak away. "He sounds like a man who couldn't but make enemies wherever he went: *A plain-dealing villain*, like Don John in Shakespeare, who doesn't care who knows his evil and holds himself in such pride that he can't see any reason to change, because he's fine as he is."

"*I cannot hide what I am*," repeated Abigail softly, savoring the words of one of her favorite plays. "*I must be sad when I have cause, and smile at no man's jests; eat when I have stomach and wait for no man's leisure; sleep when I am drowsy and tend to no man's business; laugh when I am merry . . ."*

"And kiss whatever woman as takes his fancy, without asking what she or anyone else thinks of it," finished the clerk grimly. "A despoiler, even as Don John was of poor Miss Hero in the play, only because it amused him."

"*Let me be that I am, and seek not to alter me*," she murmured, reflecting on the deeper sin of that troublemaking canker in the lovely Arcadia of Shakespeare's imagining; the man who is utterly selfish to his own appetite and whims. Her father, she remembered, had a special voice, a special inflection, when he would read Don John's part, sneering and leering. John—her John—would for his part read the man quietly cold. As if, as poor Mr. Fenton said, other people were no more to him than faces painted in a picture. When the London papers came to Boston, she would scan their columns for mention of Shakespeare's plays in the theaters there and would wonder what it would be like to actually see these events. To see men—and women, too! for shame!—striding about the raised and lighted stage, rich in gleaming costumes, gesturing and turning; not just the circle of friends by the parlor fire reading those words . . .

She frowned and halted, the wind lashing the heavy folds of her cloak. "Mr. Thaxter . . ."

Absorbed in his own thoughts, he'd gone on a few steps and now turned back hastily. "M'am?"

"There are no theaters in Boston: there never have been."

He missed her point. "No, m'am, of course not—"

"Then what are actors from Bridgetown doing here?"

Thirteen

John was home when she and Thaxter reached the house chilled and tired from a day's long ride and out of temper that Abigail had not been there to greet him. It wasn't until supper was over that he recovered his good humor enough to relate the facts, as he'd gathered them, of his case in Haverhill: Mary Teasel's prickly independence of spirit that had alienated most of the men who would sit on her jury, Ham Teasel's irruption into the local inn one night to seize John by his coat-lapels and promise him a beating out of hand if he continued to *meddle in what ain't your business.*

"Good Heavens, John, what did you do?" Abigail asked, alarmed, and John turned a little pink in the lamplight.

"Oh, just leaned to the side to put him off balance and hooked his foot." For all his verbal pyrotechnics when out of temper, John was not a violent man, and she could tell that the thought of something that even came close to a tavern-brawl scratched his touchy dignity. "By the time he got to his feet again the innkeeper's brother and nephews were on him and put him outside, but I shall have to watch myself, when I go back up for the trial at the end of the month."

Still, with one thing and another, it was breakfast the following morning—mellowed with the fresh bread that she'd tucked into the oven just before bed—before he asked after the events of her week and heard what Matthias Brown and the Heavens Rejoice Miller had had to say about Sir Jonathan's activities on his return from Maine. "That note that was waiting for me when I came in yesterday evening—when you, sir, were so high-handed as to suggest that my wifely duties ranked above the call of my country's need—"

"I said I was sorry."

She mouthed a kiss at him. "Well, the note was from Lieutenant Coldstone, saying he's arranged to meet Thurlow Apthorp at four this afternoon at the Pear Tree House"—she produced the communication from her apron pocket—"and would the both of us care to join them there and see what there is to be seen?"

"Good Lord, woman, why didn't you speak of this last night?"

She paused with raised eyebrows in the act of handing Johnny his coat—at six, the boy refused all assistance in dressing and preparing himself for school—and returned, "Because I know better than to poke at a snarling bear, sir, for fear of getting my hand bit." Johnny also had reached the age of refusing maternal kisses as "babyish," so waited patiently while she kissed Nabby and straightened the girl's cap and cloak, then held out his hand to be gravely shaken by both his parents.

"Acquit yourself well at school, son," instructed John.

"And keep your sister's hand," Abigail added, though she

knew her son would dispense with this badge of infancy the moment he and Nabby were out of sight of the front door. Besides, Nabby would fall back to walk with her friends, and Johnny dash ahead to run with his.

But knowing how busy were the town's ice-slick streets in the first flush of daybreak, she couldn't leave the words unsaid.

As soon as the children were out of the kitchen, John rose from his chair and put both arms around Abigail's waist from behind. "I shall bite you, m'am, and to good purpose." Smiling, she held up her hand to him to let him do so, stepping apart from him with the skill of long practice as Charley came charging into the room, with Pattie—leading Tommy—at his heels.

John helped her with the dishes, then retired to his study when Thaxter arrived, to sort through the conflicting stories and rumors about the conduct of the Teasels, and parse out what should be done about the half dozen other Essex County cases that would be decided at the same session. Only after the kitchen was clean, and Abigail had swept and mopped and dusted abovestairs—not that any house could be kept clean of soot-smuts and the smell of smoke, in the shut-up months of winter—and sent off a note via Pattie to Dr. Warren and another to Paul Revere, did she return to her husband's study, to finish her report on what she had put together of Sir Jonathan's nature and activities.

"According to our fine lads from Maine, Cottrell kept himself much to himself while he was there," she said. "He went once to Georgetown Island, to confer with Mr. Fluckner's agent there, but he habitually went about with a couple of Mr. Bingham's hired men for escort. Eli Putnam—who, Mr. Revere tells me, is in hiding with Ezra Logan out on Hog

Island—has further reported that there wasn't the smallest whisper of scandal about Cottrell while he was there. Evidently either he didn't fancy the ladies of Maine, or they didn't fancy him."

"It doesn't sound like that's ever stopped him before," sniffed John.

"Perhaps they weren't helpless enough. Or maybe the black eye Miss Fluckner gave him served him as a reminder every morning when he looked in the mirror."

"Hmm." John settled back in his chair and with his penknife scraped a thin paring from the edge of his quill-tip to adjust the flow of the ink. "And nothing from Miss Fluckner herself?"

"A quite remarkable list of every dance that was played at His Excellency's ball that night, the order in which they were played, and the men Miss Fluckner danced with, delivered yesterday by Philomela. Mrs. Sandhayes's tally of who was in the cardroom when—if the woman keeps count of other peoples' aces the way she recalls who was present around the table, she must be an absolute demon at vignt-et-un—is rather less complete, I gather because she had promised not to let Miss Fluckner alone to face Sir Jonathan and kept returning to her side."

"Little realizing that neither had a thing to worry about," muttered John, "because the guest of honor had the best of all possible reasons for being late to his own ball. Has a vessel come in to take Harry to Halifax yet?"

"Not yet." Abigail prodded the study fire grimly and hung the poker back on its hook at the side of the grate. "Not in weather like this. John—Mr. Fenton spoke yesterday of seeing some actors who had been in Bridgetown at the same time as Sir Jonathan here in Boston. Does that sound as odd to you as it does to me? What would actors be doing in Boston?"

"On their way to Halifax, perhaps?"

"But there's nothing *in* Halifax. Certainly not a theater. Only the shipyard and some troops and the local fishermen, who wouldn't lay out half a copper to see the Antichrist defeated on Judgment Day. The last few weeks of February—before Cottrell left and Mr. Fenton took sick—were extremely cold but quite clear. They would not have been forced to put up here because of bad weather. Would not actors have gone rather to New York or Philadelphia?"

"You're right." John laid down his pen. "'Tis odd. I'll be at the Green Dragon tonight"—he spoke the name of the tavern where the Sons of Liberty often met in the evening, sometimes only to drink ale and talk politics in the long upper room, sometimes for darker purposes—"I'll ask Sam and Revere if they can find out who these men were, and when they left town. Did Fenton speak to them, did he say?"

Abigail shook her head. "It didn't strike me as curious until after I'd left him. But I think he'd be agreeable, for me to see him again."

"Do that," said John. "Ask him when he saw them—it has to have been sometime before he took sick on the twenty-fourth—and if he spoke to them. God knows, Sam has informants all along the waterfront, and if there's a tavern-keeper on the docks that's a Loyalist, I'll—I'll leave you and marry him. Sam can learn, quick enough, if these actors were still in Boston on the fifth. 'Twill give me something to say to him when he begins to pester me about what we're to do to keep young Knox from being sent to the gallows."

By dint of concentrated exertion, Abigail had the beds made, at least some of the mending done, and dinner ready at three when Nabby and Johnny came in from school and John emerged, ink-boltered and cranky, from his study. Thanks to Abigail's message to Revere, when Lieutenant Coldstone knocked at their door promptly at four, he was followed by a gaggle of stevedores and layabouts who presumably had instructions to keep freelance patriots from molesting him and Sergeant Muldoon. Coldstone looked as annoyed about this as Johnny did when Abigail told him to hold his sister's hand, but the last thing anybody needed at this point, Abigail reasoned, was for a British officer to be beaten up in the street.

The impromptu bodyguard fell back when she and John, cloaked and scarfed to the eyes, emerged from their front door, but she was conscious of them trailing at a distance as they followed Treamount Street to the Common.

Thurlow Apthorp—a youngish man whose name Abigail recognized as connected with real estate speculation both here and in the countryside around Cambridge—met them on the ill-graveled drive. "I sent word to Mr. Elkins—both here and at his accommodation address—of your request to see the house, sir." He bowed to Coldstone, then, upon the officer's introductions, shook hands with John and bowed over Abigail's hand. "It is Mr. Elkins who has leased the house, for a year at fifty shillings the quarter. He gave me to understand that he travels a good deal, and there would be long periods when he would be away and the house locked up."

As they walked up the drive, Abigail reflected upon how Apthorp—a scion of the great merchant family—simply ignored Sergeant Muldoon, as he would have ignored one of Thomas Fluckner's footmen, or a tree-stump if one had happened to be near the place where they met. *Like they were just faces in a painting*, Mr. Fenton had said of his master's treatment of himself, of servants, of the workers at inns . . .

Of utterly no account.

What had Cottrell made of the rough and grubby Matt Brown cornering him at the local tavern in Maine and threatening him with mayhem, not about a woman—which Cottrell was clearly used to—but about the land that was the only thing these men and their families had? Had he written to Hutchinson about that confrontation? To anyone?

Was that something that he considered simply part of the cost of getting ahead in the world, along with informing on smugglers not useful to his interests, putting men off their farms, and paying off the families of girls he'd seduced?

He was what he was, Fenton had said, with the same resignation Abigail had schooled herself to feel about her mother's blindness where her brother was concerned. *Let me be that I am, and do not seek to alter me.*

The house smelled damp and faintly moldy. After the wind outside, the atmosphere within felt heavy and still. A trace of smoke seemed to cling to the walls, but nothing like the stuffy reek of a house that has had candles and fires burned in it day in, day out since November. "Who is this Mr. Elkins?" John asked, as Thurlow Apthorp led them into the wide central hallway—an open well up to the second floor in the English fashion, and impossible to heat—and thence right into a small but handsomely furnished drawing room.

"A London gentleman, well-off it seems, seeking to establish trading connections here in Boston." Apthorp shook his head. "Myself, I think the man's a fool. After what happened with the tea-ships, this town will be fortunate if the King doesn't close the port entirely to teach its more violent spirits a much-needed lesson."

"Did you tell him so?" inquired Coldstone.

"I did. He only shrugged, and said he'd take the house

in any case, and have a look about. I'd have thought—" He frowned. "I'd have thought there was something smoky about the fellow—a French agent, maybe—except he had letters of introduction from half the planters in Bridgetown, men my uncle has had dealings with for years."

"Bridgetown in Barbados?"

Abigail's glance touched John's, then Coldstone's, as the young officer asked the question. Like them, she felt herself come alert, as if at the sound of a foot on the stair of a dark house reputed empty.

Unaware of this quick and silent communion Apthorp nodded and led the way into the dining room. "This is the only room he had furnished up properly. Even the bedroom's got merely the bed in it, and a washstand . . ." The men passed through the length of the drawing room after him. Abigail lingered for a moment in the doorway to the central hall, wondering what it was that she smelled—or almost smelled—in the place. The trace—the thinnest whisper—of mortal sickness: vomit and blood-laced human waste. She looked around her at the double-high room, eerie with curtaining shadows. The doors on either side of the hall opened into chambers whose windows were shuttered, leaving the hall itself drowned in dimness, as if the gloom had settled like water into its lower half. A wide stair rose straight along one wall to a sort of gallery above, off which doorways opened into other chambers. These, unshuttered, admitted the day's gray pallor secondhand into the upper portion of the hall. A window above the door itself shed some light, but the effect was depressing and rather disconcerting, as if someone had read a book on the fashions that the English preferred in their houses without thinking through what would be needed to make the design livable here in another land. If one shut those upstairs doors, it would turn the whole of this hall into a gloomy pit.

". . . wanted a place to meet with gentlemen—in the timber trade, I believe he said," she heard Apthorp's rather light voice echo from the dining room. "But I never heard of him doing it . . ."

Abigail knelt for a closer look at the carpet. English, with a looped pile, and probably thirty shillings. It showed a little wear and some caked mud, as far as she could tell in the dingy gloom. But there was no sign that a man had died upon it—something which she knew would be difficult to hide. The oak floor elsewhere in the hall was clean as if recently mopped.

She got to her feet as the men reentered through the door at the back of the hall and followed them into the unfurnished parlor and the bare-shelved library on the left side of the front door. "What did Mr. Elkins look like?" she asked, and Apthorp frowned.

"An average sort of young chap," he said at length.

Abigail bit her lip to keep from saying, *Can you be less specific?* and Lieutenant Coldstone—evidently long used to winkling information from those not used to describing others—inquired, "Thin rather than fat?"

"Oh, thin, I should say."

"Tall rather than short?"

"Tall," said Apthorp promptly, though at an inch or so under her own height, Abigail reflected, the man would probably describe Lieutenant Coldstone as tall . . .

"My height?"

Apthorp's frown deepened. He'd clearly never even thought about it. "I should say so, yes."

"Taller?"

"Maybe a little taller—"

"Or shorter?"

"A trifle."

"Dark or fair?"

"Fair. Well, his hair was always powdered, you know. Dark brows, I think."

"Dark eyes or light?"

"Light."

Except for the difference in the height he had just described Sir Jonathan Cottrell, or Lieutenant Coldstone, or Dr. Joseph Warren, or the Heavens Rejoice Miller for that matter if one wanted to stretch the point. Abigail followed the men up the stairs. "If you thought to yourself what a fool Mr. Elkins was being for proposing to set up as a merchant," she said, "he must have rented the house later than December."

"Seventh of January," said Apthorp. "He arrived on the *Lady Bishop*, from Bridgetown. Myself, if 'tweren't for the cost of the thing, I'd have said—Well . . ." He glanced apologetically at Abigail.

Abigail sighed inwardly, and said, "Excuse me just one moment, gentlemen, I seem to have mislaid my handkerchief. Please do go on . . ." She stepped out of the bedchamber into which he'd led them—the only one furnished in the house, and that, as he'd said, only with a washstand and an uncurtained bed. She heard their voices murmur as she moved about the hollow square of hall at the top of the stairs—like a viewing-gallery of the hall below—off which all the bedchambers opened, putting her head through each door in turn. The empty rooms smelled strongly of damp plaster and mold. Not even the smell of mice, nor their furtive scurry. Clearly, no one had had anything resembling food in this place for years.

As Apthorp showed them up into the attics, John fell back to her side to whisper, "His private theory was that it was the sort of thing a very wealthy man might rent in which to rendezvous with a mistress."

"Catch me, John, I think I'm going to faint with shock."

"Any New Englander—and I don't care how rich he is—*would* faint with shock at the thought of paying fifty shillings the quarter for a house this size in which to meet a woman now and then, when he could get a perfectly serviceable room and bed at the Queen of Argyll down by the wharves for tenpence for the evening with the woman thrown in *gratis*."

"Then our Mr. Elkins was clearly willing to pay the difference for one thing that he would have here, that he would not have at the Queen of Argyll."

John nodded, as they emerged into the dense gloom of the attic, empty and icy and echoing as Apthorp, Coldstone, and Muldoon walked its length with candles held high and showing nothing but last summer's cobwebs. "Solitude," he agreed.

Fourteen

They descended to the cellar, as empty as the attic and twice as cold. "Nice wide stairs," remarked Abigail, who had frequently spoken to John on the subject of their own cellar, which even the Spanish Inquisition would have rejected as a dungeon on the grounds of excessive discomfort to the prisoners.

"I wondered why the kitchen was so chill, with such a draught from below," he responded. He thought the cellar at Queen Street was just fine.

The gold of the candle-flame touched the edges of a bucket, suspended by a pulley over a covered well in the center of the floor. "What's the box for?" asked Coldstone, nodding toward a small, closed cabinet with a ring in its top that sat near the bottom of the stair, like a good-sized breadbox but more sturdy.

"'Tis a wine-chest, sir. You see the ring at the top, that can be hooked in place of the bucket, so that it can be lowered down into the well to just above the level of the water. The property has no icehouse, you see. The well itself is only useful in the summer season, of course. It freezes hard this time of year."

"Very ingenious." At Coldstone's gesture, Sergeant Muldoon moved aside the cover, and all five of them—Muldoon excluded—leaned over the narrow throat of darkness. Coldstone removed a candle-end from his pocket, lit it at Apthorp's branch, and threw it down. It landed with a muted clunk, and Abigail saw for an instant a tiny circle of glittering ice around the flame, until it heated the surface sufficient to make a little melt-water, and so extinguished itself.

There was no wine in the wine-chest, and by the old cobweb that linked it to the wall, the contrivance had seen no use since the summer at least. "I don't think your Mr. Elkins ever occupied this house," Abigail remarked as they climbed the stair to the kitchen again. "At least he never slept in that bedchamber. Without bed-curtains, at this season, he'd have frozen in his sleep."

"Yet there's been a fire in this room," pointed out Coldstone, indicating the wide hearth, the small stock of cordwood in the box beside it. "The hearth has been cleaned and tidied—" He took from a shelf the white and blue German teapot, the neatly placed saucers and cups, and ran a fastidious finger along the dustless handle.

"Mr. Elkins paid extra to have certain amenities like the tea service and a set of sheets upstairs. Of course he'd fetch along his own tea and things, and silver, too, if he wanted it."

Abigail turned over in her hands the plates and bowls, the Japan-ware tray and the little warming-lamp. All were clean. *I'm missing something*, she thought. *Something I've been told . . .*

"Had he a servant?"

"He must have, mustn't he?" Apthorp regarded her in some surprise at the idea that a man able to rent a house for ten pounds a year would not have a valet.

"What sort of horse does he ride?" she asked, and again, Mr. Apthorp looked blank.

"I haven't the least idea, m'am. He's always come to my house afoot. I don't even know if he keeps a horse."

"By the appearance of the midden by the stables," said Abigail, "someone has done so."

Entry into the stable itself confirmed this, but not much more. Trampled straw heaped two of the stalls. Scattered oats—and a small quantity in the feedbox—had drawn the rodents from the fields around about, which had not been evident in the house, and the faint smell of horse-piss spoke of a fairly recent date of occupancy. By the same token, Abigail guessed that if horses had been here as recently as the fifth of March, they hadn't been here much later.

"You say Mr. Elkins has an accommodation address," said John, as they crossed to the house once more. "Is this how you generally communicate with him?" Through the gate and out across the fields in the direction of town, Abigail could see the wet-black roofs of the gaggle of taverns and houses that lay along Green Lane at the foot of the hill, but no trace of their earlier escort. Perhaps, like Hev Miller and Matt Brown, they had taken refuge at the Dressed Ship.

"Yes, sir. I write to him care of the taproom at the Man-o'-War, in Ship Street across from Clark's Yard. A Mrs. Klinker owns the place, sir. A clean and respectable establishment, as such places go." Apthorp sounded as if he feared they would judge him harshly by the place to which he sent his letters.

"Odd, isn't it? To spend fifty shillings a quarter for an address and then receive one's letters in a common tavern?"

Apthorp shook his head. "'Tisn't my business to say what's odd about another man, Mr. Adams. He wants it that way and is willing to pay, so I'm sure he has his reasons."

"When next you hear from Mr. Elkins," said Coldstone, "please notify me—and Mr. Adams—at once, if you would, sir. I should very much like to speak with him. Is it your intention," he added to Abigail, once they had parted company from Mr. Apthorp and were on their way back to Rowe's Wharf in the deepening dusk, "to speak to Mr. Fenton again soon, Mrs. Adams?"

"I will write His Excellency, and Mr. Buttrick, this evening to ask if 'twould be convenient for me to do so tomorrow."

"Do so, if you would, m'am. You may add Major Salisbury's name to that request, if you have any concern that Governor Hutchinson might refuse you admittance to his house. You have never told me," he added, as they left the bare back-slopes of Beacon Hill behind them for the muddy ice of Green Lane, "how you came to know of this place and of Sir Jonathan's presence there on the day of his death. We shall need sworn witnesses, you know," he went on, with a disapproving glance at John, "if we are to bring the matter before the Admiralty Court—or even the Massachusetts General Court."

"Witnesses shall be forthcoming," said John. "Once we know enough of our direction," he added, as Coldstone opened his lips to make some observation about the handiness and reliability of Massachusetts witnesses, "to be sure that our witnesses will not find themselves under arrest."

Coldstone looked as if he were going to speak again, then

closed his mouth and paced on for a time looking straight before him. Abigail noticed as they passed Green Lane that their bodyguards were back. Two men coming up from the direction of the waterfront caught a glimpse of Muldoon's crimson uniform and started to cross Treamount Street to them, and one of the men who'd been trailing them all afternoon loafed casually over and caught the two patriots by the arms. Coldstone gave no sign that he'd seen this defense, but Abigail thought his shoulders stiffened beneath their dark military cloak.

At length he muttered, "This is ridiculous."

"I agree, sir," John replied.

"I don't speak of the fact that a King's officer, legitimately pursuing the King's duty, needs a corps assigned by the local incendiaries to enter this city without being assaulted—"

"I did not think that was what you meant, sir." John glanced sidelong up at the officer at his side. "For myself, I consider it not ridiculous, but appalling, that a question of politics—of whether or not Englishmen living in Massachusetts should enjoy the same liberties as Englishmen living in London—has so preoccupied and distorted the minds of both sides that the business of justice cannot be pursued because neither side can or will trust the word of the other. With the result, as we have seen, that a criminal feels safe in murdering a servant of the King within a hundred feet of the Governor's house."

Coldstone moved his head a little at that, and something in the look of his eye made Abigail say, "If he *was* murdered in the alley. Did you smell anything in that house, Lieutenant? In the front hall?"

"I did," he replied grimly. "And I have fought on enough battlefields and walked through enough hospital-tents to know what death smells like. Yet as I can think of no reason why a killer would carry a murdered man a quarter of a mile to dump his body on the Governor's doorstep, when a quarter mile in the other direction would bring him to the ice-covered river where a body could lie undetected until April, I can only conclude that whoever died in that hall, it was not Sir Jonathan Cottrell."

Lord bless you, m'am, don't stand there lookin' at me like I'm going to stick my spoon in the wall this second." Mr. Fenton blinked sleepily at Abigail as she stood in the doorway. When she came close, she saw that even in the washed-out gray daylight that came through the attic window, the man's pupils were contracted to the size of pinheads; the bottle that stood on the table beside his cot must contain an opiate of some kind. "Your good Doctor Warren didn't tell me anythin' I didn't suspect already. At least he give me somethin' for the pain, God bless him."

Abigail brought up the broken chair, and John—as Thaxter had done two days before—sat tailor-fashion on the floor with his notebook in his hand. "Are you in much pain?" she asked gently, and Fenton moved his head, as if in a denial that the sweat on his face and his stertorous breathing belied.

"Not to speak of."

Even had Mr. Buttrick not warned her, when he led her and John through the servants' hall and up the backstairs, that Dr. Warren had pronounced the man beyond help, Abigail thought she would have known at the sight of him that he was dying. Under a sheen of sweat, his face was swollen almost unrecognizably from the man she'd spoken to only Monday evening, and in the daylight the progress of the jaundice had turned his flesh nearly orange. His voice was barely a whisper. When she took his hand—puffy with dropsy, though the wrist above it was wasted from the starvation of long illness—it felt chill and limp, like a dead man's hand already.

"Mr. Buttrick said you had a thing or two you wanted yet to ask," Fenton prompted her after a moment. "Don't fret after me, m'am—happens to everyone, I've heard tell. His Excellency sent his pastor in, for me to make my peace—" He managed a crooked grin in spite of the pain. "Leastwise I know now for certain there's no danger of meetin' His Nibs when I gets to the other side. I know which way *he* went. How's things look for your friend?"

"Unpromising," said Abigail softly. Beyond the unceiled slant of the roof, the wind flung handfuls of sleet upon the shingles. "When last we spoke you mentioned actors from Barbados—What were they doing in Boston? Surely it's a strange place for actors to come?"

"Oh, Palmer said he'd got word his sister, who'd run off two years ago with a sea captain, was now in Boston, and he was in search of her. A sad tale, but not so unusual. I've heard its like a dozen times. Cassandra, her name was—"

"You spoke to him, then?"

"Lord, yes. Had dinner with him and his lady friend at the Spancel."

"When was this? How long before Sir Jonathan left for Maine?" she added, realizing that there was a good chance Mr. Fenton was no longer aware of how long he himself had been lying here ill.

"Just the day before. I'd packed most of his kit. He was off that evening for a meeting with these great friends of Fluckner's about yet another claim that had popped up about these lands in Maine, one that none of 'em had ever heard of before. He was in a rare taking over it. Fellow'd have to be tracked down and bought off, he said—I knew he wouldn't be in until late. Mr. Palmer walked into the Spancel just a few minutes after me, with his woman on his arm, and asked, was it true we was stayin' in the Governor's house, and would the folk there know about this fellow Jellicoe who was supposed to have run off with Cassie? One thing led to another. You know how it is, when you scrape acquaintance, not knowin' anyone in the town."

"It must be a lonely life, traveling," said Abigail softly. *You know how it is*, he had said, and yet she didn't. It came to her that she had never lived anywhere where she had not had family and friends already waiting for her when she arrived. Even when she and John had first moved to Boston from Braintree, the whole tribe of Quincy, Tufts, and Smith cousins and uncles and aunts had all been waiting to greet her, not to speak of half a regiment of Boston Adamses. She thought of Lieutenant Coldstone, crossing the Atlantic in a troop-ship—of all those men on Castle Island—coming to this strange country where they knew no one and where they were automatically loathed . . .

"You gets used to it." Fenton's breath caught with a stab of pain, and his hand closed hard on hers for a moment. "And you learns. I'd seen Palmer on the stage, an' here and there about the town—Bridgetown's about the size of a market-village back home—but never to speak to: very grand, he was. Yet cast him adrift, and he was glad enough of seein' any face he knew that he bought me dinner and a couple good glasses of ale."

"Did he say how long he was staying in Boston?" John asked, and Fenton shook his head.

"Long as it took him to learn whether his sister was here or not, I reckon. They'll be gone by now."

"Did your master ever speak of a man named Elkins? Toby Elkins?" asked Abigail. "'Twas his house that Sir Jonathan visited on the day he returned."

Again Fenton shook his head. His face twisted, and Abigail found a spoon on the little table and poured a measure of the laudanum into it. "Another," whispered Fenton, when he'd drunk it. "If you please—the pain catches me . . ." After the second dose he seemed to sink deeper into the bedclothes, like a wrecked ship settling. He whispered drowsily, "Thank 'ee, m'am. It's good not bein' alone."

When Fenton had sunk into opiated sleep, John and Abigail slipped silently from the room and in silence walked back to Queen Street. Though it was only midmorning, Abigail felt strange, as if it should have been night when she sat beside the dying man. Had he family back in England? she wondered. How would anyone find out where to write to them, to tell them their son—brother—uncle—was gone? It crossed her mind to think of John, in his long and frequent travels, riding for days sometimes on the muddy roads in the western woods to one county court or another: out to Worcester, up to Haverhill, through those deep primeval forests untouched since God called them into being.

If he were taken sick, she thought, looking sidelong at that blunt, round face, that burly shape in the bundle of his cloak . . . *If he were taken sick, would anyone there know to write to me?* The thought of such a letter turned her cold inside.

John, too, was deep in thought as they walked, though his mind followed other roads, for in time he said, "No Elkins. I wonder if Sir Jonathan spoke of the man to your friend Miss

Fluckner, or to that blithering gooseberry of hers. He doesn't sound the man to tell his business to a woman . . ."

"It may not have been business."

John raised his brows.

She shrugged. "Mr. Elkins may have been a professional procurer, for all we know . . . It certainly doesn't sound as if Cottrell indulged himself much in Maine." Her voice turned dry. "It would fit with everything else we've heard of the man."

"In that case, would not Elkins have arrived with a young lady?"

Abigail shook her head. "Would he? I have no idea how such matters are arranged."

"They aren't," said John. "Not in Boston, anyway—at least not on so opulent a scale. Yet I find it curious," he added softly, "that there *is* a young woman missing . . . a young woman, moreover, upon whose virtue Cottrell made at least one attempt and possibly more. It answers nothing of how and why Jonathan Cottrell died . . . but I would very much like to know where the woman Bathsheba was during the eight days between her disappearance and Cottrell's return."

He turned down the little passway that led from Queen Street into the yard behind the Adams' house, narrow and muddy and smelling of the two cows that traversed it twice a day to be led out and grazed on the Common. In general, John—or Thaxter, if John were out of Boston—would rake out the cowhouse in the afternoon, just before the town herd-boy brought the cattle down Queen Street for the children of their various owners to fetch in for the evening milking. This morning, however, having put off the start of his day's work thus far, as soon as they came indoors, he kissed Abigail and went upstairs to change clothes, while Abigail herself shed her pattens and donned apron and day-cap to start preparations for dinner. "There's two notes for you, m'am," reported Pattie, coming into the kitchen with a broom and duster in hand and Charley and Tommy at her heels.

One, from Lieutenant Coldstone, simply reported that Mrs. Klinker of the Man-o'-War knew nothing of Mr. Elkins save his occasional visits to retrieve or dispatch mail, a convenience for which he paid her fivepence a week and had done so since the first week of January.

The other, from Dr. Joseph Warren, requested the favor of an interview, when it would be convenient.

She sent a note via one of Tom Butler's prentice-boys next door, and the young doctor himself arrived that afternoon, just as she, Nabby, and Pattie finished mopping down the kitchen after dinner. John, who liked an after-dinner pipe once his portion of the cleanup was done, rose from the hearthside settle and held out a hand to the slender young man: "God bless you for seeing to that poor servant, Warren. Good Lord, what is it that he's contracted? That's no *grippe* . . ."

"Nor is it," said Dr. Warren quietly. "It's what I wished to speak of to you." His clear gray eyes touched Abigail, included her in the statement, and the three of them moved to the fireside corner, away from where the tactful Pattie was settling the children to their lessons at the table.

"'Tis not some kind of tropical fever?" asked John worriedly, keeping his voice low. "I've heard of a jaundice like that in the Caribbean. The man was recently in Barbados, and indeed the night before he was taken sick had supper with an actor from Bridgetown—"

"Except that he had no fever," said Warren. "He had

supper with a man he'd known in Barbados—had his master known him?"

John shook his head.

"And half a day later, he was taken sick," continued the doctor softly. "So that he could not accompany his master to Maine, nor be at Hancock's Wharf to meet him when he returned. What does that sound like to you?"

John said nothing. His eyes went to Abigail's, then returned to their friend.

Abigail said, "You're not saying he was poisoned?"

"The symptoms sound precisely like certain mushroom poisons I have read of," said Warren quietly. "They're slow-acting and slow to begin their action—an advantage when someone doesn't want to be associated with the onset of the symptoms. Had not this man's master been murdered, the idea would not have crossed my mind at all. But Fenton's illness seems mightily convenient for it to be simply jaundice and *la grippe.* It might be well," he added, "to find this actor from Barbados with whom he supped, and learn if he was as ignorant of Sir Jonathan's affairs and company as Mr. Fenton seemed to think he was."

Fifteen

'Tis a long way," said Sam Adams thoughtfully, "from guessing the servant was poisoned, to finding who it was that thrashed the master and left him to die of cold in a ditch. That distance is longer still, if this British colonel has the word of a good, rich Tory's dogsbody about who was seen near the alley late that night and a conveniently dropped scarf to back him up." He knocked the ash of his pipe into the kitchen fireplace, a stone archway considerably larger than that of Abigail's more modern kitchen on Queen Street, and smiled his thanks as Bess, plump and graying, brought in coffee from the pantry for those gathered around her hearth. Wind howled eerily in the hollow of the chimney overhead. Sleet spattered on the gray windows like a rain of stones.

Paul Revere said, "I take it you want us to locate this Palmer."

"It shouldn't be difficult." John leaned forward to tong a coal from the fire and applied it to the bowl of his own pipe.

He was crowded cozily against Abigail on the old-fashioned settle that flanked the fire. "An actor's a rare bird in these climes. He'll have caught someone's attention." Sam's house on Purchase Street—one of the most venerable in Boston—in which he had been born, was constructed in the antique style, so that the whole northern wall of what had been old Josiah Adams's original "keeping room" was wrought of stone, with the fireplace so great that Bess knelt inside it to do the cooking. The settles were built along the fireplace's rough stone inner walls, and afforded draft-free, if rather smoky, seats on afternoons like this one, with a sudden gale driving in off the bay.

"Indeed he did," agreed the silversmith. "At least, if he's the same who was at the Horn Spoon in Ship Street, back in at the start of the New Year."

"Can you confirm that?" asked John. For her part, Abigail felt no surprise that Palmer was already located. The Sons of Liberty, in its way, had grown out of the less formal network of gossip, friendships, and ward-level political alliances that had existed in Boston since time out of mind. In a community where a good third of the men were involved in the smuggling trade, people kept an eye on who was coming and going in the town, and people talked: to wives, to brothers, to friends met in taverns—those same taverns where men of compatible politics would meet after supper, in order to feel themselves a part of the greater community before going home to their wives and their beds. The women whose husbands ran the waterfront taverns—or who ran them themselves—talked, too: to sisters, to friends met at the market or outside the church. An actor from Barbados would be noted and commented upon ("Lord, the buttons on his waistcoat all covered with paste diamonds, 'twould fair blind you across the room!"), even as, these days, any outspoken Tory who seemed to be powerful or connected with the Army would be duly mentioned to Sam or Revere or Hancock or Ben Edes or any of the other men who made up the inner circle of the Sons.

The Sons of Liberty took good care to know who came and went in Boston.

"You wouldn't know if he's still there?" inquired Sam, and Revere shook his head.

"I'd have heard if he were, but I'll ask. I'll ask after his lady friend, too—Mrs. Nevers at the Spoon said there was a lady with 'that actor fellow,' as she called him—"

"A woman?" asked Dr. Warren, crowded onto the settle at Abigail's other side. "Or a lady?"

"A lady, she said. Well-off, and paying all 'that actor fellow's' bills. I'll ask, too, after this Elkins, while I'm down there. The Man-o'-War's only a few yards from the Horn Spoon—though God knows every sailor and smuggler uses those Ship Street taverns as accommodation addresses. Still, if Elkins is paying fifty shillings a quarter for a house he doesn't live in, where *is* he living?"

"Check with the gate-guards," suggested Abigail. "And the ferrymen. He may in fact be traveling, though it didn't look to me like anyone had ever actually stayed at that house. Even if we *could* prove that poor Fenton was poisoned," she added quietly, with a glance at Dr. Warren, "you're right, Sam, that we're as far as ever we were from proving that Harry Knox didn't brain that—that *weasel* Cottrell. But if we can start finding these other people—Palmer and Elkins—we can perhaps show that wretched Colonel Leslie that Harry wasn't part of the . . . the conspiracy."

John sniffed, and rose to his feet, even his short height nearly brushing the roughly corbelled bricks of the huge fireplace. He strode across the hearth in his best courtroom manner, hands gripping his lapels as if he were clothed in an imaginary robe: "Gentlemen of the Admiralty Court," he boomed, "I shall now prove to you conclusively, and beyond the shadow of a doubt, that Sir Jonathan Cottrell was not beaten to death by the man whose sweetheart he attempted to dishonor—by the man who shouted in the presence of these ten witnesses that he would kill him—but was in fact the victim of an elaborate conspiracy whose nature we have been unable to determine and whose minions have slipped away through our grip . . ."

As Revere, Dr. Warren, Sam, and Sam's fifteen-year-old son—present on a little hearth-stool—all applauded wildly and raised their mugs and shouted, "Not Guilty, upon mine honor! You have convinced us, sir! Of course 'twas a conspiracy, the villains! Set the lad free!" Abigail flushed a little, and waved at John—

"Don't be an idiot, John!"

But she knew he was right.

A little later, as she and John were wrapping up to take their leave of the house on Purchase Street, she said to Revere, "Whilst you're asking after Palmer and his extremely obliging patroness, would you ask if anyone has heard anything of a woman named Bathsheba? Fluckner's servant-girl . . ."

"The one who went missing, yes." Revere nodded—of course he'd read the advertisements. Revere read everything. "She's not been found, then? I see Fluckner has quit advertising."

"She disappeared two days after Cottrell left for Maine," said Abigail. "On Thursday, Miss Fluckner found nearly twenty-five pounds hidden in her room—most of it in British coin. It can only have come from Cottrell."

Revere's eyebrows shot up at the sum, and he nodded. "I'll see what I can learn. What became of the money?"

"I sent it to my father," said Abigail, "to arrange for the purchase of the woman's two babies, and their care. I can't imagine what she knew about Cottrell, or what she could have learned. But I suspect that she's met the same fate that will take poor Fenton very shortly."

The silversmith nodded. "Whoever these people are," he murmured, "they seem to have wanted Cottrell dead very badly . . . and to have let no one stand in their way."

"I suppose not. But how *could* a Negro servant-woman stand in the way of anyone killing a King's Commissioner? I can understand having Fenton put out of the way, so that Cottrell would be alone on his journey to Maine. But why would that poor girl have needed to die?"

"When we learn that," replied Revere, "we shall have a much better idea of who it is we're looking for."

Abigail relayed the gist of this debate to Lucy Fluckner on the following day, carefully omitting any reference to the money they had found in Bathsheba's rooms or to whom, exactly, was going to do the inquiring about Palmer, because Margaret Sandhayes was hobbling beside them, with surprising agility, on the frozen mud of the elm-treed Mall. Lucy flung up her hands in exasperation. "What are they going to say?" she demanded, when Abigail had done. "That Harry just *happened* to blunder into a conspiracy and murdered Sir Jonathan before these other villains could get to him?"

Yesterday's gale had blown itself out in a chilly, glittering morning. Any who could afford to set their work aside for an hour had done so: men in cloaks and greatcoats strode the uneven ground of the Common with the movements of slaves new-freed, or gathered around the bare and venerable Great Tree that stood in the center of the meadow. Women strolled in twos and threes between the naked elms of the Mall, chattering of babies and servants and the laundry they'd do if the weather continued this fair.

"If I know anything of the British system of justice, dear child," observed Mrs. Sandhayes acerbically now, "that is *precisely* what they'll say. What is a conspiracy in comparison with a couple of good, loud threats and an eyewitness?"

"And you think Bathsheba—" began Philomela, who had been walking quietly in the rear. Mrs. Sandhayes turned, an expression of such affronted shock on her face that a servant would put herself into the conversation of her betters—that a servant would listen to what was being said—and the dark girl drew back in confusion.

"No!" Lucy caught her maid's hand. "No, she was your friend. Please speak."

Philomela flashed a glance of crimson-faced apology at Mrs. Sandhayes, who to do her justice seemed to realize that her own reaction to a servant's putting herself forward had been precisely that—a reaction—and was herself looking slightly embarrassed.

"Dear me, Bathsheba, yes," she murmured, and Philomela seemed to take this as an admission of mitigating circumstances.

"Do you think then that Bathsheba was upset—was frightened—because she had learned something of this conspiracy against Sir Jonathan?"

"Did she speak of it to you?" asked Abigail.

Philomela shook her head.

"Where would she have learned of it?" put in Lucy eagerly.

"Bathsheba used to go about with you, Margaret—did *you* ever see anything? Hear anything? Did you ever go near that house on Beacon Hill, where Sir Jonathan went the day he was killed?"

"On that side of the town?" Mrs. Sandhayes looked so startled at the idea that it was almost comical. "Have you seen the place? By what Mrs. Adams tells us, it's at the antipodes, with nothing near it but churches and distilleries!"

"Not precisely the ends of the earth," said Abigail, amused at her dismay. "'Tis only over that rise of ground over there, about a half mile . . . Yet you're quite right, Lucy. Bathsheba may have heard or seen something that meant something to her—that would mean something to a native Bostonian, perhaps, which would be lost on someone not from this town."

Mrs. Sandhayes arched her eyebrows—clearly there was nothing that a black servant-girl could see that would escape an Englishwoman—but Lucy said, "Where did you go on that Thursday, Margaret? On the day all the fuss took place, with me, and Harry, and Sir Jonathan—" Her cheeks suddenly flushed, with remembered anger, and she looked away. Past her—beyond the bare double line of trees that bordered the western edge of the meadow—the little hill crowed by the town Powder-Store rose, disused now that its successor was being built, like a solitary and dilapidated prison-tower in a fairy tale.

The little stone watchhouse stood at the hill's foot, in use mostly at night, and visible beyond it was the straggly copse of brush and trees, where Sir Jonathan had lain in wait for the girl.

Not because he cared about her, reflected Abigail, studying Lucy's half-averted profile. *Not because he was in the slightest interested in who she was or what she thought.* The one he had wooed had been her father. Secure in the assurance that his engagement to several thousand acres at least of land in Maine would be announced upon his return, he had only wanted to make his unwilling fiancée unmarriageable by anyone else until his return.

Did he really think Harry would repudiate Lucy if he learned that she'd been possessed by another man?

The look in Lucy's face when she spoke his name, the way Lucy would saddle her own horse to escape the house, the storms of temper that punctuated her relationship with the father who regarded her as a pawn to consolidate his own financial empire: these fit together as Abigail studied this big, clumsy girl who seemed so out of step with the genteel world of wealthy Boston. Against the brightness of that open sweep of hillside, Lucy had the look, suddenly, of a captive herself. With her unfashionable snub nose, her unromantically round pink cheeks and sturdy shoulders, she seemed to Abigail a creature who should have been born into a different world, a different station—a woman who belonged to the open country and the wild spring sunshine a great deal more than she belonged in the elegant drawing rooms of her father's house.

"I was out with Caroline Hartnell," Mrs. Sandhayes replied. "Do you know her, Mrs. Adams? A *delightful* woman—But it wasn't until the day after, you know, the Friday, that Bathsheba seemed to come all to pieces."

"Was Bathsheba much acquainted with her woman?" Lucy asked, turning back to Philomela. "Gwenifer is her name—?"

"Gwen, yes," agreed the dark girl. "Gwen Pugh."

"Would *she* have noticed anything, do you think?"

"Heavens, child, don't start again with prying into servants' tittle-tattle! These things get about . . ."

"I can certainly ask her," said Abigail thoughtfully. "Though you're probably right, Mrs. Sandhayes—" She turned tactfully to include the indignant chaperone. "Unless we find some definite—and spectacular—evidence of conspiracy, 'twill be hard to convince an Admiralty Court of anything except that the villainous citizens of Boston are out to cast up a smoke screen . . . *again.* From these"—she held up the notes that Lucy and Mrs. Sandhayes had given her, the last of their assembled compilations of who they could remember being where, when, at the Governor's ball—"it doesn't appear that anyone was markedly absent or noticeably late—except for Sir Jonathan, of course."

"Well, the Sumners were late, but they're always late," amended Lucy. "And anyway the four of them came together, and I can't imagine old Mrs. Sumner helping her son and daughters lie in wait in an alley to murder a man. I'll keep up my program of spying," she added stoutly, "and even drink *tea* with all Mother's friends, to get them to gossip about Sir Jonathan, but I haven't learned anything yet."

Margaret Sandhayes beamed. Evidently gossip and tittle-tattle with the wealthy were a completely different issue than the same tactics used upon servants.

"I don't suppose there's a chance of you speaking to Mr. Wingate . . ."

Lucy's jaw hardened and she looked away again for a moment. "Father's sent him to Philadelphia," she said, her usually bluff tones muted with distress. "He thought of that. I tried to talk to him, you know—to Father, I mean. About Harry. About what they'll do to him."

Sudden tears threatened her voice and she forced it steady. "Father just says—I think he really believes it—*Good Lord, they'll never actually hang the boy . . . no matter what he was doing out in the alley at that time.* Because of course he pretends that he didn't put Mr. Wingate up to it. *All that'll happen is he'll spend a few weeks in irons, which I daresay the boy deserves.*" Her voice flexed and fluffed in an imitation of her father's gruff tones, then broke again. "He really, honestly sees it as a kind of—not a practical joke, but a comeuppance, because of Harry's politics. *He should be more careful who he's seen with, or he wouldn't be in this trouble*, he says."

With an angry gesture, almost like a blow, she scrubbed the tears from her eyes and stood staring out across the pale sunlight of the Common, the illusion of light and space.

"I've tried to speak to him as well," added Mrs. Sandhayes hesitantly, when Abigail opened her lips to utter some very unwise words and then closed them again. Considering she was a guest in the Fluckner household, Abigail guessed that she had had to pick her words very carefully. "I was never so close to anything as I was to striking the man over the head with my stick! It's true—all he wants to do is get poor Mr. Knox out of Boston for a time . . . Just as he's sent away that wretched little clerk of his. Just as he'd arrange for any prentice-boy to be sent away by his master, if that boy started sending flowers to Miss Lucy, or a sailing-man to be shipped out. It is what they do," she added, and her green eyes suddenly narrowed with an uncharacteristic flicker of anger, "the friends of Parliament. The friends of the King. If there's trouble, they arrange for there not to be trouble anymore."

And for a moment, Abigail felt that she had stepped around the corner of a screen to see what lay behind the lame woman's smiling and empty-headed cheerfulness: like the sudden sight of a disfiguring scar.

The next moment Mrs. Sandhayes smiled blithely again and shrugged. "I suppose the silly man feels that Lucy will forget Mr. Knox if he's not right there beside her, and fall madly in love with someone else. Honestly, Mrs. Adams, men can be such *asses* sometimes!"

"Papa isn't—" Lucy began unhappily, and then fell silent, looking away again as if unable to bear the company even of friends. "I love Papa." And in her tone was the whole of her grief, that one man she loved would find abhorrent the other man she loved, not because Harry was a drunkard or a monster or a thief, but only because he worked with his hands. Because his father had been poor.

"Of course you do, dear child." Margaret Sandhayes took a lurching step toward the girl, propped one cane against her panniers, and put her arm around Lucy's shoulders. "Just because you want to take someone and shake some sense into their heads doesn't mean you don't love them . . . And just because they're acting like a complete *booby* doesn't mean they don't love you. It will work itself out, child—" She shifted her position a little, which caused the propped stick to fall; Abigail caught it neatly, before it struck the frozen path. "Come," she said. "Let's go up to the top of Beacon Hill, as long as we're out here. You'll feel better."

Together, the four women left the bare trees of the Mall and made their way by those frozen and houseless lanes to the top of Beacon Hill, to see the whole of the bay spread like a world of blue black diamond beneath their feet, pricked with a thousand flecks of white and tufted with islands: violet, gray, and brown. Below them on the Common, children launched a kite on the cold sea breeze; their voices skirled shrill as birds, as the boatless sail whipped and whirled aimlessly, then swooped suddenly upward, as if it had all at once discovered what it meant to be able to fly free.

"A ship!" cried Lucy, pointing, and there she was: black

hull, white sails, floating among the islands with breathtaking lightness. She fished in the deep pocket of her cloak for a spyglass. "You don't think it's word from the King, finally, do you?" She sounded excited rather than scared. "About the tea? About what's going to happen?"

Even before she could focus the glass, however, Mrs. Sandhayes replied softly, "It's early for that, child. No, I think this must be the *Incitatus*, up from the Indies, on its way to Halifax."

Sixteen

Parting, Lucy promised to write to Mrs. Hartnell the moment she got home. "I *beg* of you, be discreet, child," pleaded Mrs. Sandhayes. "You have no *idea* what the *slightest* breath of scandal can do to your reputation—"

"Oh, pooh! Everyone says terrible things about Belinda Sumner behind her back and yet she's received everywhere—"

"Belinda Sumner is married," said Mrs. Sandhayes firmly. "And don't expect too much of Caroline Hartnell. She's stupid as an owl and wouldn't see a conspiracy if twenty cloaked Venetians surrounded her with daggers."

So much, thought Abigail, *for "dear friendships" among the Tory gentry of the town.*

But the Fluckner fortune, even if it attracted parasites like Sir Jonathan Cottrell and caused Lucy's father to look askance at the suits of honest tradesmen, had its uses. Soon after dinner Philomela knocked diffidently on the back door of the Adams' kitchen, with a note from her mistress saying that the stylish matron—wife to one of Boston's wealthiest ship-owners—would pay a "morning call" at Milk Street the following day.

"She'll have Gwenifer with her," promised Philomela, as Abigail refolded the note and tucked it into one of the drawers of the kitchen sideboard. "She won't stir from the house without her."

"That scarcely gives the poor girl time to do her work, does it?"

"I shouldn't think so, m'am, no," replied the young woman, with a noncommittal politeness that some of her so-called social betters, Abigail reflected, could do well to imitate.

"Is she so frightened of the outside world?"

"I don't think so, m'am. Sheba told me that Mrs. Hartnell and other friends of Mrs. Fluckner have all heard that no English lady will go out without a maidservant to lend her consequence."

"Consequence indeed." Abigail sniffed. "Yet I suppose it spares me the awkwardness of letting Mrs. Hartnell know that it's her maid I need to speak to, rather than her all-important self. Was Bathsheba a friend to this girl Gwen, then?"

"They were friendly." Philomela gave the matter a moment's thought. "Bathsheba used to be Mrs. Fluckner's own maid, you see, before she had Marcellina, so when Mrs. Sandhayes came to stay with us, Mrs. Fluckner would have Bathsheba go about with her, for that same reason—which was very kind of her, toward Mrs. Sandhayes, but very hard on Sheba who had only just had Stephen. But Sheba would say, there's no cloud without silver lining, because Mrs. Sandhayes was very generous with her tips—"

"How so, if she's not a wealthy woman?"

Philomela sank her voice and glanced toward Pattie, who was drying plates at the table. "She cheats at cards, m'am."

Abigail said, "Ah."

"So in any event," Philomela went on in a more normal voice, "after Mrs. Hartnell took up Mrs. Sandhayes, Sheba and Gwen were much thrown together, and you know how it is. Unless a woman takes against you for some reason, you do fall into friendliness with those you see often, do you not? When they would go about together, down to the wharves, or take Mrs. Hartnell's carriage out into the country, then Sheba and Gwen would sit up on the box with the coachman, which sounds finer than it actually is," added the girl with her faint, quick grin, "when the weather is as it was in February. Sheba said she and Gwen used to share cloaks and hug together sometimes to keep warm."

"Hmm." Abigail dipped into the little jar of hard money on the sideboard for a tip.

The uncovering of Bathsheba's strange hoard had served to remind her that other servants in that household might be saving up their tips and perquisites, too, in the hopes of building some defense against the misfortunes of the world. And perhaps, she reflected, that was exactly how Margaret Sandhayes viewed her cardsharping.

The money seemed to remind Philomela as well, for she turned upon the threshold, and said, "I wanted to thank you again, Mrs. Adams, for arranging with your father and Mr. Greenleaf to buy Sheba's children. Mrs. Barnaby told me this morning that Mr. Greenleaf had offered for the pair of them—"

"'Tis nothing," said Abigail. "If ill has indeed befallen to their mother, they'll at least have food and a roof above their heads. I know Silas Greenleaf. He is an honest man who will give those children their freedom when they're of age to seek their own fortunes, and he'll not split them up. Whyever that money was offered to Bathsheba, it will have been used for the reason she took it: to save them."

Mrs. Caroline Hartnell!" murmured Pattie, profoundly impressed, when Philomela had gone and Abigail returned to the kitchen table. Johnny and Nabby had carried the clean dishes to the sideboard and were bringing out their schoolbooks and slates. "What shall you wear tomorrow, m'am? I can curl your hair—"

"You'll do nothing of the sort," retorted Abigail, settling herself on the other side of the table with the household daybook, where she could reach the inkwell that stood between the children. "And I shall dress as I do for Meeting, in my best bib and tucker. I don't curl my hair for Meeting, and I'm certainly not going to give a morning call more time and attention than I do a morning spent with God."

"Why are they called morning calls, if they take place after noon?" inquired Nabby, raising her blue eyes from *The Pilgrim's Progress.*

"Because women are silly, and live in sloth and sin," Johnny proclaimed. "Rich ones, anyway," he added quickly, seeing Abigail's eyebrows lift. "All they think of is their dogs and their dresses."

"I rather think," corrected Abigail mildly, "that 'tis because dinner used to be eaten at noon . . . and people used to get up just after midnight, to be about their morning's business, isn't that so, John Quincy?"

The boy nodded importantly and returned to his Latin

while Abigail unfolded and perused again the notes that had been waiting for her when she'd returned from her rendezvous with Lucy and Mrs. Sandhayes that morning.

My very dear Mrs. Adams (Lieutenant Coldstone had written)—

Enquiries with the harbormaster have yielded no one by the name of Elkins as having come ashore from the Lady Bishop, *nor from the* Speedheart, *which was the other ship in port from Bridgetown at the end of December and upon which Sir Jonathan Cottrell took passage. Nor is Elkins or anyone of his description listed as passenger on the* Juno *from Halifax, or the* Polly Amos *out of London, which were in port at about that time. Androcles Palmer is listed as a passenger on the* Lady Bishop. *Needless to say, if Mr. Elkins entered Boston by land, or came up from Barbados (if that was his place of origin) to another town on this coast and entered Boston on a coastwise trader like the* Hetty, *I would have no record of him. Make of this what you are able.*

Your ob't,
J. Coldstone
Lt. Kings 64th Rgt. Ft

And from Sam:

Palmer packed up and left the Horn Spoon on Thursday the 24th February. Men have asked about the district for an Englishman of his description, and none thereabouts have seen him, under that name or any other. A woman named Cherne—tall and handsome, dark-haired and of a strong cast of feature, well dressed and appearing in the mid-forties—paid for his room and his meals, and was much with him, though she herself did not stay at the inn but the first night. I venture this is the lady friend of whom poor Fenton spoke, unless there were more than just the one. None at the Horn Spoon remarked on one of Elkins's description, though the Man-o'-War lies but yards away.

Abigail folded the notes, turned them over and over in her hands: *Drat those wretched actors. Changed their names and moved their goods across the street or down two doors*—that portion of Ship Street boasted more taverns than the rest of Boston put together—*and how could we tell?*

The thought returned to vex her the following day, when—properly gowned in dark, well-cut wool and wearing, as she had said, her best bib and tucker—she sat drinking peppermint tisane in the Fluckner drawing room, making conversation with Hannah Fluckner and contemplating again the portrait of that sweet-faced lady in her youth. A pity, Abigail reflected, one could not acquire decent miniatures of such lesser personalities as the elusive Mr. Elkins or Androcles Palmer, to show to innkeepers who might never have heard the names but might well recognize the faces. Not that the miniatures would be an invariable help, she amended, returning her eyes to the portrait with a certain amount of regret. When the portrait's original asked her politely, "A penny for your thoughts, Mrs. Adams," she said, "I was only thinking what a shame it is, that no one in New England seems to be able to paint faces that look anything like the actual people."

"La, I protest, Mrs. Adams!" cried Mrs. Hartnell. "'Tis a fine, big portrait, and very handsomely done! Mr. Stanley—the man who painted it, and such a very gentlemanlike man he was!—did one of me, in my green and white satin—Do you remember my green and white satin, Hannah? La, such a *crack* as we thought it, with those great dowdy panniers—"

Abigail listened politely to the subsequent description of various recollected toilettes, but it was clear to her that it had never crossed the minds of either woman that the business of a portrait was to portray not the cost of the sitter's clothing, but those individual differences of eyebrow and chin and lip that distinguished the rather saturnine Margaret Sandhayes from the fragile and flighty Caroline Hartnell.

Neither pretty; both fairish rather than fair; both slender rather than beefy of build. Even as portraits missed the differences of feature, the fashionable layers of paint and powder blurred them, concealing the natural hues of complexions as well as their flaws under white lead and cochineal. How *could* you describe a woman, she reflected, if the main thing you saw about her was not her face, but the elaborately curled, puffed, and swagged white meringue of powdered hair that surrounded it? A describer would fix first on, *One lady was a cripple, the other two were sound*, and then *perhaps* might notice, *One lady had a tiny tricorn hat pinned to the summit of her coiffeur, the other two had silk flowers.* Certainly this was how Margaret Sandhayes had remembered those who came in and out of the cardroom and the ballroom: *the gentleman in the violet waistcoat, the lady with the coiffure Aux Rêves Sentimentales* . . . Only later had Lucy's scribbled hand filled in the names. Even those who did notice features might only say "big nose," which could describe either the Hartnell aquiline or the Sandhayes inquiring beak. And in fact, Abigail suspected, only people like John, who were used to analyzing faces, would consciously register that the uncomeliness of feature common to both women stemmed from large noses at all, or that one had a chin that was far too weak for beauty, the other, far too strong.

Mrs. Hartnell concluded her breathless and extended account of her most recent shopping-trip and turned to Abigail at last. "Now, dearest Margaret tells me you've taken an interest in that sweet little Bethlehem girl—"

"Bathsheba," corrected Lucy, ignoring her mother's admonitory glare.

"Bathsheba, of course! Brain like a sieve, Mr. Hartnell is forever telling me—How very extraordinary that she would run away like that, you're always so kind to your Negroes, Hannah. Positively spoil them, *I* say—" She laughed, as if her own observations were always the height of wit. "Well, it's very kind of you, for all that, seeing that the children go to a good home, poor brats. I am *terribly* fond of children, you know, Mrs. Adams. My own are the heartbeat of my life, you may ask any of my friends—"

Mrs. Sandhayes nodded, although she had imparted to Abigail on other occasions that her friend was unhesitating in her choice of her own convenience and pleasure over that of any of her children, having dispatched every one of them back to England for schooling at the earliest possible moment.

Abigail said, "Indeed," and continued into the split second that the other woman was drawing breath to expand on the topic, "but I have the theory that she may in fact be in hiding. Mrs. Sandhayes said that she seemed upset and frightened on the day before she fled. I understand that you had been out with Mrs. Sandhayes that day, and she has told me *how much* your observations are to be trusted—"

Not, in fact, a lie, she comforted herself.

"Did you see anything, on that Friday when you were out, that seemed odd to you? Out of the way?"

In the far (and coldest) corner of the room, where Philomela sat sewing with the dark-haired, diminutive girl whom Abigail guessed had to be Mrs. Hartnell's Gwen, Abigail was conscious of quick movement. She turned her head to see Gwen look up and swiftly meet her eyes. Then, as quickly, the girl bowed her head again over her work. But Abigail knew she was listening.

"You remember, Caroline," prompted Mrs. Sandhayes. "It was the day we went down to Merchant's Row, and you found that astonishing piece of French lace, for truly *dagger-cheap*, and the pink satin shoes with the paste buckles—"

"Yes, yes, yes, of course!" cried the other woman. "How could I forget?"

"We were simply *hours* in that warehouse, and in the shops on the wharf," said Mrs. Sandhayes. "Afterward I was half-froze and my feet felt as if I'd been bastinado'd, but I wouldn't have traded for anything, you know." And she smiled.

"No, no! Such a *delightful* day!"

"When you came back to the carriage," said Abigail, wondering how even Mrs. Sandhayes's devotion to fashion and "good society" could compensate her for even an hour of this woman's conversation, "did Bathsheba seem upset or distressed in any way?"

"I don't think so." Mrs. Hartnell frowned uncertainly. "And surely—"

"But we didn't leave them with thc carriage, dear," put in Mrs. Sandhayes. "Remember? We knew there would be a great many things to carry."

"Of course!" Mrs. Hartnell broke into a smile. To Abigail, she confided, "*Dear* Hannah has been *so* generous, making sure poor Margaret has had a servant to go about with her. Really, not everyone would be so considerate of a guest." She smirked happily, and Abigail was conscious of the sudden, slight rigidity Mrs. Sandhayes's smile, at the reminder of her condition—and of the fact that for three months she had been living on Thomas Fluckner's charity. "*How* she can have managed on the ship from England I can *not* imagine—"

"My dear, I lost the use of my legs, not my hands or my voice." The thinnest touch of acerbity speared through the habitual sweetness of the Englishwoman's tone. "It isn't only servants who are willing to help a woman who is having trouble carrying her luggage."

"Yes, but when one hasn't a sou, one finds even the *greatest* gentlemen are so much less obliging," responded Mrs. Hartnell blithely, and Abigail could not suppress the reflection that the chaperone was being paid back for some of her remarks in Philomela's presence about the moral character of the servant class.

"So Bathsheba and Gwen were with you, pretty much, all that morning?"

"Indeed they were."

"And you saw nothing amiss in Bathsheba's behavior."

Mrs. Hartnell frowned, more as if trying to decide why anyone would notice a servant's behavior in the first place, than to recall what it had been on a day over three weeks ago.

"As you generally walked in the lead"—Mrs. Sandhayes smiled—"except of course when you so kindly took my arm in the crowds—I doubt you'd have had much chance to observe poor Bathsheba. Gwen, my dear—" She raised her voice slightly and beckoned Gwen Pugh from her corner, while her friend went back to feeding tidbits to Hercules, who all this time had been sitting happily on her lap and drooling into a hundred shillings' worth of point lace.

"This is Mrs. Adams," she introduced kindly. "And she is

trying to discover what might have happened to Bathsheba. Do you remember the Friday Mrs. Hartnell and I went down to Hutchinson's Wharf together? The last morning Bathsheba went out with us, before she ran away?"

The girl—who seemed to be in her early twenties, and was small and dark and rather shy—replied hesitantly, "I don't remember clearly, m'am." The coffee brown eyes went from Mrs. Sandhayes to Mrs. Hartnell, then swiftly, briefly touched Abigail's before lowering to the carpet again.

"You do remember that Bathsheba seemed upset and forgetful, though? Mislaying things and missing the way walking back to the carriage?"

"Yes," responded the girl obediently. "Yes, I do."

"But she didn't say what was troubling her?"

"No, m'am. That she didn't."

"And you didn't see anyone speak to her, or give her anything, did you?"

"No, m'am." Given the firm tone of the Englishwoman's voice, it would have been astonishing, thought Abigail, had the girl had the courage to say anything else.

Rather vexed at this high-handed appropriation of what was supposed to be her investigation, Abigail asked, "Would you say that you were friends with Bathsheba, Miss Pugh?" and the maid looked up again, as if startled to be asked anything about her feelings at all.

"Yes, m'am. Bathsheba, she was all right. She told me who was the best tooth-drawer to go to, when I'd cracked my tooth on—"

"Gwen, I'm sure Mrs. Adams does not need details of your dental history," laughed Mrs. Hartnell. "Really, the things servants will come up with if you encourage them!" Gwen's cheeks colored, and she looked down in shame.

"Did Bathsheba ever speak to you," asked Abigail gently, "of anyplace she would go—or anyone she would go to—if she were frightened, or in trouble? Was there anyone in Boston, or in the country round, that she had whom she trusted?"

"Mr. Barnaby, m'am," said the girl promptly.

"'Tis quite true," put in Mrs. Fluckner. "Barnaby is very much the father to all the servants, which is of course as it should be. And speaking of servants—"

"That will be all, Gwen," dismissed Mrs. Sandhayes. And the discussion of the enormities of the lower classes flowed over the tea table like an inexorable river. Abigail settled back and sipped her peppermint tea (on which both Mrs. Fluckner and Mrs. Hartnell had twitted her, as if standing against the King's monopoly were some mental maggot or hobbyhorse), dissatisfied and troubled and very well aware that Mrs. Hartnell had told her very little, and Gwen, nothing at all.

Which was odd, given that most people were delighted to talk about events, particularly events connected with murders, disappearances, and conspiracies.

Or did Caroline Hartnell—like Margaret Sandhayes—simply consider her a provincial busybody?

Abigail's eyes went back to the portrait of Hannah Fluckner—which could have been the depiction of any twenty-year-old girl some eighteen years ago—and then, troubled, to the two maidservants sewing in their corner. And so doing, her gaze crossed that of Gwen Pugh, and she saw in the girl's dark eyes the wretched uncertainty of one who had lied, and knew she lied . . .

. . . and yet dared not speak the truth.

The maid turned her eyes quickly away.

Mrs. Sandhayes chirupped, "More tea?"

Seventeen

"To lie about one's activities is scarcely evidence of a conspiracy to murder a man she doesn't know," John remarked, when Abigail told him the tale of her morning call over dinner. "The woman might simply have been meeting a lover—"

"The two of them were in it together," insisted Abigail. "Rather, I should say 'twas the Sandhayes woman who did the lying, for Caroline Hartnell quite clearly hasn't the brains to find her way back from the outhouse if she ventures forth without a guide."

John spooned Indian pudding onto the plates as Johnny passed them to him. "Nor does she need brains," he replied. "Mrs. Hartnell is wealthy. Her husband is a member of the General Court and a friend of the Governor, and her friendship assures that Margaret Sandhayes will not be treated in this town as the charity case that she is. No, you shall not have more molasses, Charley—that is all the molasses that a boy of your years should eat." He turned from his middle son—who knew better than to argue the point—back to Abigail.

"We are in large part as people treat us, Portia. The difference between a woman who accompanies a wealthy young lady about town to keep would-be suitors at a distance, in trade for a roof over her head and a pittance of money, and a woman who does precisely the same thing as a kindness because she is a guest of the young lady's family is—incalculable. And the difference lies entirely in whether that woman is welcomed by the family's friends or is regarded by them as a very intelligent servant."

"But for a woman of Mrs. Sandhayes's intelligence to participate in a cheap intrigue—"

"So far as I've been able to ascertain," John said, "Margaret Sandhayes came to this town this winter with very little beyond a respectable wardrobe and a couple of letters of introduction: nothing to live on or by. Yet she's a proud woman and obviously of good family. She would readily admit that Philomela and Barnaby are intelligent . . . and I daresay she would rather die than be regarded as their equal."

"There is no shame in it."

"There is no shame in it for *you*," John replied. "Nor for your sisters, nor any of the women you know, because Massachusetts is not like England." He finished his corn-pudding and rose, Nabby springing to her feet and gathering up the plates while Tommy in his raised chair—quick to observe his mother's preoccupation with her conversation—gravely applied palmfuls of molasses to his own cheeks.

"We demand the rights of Englishmen, in Parliament and before the King, but we are not like them," John went on. "'Tis what they don't understand. We know in our hearts—men and women both—that we can always find some honest work that will feed us, even if it be breaking flax in some backcountry farm. 'Tis not the same in England. We forget that."

"How do we go about finding the truth, then?" Abigail folded her napkin, her thoughts far beyond the warm kitchen and the bright, icy slant of the evening light upon the wall. "We have no idea how long until the *Incitatus* sails, but it can't be more than a day or two. And all we have learned is who *couldn't* have had to do with Cottrell's murder—a formidable list of the 'best people' in the town"—she drew out the several amended tallies put together by Lucy and Mrs. Sandhayes—"plus the two men who had the best cause to thrash him, whether or not he froze to death afterward. Three men, I should say, counting Harry. Thomas Boylston Adams!" she added, suddenly aware of her youngest child's experimentation with molasses as facial decoration and hair restorant. "If this is the purpose to which you put your molasses, you shall have no more of it!"

"I'll take his, Mama, please." Charley stood up on his chair in his anxiety to be heard. "I promise I won't put it on *my* hair!"

There was a pause in the adult conversation, as Abigail cleaned up her son while Johnny, Nabby, and Pattie cleared the table, put the leftovers in the pantry, spread towels, and poured water from the boiler for the washing-up. Thaxter, returning from his mother's house, dropped the afternoon post on the sideboard and said, "One from Haverhill, sir. It looks like Mrs. Teasel's hand," and this John read while Abigail led the cleaning-up, then bundled the older three children up tightly for an excursion to the Common.

But her mind was on the *Incitatus*, lying at anchor off

Castle Island with its white sails folded like a Death Angel's wings; on Margaret Sandhayes's firm determination to avoid the impropriety of interviewing the servants of people socially useful to herself; on the shadowy cavern of the front hall of the Pear Tree House and the trace of stink lurking in its gloom that whispered like a trapped ghost, *Someone died here . . .*

John said, "Damn."

Abigail looked up.

He held Mrs. Teasel's letter, but his eyes were on Thaxter's, who had read it over his shoulder. Their faces were grave.

"What is it?"

John put down the folded, much-crossed sheet. "The body of Mary Teasel's husband was found in the kitchen of his house—*their* house"—he turned the sheet to look at the date—"Tuesday evening. I'll have to go. Pray the weather holds—" He crossed to her, put his hand on her waist to kiss her on his way to the hall, the stair, the bedroom to pack—

"I won't," she said softly. "I can't."

His round blue eyes widened at this—if the weather didn't hold it meant thirty miles in cold and sleety gale, and undoubtedly finishing the journey in the dark—and then he remembered. He said softly, "Ah."

If the icy good weather remained, the *Incitatus* would sail for Halifax within days, with Harry in chains onboard. And once he'd been tried by the Navy Court—and, given the feelings of the British military since the dumping of the King's tea, convicted—Abigail suspected that nothing would prevent the young man from turning King's Evidence against Sam, against Dr. Warren, against John and dozens of others, to keep his own neck out of a noose.

* * *

By dark the wind had risen. Ironing John's shirts by the blaze of the kitchen hearth, Abigail heard it moaning in the chimney and quoted the Book of Kings: "*Behold, there ariseth a little cloud out of the sea, like a man's hand.*"

And John, sorting through the papers he would need to take with him in the morning, grumbled the next verse, "*Prepare thy chariot, and get thee down, that the rain stop thee not.*" It was a long way to Haverhill.

The post had also brought a note from Paul Revere, reporting a complete lack of result in his search for either *a tallish dark-haired thin gentleman, blue or green eyes, seen in the vicinity of the Man-o'-War on Ship Street and going possibly by the name of Elkins* or *a slender gentleman a little under middle height, dark hair, blue eyes, a dimple in his chin, gentlemanly speech and bearing; possibly wearing a yellow waistcoat embroidered with violets* . . . which was discouraging but not altogether surprising. Toby Elkins had come out and told his landlord that he would often be away from town—who knew what that meant? And put an actor in a sailor's slops or a footman's livery and Androcles Palmer would vanish as if he had never been. What actor drew breath who could not assume the bearing of a footman or a lord—or a lady, for that matter—at will? The descriptions were no more informative than the portraits on Hannah Fluckner's drawing-room wall.

Frozen sleet had begun to hammer the window-shutters when someone pounded on the back door, and Pattie came back into the kitchen a moment later with the same young footman who'd brought Abigail Lucy's note a week before. Abigail gave him a silver bit, because it was raining so hard, and after she'd read the note, she wished she'd given him two.

Mrs. Adams,

This evening we have had music at the Gardiners' and I have only just got home, after gossiping with Fanny Gardiner and Belinda Sumner, who wish nothing better than to speak ill of the Dead which I encouraged them to do. It is perfeckly true what Lt C said of Sir J, that he seduc'd a young lady of good family who hanged herself, and Margaret, tho she did not know Sir J was the man in questn, tells me that this girl's sister so griev'd the loss she too died at her own hand. I askt was there a brother or a father, and some say no and some say yes, but the sister had a lover, whose name was Tredgold, and Fanny Gardiner (who is from London) says, t'was on this Tredgold's account that Sir J had himself sent first to Spain, then to Barbados.

This was in 1766. Would Mr. Fenton know of this, and be able to tell us, what this Mr. Tredgold looked like?

"Eight years is a long time," murmured Abigail, when John had read the note over her shoulder. "*Would* a man pursue across the ocean the one who brought his sweetheart to death from grief? Would you?"

Abigail knew any number of men who would fall over themselves with gallant affirmatives: ungallant, untactful, and truthful as a cudgel, John stood for a time in thought, turning over in his mind what he would *actually* do.

Like Don John in the play, thought Abigail, with an inner smile—because it clearly didn't even cross John's mind that he needed to profess his love or his loyalty, when that wasn't the question. *Another man who eats when he has stomach and asks no man's leave . . . laughs when he is merry, sleeps when he is drowsy . . . and lives his truth though it bring the world to ruin about his ears.*

"I think a great deal would depend on who this bereft suitor was," said John at length. "Was he a gentleman of independent means? Or did he have to work for the money it would cost him to take ship—a consideration that I notice rarely vexes the heroes of novels." He gathered up the shirts and bore them upstairs, where his portmanteau lay unfolded upon the bed surrounded by four times as many books as could possibly fit into its volume. Abigail followed. By the dim tallow candles that flickered odiferously in the draught, he packed the books first, then folded each shirt carefully into the smallest possible packet and attempted to ram the packets by main force into the corners.

"I suppose 'tis one reason the great epics are all written about kings and noblemen," reflected Abigail. "One cannot quest far on foot with a few shillings in one's pocket. Even Don Quixote was of noble blood."

"I think the point of *Don Quixote*," returned John grimly, "at least in this instance, is that behavior that is considered acceptable, if eccentric, in a nobleman is ludicrous—or criminal—in the Sancho Panzas of this world . . . Like seducing girls and abandoning them. Would your Lieutenant Coldstone know more about those involved?"

"I shall certainly write him first thing in the morning to ask."

After seeing John off in the wild bluster of morning light, Abigail wrote a brief note to the Lieutenant and carried it down to Oliver's Wharf at the foot of King Street, whence it was usually possible to find someone going from the town out to Castle Island at most hours of the day even in weather like this. Ascending the slope of the street again, it crossed her mind as she approached Customhouse Square that only a short walk along Cornhill would bring her to the Governor's house, where Mr. Buttrick might tell her how Mr. Fenton fared.

She could not, she knew, despite what Lucy had written, put him to further question on the matter of his master's behavior and death. Her own heart clenched with anger at the thought that he might have been poisoned solely as a ploy, a means to be sure that Jonathan Cottrell would be alone when he stepped off the *Hetty* on his return. Yet he had helped her, and she felt a kind of sad protectiveness toward him, lying in that dim attic room listening to the wind howl around the eaves.

What would it be to know one was dying, surrounded by strangers in a town on the other side of the ocean from one's native land?

Yet as she crossed the square, she heard the far-off clamoring of voices down Cornhill in the direction of the Common and saw a small squadron of constables hastening along the street in that direction, trailed by a crowd of apprentices and boys. *Some trouble somewhere*, she thought. *Thank heaven Nabby and Johnny will have reached the school by this time . . .*

"Mr. Thaxter heard shouting in the street and has gone to see," provided Pattie, the moment Abigail came into the kitchen. "Shim Walton"—she named Thomas Butler's apprentice next door—"says a man was shot." She sprang to the hearth in time to catch Tommy before the child could precipitate himself into the fire.

"A Tory," provided Charley, who had not the slightest means of knowing this piece of information. "Bang!"

"Bang indeed," murmured Abigail, and fetched out her pastry-board. The thought crossed her mind that if news *had* arrived about Parliament's reaction to the Tea-Party at last—and if there was genuine trouble over it—Thaxter could be sent galloping after John. Heaven only knew how that news—and whatever mob reaction was triggered in Boston in response—would affect Harry's verdict. Perhaps there was some way the *Incitatus* could be disabled in port . . . Though with spring advancing, another ship was sure to arrive soon.

She dropped lard into her flour, two knives deftly flashing as she cut it smaller and smaller. The wreckers themselves might well be caught, too, multiplying the number of frightened men apt to turn King's Evidence . . .

The shouting in the street was definitely coming up Queen Street. Her eyes met Pattie's: "Get them upstairs." Charley had already put aside the battle royal he'd been conducting between two walnuts and stood by the table, listening with widened eyes. Johnny, Abigail reflected, would hear the tumult with that strange eagerness, that readiness to fight, shining in his face . . .

Charley was scared.

Pattie scooped Tommy up and took Charley by the hand, just as someone knocked sharply at the front door.

Abigail said, "Go." She dropped a towel over the flour, dried her hands on her apron as she strode down the hall. Just as she opened the door Thaxter—panting—slipped out of the mob and into the hall at her side.

"Mrs. Adams—"

Two constables were immediately behind him, and a man whose blue military cloak didn't quite conceal the uniform of Major of Artilleryman from the shore battery. It was one of the constables who spoke.

"Mrs. Adams?"

"I am she."

He held up a folded square of paper. "Did you send a

message across to Lieutenant Coldstone of the King's Sixty-Fourth Foot, at Castle Island, bidding him to meet you?"

"I did." *What on earth—?*

"He was ambushed and shot in the Common. You're not under arrest by any means, m'am—" That was for the benefit of the growing crowd of men behind them. "But we've been asked to bring you before the magistrate of the ward, to explain why your summons was in his hand at the time."

Eighteen

Is he alive?" For the moment it was all that she could think of: that cold-blooded, oddly compassionate young man dead, far from the family that he cared for. *I'll have to write to them*, she thought . . . Then the constable's words sank in: "In his *hand*? I only gave that note to—" Her mind stalled on the name of the fisherman she'd handed it to . . . Geller? Gilson? One of John Hancock's part-time smugglers . . . "I only sent that note across to the island an hour ago."

"Do you deny that this is the note that you sent?"

Lieutenant Coldstone,

A shocking piece of information has come to me that I do not know what to do with. Meet me beneath the Great Tree on the Common at nine tomorrow morning.

Abigail Adams

Abigail blinked, trying to shake herself free of the sense of being in a dream. The handwriting was so similar to her own that for a moment she wondered, *COULD I have written that and not been aware of it . . . ?*

Don't be silly, Abigail. This is not a romance.

"When had he this?" she asked. "I do deny it—"

"Do you deny that it is in your hand?"

"I—"

"The hand is very similar to Mrs. Adams's." With John's best courtroom manner, young Thaxter took the note from Abigail's fingers. "Yet it is not her own." The stolid young clerk held the paper to the light for a moment, then handed it back to the constable. "I've already sent for Mr. Adams—"

Abigail regarded him in surprise—as far as she'd known, Thaxter had been at the jail interviewing another of John's clients—but his eyes met hers and he nodded.

"He'll be on the Salem Road—I sent a man after him. He should be back within the hour, sir. You could return, or—"

"No, please come in." With a rush of gratitude for Thaxter's unimaginative presence, Abigail straightened her back and stepped aside to let them pass. "You must be freezing, all of you. Lieutenant Coldstone—"

"Is unconscious, m'am." The artillery officer hesitated before crossing the threshold, but the crowd was growing thicker, and the wind streaming in from the bay was sharp as broken clamshells. "He has been taken to the Watchhouse on the Common. The regimental surgeon has been sent for."

Thaxter ushered them into John's office, his matter-of-factness putting the men in the position of ordinary clients. Mistaken rather than sinister. As he did so, she whispered, "Who did you send?"

"Jed Paley, on that spitfire mare of his. They should catch him no matter how far he's got."

"What happened?"

"I was at the jail when the town herd-boys ran in looking for the constable. They were shouting that someone had murdered a lobsterback in the Common—one of them said that a note from you was in his hand."

With my signature on it for all the world to see . . .

"Even a Whig surgeon would not assassinate a British officer if he were brought in to care for him, you know," Abigail pointed out to the artilleryman and removed her apron. "Not with all of you looking on. Would you gentlemen care for some hot cider? Or have you orders not to let me out of your sight? Ah, Pattie—These gentlemen have come to arrest me for setting an ambuscade to murder Lieutenant Coldstone this morning. I'm pleased to say I did not succeed."

"Mrs. Adams was with me all the morning," announced the girl, with commendable promptness.

"No, dear, you're forgetting that I went down to the wharf an hour ago, to send the Lieutenant a note," Abigail corrected her. "Which must be still on its way to Castle Island—"

Unless the boat capsized in this weather. Had Abigail been a swearing woman, she would have done so at the thought.

"Miss Clarke." The senior of the two constables held out the note to Pattie. "Is this your mistress's hand?"

"No, sir," stated Pattie, before she unfolded the paper.

"But 'tis very like," said Abigail.

The girl looked at the paper, uncertain about admitting anything, then nodded. "Yes, m'am."

No wonder the British complain Massachusetts witnesses never tell the truth!

"Mr. Thaxter," said Abigail, "is there a way that I can go

to the Watchhouse to see how Lieutenant Coldstone does, without prejudice to my cause or the construction placed upon my action that 'tis an admission that I'm submitting to arrest? I—Oh, Mr. Revere, thank goodness!"

All the men turned, as Paul Revere—who had come in as usual through the kitchen—appeared in the study door. The artillery officer scowled—evidently familiar with his name—but the constables greeted him as an old friend and thrust the incriminating evidence into his gloved hand.

"It reached Lieutenant Coldstone on one of the last of the provision boats yesterday," said the senior man, whom Abigail recognized as one of those men long active in ward politics in the town. "His sergeant says they came ashore at Rowe's Wharf on the first boat—"

"Sergeant Muldoon is with him?" broke in Abigail, relieved, and the constable nodded.

"The Lieutenant left Muldoon in the Mall near the work-house and crossed the Common toward the Great Elm alone, with the words to the effect that the note said nothing of another's presence. Sergeant Muldoon said the Lieutenant had almost reached the elm when he heard a shot and saw the Lieutenant fall. He ran toward the place. He said he did not notice anyone fleeing and had no idea from which direction the shot came. But the Powder-Store is somewhat less than two hundred yards from the elm, at the top of a hill, and that hill, and the copse at its foot, would have covered a single attacker's retreat."

"Good shooting, whoever he is," Revere commented. He went to the desk, and from the top of one of the neat stacks of correspondence there took a letter that Abigail had written to John some weeks ago, when he was at a trial in Worcester. "You generally sign yourself *A.A.*, do you not, m'am?"

"It is my usual signature. Sometimes I'll sign *A. Adams*, but not as a common thing."

Revere held out both papers to the senior constable. "See how the line widens at the tail of the *g*," he said, "where the forger tries to imitate the curve of Mrs. Adams's hand, and where the *g* in *great* stands isolated from the *r*? Mrs. Adams's hand connects it there, and there. The shape of the tail is completely different, too, as you will notice."

While trying to recall whether she habitually connected her *g*'s to their parent words or not—or whether these so-called *proofs* were in fact just slips of a badly cut pen—Abigail reflected that had that difference not existed, the sharp-eyed silversmith would have found any of a dozen others. He was a man used to looking for details, but it was a lawyer's riposte, one that she—and Revere—had seen John use any number of times to parry an enemy's attack by throwing doubt upon the evidence. By the constable's frown of concentration—and his slow nod—she could see that it worked.

"Might we go to the Watchhouse?" she asked. "Lieutenant Coldstone is my friend . . ." She bit back the words, *And I trust there are enough of you gentlemen to prevent me from murdering him on sight.* Knowing the constables, they would undoubtedly take her seriously and arrest her on the spot.

The Watchhouse that stood at the foot of the Powder-Store hill was barely larger than Abigail's bedroom, a single whitewashed chamber with stone walls and a fireplace that wouldn't have kept a bowl of gruel warm. The Common, a quarter mile north to south and twice that end to end, was a bleak and desolate place once the sun went down, and the open fields beyond it, over the slopes of Beacon Hill, largely deserted. The Hancocks and Olivers and Apthorps who held the great houses along Beacon Street wanted to make sure that in the event of trouble that their own servants couldn't deal with, there would be constables within call.

As if the winds had whirled away Thursday's strolling ladies and kite-flying children, the town pasture lay nearly empty under the scudding morning sky. The town cows, left in charge of the youngest and lowest-ranked herd-boy, were being slowly brought up from the other side of the meadow, and all the older herd-boys had already joined what amounted to a scattered crowd that milled about the Watchhouse. It was the usual Boston Mob, Abigail noted: prentice-boys and dock-laborers, and men who looked like tavern-servants. The eyes and ears of the Sons of Liberty . . . and of the smuggling-bands operated by half the merchants in Boston.

A number of these individuals were shouting insults and throwing stones and frozen cow-dung at the stolid red-clothed form of Sergeant Muldoon, who stood before the Watchhouse door with his musket at his side. One or two hooligans broke off at the sight of the artillery officer who had accompanied the constables to Abigail's door, but the presence of a woman with them seemed to act as a deterrent to anything but shouts of "Fucking lobsterback!" and "Murdering pigs!"

"Excuse me a moment, m'am, gentlemen." Revere strolled over to them. The shouting ceased at once, and the little knots of men and boys retreated. Some moved off around the hill, or into the brushy copse at the hill's foot, but Abigail could feel their presence, like a tension in the air.

Muldoon kept his eyes very properly on the copse but spared a glance at Abigail as she came to his side; blue eyes troubled at the sight of her. "I shall want to speak with you later, Sergeant. Is that permitted, Constable?"

Rather than coming anywhere near the Watchhouse, Revere moved off, pacing the distance between the infamous copse and the Great Tree. Abigail knew why but considered the caution unnecessary. Did he *really* think the artillery major, unsupported by troops, would be such a fool as to attempt to arrest him in the teeth of the mob?

Lieutenant Coldstone had been laid on the table before the fire in the little building, with a third constable beside him on one of the room's battered benches. This man jumped to his feet as Abigail and her party entered. "He's still breathin', sir—" He was an elderly man, with an accent of Ireland and a palsied quiver to his hands. Abigail couldn't imagine what help he'd have been had the layabouts—or the murderer himself for that matter—decided to rush the place and finish what the unknown assassin had begun. "I can't wake him." The room stank of blood, rum, and the burned hair that presumably the old man had used as makeshift vinaigrette. Someone—Muldoon?—had covered Coldstone with the young officer's military cloak, to which had been added one of the constables' greatcoats.

Abigail said, "Open the shutters," which had been closed, presumably out of fear that the crowd would break the grimy glass. Compliance by the constables with this request didn't help matters much. The windows were small and set high. Given the general dimness of the morning, not a great deal was visible in the gloom. Every lantern the Watchhouse possessed had already been lighted and pressed into service around Coldstone on the table, giving his body the curious appearance of some arcane sacrifice laid on an altar. His wig, smeared with mud, lay on one end of the bench. In the frame of his short-cropped pale hair his face seemed white as bleached wax, his brows—which normally appeared rather mouse-colored—now almost black by contrast. Under the cloak his coat had been pulled off his left shoulder and arm, and his shirt cut away and torn up to make a dressing.

"Bullet's lodged, sir—m'am—" The elderly constable divided a doubtful glance between his commander, the artillery officer, and Abigail. "Bled somethin' horrible, he has—"

Thaxter bent over to look, and said, "Damn," and Abigail put in, "I hope some of that rum that I smell was used to cleanse the wound?"

"'Twas, m'am," affirmed the elderly constable. "I did a trifle of work with the surgeons, back durin' the war."

"Who knew about the message that you sent Lieutenant Coldstone, m'am?" asked the officer, speaking for the first time.

"No one," insisted Abigail. "That is, the message I sent was not the one that he received last night. I sent mine first thing this morning and doubt that it has reached Castle Island even yet. And in it I asked merely that he might name a place and time for our interview, in some public place, as my husband is from—Lieutenant!" As she had spoken, her hand had been on Coldstone's wrist, feeling for the swift, thready pulse; so it was she felt his arm move, even as she heard the agonized intake of his breath. "Give me that rum."

The elderly man pressed it into her hand. Coldstone coughed on the sip she gave him, and turned his face aside, a sentiment for which she could scarcely blame him. "Can you hear me, Lieutenant?"

His eyelids flickered, and he nodded. The Watchhouse door opened and yet another constable entered, carrying—Abigail was delighted that someone had shown this much sense—a couple of blankets, obviously fetched from the town Almshouse at the end of the Mall—and a number of billets of firewood.

"Did you see anything of the man who shot you?" Abigail asked, and the artillery officer stepped up beside her, with the air of one who would have put her bodily out of his way, if he could have.

"One of the damn Bostonians learnt Mrs. Adams had sent for you," he said, leaning over Coldstone, "and lay in wait."

Abigail opened her mouth to protest yet again, then shut it. The man clearly had his own ideas of what had happened, and it would be useless to argue.

"You lie quiet, sir. You've taken no mortal hurt. We've sent for the surgeon—"

Abigail backed away and slipped through the door. Thaxter was talking softly with Muldoon; Paul Revere was nowhere to be seen. Muldoon asked, "How is he, m'am?"

"That artilleryman says the Lieutenant isn't mortally wounded—Who is he, anyway?"

"Him? One of the officers at the South Battery. When himself went down a couple of the herd-boys came runnin', an' one went to fetch the Watch whilst t'other helped me get the Lieutenant here. The constables must've gone for the nearest officer they could think of. Before we even tried to shift him I packed the wound with everythin' I could lay hand to—" Abigail noticed for the first time that Muldoon was missing his neckcloth. "But he's lost a fair river of blood. What was it made you send to ask for a meetin' here, m'am, if you don't mind me askin'? There's not someone watchin' your house, is there?"

Abigail explained for what felt like the dozenth time that she had had nothing to do with the message that had brought Coldstone to the Common, then asked, "Where was he shot from? The bushes below the Powder-Store?"

"Got to be, m'am. 'Tisn't an inch of cover that would hide a man any closer. And further off, Robin Hood himself couldn't hit at the distance, not if he had a telescope and a magic gun from the King of the Fairies."

"And of course anything resembling tracks would have been trampled out by this time by Sam Adams's pet mob—"

The sergeant took his eyes off the little knots of men still moving about in the vicinity long enough to give her a quick grin. "Wouldn't be no tracks anyway, m'am. The ground's like flint. Well, here's someone in a hurry," he added, as a horse burst at a clattering canter from the bare trees of the Mall. "Let's hope 'tis the surgeon—"

"It isn't, though." Abigail shaded her eyes. "It's Mr. Adams."

How she knew it at this distance she wasn't sure—he was riding a horse unfamiliar to her—but sure enough, when he came a little closer, she identified the caped gray greatcoat and mud-spattered top boots. She lifted her arm to wave, and he drew rein beside her and flung himself from the saddle to catch her in his arms. "Nab, are you all right?"

"I'm well—"

"I can't leave you for half an hour before you're arrested—and for murdering a British officer—!"

"As I have explained to all those gentlemen in the Watch-house," sighed Abigail, "I had nothing to do with it. But someone went to a good deal of trouble to see to it that the British think I did. I'm beginning to know how poor Harry feels! Now *that*," she added, shading her eyes and looking in the direction of the other end of the Mall, "will be the surgeon."

Several of the assorted stevedores, layabouts, smugglers, and such, appeared as if by magic from the copse and the hill-side as the three crimson-coated riders drew near, but there was not even shouting. The absurdly young officer saluted Muldoon and left his escort on guard outside; John—no coward but no fool, either—stepped back and nodded in the direction of the copse at the foot of the hill.

Abigail shook her head. "You go," she whispered. "I'll be all right."

"There'll be trouble, if they try to arrest you—"

"They won't try to arrest me. They haven't a leg to stand on—and if I know Mr. Revere, reinforcements are already on their way."

When she reentered the Watchhouse, the youthful surgeon was examining the wound by the clustered light of the lanterns, but at least, Abigail reflected, he didn't suggest that his patient be bled, puked, or given emetics to regulate the balance of his bodily humors.

"We should get him to the camp before I attempt to remove the ball," he said, straightening up at last. His speech, like Coldstone's, was that of the gentry class: Abigail wondered if his parents, like the Lieutenant's, had not been quite able to afford professional training for their son and so had apprenticed him to an Army surgeon instead. Looking around him, he registered a moment's surprise at the sight of a woman in the place, then stepped over to her and bowed. "Lieutenant Dowling, m'am, at your service . . . Can you tell me, if there is some herb—some poultice that the local midwives use—as a sovereign for cleansing a dirty wound, or as a febrifuge? I have often found these old remedies to be of great use, but unfortunately I only know them for the Indies."

"Willow-bark tea will bring down a fever," Abigail began.

The artillery officer broke in, "Really, Lieutenant Dowling, do you think that's wise?" And in a lower voice, "'Twas this woman who lured Lieutenant Coldstone into the trap! Her husband is the head of the Sons of Liberty!"

Exasperated, Abigail snapped, "Mr. Adams is nothing of the kind! You're thinking of the *other* Mr. Adams—"

And in a thread of a voice, Lieutenant Coldstone added, "'Tis true." His hand stirred toward her. "Mrs. Adams—"

"Hush," said Abigail. "Lie quiet. They'll be taking you back to the camp—" For the soldiers that young Lieutenant Dowling had brought with him now entered, with a makeshift litter of poles.

Coldstone shook his head. "My sergeant—?"

"Is well," said Abigail. "The shot was meant for you." She stepped close, avoiding the soldiers as they prepared the litter. "I sent you no note, Lieutenant. That is, I *did* send you a note, but 'twasn't the one you received: that was a forgery."

"What news?" he murmured. "*Shocking news*, you said—"

She bit back her protest that she'd had nothing to do with that particular communication, and only said, "I shall tell you later, Lieutenant. All is well for now." She laid her hands over his and through both pairs of gloves could still feel how cold his flesh was. "But I must have your permission to see you—" She glanced at the artillery officer, who was frowning at her in a way that presaged future welcome by the authorities in the camp.

Coldstone nodded. Encouragingly, Lieutenant Dowling bent over him and said, "It will all be well, Mr. Coldstone. Beyond the loss of blood there is no mortal hurt."

He started to withdraw, with a sign to the soldiers to proceed, and Abigail laid her hand on his sleeve. "Pray, sir, tell no one that."

"I beg your pardon, m'am?"

Her glance went to the artillery officer, to the constables, calling them close. “Please, listen to me, gentlemen. Tell no one that Lieutenant Coldstone’s hurt is not mortal.” And, when they looked at her blankly: “Do you not see? A trap was laid for him, by whom we know not. Nor do we know when they will strike again, or how. Let no one see him—”

“Really, Mrs. Adams!” exclaimed the artilleryman. “In the safety of the camp—”

“As few as may be, then . . . and myself.”

He looked as if he had something else to say about that, but Coldstone whispered, “Let it be as she says. She is right.”

“Enough now, sir.” Lieutenant Dowling stepped forward again, a trifle diffidently, and signed again to the soldiers. “We must take you across to the island, before the gale freshens further. Mrs. Adams—” He turned to her as the men began, with the competence of those who’ve handled the wounded on the field of battle, to shift Coldstone over onto a litter. “Is there one in Boston who deals in these herbal simples you’ve spoken of? In the islands it was the Negro midwives, and one had to go to the slave-dances to find them—”

“I shall make up a packet for you,” she said, “and have it sent across before the day grows dark. I grow them myself, and dry them—my mother, and my mother-in-law, send others across from our family farms.” She flinched, as a cry was wrung from the patient when they settled him on the litter, and she turned to take his hand again. “Remember, when they carry you out, to do your best to look like a dying man, sir,” she instructed briskly, and Coldstone managed the flicker of a smile.

“Endeavor—to convince . . .” His fingers closed weakly around hers. “News,” he said. “What was it? *Shocking*—”

She shook her head, “Later,” she said. And then, when he

gripped her hand as she tried to draw it away: "The name of the girl who hanged herself over Cottrell. What was it?"

"Seaford." His eyelids slipped closed again. "Sybilla Seaford."

"And her sister?"

Breath and consciousness went out of him with a sigh.

Nineteen

If the would-be killer were watching, Abigail knew it would be better to have herself taken out of the Watchhouse surrounded by constables, as though she were under arrest. But she could think of no way to do this without having the rabble attempt to rescue her—certainly she could think of no way to convince the harassed artillery officer to go along with the charade. The soldiers who manned the British batteries at either horn of the mile-wide crescent of Boston Harbor seldom emerged from behind the palings of their garrisons, and with good reason. Vastly outnumbered, it would not take much of a confrontation for someone to start shooting . . .

Which is all we'd need, with the King and Parliament convinced we're a rabble of traitors because we refuse to submit to arbitrary taxes.

It was all Harry would need, she reflected a moment later, when he came before the Admiralty Court—

No. She thrust the thought from her mind. *We can't let it go so far. One way or the other, we cannot let him be taken aboard the* Incitatus . . .

But as she followed the stretcher-party out the door of the Watchhouse, she could think of no way of stopping the event.

Coldstone had promised he would try to be appointed for the defense. She shivered as she looked down at the young man's waxen face. And shivered again at the thought that the would-be killer was a good enough shot with a rifle to hit a man at nearly two hundred yards—

—and that Lieutenant Coldstone might not have been the man's only target.

Fortunately, the Common was the widest space of open ground in Boston, and the only possible cover—the copse of brush at the bottom of the Powder-Store's unkempt hill—had been thoroughly overrun with prentice-boys, ruffians, and smugglers, and probably thoroughly searched by Paul Revere as well.

She saw she had been right, too, in her guess that Revere would send for reinforcements the moment two other soldiers appeared on the scene. The mob formed a loose ring around the little cluster of stretcher-bearers, constables, and soldiers, at a distance of about twenty yards: idly loafing, looking about them as if they had by coincidence all decided at once to take a walk on the Common that morning. But many of them carried cudgels, or the short clubs used by the men at the ropewalks for beating cable; some openly bore guns. She knew that they'd stay with the shore party down to Rowe's Wharf.

"'Twill be a savage crossing for poor Coldstone," she murmured to John, who came forward out of the ring of men, leading his borrowed horse, as she fell back from the stretcher-bearers. "But I suppose if we were to offer Lieutenant Dowling the spare room in which to remove the bullet, and to keep the Lieutenant there to recover, that artillery captain would suffer an apoplexy."

"As would Cousin Sam," returned John. "Not to mention every one of our neighbors, when I ride out for Haverhill Monday morning. Will you never cease being a scandal, woman?" he asked, with a grin at Abigail's shocked expression. "For a good Christian you've a surprising innocence of heart."

"*Honi soit qui mal y pense*," she retorted.

"Then shame upon the whole length of Queen Street, because *mal pense* is precisely what everyone will do . . . and *does*, given your penchant for making friends with handsome British officers. Besides," he added, clearly enjoying her outrage at the thought that anyone would read scandal into her meetings with Coldstone, "you'd never separate that sergeant of his from him, and what would we do with the man? Let him sleep in the kitchen? Then there'd be trouble from one end of the town to the other, about British troops being quartered upon civilians—"

They followed the litter-bearers down Winter Street and past the Governor's house on Marlborough Street, men and women coming out of homes and shops to gawk—and some to join the mob. Abigail saw Revere and Ben Edes—the publisher of the *Gazette*—and young Robbie Newman in the crowd, and at one point thought she glimpsed Cousin Sam. But the Sons of Liberty had no intention of permitting another Massacre. The four soldiers clustered more tightly together but did not break their disciplined step, and in the whole of the company, no one shouted.

There was only a low murmur, like bees when a hive swarms. For her part, Abigail felt uneasily conscious of the number of upper windows they passed between, and as the houses thickened on either side, she walked closer to John.

"I'm sorry you had to return."

"It couldn't be helped. I'd hoped to have Sunday there to walk about and see the town, but if I leave at first light Monday, 'twill be the same." Abigail reflected guiltily that had the weather worsened today, while he was on the road, he would have had the choice of passing the Sabbath at some point in between. Now he had lost that leisure, and the thought of obliging him to do thirty hard miles, in so rough a gale, in order to reach Haverhill on Monday was as bad as the thought of poor Lieutenant Coldstone being tossed and thrashed on a military launch between Rowe's Wharf and the island camp.

"I would stay here if I could, Nab. Yet I fear they'll have put Mrs. Teasel in the town jail, and God only knows where and with whom her children will be disposed—"

"I'll be well, John. You know Sam will keep an eye on things." Privately, given the spattering of rain and sleet that began as they detached themselves from the mob and made their way along Cornhill to Queen Street, Abigail was just as glad John had returned. The rain was sweeping in from the north and east, and would have made the road even as far as Salem a nightmare. By Monday it might be easier.

Or impassable.

"Pattie's making dinner," announced Nabby, hugging her mother as the family entered the kitchen. "Stew and Indian-bread—Did the constables arrest you, Mama? Shim Walton says they did. He said they'd take you over to the Army camp, and if Papa came back and tried to get you out, they'd arrest him, too—"

"As you see," smiled Abigail, "I was not taken over to the

Army camp, and your father is perfectly safe and will be going to Haverhill on Monday. No one is arresting anyone."

"But that Lieutenant was murdered," said Johnny, with a six-year-old's ghoulish anxiety not to be cheated of at least a little bloodshed. "Was he not?"

Abigail started to say, *Of course not*, and then considered how much information the Sons of Liberty—and perhaps others—gleaned from the tales told by children in the streets. She said, "We won't talk of it now, Johnny. Help your Father with—Is that Mr. Paley's horse you borrowed to ride back on, John? Pattie, I cannot thank you enough—" She stripped off her cloak as she said the words, put on her apron and house-cap.

While John fretted and reviewed with Thaxter all the details of the Teasel case that had to be dealt with, Abigail made up a packet of willow-bark and Saint-John's-wort, yarrow and coral bells, for young Lieutenant Dowling, but guessed that no one would be crossing to the island this afternoon. As she packaged up the mild-smelling simples, she found her thoughts returning to Braintree, where her sister-in-law and John's redoubtable little mother—a widow now on her second husband—had grown these things and sent them on to her. Closing her eyes, she felt for a moment that she could reach out and touch not only the warm summer afternoons on the farm there, but the peace of a world separated from Boston's politics, Boston's grime, and Boston's violence. What were the analogous plants in Barbados, she wondered, that young Lieutenant Dowling sought out the Negro midwives to buy?

Was this something she could ask him in her note, and would he respond?

The rain increased, hammering the black, wet roofs of the

town, driven sidelong by the northeast wind. As she chucked wood onto the fire after dinner, while John brought in bucket after ice-cold bucket of water to heat for the family baths, Abigail wondered how Harry was faring in that dank and icy cell. Both Billy Knox and Lucy, she knew, had tried to get food, books, and clothing to him, and had had them sent back. Had the Provost Marshal let him keep even what she'd brought him?

They must have. They couldn't . . .

A dark shape crossed the wavering gray curtains of the rain, loomed by the back door. Abigail hastened to open it and saw that it was Philomela. "I can't stay but a moment, Mrs. Adams," said the girl, "and such an uproar as there is, over this shooting, and Mr. Fluckner claiming 'twas only to be expected with traitors going unpunished everywhere in Boston, and Miss Lucy—" She shook her head, and held out a note. "But Miss Lucy said that you would want to know this, m'am."

Mrs. Adams,

Mr. Barnaby told me his brother-in-law sent him word today that poor Mr. Fenton died in the night.

Yrs faithfully,
Lucy Fluckner

On those nights when John knew he must rise betimes, to be ready to take to the road the moment there was light enough in the sky for the ferrymen to make out the crossing to the mainland, he could fall asleep quickly and sleep like the dead.

Abigail wasn't sure what woke her in the small hours of Monday morning. The rain that had hammered Boston through Sunday morning had gradually lightened, though the wind remained strong—but she was used to the sounds the house made on windy nights.

Something in her dream, then? A troubling dream about sitting at David Fenton's bedside, listening to his whispered ramblings. Only sometimes it wasn't the servant who lay dying in that dark and chilly attic room above the Governor's house, but Lieutenant Coldstone, very young and vulnerable-looking without his wig. Folded notes littered the blanket all around him, all of them in her own handwriting: she kept opening and reading them, looking for the one she had actually written, filled with a despairing sense that even if she found it, she could not prove the others had not been written by her as well. If she failed, they would send her to Halifax to be tried and hanged, unless she betrayed John and her children, her sisters, and her parents. . . . The ship was at the dock, waiting for her, dark masts swaying in the wind, rigging creaking—

She heard something in the house below her and knew it was the cover being slammed on the well in the cellar.

Her eyes opened to the inky darkness of their curtained bed.

How foolish. There's no well in our cellar.

John's breathing was slow and deep and utterly peaceful at her side. A restless sleeper at the best of times, she wanted to reach across and shake him out of sheer annoyance.

Messalina, she thought. Whoever had invented the phrase *graceful as a cat* had never seen Messalina hunt.

But even as her mind framed the thought, she knew it wasn't the cat.

The fire had been banked; the bedroom was glacial and dark as Erebus. Yet in nearly two years of residence, Abigail had learned the exact number of steps that would carry her to its door, and that door's exact relationship to the bed. Charley had been barely a year old when John had bought this house, and Johnny only four. At such ages there were nightmares beyond the power of a mere older sister to hold at bay. Charley especially was prone to them, and within the first weeks here Abigail could traverse the house from the room where she slept with John—and in those days tiny Tommy as well—to that shared by the other children, in utter darkness.

She gathered up candle, striker, flint, and slipped into the hallway, where she stood listening for a time in the darkness. No sound from the children's rooms. In any case, something about what had wakened her—if it had been a sound that had done so—had said to her, *Deeper in the house.*

In the hallway she stooped to strike light, where the new tiny brightness wouldn't wake John (*as if the Last Trump would wake John . . .* !). When she stood, she knew what was wrong. The candle-flame leaned, ever so slightly, to the left, toward from the tight, square spiral of the stair. It straightened almost at once, but Abigail knew every chink and draft and crochet of the house. The door at the bottom of the stair never fit quite right, especially in the winter; in the daytime, when there was coming and going from the kitchen, close it how she would, there was always a whisper of a draft.

There was a window open downstairs.

She thought—and later could not believe she could have been so stupid—only that in barring the shutters, Pattie had been hasty. There was one in the kitchen whose bolt never fit quite right into its slots. Just as it had simply failed to occur to her that anyone could or would attach scandal to her friendship with the extremely comely Lieutenant Coldstone, it never crossed her mind that a window would have come open in the middle of a very windy night due to anything but accident. What she should have done, she knew in hindsight, was to go back into her room immediately and fetch John, dawn departure or no dawn departure.

What she did was descend to the kitchen, soundless as a ghost in her quilted blue nightgown, and cross to the window in question—which *was* open, shutters and casement both—and reach out to pull the shutters closed.

She didn't know what made her turn. Messalina, she later thought—the cat came bolting out of the pantry, fleeing for the hall door, which Abigail had left open behind her . . . Turning, she saw in the almost total gloom the unmistakable shape of a man standing in the pantry.

Her start gave her away, and her first instinct—always her downfall—was to cry, "Here!" almost as if, like a disobedient child, he would surrender.

Instead he rushed her. He covered the distance with snake-strike speed, and Abigail—at first immobilized with shock—snatched up the nearest object to hand—a chair—and swung it at him with the whole strength of her back. He dodged, lunged, and Abigail had time only to think, *I've seen him before*—when the candle was struck from the table where she'd set it, and strong hands grabbed her shoulders, swung her in the darkness. Abigail twisted, grabbed at the man's head—felt her hands seize an ear and heard the hiss of agonized fury in the second before she was slammed to the floor on top of the chair.

She cried out with pain, and then, belatedly, screamed at the top of her lungs. Somewhere upstairs she could hear John shouting "Nab? NAB—!!" and she screamed, "MURDER!"

because it was easier than screaming *Burglary*! And she didn't think of it and was in too much pain in her ribs, her knee, her head. She could hear her burglar blundering and scrambling close by—trying to find the window—and she screamed again, hoping to get not only John but Tom Butler from next door. It was too dark to see anything, but she felt the cold and smelled the wind when the burglar succeeded in slamming open the shutters, and she heard the splat when he got through the window and fell.

I hope he's broke his leg . . . Then she heard his footfalls slap-slap-slap on the mud of the passway, and out to Queen Street.

John flung himself through the kitchen door, and she shouted, "I'm all right! He's gone!"

John had a candle and a stick of firewood held like a club, and was already halfway to the window. He wheeled, dropped to his knees at her side. "Nab—"

"I'm all right." This wasn't entirely true. She felt like she'd fallen out of a tree, in more pain than she'd been—with the exception of childbearing—since her own childhood, and she fought not to weep for fear it would frighten him. He caught her up in his arms, and she heard more footsteps pattering upstairs, followed by the caroming of slight bodies off the stairwell walls and Pattie's cry, "Johnny, no!" and then a wild clatter: Johnny had obviously come downstairs armed.

"You're bleeding." John caught her hand. Pattie brought another candle into the room and, with commendable presence of mind, went straight to the candle-box and set a dozen on the table beside which Abigail and John sat, next to the felled chair.

Abigail looked at her hand. There was blood under her nails. "I think it's his." With John's hand beneath her arm she got unsteadily to her feet, and the children—who had hung back in shocked horror at the sight of their mother sitting on the floor, bruised and disheveled in her robe—flung themselves on her, Charley and Tommy bursting into loud tears.

There was of course no question of anyone getting to bed that night. John listened to her account of the robber with a detached attention that Abigail found far more comforting than repeated assurances of thankfulness that she'd taken no hurt, interrupted almost at once by the arrival of Tom Butler from next door and both his apprentices, armed with a pistol and a very fearsome hammer. He was succeeded almost at once by Ehud Hanson—a shoemaker who lived on the other side—his younger brother, and his formidable wife, also armed; the Watch arrived minutes later. While Abigail was assuring them all that she was well ("And get those children to bed, Pattie, please—"), John checked the drawer of the sideboard in which the household cash was kept. "He didn't get that, in any case," he remarked, and disappeared into his study, emerging almost at once with the report that nothing there seemed in the slightest disturbed.

"You must have surprised him just as he entered and was looking his way about." John disappeared into the pantry and came out again with a pitcher of cider, which he poured into the smallest of the pots on the hearth to heat. Abigail, on the settle next to the hearth—Pattie had stirred up the fire—started to rise, then sank down again with a wince. Even sitting for a short while had stiffened bruises she hadn't known she'd acquired. Distantly, she could hear the clock of the Brattle Street Meeting-House striking four.

Mrs. Butler had put in her appearance by this time, semi-dressed and with her hair hanging in a braid, and while Abigail was reassuring her in her turn that she was well and stood in no need of assistance, John disappeared again, to come back downstairs a few minutes later dressed, wigged, and carrying his saddlebags. "*Will* you be all right?" he asked, after he'd tactfully but firmly shoved the cooper's well-meaning wife out the door. "Nab, forgive me—"

"No, you have thirty miles to ride—"

"Were I not sure that my client has spent the past three days in the town jail, I would stay, but I cannot, Nab. If it rains again, God knows how long 'twill be—"

"No, of course you must go! Wherever her children are, you know no one in town will be caring for them, if all are saying their mother's a murderess. I'm bruised, 'tis all. 'Tis as if I fell down the stairs." She opened her mouth to begin, *I didn't want to tell you before others, but I knew the man. I've seen him, I know it . . .*

Then she thought of the child Marcellina, and tiny Stephen fretfully sucking at the spouted milk-cup held for him by Mrs. Barnaby, and of how the world treated the children of paupers. The sooner John got to Haverhill, the better for those unknown offspring of his client.

She closed her lips again.

The light of a single candle, darkness and confusion . . . *Had* she seen her assailant before? She groped in her mind, trying to recall where, and couldn't even be sure that her impression was an accurate one. The prominent chin, the long nose emerging from beneath the shadow of his hat, the dark brows: a fleeting sensation of recognition, based upon what? One of the loafers around the Watchhouse yesterday? Someone passing in the street?

It was nearly time to do the milking. The herd-boys would be blowing their tin trumpets in the street before long. Gently rejecting Pattie's offer of assistance, Abigail went upstairs and dressed, and came down again to find John and the children devouring a scratch breakfast of the last heel-ends of Friday's bread, and the cider that he now poured steaming from the kettle. *Baking tonight.* "I shall be home Wednesday," John promised, and went out to the stable with her, saddling Balthazar while she and Nabby milked. "Thursday at latest."

Then he was gone, and in spite of herself, Abigail felt a shiver of dread, watching him ride away through the first chilly dimness of the wind-lashed dawn.

I know I saw him before.

But what did I see?

Thaxter arrived. He and Johnny did the stable chores before the two older children left for school. When they were gone and Thaxter settled in John's office to copy documents, Abigail sank down onto the settle again, with the queer shakiness of exhaustion. Just after the burglary, she had felt clear-headed and strong: *What's the matter with me now? I've dealt with worse. Those Roman matrons one reads about could defend the city's walls in the morning and bake bread in the afternoon without turning a hair.*

"Are you sure you don't want to lie down a little, Mrs. Adams?"

She looked up with a start, to see Pattie standing beside her.

"I can clean the kitchen, and get the bread started, and get you up in time to get the dinner begun, if you feel able for it. You don't look any too well."

"Maybe I will rest a little." Abigail got to her feet, and flinched in earnest. She turned toward the stairs and then stopped, something tugging at her mind—"Tommy," she said, shocked, "what have you got there?"

Though it was quite obvious that what Tommy had there

was a dead mouse. She and Pattie reached the boy in a couple of strides, though he tried to duck back into the pantry with his prize. *Messalina*, thought Abigail . . . *Did our visitor last night dodge back into the pantry and interrupt her at her kill?*

She took the mouse by the tail and moved toward the back door, then stopped again.

There was no blood on its fur. Rather, its whiskers and paws were powdered with flour . . . *Oh, not again*! Above all things, Abigail hated to have to throw out flour because rodents had somehow managed to get into it, despite every precaution of barrels and bags. She glanced back at the flour-barrel, expecting to see a telltale track that would show where it had been gnawed through . . .

And saw that the barrel was open.

Good heavens, did Pattie or I forget to close it?

She had only to form the thought to discard it.

White tracks amply showed where the vermin had taken advantage of their opportunity . . .

And down behind the barrel, another mouse lay, as dead as the one still dangling from her hand.

On the shelf above the barrel lay the longest of her wooden spoons, whitened with flour for a good three-quarters of its length, as if someone—*Who?*—had stirred the barrel . . .

Had stirred something into the barrel . . .

Abigail put her hand over her mouth and felt herself go cold.

Dear Heavens . . .

Half a day later, he was taken sick . . . She heard Dr. Warren's light voice in her mind. *What does that sound like to you?*

The man had come not to steal but, with a deliberateness that took her breath away, to kill every member of the household.

Twenty

For the love of Heaven, Nab, we don't need to be calling Apthorp into this." Cousin Sam thumped his hand on the parlor table with an impatience that rattled the half-empty cider-mugs. Not wanting to disturb the children any more than they already were, Abigail had chosen to confer with the men in this room rather than the more homey—and also warmer—kitchen. "I have a couple of friends who can get you into that house—"

"There has been quite enough breaking and entering in the past twelve hours." Abigail glanced from Sam to Paul Revere to Dr. Warren—the latter, to his credit, looked shocked at the suggestion—and then back to Sam. "Just because the man's a Tory and an Apthorp doesn't mean he's going to run to this mysterious Mr. Elkins and warn him that I want to see the inside of that house again. Besides, I need to speak to him about his tenant."

"You think it was Elkins who came here last night, then?"

Warren didn't sound disbelieving, only curious about her reasoning.

"I think I should like to see if Mr. Elkins has a wounded ear," replied Abigail. "He may not. He may have some perfectly legitimate reason for spending fifty shillings a quarter on a house he doesn't seem to be living in—which coincidentally lies within easy walking distance of where Lieutenant Coldstone was shot."

Though she was fairly certain she'd interrupted her visitor in the midst of his first task of the evening, she'd spent the hour or so between her discovery of the dead mice and the appearance of her three friends in response to her frantic notes, nailing shut and stowing in the attic not only the flour, but also the cornmeal and the cider, and her mind kept questing back to the other contents of the pantry . . .

Did poison wait for them there, too? She knew this was unreasonable but could not free herself of the panicky obsession. Greeks and Romans had poisoned one another with liquids as well as powders, and such a philtre might conceivably have been poured over or into the sugar as well . . . Would it have caused the sugar-loaf to change color?

She would have to ask Lucy, who seemed to be a girl familiar with the more lurid forms of fiction that might deal with such matters . . .

"A man lays out money like that only if he has good reason, and no good reason seems readily visible. Money also turns up in the room of the servant-girl Bathsheba, who disappeared two days after Cottrell left Boston. And now this actor, this Mr. Palmer, who had dinner with poor Fenton the night before he took sick, seems to have disappeared as well. We have a pattern, gentlemen"—she ticked off the points on her long, slender fingers—"money, poison, and people disappearing . . . I shall take Mr. Thaxter to Pear Tree House with me. Not simply for the sake of respectability," she added after a moment. "But I'm starting to find it a bit unnerving, to go about alone."

And you think this Mr. Elkins is connected with the Seaford sisters—the ones who killed themselves on Cottrell's account?" Thaxter glanced around him and drew closer to Abigail as they emerged from the relative shelter of the houses along Southack Court and made their way along the frost-hard mud of one of the unfinished streets that crossed the northern slope of Beacon Hill. The river and the Mill-Pond, which had been dammed off it, both floated with chunks of ice, and the wind that swept across them and over the hill's bare shoulder was wickedly cold. Having dispatched a note to Lieutenant Coldstone informing him of these new developments and having received from the same boatman a very polite thank-you from Lieutenant Dowling, Abigail spared a pitying thought for that very young sawbones, exiled from the warm Caribbean to ply his trade in the damp brick corridors of a fort in a half-frozen bay.

"I think he is connected with someone whom Cottrell harmed." For Cottrell—also newly come to this brutally frigid land from the mild Indies—she felt no pity. *Margaret tells me that this girl's sister so griev'd the loss that she too died at her own hand.* Heat flashed through her at Lucy's words, rage so stifling that for a moment she was scarcely aware of where she was. She loved her scapegrace brother William, for all his faults, but the love for her sisters Mary and Betsy went deeper, twined around the roots of her soul. The world being what it was, she had tried to face in imagination what it would be like were brisk, busybody Mary to die in childbed, or spinsterish, beautiful Betsy of some disease in their parents' home. Such things happened, and Abigail had prayed that should such an event come to pass, the God who had sent it would help her to bear it.

But had one or the other of these women—these souls who seemed as much a part of her as her own—died by her own hand, in shame and horror . . . would she, Abigail, be driven to end her own life rather than live without the sister she loved?

She didn't think so. Yet she found herself contemplating with a certain hellish satisfaction the image of Sir Jonathan Cottrell, beaten half to death, lying conscious and freezing for some time in that alley before the darkness took him. *Forgive me, Jesus . . .*

She forced herself to add, *And forgive him.*

And soften my heart that I may actually mean those words. Because I don't.

She realized she had been long silent. Her husband's clerk was watching her face with the eyes of one who read her thought.

"Poor Mr. Fenton spoke of a number of women whom Cottrell despoiled," she went on. "One at least had a lover for whose death Cottrell seems to have been responsible as well. A *fulyear*, Grannie Quincy says they used to call such a man: A man who dishonors women for sport. Of those women, only one—or two, if you count the poor sister—seems to have had family or friends in a position to seek vengeance for what he did. And even those, as John pointed out, may have had to wait until they had the resources to begin the pursuit."

Her iron pattens scrunched in the hard-frozen mud as they

ascended the hill toward Pear Tree House, its pink bricks very bright against the brown of the naked orchard. Thaxter put a hand, stout in its dogskin glove, beneath her elbow to steady her, until they reached the muck-drowned gravel of the drive.

"Unfortunately," Abigail went on, "it will take at least six weeks for a letter to reach anyone who knew the Seafords in England for a description of the sister's fiancé Mr. Tredgold. Another six weeks or more for a reply. And it is beyond hope that by June, this town will not be entangled in such a confusion of reprisal and counterreprisal for the destruction of that miserable tea last December, at the very least . . . and in any case," she added, "were it *two* weeks, I fear it will not save Mr. Knox."

"It may not," said Thaxter. "Yet all we need to do, really, is find a single point sufficiently telling to Colonel Leslie, for him to cancel the order for an Admiralty trial. And for that we need produce only the evidence that one who wished the Commissioner's death with sufficient resolution was here in Boston and had the means to accomplish it."

"You're quite right, of course," replied Abigail thoughtfully. "But more's the pity, you've just given a description of Harry Knox."

Thurlow Apthorp waited for them, just within the doors of the Pear Tree House. He appeared relieved to see that Abigail's escort was her husband's very respectable young clerk and not some shaggy mechanic. He seemed, too, genuinely troubled by Abigail's information that she suspected that Mr. Elkins had something to do with—or at least some knowledge of—the shooting that had taken place on the Common the previous day: "Please understand that we have no accusation to make against him," said Thaxter, not entirely truthfully but certainly within the letter of the law. "But events having taken the turn that they have, it is imperative that we speak to Mr. Elkins as soon as may be."

"There's the trouble, sir," replied Apthorp worriedly, and he shut the door to exclude the whipping draft. The tall central hall settled again into the semblance of a well filled with shadow. "Mr. Elkins has not come into the Man-o'-War to pick up his letters—"

Abigail was already aware of this fact from Sam, since a couple of the Sons of Liberty were watching the place.

"—and I've no means of reaching the man until he does." He added, as if he feared they thought such a course might have slipped his mind, "I have written him."

This, too, Sam had reported. His informants had gotten a good look at the letters waiting under the tavern's counter.

"Of course you have," said Abigail soothingly. "And the matter being one of suspected violence against officers of the Crown, your permitting us use of the house again in your tenant's absence is certainly not actionable." She looked around her again at the high walls with the single stairway leading up one side, the cold light from the window above the door lending a kind of pallid illumination to the upper reaches and almost none down below. The sickly odor of death had faded, yet she still led the way as quickly as she could into the drawing room that was the only fully furnished chamber in the house. "Has Mr. Elkins never spoken to you, when coming or going from the town, of which direction he would travel in? Or of where he might have been, ere coming to New England?"

"Britain, I've always assumed. At least, he always paid me in British coin."

"What, all of it?" It was the other question she had meant

to ask, and Abigail felt a little as she had when, as a child, she'd pegged the bull at darts three times in a row, something even William couldn't do.

The householder nodded, and Abigail's glance crossed Thaxter's. Then Thaxter moved off toward the dining room, Apthorp bowing to Abigail to precede him . . .

She paused, frowning at the closed door behind her. "Did Mr. Elkins say why he had the latch removed from this door?"

"Latch?" He stared at her in surprise.

Abigail's gloved fingers brushed the holes in the wood of the door itself, and its frame. "Was there not a bolt here?"

Apthorp shook his head: "Why on earth would anyone want to bolt the door to the *drawing room*? Good Lord," he added, bending closer to look and squinting a little—Abigail realized he was nearsighted. "Well, bless my soul." He straightened again, regarded Abigail—and Thaxter, who had turned back from the dining room door—in bafflement. "Was a latch put on the other door?" Apthorp hurried across the drawing room to see. "What an extraordinary thing to do—"

He looked at the door into the dining room, then opened it and checked the other side. Abigail followed—rather carefully, as the shutters still covered the ground-floor windows—and checked as well. "Odd." She crossed back to the door into the central hall, knelt in a rustle of quilted petticoats, and peered at the holes in the gloom. "It looks like a bolt—can you get those shutters open? Thank you! And the holes look fresh."

She got to her feet. "Let us see if other doors were used the same way."

They made a circuit of the ground-floor rooms, which were laid out around the central hall, and the pattern became immediately evident: all doors leading into the hall bore the same pattern of nail-holes on their inner sides. When the searchers climbed the stairs and checked the rooms above they found it so upstairs as well. "What on earth was the man afraid of?" asked Thaxter, as they came down the stair again. "None of the communicating doors between room and room, so he expected . . . What? That someone might be able to get into the hall—through the front door or that upper window above it—while he slept? But who?"

"And would it not have been simpler to have told his servant to bed down in the hall?" inquired Apthorp.

"I don't think we've established yet that Mr. Elkins possesses a servant," murmured Abigail, opening the dining room shutters and examining again both sides of the door from drawing to dining room. "Nor that he ever spent a night under this roof."

"It makes no sense!"

"It does," contradicted Abigail softly. "But in a context of which we're ignorant."

"The context is that the man's clearly mad," declared Apthorp. "Who would have thought it? Such a gentlemanly young man . . ."

A gentlemanly young man who KNOWS WHERE I LIVE. Who had access to at least one note in her handwriting? Abigail shivered at this thought, half guessing that as the note had been the bait for Coldstone, his murder had been almost certainly simply a tool, a means to have her hanged.

Where have I seen him? She tried to set the strong cheekbones, the long nose, into a context, and failed. *In the street? In the market?*

Why cannot I call to mind how he was dressed, where he stood, if he spoke, what sort of hat he wore?

On her search this time, Abigail looked into every drawer and jar in the kitchen, though she admitted to herself that it was hardly likely that the mysterious Mr. Elkins would have left poisons in an empty house for anyone to find. The upper floors and attic proved as devoid of poison-pots, weapons, or little chests of British coin as they had upon the previous occasion—even the attic contained none of the trunks and disused furniture that could have provided hiding-places for such apparatus of villainy. The shuttered window casements showed no sign of having been opened in years. The house being fairly new, there were no loose boards in walls or floor, and no join of truss to king-post in all the maze of rafter-work had been made to serve as a hiding-place for anything but years-old rat-nests. Boots had scuffed the dust on the floor, it appeared, only once. She found one clear track, its length and thinness seeming to echo Apthorp's earlier description of the man they sought. Nothing more.

The fact that the rather epicene gentleman the householder had described didn't sound to her capable of beating another man to death she put aside. Sir Jonathan had not been a big man, either, and if Mr. Elkins were indeed Mr. Tredgold, cold vengeance would undoubtedly have lent strength to his slender arm.

Candles were lighted, but because the house was built rather high, small, stoutly barred windows admitted a gray and dismal light to the whitewashed cellar. Like the attic it was virtually bare, containing not even the spare stores of firewood that choked the corners of Abigail's own cellar at Queen Street, much less the usual cellar impedimenta of potato-bins, broken milk-pails, and sealed crocks of vinegar, butter, and cheese.

Though the room was three times the size of Abigail's,

the place oppressed her. Despite its cover, the well exuded a dampness that seemed to eat into her bones. Even in prosaic daylight, the pulley that hung above the well-curb still had the look of some sinister implement of torture, and she felt a strange unwillingness to touch the square wine-box, as if it contained the unspeakable.

It did not, even upon second inspection.

She sat back on her heels, her breath a thick cloud and her toes growing swiftly numb. "Will you open the well?" she asked.

Thaxter lifted the heavy cover. It was designed, Abigail observed, so that it could be closed even when the wine-box was lowered into its cooling depths. This time, when Abigail dropped a lighted candle-end into the Stygian depths, it vanished with a prompt little plop—evidently the slight warming of the past two windy weeks had been enough to melt the ice. "Is there a pole, or a hook of some kind, that we can use to plumb the well?" she asked, and Apthorp regarded her again in bafflement, as if asking himself if his somewhat Gothic tenant weren't the only person in the case who was mad.

"Whatever for?"

"'Tis the only container in the house I haven't looked into," she replied. "I don't mean to leave until I've seen all there is to see."

No pole in the kitchen or the stables proved long enough, so in the end Abigail lowered the bucket-hook down on the end of its chain, weighted with a couple of small stones from the garden bound onto it with twine. More twine looped around the chain gave her a sort of leading-string by which she could drag the hook back and forth in the lightless depth. Apthorp only watched in puzzled fascination, but after a little, Thaxter asked, "What do you hope to find, m'am?"

"I have not the faintest idea. But someone was killed in this house—in the front hall, I think, by the smell of it—" Apthorp looked like he'd have visibly blenched, had the light been better. "If Mr. Elkins is as clever and thorough as he has been so far, we should find nothing—"

The hook snagged on something, held for a moment, then came free.

Abigail shut her teeth hard upon a sudden qualm of nausea at the thought of what it might be.

Twenty-one

I doubt it's a man." Abigail kept her voice steady with great effort. Her brother William—and any number of her older Smith and Quincy cousins in and around Weymouth—had outdone themselves in their efforts to shock and sicken the parson's three stuck-up daughters, and the half-wild countryside had abounded in dead cats, maggoty bird-corpses, cow-dung, and other gooey and odiferous evidences of Nature's ability to break down mortality into its component elements. Mary had gotten angry, and little Betsy had squealed and squirmed, but Abigail had regarded it as a matter of honor to meet all such attempts with calm *sangfroid*—an attitude that she guessed would stand her in good stead a few years hence, as the mother of three boys.

She felt a strange—and very ancient—stirring of gratification at the expressions of queasy horror on the faces of the two men with her.

She went on, "I felt it start to come, before it pulled loose, and it felt too light. Besides, there's no stink. How long is it, for a man's body to float?"

Apthorp shook his head. Thaxter looked too disconcerted to even attempt a response. In the back of Abigail's mind stirred the childhood recollection of Asa Shapleigh—who had been no loss to the Weymouth community—going missing and his body coming to the surface of Vinal's Pond a week or two after he'd last been seen staggering away drunk into the woods.

"What *is* it?" Thaxter asked, when at last Abigail hauled up an object limp and dripping, glistening darkly in the light of the candles and the waning afternoon light.

Apthorp, who despite Abigail's reassurances seemed to have feared that it would indeed be Bathsheba's body, only looked profoundly relieved.

Gingerly handling the sodden folds—the cloth was unbelievably cold, even through her gloves—Abigail spread it out on the cellar floor.

"A shawl, it looks like." She gently flapped the corners of the big rectangle to straighten them. "We need to dry it." As near as she could tell, it was wool rather than silk, but with what daylight there was beginning to fade, it was impossible to distinguish color or pattern. Dropped a second time, the hook clinked and scraped a little on the irregularities of the well's bottom, but encountered nothing similar: no clothing, no ropes, no shoes. Apthorp went upstairs, and after a little time came down with coarse toweling from the kitchen, and in this they wrapped the wet mass of cloth, to carry back to Queen Street.

"I suggest that you have the locks on the outer doors and the stables changed at once," said Abigail, as Apthorp locked the house up after them. "The sooner the better, though I doubt Elkins will be back. If he is indeed this Mr. Tredgold—or anyone who sought to conspire against Sir Jonathan's life—he has accomplished his end."

"But why stay in Boston?" asked Thaxter, as they descended the bare slope of the hill again. "If he was the man who attacked you last night—"

"We cannot say for certain that it was Elkins." Abigail shook her head. "Or who else might have been acting with or for him. Had I conspired to murder a man I had, perhaps foolishly, spoken of killing at some time in the past, I think I should personally make sure I had a regiment of witnesses that I was elsewhere on the night of his death . . . and that I did not announce my guilt by fleeing the morning the body was discovered."

"Exactly like Harry, in other words."

"Yes, well," admitted Abigail, "perhaps we had best reword that theory, if and when we present our case to Colonel Leslie. I suspect," she added more soberly, pausing to look out toward the harbor, where the masts of the dark ships rocked uneasily at anchor along Boston's sixty-plus wharves, "that the main reason he's still in town is that almost since the night of the murder, wind has kept all the oceangoing ships in port. If this is Mr. Tredgold we're dealing with—or only his spiritual brother—having accomplished his vengeance, he'll be returning to England now, to take up his life again—"

She paused, as the Reverend Cooper's words returned from—When?—Two Sundays ago? Three?—*How can we do good in the sight of the Lord God, if the doing of it will transform us into the Servants of Ill? Will mark us with the Mark of the Beast?*

"To take up his life again," she said softly, "if he can. If he was the local curate and has spent eight years tracking a man with the intention of doing murder in cold blood, I doubt he will find himself much suited for the care of anyone's soul."

The thought returned to Abigail later, as she found herself obsessively scrubbing and rescrubbing every apple, every potato, every carrot that she'd brought up from the cellar, having thrown down the outhouse anything edible that remained in the kitchen. This included things she knew intellectually must have been safe, like the butter in a crock still sealed (*Agrippina the Younger of Roman infamy would have found a way to poison butter in a sealed crock . . .*), and the cheese even after she'd trimmed away slices from its cut ends (*How WOULD one poison a cheese?*).

"This way lies madness," she murmured to herself as she stood debating whether the new barrel of flour, delivered through Sam's good offices, should be put under lock and key in the cellar, yet she spent the whole of the evening after dinner taking her own pulse, monitoring every ache and twinge of her joints (which, thanks to an afternoon spent in a damp cellar, were indeed in feverish pain by nightfall) and watching her children in surreptitious panic. She had told them nothing of the attempt to poison the family, but when the kitchen was cleared up and the lamps lit, she gathered them about her and informed them that the same Evil Person who had shot Lieutenant Coldstone might be also out to do them harm, and until she told them otherwise, none were to accept food or drink from anyone but herself, Pattie, Thaxter, or John.

"Will he try to poison us?" Johnny's face glowed in hopeful delight.

"This is serious, John Quincy." Abigail never used her

son's full name, save when matters were indeed grave. "'Tis no game."

"No, m'am." He tried to readjust his features. "Is it the Tories?"

"I don't know. I think so." She salved her conscience with the fact that the money in the case definitely pointed to the British, and that was Tories, if you would. "You and your sister must keep a careful eye on the others."

Nabby, standing at her side, said nothing, but slid a very cold little hand into hers.

In between her preparations for dinner, Abigail had written notes—dispatched via the various apprentices of Butler and Hanson on either side of the house—to Sam and Revere, Lucy Fluckner and Lieutenant Dowling, enclosing in the latter a message to be relayed to Lieutenant Coldstone, and this had kept her thoughts at least in the reality of what had happened, and away from speculation. But after dinner, in the last of the afternoon's waning light, she had pried loose the cover on the contaminated flour-barrel and examined it by the attic windows, observing the thick streaks of a greenish gray powder, where it had been imperfectly stirred into the pale buff contents. Had her visitor had but a little more time, he could have mixed it thoroughly enough to conceal any adulteration.

She remembered poor Mr. Fenton's sufferings: the thirst of the damned, the jaundiced agony as his liver died within him, the bloated features. She, and John, and their children would have died—in who knew what horrors?—and the blame would have fallen on some illness unknown.

Rage went through her in a wave of fever, burning her flesh to her ear-tips and hairline, and she no longer asked herself if the hypothetical Mr. Tredgold could or would have tracked Cottrell to the earth's ends to avenge the suicides of Sybilla Seaford and her unhappy sister.

Johnny. Nabby. Pattie. John . . . Her own hands shook with fury.

God's certain vengeance would be insufficiently swift. *I would wrest the weapon of it from His hand, for the pleasure of striking the blow myself, though my soul were damned for the act.*

And in the back of her mind she heard John's voice—*Would you really? Though your soul were damned for it?*

Abigail didn't know.

It was far too late for Captain Dowling to cross from Castle Island that evening, but Lucy Fluckner appeared only an hour after the arrival of a hastily scrawled note requesting the favor of an interview etc., etc. Bearing all the lamps that could be gathered, she followed Abigail upstairs to the attic where the jetsam of the well had been laid out to dry. The shawl was still wringing-wet and discolored, but the girl's face grew grave as she viewed it. "That's Bathsheba's," she said quietly, and glanced back at Philomela, her blue eyes sick with grief. "It used to be mine. There's where I tore it climbing over the palings by the stable, and see where the fringe has been burned? I caught it in the bedroom candle. It's Bathsheba's." Her gaze went to Abigail's. "She really is dead, isn't she?"

Abigail said gently, "Mr. and Mrs. Greenleaf will look after Marcellina and the baby." For Lucy had brought her the news that while all else had been going forward that day, the farmer Silas Greenleaf had arrived to take the two children back to Weymouth with him, for a childhood of hard farmwork and regular meals, until they should be old enough to be set free. "But us finding her shawl there in that house proves that her disappearance is after all connected with Cottrell's death, somehow. Think, Lucy. What *could* she have learned about Cottrell? What *could* she have seen?"

"Could Sir Jonathan have dropped, or left behind, some token or paper when he attempted to force himself on Bathsheba in her room?" Lucy—whose imagination of the scene had clearly been influenced by certain well-defined genres of fiction—glanced back at her maidservant, as the women left the attic and descended the ladderlike stair to the bedroom floor. "Something she found later?"

"That told her what, m'am?" responded the black girl. "She said nothing of it to me. Nor of seeing him later, nor of any message sent to her from him."

"But she was upset, shaken up, the day before she disappeared," the girl pressed. "You said she burst into tears in the public street, Margaret." As they reached the bottom of the flight, she turned appealingly to Mrs. Sandhayes, who had insisted on being helped up the narrow stairs from the hall, but whose lameness had met with defeat at the second ascent. "If it was something that fell or rolled, and she only found it later, or a letter that whisked under the bed—"

"Now, you know as well as I do, m'am," Philomela corrected softly, "how tidy Sheba was about her room. That time when Mr. Cottrell followed her up to her room was five days before he left Boston. Nothing would have lain on the floor, even under the bed, for that long."

"Could she have found out something about this Mr. Tredgold?" persisted Lucy, holding out her arm to help her companion down the twisting, narrow stair to the hall.

"Who?" Mrs. Sandhayes frowned.

"Mr. Tredgold. You remember me asking Fanny Gardiner

about poor Miss Seaford, and you saying that her sister had killed herself . . ."

"Good Heavens, you don't think a man would wait all these years to wreak his vengeance, like some hero of a Venetian melodrama? Thank you, dearest—" She took her sticks, which Abigail had carried for her, and hobbled painfully to the parlor fire. Pattie and Philomela disappeared together down the hall to the kitchen, whence Pattie returned a few moments later with a tea-tray of gingerbread and gooseberry tart.

"He might have needed time to gather up money for his pursuit," opined Lucy. "I think a man whose beloved killed herself for grief never *would* forget, nor forgive . . ."

"My dear—" Margaret Sandhayes raised her painted brows, and her long, rather square mouth tightened into a bitter line queerly at odds with the girlish brightness of her maquillage. "I think as time goes on, you'll learn that a man who needs to spend a couple of years gathering money to pursue revenge upon a friend of the King's, whose friends are all in a position to help the bereaved suitor to preferment in the law or the Church or some other useful profession, generally comes to the conclusion that vengeance is best left to Heaven, long before he's saved half the cost of passage to Spain or wherever it was the odious Cottrell fled to." She took a piece of gingerbread, broke it in half, lifted the cup of chamomile tea to her lips, and then set both down with a grimace.

"It's a rare man who will sacrifice his *entire* life—*all* his affairs—for the pleasure of bringing to justice a blackguard whom the King has already forgiven for his peccadilloes. Men simply have not the necessary concentration of mind."

Lucy bristled. "Harry would avenge me. Whatever the cost!"

"Indeed he would." Mrs. Sandhayes folded her hands. "Harry is different from all other men."

"What was her name?" asked Abigail, since Lucy appeared on the verge of some very unwise assertions. "Sybilla Seaford's sister, the one on whose behalf this Mr. Tredgold is or is not seeking revenge?"

"Alice? Alisound?" Margaret Sandhayes shook her head. "Something with an *A*, or maybe it was Juliana. Something like that. The scandal was supposed to be quite nasty while it lasted, but these things never do last, you know. We were living in Bath at the time, and Mama did her best to keep the details from me, though I was quite old enough to hear them. But then, our family never did move in the highest circles, and poor Mama got all her gossip secondhand. I think it far more likely that whoever it was who waited for Sir Jonathan at the end of that alley on the night of the ball, he had a fresher grievance than poor Mr. What's-His-Name and had not sailed two thousand miles in the dead of winter to appease it."

With this, Abigail was more than a little inclined to concur, particularly in light of what she knew about the behavior of men when confronted with preferment and privilege. John frequently derided the somewhat far-fetched premise of her favorite novel—Richardson's *Pamela*—on the grounds that no man would put himself through the social contortions undergone by the sinister Mr. B— in pursuit of the blameless heroine, but lying in the curtained darkness of her bed listening to the wind howl, Abigail reflected that this was not really the point of the book. More telling than the interior wrestling-match between love and lust was the behavior of those whom Mr. B—coerced into complicity with his will: the parson who, needing a way to make a living in a country overcrowded with impoverished parsons, chose B—'s patronage over moral imperatives; the servants who would sooner assist their master in raping an unwilling girl rather than lose the only means of making their own livings.

Would a man, confronted with the suicide of his beloved, risk his own livelihood—and the inevitable countervengeance of the King's so-called justice—to commit murder when that royal justice had officially ignored what was, in effect, a moral rather than a legal offense? John's powerful sense of duty had taken him away from her side tonight—and in her heart she prayed he wasn't still out on the road between Salem and Haverhill somewhere, with the sleet flying about his ears. She could not imagine any respectable hero in a novel choosing his responsibility for making a living for his family—not to mention getting his client out of jail and making sure her children weren't consigned to a cellar someplace—over staying on guard against an unspecified threat at home.

Is it madness, that throws away ALL?

The lives of the Christian martyrs—the tales of the ancient Romans—abounded in incidents of desperate self-immolation, different in kind from the obsession of which the Reverend Cooper so often spoke. *The Mark of the Beast that considers naught but his own desires . . .*

The dead King says to Hamlet, *Leave thy mother to Heaven*, before his son goes on to destroy himself, his beloved, his mother, and his best friend in the obsessive quest for vengeance, leaving his leaderless country to the mercy of a foreign usurper.

Yet could Hamlet have turned aside, knowing what he knew?

In the morning, head heavy with sleeplessness, Abigail

did her marketing, then turned her steps toward the Old North Church, where young Robbie Newman let her into the little outbuilding that had been turned into a combination jail and hiding-place for Matt Brown and the Heavens Rejoice Miller. Sam had brought her up-to-date on the story that the two Mainers had been told, about how unsafe it was for them to leave Boston yet and how the *Magpie*—in reality safely berthed at Lynn—had fled back to Boothbay, with promises to return in a week or maybe two . . .

In the meantime, the two fugitives had plenty to eat, ample gossip from every Son of Liberty with a few hours to spare, and enough seditious literature on hand to bring an empire down in flames. Abigail went over with them again every word and action of the deceased, either witnessed by the cousins or relayed to them by gossip: Had Cottrell ever spoken of a man named Toby Elkins? A woman named Sybilla Seaford? *(As if any man would give a moment's thought to a seduction eight years in the past . . .)*

She felt the nagging certainty that these men held the key to finding Cottrell's killer, if she could but ask them the right question. Yet like a key mislaid—*In a drawer? On a shelf?*—it eluded her. Was there any woman in Boothbay that Cottrell was supposed to have seduced or insulted? Or the rumor of one?

"Not even the rumor, m'am," affirmed Miller. "Right from the first, he kept his nose indoors."

"Even Hilda Sturmur couldn't get a rise out of him," added Brown helpfully. "And she's had every man around Penobscot Bay behind old Bingham's barn."

"Bingham? The man Cottrell stayed with?"

Both men nodded. "Hilda's old Bingham's milkmaid."

Brown added with a grin, "They say even Bingham's bull

turns tail in panic when he sees Hildy coming—" and got a sharp elbow in his side from the marginally more respectable Miller.

"That is, no, m'am," filled in Miller, and took a long pull of the cider Abigail had brought them. "Why seduce someone in the village when Hildy Sturmur was there and willing, and she was just beside herself not to manage him while he was there."

"I'm sure she wouldn't have boasted of it—"

"Oh, no, m'am. Hildy's not *that* kind of girl."

Abigail blinked, wondering exactly what *that* kind of girl was considered to be, in Maine.

"But she complained of him to my sister Levvy—"

"Levi?"

"Leviathan. Hildy complained to Levvy that Cottrell wouldn't so much as look her in the eye. Most people think Hildy had her eye on that gold ring he wore on his pinky, though she never did manage to get it off him. Myself, I think it was just the challenge that she likes."

"*Challenge*," said Brown wisely, "is *not* what Hildy Sturmur likes."

Maybe not, Abigail reflected, as she turned her steps homeward along the crowded wharves. But challenge was the farthest thing from what, under normal circumstances, any female would have faced, living in the same household as Sir Jonathan Cottrell.

Was the man that frightened? she wondered, holding her cloak tight around her against the gray howl of the offshore wind. Frightened even in Maine, where he was reasonably certain Harry Knox would not have pursued him? Did that fear have anything to do with the telltale nail-holes in every door that communicated with the central hall of the Pear

Tree House—doors bolted to confine someone or something in the central hall, as if in a pit?

Was it fear of the disgruntled Mainers themselves that made him so radically change his habits? Or something—or someone—else?

Twenty-two

The note that awaited Abigail in the kitchen upon her return said simply,

Mrs. Adams,

I am at your service and will await your convenience at the garrison house attached to the South Battery.

Lieutenant Rufus Dowling
Surgeon, King's 64th Foot

He must have crossed—in weather like this!—as soon as 'twere light enough to do so. Guilty as she felt about abandoning poor Pattie yet again to doubled morning chores ("Don't you *dare* do the beds or the dusting for me! I shall deal with them when I return if it means working 'til sunset!"), Abigail felt still more responsible for leaving that earnest young surgeon stranded in the garrison house at the foot of Fort Hill, particularly as the day was worsening again. She set the fish and the ducks she'd bought in the pantry shed to stay cold, checked that Tommy was dry and firmly affixed to the sideboard, and that Charley hadn't hidden any of Johnny's belongings in any of his usual places, warned Pattie to keep a close watch against dangers unspecified, kissed both little boys, and set forth again, taking the long way to the small cluster of barrack huts so as to stop in Purchase Street and obtain the company of Sam's servant-woman Surry. Though it was Abigail's repeated contention that in America—unlike in England—a woman could walk anywhere unmolested, she drew the line at venturing into even a minor group of British soldiers alone.

Fort Hill lay only a few hundred yards from Sam's house, outside of Boston proper at the eastern end of that sprawled plot of open ground that had once comprised the whole of the town's Common Land. During the wars with France, batteries had been established to guard the harbor in case a French fleet came down from Canada. Now that the French were gone from Canada, the North Battery, in old Boston proper where Ship Street ran into Lynn Street, was scantly manned. The soldiers in charge of the guns there were ferried straight across from Castle Island for their watches and straight back, and observed with invisible zeal by the ruffians, idle prentices, and Sons of Liberty who frequented the wharves. The South Battery, more isolated on its hill outside the confines of the town, had a cluster of barrack huts surrounded by a palisade, so that the men charged with keeping the Sons of Liberty from stealing the thirty-five cannon in its gun park had at least someplace to sit on bitter spring days like this one. Even before the events of last December, as tensions mounted between the Crown and those who protested its interference in the colony's government, the soldiers had learned to remain within the wooden palings on the hill's east side. There were always loafers on the wharves along the Battery March, and should any untoward number of soldiers attempt to land on Rowe's Wharf or Apthorp's or any other close by, word would flash through the town with the speed of a heliograph, and an armed mob would be waiting before the invaders reached shore.

Thus Abigail didn't blame Lieutenant Dowling for taking the better part of valor and asking that she—a respectable married woman—venture into what constituted a miniature Army camp. The sentry on the gate glanced at her and the handsome, smiling black woman who walked at her heels, and pointed out the hut where Lieutenant Dowling waited.

"Lieutenant Coldstone is well," the young surgeon answered her first question, bringing up another chair to the fire of the rather grubby little office that the post commander relinquished to him. Abigail knew women—numbering Mrs. Fluckner and her friends among them—who'd have left Surry to wait outside in the cold. Though Lieutenant Dowling would not fetch a chair for a servant-woman, he raised no objection to her simply standing close to the fire. In fact, in the way of that class of Englishmen to which he, Lieutenant Coldstone, and Margaret Sandhayes all belonged, he simply did not appear to see her at all.

He went on, "Per your request, m'am, I have kept information about his condition to the fewest possible hearers. Do you honestly think him in danger, even out at the camp?"

"I scarcely know," confessed Abigail. "I would have said, No, and assumed that the attempt upon his life was the work of some"—she hesitated, then went on smoothly—"of some traitor, perhaps, who had heard of his association with me. Did my own note—the one requesting a meeting in some place at his convenience—reach his office at the camp?"

"It did, m'am. The hands were compared and are very like. Yet if you had baited a trap with the first, why send a second? Moreover, the Lieutenant insists upon your innocence."

"I appreciate his confidence." Abigail smiled. "I had meant to bring some bread and jellies for him, but . . . Well, I would rather now be a little careful, who is seen giving food to whom." And she told him of the events of Sunday night. "'Tis the opinion of my medical friends that the death of Cottrell's servant Fenton resembles in its symptoms the effects of the death-cap mushroom. My friends found it suspicious that there was no fever, nor were others in the Governor's household sick with like symptoms."

"Poison?" Dowling frowned. "Why would anyone poison a servant?" Unspoken was the question, *Why would anyone bother?*

"Why would anyone poison me or my family?" returned Abigail. She brought from her marketing basket the little packet of paper, carefully folded and sealed, that she had carried from the house. "Whatever this was, 'twas deadly enough to kill two mice almost on the spot. Dr. Warren was kind enough to conduct a postmortem on one of them, but all he could say was that he found neither corrosion nor internal bleeding. It has been a little mixed with the flour in the barrel," she added, as Dowling tapped the contents of the crock out onto a dry saucer. "'Twas the darkest place I could find, of the half-mixed streaks."

"It seems to be vegetable." The surgeon stirred it with the tip of his penknife, then carried it to the window's light.

"I was wondering," said Abigail, following him, "if 'twere familiar to you from the West Indies?"

Dowling bent his head close to the saucer, and sniffed, carefully. "By the color it looks a little like oleander," he said at last. "Yes, it is grown in the Indies, in gardens; also in Italy, though it's originally an Asian plant. A virulent poison." He shook his head, sparse fair eyebrows tugging together. "I have known men to die from having spitted meat on its twigs to cook. Yet Sir Jonathan himself wasn't poisoned, but beaten—by the look of the bruises on his head and shoulders—and left to die of cold."

"I would say," said Abigail, "it might be because the killer feared Sir Jonathan would recognize him if he somehow introduced himself into Governor Hutchinson's party that night. Or it may simply be that he had not the clothing, nor the manner, to pass himself off as someone who would be welcome in the Governor's house. The merchants of the town all know one another, and might be quick to spot a stranger. Where were you stationed in the Indies, Lieutenant? And how long ago?"

"I've been on post here six months." He returned to the fire with her, and carefully wiped his penknife on a corner of his pocket-handkerchief, which he then knotted, as a reminder—Abigail assumed—not to do anything further with that cloth until it had been washed. A virulent poison indeed. "I was in Kingston four years."

"Did you ever hear of an actor in those parts named Palmer? Androcles Palmer?"

"I saw him in *The Jew of Malta*, if he's the man I'm thinking of." The young man smiled at the recollection. "He played about six roles—all of them poisoned by the said Jew—and was one of the best things in the performance, which was shockingly bad . . . at least it seemed so to me, since I was seventeen years old and was used to Garrick and Woodford.

He's one of the men poor Coldstone has been seeking word of, isn't he? I seem to recollect that he's partner with a man named Blaylock—the fellow who did the Jew himself—and they tour the colonies every few years."

"Do you know anything of him?" Coldstone—and Revere, who had done militia service—had both told her how gossip about anything and everything would be handed round military posts, by men with too little to do and too much time to do it in. "To his credit or discredit?"

"To his credit," said Dowling, with a grin that made him seem even more boyish, "he was one of those actors who can change not only his makeup and wig, but his posture and voice and the way he walked. On stage I could tell by his stature 'twas the same man, but otherwise, he would go from a cringing slave to a bawling soldier to a pious nun. To his discredit, I understand the man is what my sisters call a *thoroughly bad hat*: a cheat at cards, they said on the post, and a thief of his partner's share of the profits. Rumor had it that the only reason poor old Blaylock keeps with him is because he's very good, and Blaylock, bless his ranting and his tears, is *very* bad. If they've parted company by this time, I shouldn't be surprised."

"Would rumor put it past him, to murder a man, if he were paid to do it?"

"I don't think so." The young surgeon considered the matter. "I don't know, really. It's a hard thing to say of a man, you know? Especially one who's not here to defend himself. My impression is that he would have to be very well-paid, and the murder a very safe one, for everyone said he's the most arrant coward who walks the earth. I can't see him thrashing Sir Jonathan, for instance."

He frowned into the pitiful fire. "Not that he wouldn't

walk off and leave him lying, I don't believe—but I think that, given his choice, he would pick some other way to punish him. Beating a man and leaving him in an alleyway is . . . is only incidentally conducive to death, you know. Sir Jonathan would very likely have lived through a night less cold, for the contusions on him were all quite superficial."

They were what a man would have sustained, Abigail reflected uneasily as she made her way back toward Queen Street, who had been beaten up by the large and angry sweetheart of a woman he'd insulted. Only the offended sweetheart had been busy that night, printing up the broadsides at present lodged in her attic, and Paul Revere's, and a dozen others in the town—broadsides calling all men of courage to be prepared to stand against the tyranny of the Crown. Not an argument one could present in one's own defense.

"Like as not the wretched actor's halfway to New York by this time," muttered Abigail. "And will be on his way back to the West Indies, or to London, by the time a letter reaches the proper authorities."

"I don't know about proper authorities, m'am," said Surry, pacing calmly along a half step to Abigail's rear. "But Mr. Sam's had the word out since last Wednesday, when Dr. Warren first said that that poor manservant had been poisoned by this Palmer, and them friends of his travel faster than any postrider in New England. If Palmer's above the ground, they'll find him."

"How, among all the men in New England?"

They paused by the gate of Sam's dwelling; Bess's voice could be heard from the yard, singing a rather disreputable sailor's song with her daughter Hannah. Surry smiled. "Among all the *honest* men in New England, they'd have a problem, m'am," she agreed. "That actor fellow might be able to pass himself off as a Turk or a nun or a friendly fellow that's safe to have a meal with, for a short time. But low blood and a low mind is going to come out, sooner or later, and I'm willing to bet you, acting is all the man can do. The weather bein' what it is, we know he's not took ship for England because *nobody's* took ship for England. Which means he's on his way to New York or Philadelphia, because that's the only place he'll find work, unless he's set on livin' off this Mrs. Cherne—whatever *her* real name is—that Mr. Sam said was payin' Palmer's bills at the Horn Spoon. The Sons'll find him, m'am. Don't you worry about that. There aren't that many places an actor can be. And then you bet they'll ask him who was the one who paid him to make sure Mr. Fenton wasn't with his master when his master come home from Maine. And they'll ask him so he'll fall all over hisself to answer."

Abigail knew Surry was right about that. Heaven only knew what the slave-woman—the sole remaining fragment, along with the house itself, of the patrimony that Old Deacon Adams had left his brilliant, scheming son—thought of the Sons of Liberty, in her heart.

Bess, when she came to the gate at the sound of Surry's voice, understood Abigail's excuse that she had to return home to begin dinner, for the older children would be home from school soon. "Sam has everything well in hand, dear," declared Bess reassuringly, and pressed upon her a twist of paper containing a couple of spoonfuls of smuggled tea: "If you mix it with chamomile, you can get at least four pots from it."

Sam has everything well in hand . . . Abigail shivered, as she hastened her steps along Long Street, the sharp gales off the harbor whipping her cloak and turning her toes and fingers numb.

Except how to get Harry Knox out of the grip of the British. Except any assurance that, faced with the noose, the young bookseller wouldn't turn King's Evidence once he got to Halifax where the Sons of Liberty could not take their revenge. Harry, Abigail knew, was committed to the cause of colonial liberties and to the concept of the colony's self-government, free of interference from the King's Commissioners and the King's bosom friends. He was committed, moreover, to the friendships that made up the heart and soul of any normal man: to Sam and Bess, to Dr. Warren, to Paul and Rachel Revere, to Robbie Newman at Old South, to herself and John. To the people he'd known in his home town of Boston all his life.

She knew also that once a man was hoisted on the gallows, it took twenty long minutes, dangling, kicking, at rope's end, to suffocate to death.

She remembered how Revere had joked about breaking Matt Brown and Hev Miller out of the Boston jail; how her brother's friends had gotten him out of the place almost casually, as if he'd been locked in a cupboard or a cellar. In Boston it was generally known that the King's Commissioners couldn't take a smuggler, because of the providential appearance of large numbers of armed dockside types—the chief reason that the Crown had begun to prosecute smugglers in Halifax.

Walking along Purchase Street, Abigail could look out across the bay and see the *Incitatus*, riding at anchor off Castle Island. Waiting for the wind to change.

"Mrs. Adams?"

A girl who was passing her as Abigail turned the corner into Queen Street halted on the pavement and put back the hood of her cloak. Under a neatly starched white cap, black curls flickered in the tug of the wind.

"I'm Mrs. Adams, yes." Abigail wondered why the wide brown eyes, the heart-shaped face were so familiar . . .

"Miss Pugh," she said.

"I've waited for you, m'am—Miss Pattie let me in—but I couldn't wait no longer." The girl cast a frightened glance back in the direction from which Abigail had come—the direction of the Common, and the handsome houses of the rich along Milk Street and Beacon Hill. "Mrs. Hartnell, she'll be askin' after me, and I don't dare not be there—"

"I shall accompany you," said Abigail promptly, "that you may lose no time. I'm sorry I was from home. Had I known—"

Gwen Pugh shook her head, "Oh, not your fault, m'am, no, please. I saw the chance, when Mrs. H was still abed, after being up all hours playing cards." They crossed by the Customhouse and turned along Cornhill again, stepping quickly on the slippery cobbles. "I had to find you, and speak, m'am. I didn't know Sheba well, but she was that kind to me, not just about the tooth-drawer but afterward, when I was in so much pain. And the way she spoke of her little girl, and how worried she was about her baby when she had to go out with Mrs. Sandhayes—" She shook her head. "Though she was a Negress and all, I did so much feel like I was home again, with my own sister and baby brother. And Mrs. H has been so very kind to me also, and took me in when I was barely a mite, when my mamma died, and didn't know no manners or how to sew or iron, and had me taught . . ." Anguish at her own disloyalty pulled at the girl's face. "But she lied to you."

"Yes," said Abigail softly. "I thought she had."

"Bathsheba, she wasn't upset or frightened or anything else they said that Friday, just vexed that she had to be away from baby Stephen again. When Mrs. H and Mrs. S would go out together, it would be hours before she was able to go home again, and the poor little thing would be crying from hunger, which always made Mr. F wild. But Mr. Hartnell, m'am—Well, after last time there was almost a scandal, about Mrs. H and that Mr. Smyles from New York, he took on pretty severe. The only reason he'd let her take the carriage, you see, was if she went with some other lady."

"I see," murmured Abigail, disappointed but not surprised. Mrs. Sandhayes wanted social recognition and friendship with a wealthy woman who was too stupid to keep track of her discards playing loo. Mrs. Hartnell wanted a respectable-looking stalking-horse for her *amours*. Yet Philomela and the Barnabys had described Bathsheba as profoundly upset by Friday *evening*. Had she dissembled to this girl? Found some message awaiting her on her return to the Fluckner home? Or learned something in some other fashion after she got there?

"So in fact, Mrs. Hartnell was going out to meet a lover. And you, Mrs. Sandhayes, and Bathsheba were only out to provide a good story for her, lest anyone ask."

"'Twasn't that, m'am," said the girl earnestly. "Though Heaven help me, I've done that these five years, *and* put up with some of her men-friends, when they thought she wouldn't see . . . And she means no harm by it, m'am. She truly doesn't. You'd have to know her—" She stopped herself. "The thing is, m'am, we weren't with Bathsheba hardly at all that day. Nor most days when we'd been out together. We'd walk out by the Common, usually, and there's a Mr. Vassall that would drive by and take us up—Mrs. Hartnell and myself—and drive us out to Roxbury, where he has his house."

Abigail said, "T'cha!" in disgust. What had John said?

Very little beyond a respectable wardrobe and a couple of letters of introduction: nothing to live on or by . . .

So in fact Bathsheba *could* have seen something . . .

"And she'd leave her so-called friend to loiter about—staying out of sight, I daresay, so that there could be no comment—until she was ready to come home. Your mistress is very fortunate indeed that her useful friend isn't of a nature to demand hush-money. Were walking as painful to me as it is to her, I should certainly feel justified in asking for a compensation for—"

"Oh, no, m'am," corrected Miss Pugh. "The thing is, Mrs. Sandhayes couldn't ask for hush-money, for she was meeting with a lover herself."

Twenty-three

For a moment Abigail could only stare. Her instinctive thought—*How could a crippled woman*—? dissolved at once in anger at herself. The poor woman did everything a normal one could do, except dance, with a zest that made a mockery of the fate that had robbed her of that pleasure. Goodness knew a woman didn't have to skip and scamper to enjoy the embrace of a lover. Though her upbringing cried sternly to her that such behavior was reprehensible (as her own, she had to admit, had been with John, when they were courting . . .), if Mrs. Sandhayes had met a man who saw the intelligence of her eyes, and not the threadbare dresses and the gold-headed sticks—the more credit to him!

"Are you sure?"

"Oh, yes, m'am. More than once, when Mr. Vassall brought us back again at the end of the afternoon, we'd see them coming down Cambridge Street, this man and Mrs. S in a chaise, with Bathsheba sitting up behind . . ."

"Cambridge Street?" Abigail blinked, wondering if her thoughts upon the Pear Tree House had led her hearing astray.

"Yes, m'am." They had reached the head of Milk Street, where the houses began to thin and the garden walls along the unpaved way showed treetops above them here and there, the orchards of the well-to-do. The Governor's house, where Lucy Fluckner had waited uneasily for the arrival of a lover for whom another had also waited in the alley, stood opposite, bland and handsome behind its twin lodges. Gwen Pugh nodded past it, in the direction of the Common only a few hundred yards away. "He had a house, Bathsheba said—a fair big place with a ruined orchard by it—on the back-side of Beacon Hill."

Margaret Sandhayes.

Margaret Sandhayes and Toby Elkins . . .

Or was it, Abigail wondered as she walked slowly back toward Queen Street, *Margaret Sandhayes and Sir Jonathan Cottrell?*

A slender little fellow, Miss Pugh had described the unknown lover; fairish with a dimpled chin. Palmer was universally described as dark, but a different wig would alter that description in seconds—and she cursed again the shortcomings of the art of miniatures. *Shorter nor Mrs. S*, Miss Pugh had said, but then Margaret Sandhayes was a tall woman.

Toby Elkins was "tall." *But how tall is tall?*

He played about six roles, Dowling had said of Palmer. *He was one of those actors who can change not only his makeup and wig, but his posture and voice and the way he walked . . . from a cringing slave to a bawling soldier to a pious nun . . .*

Given Mr. Apthorp's vagueness about description, it was perfectly possible that young Mr. Elkins and slender Mr. Palmer were in fact one and the same man. Abigail dug through a memory sharpened by years of reading and quoting classics and the Bible for anything Thurlow Apthorp had said about when last he'd seen the elusive Mr. Elkins. As far as she could recall, nothing had been seen of the man later than Thursday, the twenty-fourth of February: the day Sir Jonathan Cottrell had set sail for Maine—unless of course that had been Mr. Elkins she had encountered in her kitchen at three o'clock on Monday morning. That same day, the twenty-fourth, Androcles Palmer had packed up his belongings and left the Horn Spoon for parts unknown. According to Gwen Pugh, that had been the last day upon which Mrs. Sandhayes had met her lover.

And if Mrs. Sandhayes was a part of the conspiracy . . .

Abigail frowned, quickening her stride.

If Mrs. Sandhayes was part of the conspiracy, how much of what she had said about Cottrell—or the events surrounding his murder—could be taken as the truth?

Certainly nothing that was corroborated by that imbecile Hartnell woman. The woman clearly hadn't the foggiest recollection that anything distinguished one shopping expedition from another, and in any case—with the prospect of blackmail hanging over her head—would cheerfully go along with anything her "friend" suggested.

Drat John, for being away!

So the whole of Margaret Sandhayes's catalogue of who came in and out of the Governor's cardroom, and when, could simply be tossed down the privy. The woman could have included or excluded anyone from her list, while smiling and chatting at the ball herself with all and sundry. She could have vouched for Palmer/Elkins to get him into the Governor's house . . .

Or, more simply still, Palmer could have waited at the Pear Tree House for a meeting prearranged that afternoon. *It wouldn't have taken much. A letter to Cottrell purporting to be from a claimant to the Fluckner land-grant would have brought the man anywhere in New England hotfoot and could have been waiting for the man on the wharf, the moment he returned. If the Sandhayes woman was in on it somehow—and that certainly explains where they obtained my handwriting!—it also explains how Bathsheba would have seen something she ought not to have seen.*

Whatever that might be.

The twenty-three pounds was only to keep her silent, until a meeting with her could be arranged for a more final solution to the problem.

Palmer—or Elkins—is still in Boston, hidden somewhere. There's some reason the Sons haven't been able to find him . . . Speculating on what that might be, she turned down the passway to her own yard, calves aching from what felt like miles walked in pattens. She mentally reviewed the abject apologies owed to Pattie, and how quickly after dinner she could abandon her rightful chores and walk down to North Square to consult with Paul Revere. He, if anyone, would be able to make some sense out of—

She stepped into the kitchen, and there was the man himself, seated by the hearth making a penny appear and disappear in his fingers, for the edification of the enraptured Charley. Sam, on the settle opposite, held Tommy on his knee, while Johnny and Nabby hurried to and fro under Pattie's direction, setting the table for dinner.

At Abigail's entrance, both men got to their feet.

"We need to see you, Nab." Sam set Tommy aside, and—as

Abigail had done yesterday—guided Abigail down the hallway and into the parlor, where a warm and welcoming fire had been kindled. Revere followed them in and closed the door behind them, a large and rather battered roll of cartridge-paper in his hand.

"We need to know." Sam handed Abigail into the fireside chair. "You've been there. Where is Harry being kept?"

"Harry—?" Abigail blinked at him, for a moment not understanding. "He's on Castle Island—"

Sam made an impatient gesture, and Revere said, "Can you show me the place on this?" He unrolled the cartridge-paper and brought a couple of draftsman's pencils out of a coat pocket, and Abigail, looking at the spread-out diagram, recalled that Revere had been one of the men who'd worked on putting the fort back into order three years ago, when the Boston garrison was moved there after the Massacre in Customhouse Square.

Something in the graveness of those dark eyes sent a chill down her back. "What are you going to do?"

"We just need to know where he is," said Sam, too quickly, "if we're to slip word to him before he's taken away. That's all."

Sam could generally make anyone believe anything he said, but this time Abigail heard the lie in his voice, even if she had not seen it in Revere's eyes.

"You can't mean to break into the fort!" Yet the crowded, bustling quay below Castle Island's main gate sprang to her mind, the jostling confusion of launches and skiffs and whale-boats that plied the harbor between the island and Boston. The constant comings and goings of provision-merchants, wigmakers, whores, and porters, and purveyors of sheep and pigs. Anyone, she knew, could walk ashore and walk into the fort itself . . .

"Good Lord, Nab, of course we wouldn't!"

He's going to exclaim, "What an idea—"

"What an idea!"

Her glance went back to Revere's face. He, too, she could tell, was thinking about how long it took a man to die on the gallows, and how long that last night on Earth would be for a young man who knew he could save himself with a handful of names.

"We're not talking about the Boston jail," said Abigail quietly. "Have you any idea what the British would do—especially after what happened with the tea, and with Heaven only knows what Writ of Vengeance already on its way from Britain—if insurrectionists, as they'll call them, tried to break into the Castle itself? What would befall them if they were caught? What—"

"Mrs. Adams," said Revere softly. "Please."

She looked up at Sam again, a second thought going through her like the chill of poison in her veins. With a deadly sense of calm, she asked, "Or were you thinking of something a little quieter?"

And she saw Sam's gray eyes shift.

Revere said, "No. We were not."

No, thought Abigail. But at some point, Sam had considered it.

For a time she was so angry she couldn't speak.

It was Revere who broke the silence. "We have to get him out, Mrs. Adams. The *Incitatus* is going to sail within hours of the wind dying down, and then our only course would be to try and take her on the high seas. She outguns anything we could float."

"You'll be killed," said Abigail. "And there will be Hell to pay."

Neither man replied.

"And I have learned some quite extraordinary things about Sir Jonathan Cottrell's murder."

"Have you learned who beat him and left him in that alleyway?" Sam's voice was flat, level, and hard as a sadiron. "Acquired evidence that will convince Colonel Leslie not to send him? Or the Admiralty Tribunal to acquit him?" It was Abigail's turn not to be able to meet his gaze. "We have no more time to wait, Nab. We have no more time to hope that what you seek will fall into your hand. We must act—one way or another."

"First tell me this," said Abigail. "When was this Toby Elkins last seen? When did he last come into the Man-o'-War?"

"The twelfth of February," replied Sam at once. "Having taken the house, and paid his rent, about three weeks before. Letters, communications, everything since then are still under the bar in the taproom. Believe me, Nab," he went on, "we have looked for this man—or a man of his description—everywhere in Boston. We have asked tavern-keepers and rich men's servants, street-urchins and merchants and the farmers in every town in riding distance, if there is an Englishman who came into these parts at any time this winter, probably from Barbados, who cannot be otherwise accounted for . . . And especially I have asked," he added, "after Sunday night, when he would have had the mark of your fingernails on his ear, for all the world to see. 'Twere Elkins, he must have been *somewhere* in the town from the time the gates were shut on the Neck until at least it grew light enough for a boat to get across the river and believe me, I had men at both the ferries and the Neck when that sun came up. And we have found *nothing*."

"That there was a conspiracy afoot, I will readily believe," said Revere, as Abigail drew breath to protest. "That this Elkins murdered the woman Bathsheba, and paid off an out-of-work actor who knew Fenton by sight to hail him at a tavern and then put poison in his food, I accept—"

"I think they were one and the same man. And I believe the Sandhayes woman is in on it—"

"It changes nothing, Mrs. Adams." He leaned toward her, strong brown fingers outspread on the stained diagram before her. "We have deduced a conspiracy but proven nothing. Nor can we prove anything until we have something in hand that will connect any of these people—whether they are two or three or even all one and the same—with the death of Sir Jonathan Cottrell on the night of the fifth of March. Until we can do that, we can do nothing—except get Harry away from Castle Island at the soonest possible moment, before the wind dies down, cost what it may. And that," he concluded softly, "is what we need to do."

Pattie tapped softly at the parlor door: "Mrs. Adams?"

Abigail rose and opened it halfway. "Get the children their dinner, and just put aside a little for me, if you will, please," she said. "We shall be here a time." Closing the door, she returned to the table, and for the next hour, she went over her visit to the Castle, step by step: guards, corridors, right turn, left turn. Cells, doors, windows. Revere made notes on the edges of the cartridge-paper, which was, Abigail saw, already laced with them. He must have worked up descriptions from smugglers, farmers, laundrywomen over the years that British troops had occupied the island—Abigail had one friend that she knew of who had made a regular study of the place, for the benefit of the Sons of Liberty. She heard Thaxter's voice in the hall as he returned from his own dinner, heard the clunk of John's office door shutting, and knew the afternoon was getting late.

Half closing her eyes, she made herself see again the corridor leading to Harry's cell, the window's size and height, the lock on the door. A craftsman himself, Revere had a good eye and a good memory for the tiniest of details: Who had the cell key? Where was it kept, in Coldstone's office? Did the window of Harry's cell have shutters? Bars? Glass? Could a man of Knox's substantial frame get himself through it? (Abigail thought not.)

As the description took shape and Abigail studied the calm, dark face bent above the map opposite her, she thought, *He's going to lead the party in himself.*

"You say we mustn't let Harry be taken for trial to Halifax," she said, when Revere was done, "lest being found guilty, he turn King's Evidence rather than hang. Yet how much do you multiply their captives—multiply those who will face that same choice—if you carry through with this plan?"

The silversmith paused in rolling up his paper and grinned. "Then we mustn't let ourselves be taken, must we?"

Nabby and Johnny had already finished cleaning up after dinner when Abigail and the Sons of Liberty passed through the kitchen. Both glanced up from their schoolbooks and slates at their mother's face, and hesitated to speak to her as she walked her guests to the door into the yard. Neither Charley nor Tommy were so discreet, and neither approved of their mother's preoccupation with matters that did not concern themselves. Tommy flung himself against the leading-strings, wailing, as Charley—free—clung to her skirts. Abigail couldn't keep from smiling and ran a hand through Charley's curls. But her eyes were somber as she bade Sam and Revere good afternoon.

"When shall this take place?" she asked softly, and Revere began to reply, but Sam cut him off.

"We haven't decided." For a man as friendly and gregarious as Sam quite genuinely was, he kept matters concerning the Sons of Liberty tight-shut in some battlemented corner of his mind. "With no moon in sight, 'tis a challenge at the best of times, even were we not going out against an inshore gale. 'Twill be soon."

He turned away, but there was a flicker of grimness in his eyes, an anger, that made Abigail touch Revere's sleeve: "*Do* you believe me?" she asked. "That there was a conspiracy—a very well-planned one—to . . . to *surround* Cottrell and run him to earth? Else why try to kill me? Why lure Lieutenant Coldstone ashore, where he could be shot at?"

"That could have been anyone," pointed out Revere, with half a grin. "I think you could even get Sam to take a shot at an Assistant Provost Marshal, if he could be sure there was no way he would be connected with the crime. You think Elkins—or Palmer—was the one who entered the house Sunday night?"

"I'm sure of it. I marked him—"

"You did well," said Revere. "It gives us another—What? Three days? Four days?—in which we can prove the connection, before the marks fade." Turning his head, he studied the mottled dark roof of the evening sky above the houses, listened to the moan of the wind in the tangle of yards and alleyways that made up this close-built heart of the town. "Whether the wind will hold that long, God knows." He donned his hat in order to lift it to her and, pulling his scarf close about him, hastened across the yard to where Sam waited in the passway, the stray whirls of the wind, even in that protected spot, tearing at the smoky stream of his breath.

Three days, thought Abigail, as she turned back toward the kitchen. *Four days. If the wind holds . . .*

Her younger sons clutched triumphantly at her skirt, as if they knew—she reflected bitterly—how signally her investigation had failed.

Palmer is a dark man and Elkins is tall and fair. And Margaret Sandhayes is somewhere in between them. Put a gray wig on his head—as Sam did for Hev Miller—and a patch on his eye, and all anyone will see is the gray hair and the eye patch. What had she said, only days ago? *Money, and poison, and people disappearing . . .*

But I knew him. That shocked twinge of recognition that had lanced through her as she'd seen the poisoner's face in candlelight would not leave her mind. *I saw him and I knew him.*

Where have I seen him before?

I marked him. I have three days—four days—until the marks fade . . .

Abigail halted in the door of the icy pantry and stood for a moment, looking across the table where Charley was attempting to get the attention of Johnny and Nabby away from their slates. Johnny shoved his little brother impatiently—Charley shoved back, making the chair he stood on tilt perilously . . .

Abigail moved to cross the room, to break up the inevitable tussle—*Just what the lad needs, another black eye when his last one's barely been gone a week . . .*

She stopped beside the table and stood for a moment, very still.

What was it Coldstone had said to her, in that dank little cubicle of his, the morning after Sir Jonathan Cottrell's body had been found?

"Thaxter," she called, and walked to the doorway of the hall, catching Charley as he did, in fact, overset the chair.

Her husband's clerk put his head through the office door.

"Thaxter, dear, I'm desolated to ask it of you at this hour"—she set her middle son on his feet and kept a firm grip on his hand—"but could you get your coat on and take some messages for me? You can go straight to your mother's after, but I think these really need to be sent tonight. Pattie—" She looked around, but Pattie had gone scampering out the back door, which had not closed properly, to catch Tommy before he made it across the yard to the passway to the street.

Honestly, I understand why ladies are never the heroines of anything, they simply cannot get away from their kitchens long enough to rescue anyone . . .

"Nabby, hold on to your brother until I get these notes written, and then Charley, yes, you shall have a story . . ."

One note was to Lieutenant Jeremy Coldstone on Castle Island.

One was to Lucy Fluckner.

And the third was to Dr. Joseph Warren.

Twenty-four

Abigail jerked to wakefulness and lay with pounding heart.

Blackness.

Silence.

Was it a sound? She saw again the open window in the kitchen on Sunday night, the dark form against her candle's feeble glow, the dead mice beside the barrel of contaminated flour . . .

John dead. Johnny dead. Nabby dead . . .

What had waked her?

A shutter banging?

A footfall?

She slithered from under the blankets and out through the curtains, shuddering in the cold, which seemed deeper and more intense than it had for two weeks now. Wrapped herself in her wool robe, scuffed slippers on her feet. Padded, silent as breath, to the door of her room and opened it, feeling rather than seeing the change of air in the dark of the hall.

She'd dreamed of Paul Revere, of Dr. Warren, of other men she knew—dreamed of John, though she knew he would never undertake anything so mad-brained as what Sam proposed . . . Dreamed of them rowing across the choppy water of the bay, headed under pitch-black cloud-cover for Castle Island and death.

Was that what she had heard? Shots, cries . . . Impossible, across three miles of open water.

Then what sound—?

She was halfway to the stair before she realized that what had waked her was not sound, but stillness.

The wind had died.

Her candle-flame burned straight upright in its lantern when she crossed the yard two hours later, at the first crowings of Arabella Butler's rooster. The new moon had set already, behind the breaking clouds. Thin starlight showed her her own breath.

Dear God, protect them . . .

Their Majesties—as she sometimes called Cleopatra and Semiramis—blinked sleepily at her as she entered the cow-house, waked before their usual time but accepting of it. Abigail was a poor sleeper and often rose at such an hour to do the milking and start her work rather than waste another three-quarters of an hour in bed in an unprofitable quest for further sleep. Their eyes flashed gold at her in the dark; the thick smell of hay was deeply comforting.

First light saw her hastening along Queen Street, when in other houses the kitchen-fires were just being lit. The market-square looked queer in twilight this early, without the booths and barrows she was used to seeing on Mondays and Thursdays. But life was stirring along the quays, as men called back and forth among the fishing-boats and warehouses—*Maybe we'll get down to Charleston this time . . . Looks to be clearing . . . Jaysus, we've had the hold filled for a week! If we're caught in harbor again, Cap'n'll have a seizure . . .*

At Castle Island they'd be loading the *Incitatus.*

Paul Revere was eating breakfast when she rapped at the kitchen door.

Just the sight of him as Young Paul opened the door for her—the shutters in the front of the house were not yet taken down—flooded her with relief, like a benediction: "You didn't go."

"Blasted smugglers were taking a cargo across to Lynn with the boat—!" His dark eyes fairly glittered. "And now—"

"Now I think I know at least a part of what happened," said Abigail. "At least enough to make an argument for the Provost and Colonel Leslie. But I must get word across, and quickly—what time does the tide go out?"

"It won't turn 'til near noon."

"Good," said Abigail. "Will you come with me to Old North? I need to speak to our brave boys from Maine."

Matthias Brown was still asleep when Revere and Abigail crossed Sun Court to the church; Hev Miller was helping Robbie Newman take down the shutters on the vestry, and explaining in intense detail just why his mother's way of cooking canvasback duck with woodchuck-fat was superior to and more healthful than the Boston way, not meaning any disrespect to Mrs. Newman . . .

He listened to the question Abigail put to him and shook his head. "No."

"Had he any remnant of it? Any mark whatsoever?"

"No. I don't see how he could have gotten one," the Mainer added. "The man wouldn't have put up a fight if you'd walked up and spat in his face. Is there a chance Matt and I might be getting back to Boothbay, now the wind's turned to the north?" he added, looking over at Revere. "Matt and I took a turn along Ship Street yesterday, and I'll swear we saw the *Magpie*, tied up at Burroughs's Wharf—"

Revere glared at Robbie, who made a helpless gesture: "I couldn't see the harm in it—"

"A few days more," promised Abigail. And to Revere, "'Tis no matter, in fact 'twill help. Can you go find it there, and ask young Mr. Putnam if he'll take us across to the Castle, the moment the tide turns? I shall be at the wharf at half past eleven—"

She had hoped to find notes from Dr. Warren, or Lucy Fluckner, or both, upon her arrival at her home at half past eight. Instead, when Abigail entered the kitchen she was startled to see Mrs. Sandhayes rise awkwardly from the table. "Please forgive me, Mrs. Adams, for calling at such a horrifying hour," she said, holding out her hand. "I must speak to you. I have used you dreadfully—as I find that I have been used myself."

Abigail was silent, regarding that beaky, over-painted face, the red mouth set and the green eyes filled with an expression of chagrin. She asked, "By Palmer?" and Margaret Sandhayes nodded. "Or Elkins, if that was his name—or was it Tredgold?"

Pattie's footfalls reverberated dimly from upstairs, trailed by Charley's toddling steps. Tommy, tied by his leading-strings to the leg of the sideboard, left off trying to undo the knots and stood up, holding out his arms for his mother: "Mama!"

"Who? Oh, the Seaford girls, yes." Mrs. Sandhayes shook her head. "To be honest, Mrs. Adams, I don't know. Your lovely handmaid said I might wait for you in the parlor—?"

"Mama!" crowed Tommy urgently.

"Of course." Abigail kissed the boy, stood again—Tommy began at once to wail his protests—and picked up the teapot and her guest's half-drunk cup and saucer. In the parlor a lively fire had been kindled to warm the room. A second cup, pristine, sat on the tray beside a small plate of gingerbread. God bless Pattie, for thinking of everything.

"I had this"—from her pocket, Mrs. Sandhayes drew a folded sheet of paper, which she handed across the small table to Abigail—"last night. Brought to the back door as usual by a boy picked at random off the wharves—at least, the whole time I knew Mr. Palmer, if that was in fact his name, it was never the same boy."

"Last night?" Abigail unfolded it.

Mags, it said, in a sprawled and jagged hand, *sorry to do this, my dearest dove, but the time has come for us to part. There's a man come forward, that says he saw me follow Sir J from the wharf to the house, and I can't risk staying. Thank you for all the help you've given. Perhaps we'll meet again. A thousand kisses—A.P.*

Abigail looked up, frowning, as her guest poured her out a cup of the yellowish chamomile tea.

"You must be frozen." Mrs. Sandhayes pushed the plate of gingerbread nearer. "Did you make this gingerbread, my dear? I used to make a fair gingerbread myself." She sighed, bitter and weary, and sipped her tea. "I thought—Well, I'm well served, I suppose, for believing the man."

"What did he tell you?"

"That Cottrell had—*ruined*, I suppose the novelists would say—his sister . . . though I suppose it is stretching the truth a bit, to speak of *ruining* an actress. She was caught with child, and being very young and inexperienced, I suspect she let matters go a little too long before she took steps to resolve the matter, and the long and the short of it was that she died." The Englishwoman's hand strayed nervously to the black Medusa cameo at her throat, rubbing it, as if it were a talisman of some loss of her own. "She was the only person he had ever cared about, he said, and it enraged him that no one would so much as chide the man for his deed. I was angry for his sake, and for hers—but more than that, I'm ashamed to say I . . . I simply enjoyed being part of a conspiracy."

"Why you?" asked Abigail. "What part had you to play, if you'd never exchanged a word with Cottrell?" She set the note down, groped for the teacup, and picked it up.

Raising her eyes, she saw—for one instant only—the intentness with which Mrs. Sandhayes watched her, before the other woman turned her eyes away.

Arrested by that expression—coldly eager and almost inhuman—Abigail's glance went to Mrs. Sandhayes's own half-empty cup and she thought, *She cannot abide chamomile.*

And then, as if she'd opened a box and seen all the events stored there like game-tokens: *She came to Boston sometime after Christmas, at the same time as Androcles Palmer, and Sir Jonathan Cottrell . . . From where?*

If she's a part of this conspiracy, this may ALL be another lie.

She put the cup to her lips, raised it as if drinking, her lips pressed tight shut, and tried through a surge of panic to remember what Lieutenant Dowling had said about oleander's deadliness. She set the cup down and immediately rested her chin on her hand as she studied the note, in such a way as to unobtrusively wipe her lips . . .

The paper on which the note was written looked like the same kind used in the Fluckner household. The ink, too: blue black with a good color to it, not the thinner sort used by John for drafts and documents of little importance. She was conscious of her heart pounding, of a shivering coldness rushing through her body. *If EVERYTHING she has said is a lie . . .*

Raising her eyes again, she became aware that Mrs. Sandhayes had changed the way she dressed her hair. No one—no grown woman that she knew, certainly no woman with the slightest pretension to fashion—wore her hair to cover her ears. The schoolgirl curls that the chaperone had induced to cluster around her face, hanging down from the more fashionable side-rolls of hair, were grotesque in the extreme, but grotesque in a different manner than the woman's usual swagged fantasias of poufs and powder. As if her eyes had changed their focus, it seemed to Abigail that she could see through the gaudy makeup, to the severe—almost masculine—bone structure of the face, the strong chin and long nose . . .

She said, in a tone of surprise, "What on earth did you do to your ear?"

Mrs. Sandhayes's left hand jerked toward that mass of curls, and as she touched them, Abigail saw that indeed the lobe of the ear was scabbed as if recently torn. With swift deliberation she raised her teacup to her tight-sealed lips again, made the pretense of drinking. Anything to put Mrs. Sandhayes off her guard—to put her at ease and make her think the danger is already taken care of—

Her visitor was watching her now with narrowed eyes, though her laugh was as empty and sparkling as ever. "Would you believe it, when I was dressing these silly curls—Did you ever see anything so foolish? Yet I understand they are all the rage now in London!—I caught the comb in my earring, a silly girl's trick—"

"Oh, heavens—" Abigail made herself laugh, too, then drew a deep breath, pressed a hand to her bosom. "You must—forgive me. I feel suddenly queer—" *What are the symptoms of oleander poisoning?* "Pattie—" She staggered to her feet, and Margaret Sandhayes, with not the slightest effort to reach for her walking-sticks, sprang up like a panther, rounded the table, seized her by the arm, and shoved her back into her chair with one hand, and produced a pistol from her pocket with the other.

The walking-sticks clattered unheeded to the floor.

Well, of course she'd have lied about not being able to walk—

"If you'd drunk oleander, you would be retching your heart out by this time."

Abigail forced herself to look away from the pistol, and up into Mrs. Sandhayes's face. "Is oleander what you gave to Jonathan Cottrell?"

"Oleander is swift," said the Englishwoman quietly, her pistol never wavering. "I did not wish him to die swiftly."

At her words, Abigail saw with sudden and terrible clarity the square front hall of the Pear Tree House, like a great square well with doors to the rooms around it: west, east, north, and the front door facing south. Saw the telltale holes where bolts had been put on every door that would provide escape, upstairs and down.

She gave him the poison, got him into the hall . . .

And stood there on the stairs to watch him die. Not swiftly.

If he'd tried to mount the stair, she had only to retreat into one of the chambers, which communicated with each other and were all locked in their turn.

A chill went through Abigail at the deliberateness of it.

As deliberate as the poisoning of a whole household, when it looked like one member of it was getting close to the truth.

As deliberate as killing the servant in order to make sure no one met the *Hetty* at the wharf and saw that the man who got off was not, in fact, Sir Jonathan Cottrell.

Sandhayes nodded at the cup. "Drink it."

"What did you use on him?" asked Abigail conversationally, though her heart was racing so that the tips of her ears felt like they were on fire. "Not death-cap mushroom, like poor Mr. Fenton, surely—Put that pistol down, m'am, you know perfectly well you can't shoot me."

"Can't I?" Mrs. Sandhayes raised her brows.

"Well, you can't very well go claiming to Pattie that I fell over and died of sickness if I've got a bullet-hole in me—"

"I won't have to," replied the Englishwoman. "All I'll have to do is scream for Pattie, and she'll come rushing downstairs and through that door. I can crack her skull with the butt of it while she's bending over you. And unless you drink what is in that cup, Mrs. Adams, I assure you that after shooting you, and disposing of the helpful Pattie, I will then cover my tracks by setting this house afire, and leave your little sons upstairs to burn."

Abigail stared at her, open-mouthed in shock. "And that is what Sybilla would have wanted you to do?" she asked after a time.

"Don't name her to me." The older woman's eyes flashed with a cold green light. "You know nothing about it."

"I know what I'm hearing," replied Abigail. "Listen to yourself, woman! You honestly feel you can simply kill a man—"

It was Mrs. Sandhayes's turn to stare. "Listen to *your*self, Mrs. Adams. You honestly think that the man who raped a sixteen-year-old girl for his own amusement—only it was not rape, but murder, when she found she was with child—should walk away *free*? Or are you just like the men whose company you so clearly prefer? It's perfectly all right to burn the hide off a man with boiling tar, or to thrust his wife and children into a life of poverty and ignorance by destroying his shop or ruining his business in the name of politics, but for actual *justice*—for the redress of human wrongs—you have little time." She shifted as Abigail glanced toward the door, brought the pistol up closer. "Besides," she added after a moment, "that isn't poison in that tea—or whatever it is your girl gave me. It will make you sick and then put you to sleep for twenty-four hours, until I am well away from Boston. That's all. I just need time."

No, thought Abigail. *What you need is an open road back to England, and to the family and the life you left . . . something you won't have if there's ANYONE who understands how you poisoned a man on the night you were at a ball in plain sight of two hundred people.*

And the note I sent to Lucy yesterday told you that's exactly what I am.

She took a breath, and made her shoulders relax as if in acquiescence; turned her face slightly away. Her hands were shaking so badly she wasn't sure she'd be able to grip anything. *You can do this . . . you can do this . . . O God, help me do this . . .* She was aware of her adversary close at her elbow as she turned back toward the table, of the pistol against her side.

"Did Cottrell know it was you?" she asked, and Mrs. Sandhayes sniffed.

"After he'd drunk it I told him. Before—How would he have recognized me? He never spared a glance for me whilst he was seducing my—"

In what she hoped was a single movement, Abigail hurled the tea from the cup into Mrs. Sandhayes's face, ducked sideways, and swept her leg with all her force at the other woman's feet. Their petticoats tangled, Mrs. Sandhayes staggered, and the gun went off with a noise like the break of doom in the little parlor. Not even sure if she'd been hit or not, Abigail grabbed a leg of her chair and hurled it at her assailant, tripped as her petticoats snarled in the other chair, and took a kick in her side as she fell that left her gasping.

Trying to roll to her feet she heard the other woman's steps in the hall, racing for the kitchen—

"Tommy!"

Abigail sprang up, fell against the wall, dimly conscious of the clatter of Pattie's feet on the stair and a jumbled crashing from the kitchen.

Tommy screamed.

Abigail jerked open the kitchen door and smoke poured out into her face. Her first terrified impression was that the whole room was ablaze—her second, knowing that there hadn't been time for such fire to take hold, was of a dozen small fires where the logs from the hearth had been hurled into the room, against the table, the chairs, the sideboard where Tommy was tied.

The back door was open, but Abigail saw nothing of that in that moment, only the burning wood under the sideboard and the fire licking greedily up. She flung herself to her knees beside her hysterical son, "Stay still!" she commanded, which of course the terrified child didn't, as she ripped and wrenched at the long cloth tapes. She sprang up, half choked on the smoke swirling around her, wrenched open the knife-drawer, seized the first blade that came to hand.

She heard Pattie scream and had the confused impression of somcone behind her as she slashed through the leading-strings, half turned as hands grabbed her—*I thought she'd gone—*

She barely got a glimpse of the man who flung her to the floor, before she was smothered in darkness.

Twenty-five

Abigail slashed, kicked, and struck out with the knife that was still in her hand. An Irish voice swore, "Mother o' God!" and what Abigail realized was a man's cloak was pulled clear of her head. Somewhere—outside?—she could hear Tommy screaming, and the kitchen was filled with smoke and the smell of wet ashes and brick.

Lieutenant Coldstone, her neighbors Tom Butler and Ehud Hanson, and three extremely rough-looking men who looked like rope makers—presumably, Abigail reflected, the Sons of Liberty who'd followed Coldstone from the wharf—were raking together the pile of firewood, over which someone had dumped the contents of the kitchen water-jar. The Lieutenant's left arm and shoulder were strapped tight in a sling, and his face was nearly as white as his wig with the exertion.

Abigail gasped, "Where's Tommy?"

Sergeant Muldoon, kneeling at her side sucking the blood from his slashed hand, said, "He's outside with Miss Pattie, m'am, and fine as thruppence . . . Beggin' your pardon for handlin' you so, m'am, but your skirt had caught."

"Did you catch her?" Abigail seized Muldoon's arm, and the young man lifted her to her feet as if she'd been a ten-year-old girl. Staggering, she looked down and saw that yes, the whole right side of her skirt-hem was burned away, the petticoat beneath charred. She had neither seen nor felt a thing. "Margaret Sandhayes," she added, as Muldoon and Coldstone helped her to the back door, beside which not only Pattie but Charley sat on the log bench, Pattie cradling the sobbing Tommy in her arms. Tommy reached out for his mother, howling in terror. "Only I think her true name is Seaford . . ."

"Margaret Seaford?" said Coldstone.

"The girl Sybilla's sister? She told me the sister's name was Alice . . ."

As the words came out of her mouth, Abigail felt like kicking herself, because of course the woman would have told her the dead girl's sister was called Helen of Troy rather than Margaret. A woman who had patiently counterfeited lameness to make others assume she could not be a killer would not have committed the mistake of giving her rightful name.

It seemed to her that every neighbor for blocks of Queen Street swarmed the yard, and that a dozen more of Sam and Revere's rougher henchmen were coming in and out of the kitchen, clearing out the wet wood and the few chairs that had been aflame.

Coldstone reached out suddenly to lean against the wall beside her, and she caught at his sleeve, even as she pressed her weeping son's head to her shoulder. "She poisoned Cottrell," she said quickly. "Not the night he was found, but ten days earlier, the day he was to leave for Maine—and got Palmer to take his place. The body was kept down the well in the cellar of Pear Tree House. Frozen, like pork in the pantry, so the death could not be traced to her—"

"She told you this?"

"She told me she poisoned Cottrell, for what he did to her sister. I'll take oath on it—"

"You shall have to. Sergeant, go to the Battery, get as many men as they can spare—if"—Coldstone added, glancing about him a little grimly at the incipient mob in the yard—"these gentlemen will permit it . . ."

"Ben!" Abigail stretched out a hand to a man she recognized. Ben Edes, who printed the *Boston Gazette*, was dressed as if for a rough day's hunting, or for the street rowdiness of Pope's Night. Ink still blotted his hands. "Ben, go with the Sergeant, make sure no one hinders him, or the soldiers he brings—"

"Why trouble the King's good servants, Mrs. Adams, Lieutenant?" Edes cocked a wise, dark eye at Coldstone. "If you're able to make an arrest of the—woman, is it?—who did this to Mrs. Adams, we're all the *posse comitatus* you'll need."

Coldstone's upper lip seemed to lengthen with his disapproval, but Abigail said, "He's right, Lieutenant . . . There, there, sweeting," she added, as Tommy, sensing himself ignored, began to howl again. "'Tis well, Mama's here—And don't trouble going back to the Fluckners'. Margaret Sandhayes will have headed straight from here to the wharves, for whatever ship is leaving for England with the tide."

"That'll be the *Saturn*," put in a huge, unshaven laborer unexpectedly. "They've been loaded and ready this week at Wentworth's Wharf, and Captain Nesbitt wearing out the deck-planks pacing to be off."

"Some one of you—Jed," she added, turning to one of the prentice-boys whom she knew. "Run to Burrough's Wharf and tell Eli Putnam on the *Magpie* sloop to be ready to sail in ten minutes—"

Tommy, as if sensing that the next event would be his forcible detachment from the mother he adored in the midst of this confusion and pain, tightened his grip on Abigail's dress and hair. Only then did she become aware that her hair had come unraveled from beneath its cap, with thick dark waves hanging over her shoulders and back; and she looked around at Pattie, knowing she would indeed have to abandon her son.

Of all these men—including Lieutenant Coldstone and Sergeant Muldoon—only she would be able to recognize Margaret Sandhayes.

And without testimony against Margaret Sandhayes, the one who would be leaving on the tide would be Harry Knox.

Tommy whimpered, "No—" as Abigail gently tried to pry his tiny hands loose. "Mama—"

She could scarcely blame him—had John been present, she reflected, *she* would probably have clung to *him* and whimpered as well.

"Here," said Muldoon, "we can take the boy along, can't we? Poor tot's had grief enough for the day, wi'out havin' his mum leave him again."

"Me!" added Charley, running to catch Abigail's charred skirt as she rose. "Me!"

So it was that Sergeant Muldoon carried the ecstatic Charley on his shoulders in the midst of the mob that followed Coldstone and Abigail down to Wentworth's Wharf, and Abigail bore Tommy, his blue eyes wide with delight. At some point during the walk from Queen Street to the long waterfront, Paul Revere joined the mob and nodded a friendly greeting to Lieutenant Coldstone, whose crimson coat, like Abigail's clothing, bore the marks of the fire.

Abigail handed him the note that Pattie had given her just before the mob left the house—*I found this in the knife-drawer, m'am, and I don't know how it got there, for I'd left it on the sideboard for you . . .*

Where Margaret Sandhayes read it the moment you were out of the room.

The note was from Dr. Joseph Warren.

My dear Mrs. Adams,

The problem you put to me is a curious and interesting one, and one with which I have no firsthand knowledge. That said, I will venture to affirm that were a man's eye to be blacked—or in fact were any other sort of severe bruise or contusion to be administered some hours before death—and the body subsequently frozen, the "mouse," or other bruise, would remain visible when the body thawed, in the same state of appearance it was when death occurred. Bruises are occasioned by blood leaking from broken capillaries into the surrounding flesh, which engorges and darkens. At length, the blood is reabsorbed into the living tissue, an effect which would not take place in the dead.

I trust this solution will have bearing upon the case of Sir Jonathan Cottrell, and result in the freedom of our friend?

Yr ob't,
Dr. Joseph Warren

"Lieutenant Dowling is a good man," remarked Lieutenant Coldstone, when Revere passed the message to him in turn. "Yet he was very young when he began his apprenticeship in Army surgery, and that, in the West Indies, where he would have no opportunity to observe the effect of cold such as New England's upon bodies that had been subsequently frozen. I daresay the duskiness he remarked in the corpse's hands and feet came not from freezing, as he surmised, but from the body's having been hanged down the well. From the hook that supported the wine-chest, I presume."

"Was there the mark of a rope beneath the arms?" asked Revere.

"She'll have padded it," replied Abigail, unhesitatingly. "And made sure to carry the rope away with her, when she finally pulled the body up. By taking it on Mr. Howell's horse to the head of Governor's Alley in the small hours of the Sunday morning, she unimpeachably proved herself to be at the ball—in the presence of at least two hundred witnesses—when the death *must* have occurred . . ."

"Even had anyone thought to ask if her crutches—or her name—were genuine," mused Coldstone. "Not considerations which occurred to me, I must admit."

"Why would they have? She kept Bathsheba's body in the well, too, for a time, though the water hadn't frozen then. If you drag the Mill-Pond, Lieutenant, and the marshes west of the Common, I think you shall find beneath the ice the body of the actor Androcles Palmer, and probably that of a young Negro woman named Bathsheba. Palmer bore enough of a resemblance to Cottrell to pass for him for ten days in Maine, among men who had never seen the real Cottrell. He lacked only the black eye Cottrell had acquired on the day of his supposed departure. Perhaps I should have realized his behavior there was uncharacteristic—he refused to steal a kiss from a milkmaid even when it was practically forced upon him—but I didn't. I only thought he was too afraid of Mr. Fluckner's irate tenants."

"Whereas I daresay," put in Revere, "he was far too afraid of Mrs. Sandhayes. I'd be. If the woman knows what a scruple is, she hides the knowledge well."

"As I remember the scandal," said Coldstone quietly, "the Seaford girls' parents were dead; Sybilla was ten years younger than her elder sister, who raised her as a mother would. According to my mother—who knew the family—Margaret Seaford was a woman of iron will and strong character. Her single suitor had been engaged to her for eight years, without bringing matters to a conclusion, at least in part because Sybilla could not endure it that another would share her sister's love. Sybilla was Margaret's only weakness, my mother said; but the attachment was a weapon that cut both ways. Margaret would not share Sybilla's love with a suitor, either, and the girl was"—he hesitated, like a man seeking a word—"ripe, I suppose one could say, to be seduced by a man observant enough to play upon her desire to rebel against her sister's domination. This at least was my mother's judgment of the matter," he added, a sudden self-consciousness cracking his usual calm façade, as if speaking of his mother in this crowd of jostling hooligans on Boston's wharves would bring her before them.

"Your mother sounds like a woman of discernment," said Abigail gently.

"I have always found her so. Damn," Coldstone added, as they came around the corner of Benning Wentworth's countinghouse and stood at the head of the wharf beyond. A couple of dockhands were coiling ropes at the far end; a porter rolled a barrel out of one of the warehouses that lined the inner end, in the obvious expectation of another ship's later approach.

Beyond the wet black platform, stretching a hundred yards into the bay, green black water pitched and chopped with the high, outgoing tide.

"Can we catch her?" Revere pointed to the white spread of the *Saturn*'s sails, just coming even, Abigail calculated, with Bird Island, two miles out in the harbor channel.

"The *Magpie*'s said to be fast," Abigail replied.

"I reckon we'll see if that's true."

The tide was running strong out of the harbor, but the wind blew from the south rather than the west. The *Saturn*, a square-rigged two-master of some six hundred tons, had been built to carry quantities of furs, tobacco, and potash in safety to the Mother Country, not for speed. The *Magpie*'s slimmer build and sloop rigging caught even the contrary wind and drove her forward like a galloping horse. Abigail clung grimly to the rail as the first chop of the wind-driven channel hit the ship . . . *I WILL not be sick* . . .

"We'll have 'em, m'am." Matthias Brown dropped from the rigging to the deck beside her, as graceful among the ropes as he was toadlike with land beneath his moccasins. "Don't you worry." He cast a glance, askance, at the British officer who stood beside her and the stolid redcoat sergeant who sat a little distance away on a coil of rope, one arm around Tommy and with the other arm firmly keeping Charley between his knees. Both boys were pale with excitement—Tommy in fact looked a little ill—but neither had allowed himself to be fobbed off with *Now, Mama will be back soon* . . . when they'd made it all the way down to the wharves with what they both knew perfectly well was one of Uncle Sam's mobs.

At least half the mob—Edes and Revere among them—had

crowded onto the sloop, competently assisting young Eli Putnam, Hev Miller, and Matt Brown in setting the sails. They now clustered the bow, watching as the distance between them and the *Saturn* imperceptibly lessened. "Wind's comin' around," someone remarked, and against the dark chop of the sea, white sails unfurled like clouds from the merchantman's masts.

"We'll have 'em," Miller echoed his cousin's words. And to Abigail, "You're saying that wasn't Cottrell who came to Maine at all?"

"I don't think so, no." Abigail clung steadfastly to the nearest line and kept her eye on the sails ahead, grimly pushing away the nauseating dizziness of seasickness that swept her like the heaving waves. "I think what happened was this: probably after considerable searching, Margaret Seaford encountered a man who could pass himself off as Sir Jonathan Cottrell. Whether this happened in England or on the Continent or in Barbados itself, I don't know, but she'd clearly built up a reserve of money by that time and had certainly been keeping track of where Sir Jonathan was stationed in his service to the King. I suspect, but I'm not sure, that at some point she had announced her intention to murder Sir Jonathan in revenge for her beloved sister's death—or that someone who knew the story remarked on it, when she took up the study of poisons. I see no other reason that she would have taken such pains to prove that she was nowhere near him when he was killed—"

"I heard from my mother that she so swore," put in Coldstone. "So it must have been common knowledge."

"Common enough to keep her from returning to her home and having the use of her property, once her revenge was accomplished," said Abigail.

"A woman of deliberation as well as passion," remarked the officer. "A dangerous combination."

"Deliberate enough to learn the finer points of cardsharping as well as poisoning, at any rate," said Abigail. "I trust, by the way, that somebody put aside the contents of my teapot where they can be examined—"

"I instructed your girl to see to it," said Coldstone. "I daresay you shall need to replace the teapot."

"Just as well. 'Twas a wedding-present from my Uncle Tufts; I never liked the thing."

"Then why'd she come after you?" Muldoon wanted to know. "Beggin' your pardon, m'am, Lieutenant . . . What'd you say in that note of yours to Miss Fluckner?"

"I asked Lucy Fluckner about Margaret Sandhayes's movements on the day Sir Jonathan supposedly left Boston," said Abigail. "I included the strictest warning against letting its subject know anything about the matter, but I daresay Mrs. Sandhayes was paying one of the servants to intercept messages from me. She knew I had discovered the well in the cellar, and she may have worried that I would eventually reason out how she could have been instrumental in the murder while attending a ball at the Governor's at the only time it could have been committed. I wonder now whether Palmer knew anything about why he was going to Maine at all. Mrs. Sandhayes was careful about her accomplices—I suspect she herself was 'Toby Elkins' who rented the house. She was certainly the one who attempted to poison me and my family."

"And you think that's why she did for that poor Negro girl?" put in Muldoon. "That the girl saw her, walkin' about in her room wi'out her sticks?"

"It may have been that simple," agreed Abigail. "Or she might have come on some item of her male disguise, or her cache of money . . . Or Mrs. Sandhayes might only have wanted to put out of the way anyone who knew about Pear Tree House and her meetings with Androcles Palmer. A promise of money would be enough to secure a meeting with a slave longing to buy freedom for herself and her babies."

"The way a letter telling Cottrell that there was another claimant to the Fluckner land-grant was enough to bring him to the Dressed Ship Tavern," said Coldstone. "And that lies only a few hundred yards from Pear Tree House. It was undated," he added grimly, "but tucked in the desk in his chamber. Damn!" he added, as the *Magpie* turned to better catch the wind, and Castle Island came into clear view off the starboard.

And Abigail said, "Oh, no—"

The sloop was within half a mile of the little round knoll of rock; the *Saturn*, already past Governor's Island and heading out into open sea. At the end of the Castle wharf, the *Incitatus*, which Abigail had seen only in tight-furled stillness, now swarmed with activity. Like ants, she could see men moving up and down the ladders, and the water around the dark hull bobbed with boats. Beside her, Coldstone had put a glass to his eye. Then he silently passed it to her, and she could see that very little in the way of provisions or water-kegs remained on the wharf.

"No—"

Abigail was aware of Revere's dark gaze, on herself and on Coldstone. Once Harry Knox reached Halifax, there was very little likelihood that three British admirals would be much impressed by tales of conspiracies of revenge. "Have you enough," the silversmith asked Coldstone quietly, "to convince Colonel Leslie to drop the charge?"

Coldstone's eyes met Revere's.

Gently, the silversmith went on, "Or is it the charge of murder that is your Colonel's principle concern?"

Coldstone's lips tightened slightly. "The charge of murder," he replied, "is *my* principle concern. Mr. Miller," he went on, "put about and take us into the Castle."

Twenty-six

The *Magpie* lay at anchor for some four hours at the wharf at Castle Island; Paul Revere and Ben Edes remained prudently belowdecks. In a fog of giddiness and nausea, shivering in her own cloak and Lieutenant Coldstone's, Abigail waited in the brick corridor outside Colonel Leslie's office, listening to the dim murmur of voices within. Muldoon fetched her hot tea and bread-and-butter. She couldn't touch the food, but the tea made her feel better and be damned to Cousin Sam's boycott.

At length Coldstone opened the door and bowed her inside.

"That is certainly an extraordinary accusation you are making, Mrs. Adams." Colonel Leslie frowned at her across his small and scrupulously tidy desk. On the office wall behind him maps of Massachusetts Colony, and of the coastline from Halifax down to Philadelphia, made buff-colored panes against the sooty whitewash; the light from the little window caught a steely gleam from a gorget on top of the cabinet.

"It is indeed, sir," Abigail replied, and was a little surprised, when she inclined her head, that it didn't fall off. "Yet *the guilty flee when no man pursueth*, and if you will but send to the Fluckner house, you will find that Mrs. Margaret Sandhayes took flight without warning this morning, upon reading the note that I sent to Miss Fluckner, which asked after Mrs. Sandhayes's movements on February twenty-fourth—that is, the day on which Sir Jonathan Cottrell supposedly departed for Maine."

And if I'm wrong, thought Abigail wearily, *and the messenger arrives at the Flucknerss' to find Mrs. Sandhayes peacefully taking tea with her hostess . . .*

Her tired mind would pursue the thought no further.

"Supposedly."

"In point of fact," said Abigail, in a voice she usually reserved for reasoning about politics with her Cousin Isaac, "Margaret Sandhayes—by her own admission to me—poisoned Sir Jonathan Cottrell at a house just north of the Boston Common and lowered his body down a well in the cellar, where it was preserved by the cold while her lover, an actor named Androcles Palmer, of stature similar to Cottrell's, traveled in his place to Maine. The previous evening, Palmer and, I think, Sandhayes had accosted Cottrell's servant at the Spancel tavern on School Street and, in the course of dining with him, dosed him with what appears to have been death-cap mushroom. The servant was too ill to join his master aboard ship the following day, and in fact he died two weeks later. When Palmer returned to Boston in the guise of Cottrell, he went, not to the house of his host Governor Hutchinson, but to Pear Tree House, which Mrs. Sandhayes had rented under the name of Toby Elkins, only a few days before Sir Jonathan's arrival in Boston."

The Colonel raised his eyebrows. A youngish man, he was handsome in his way, but Abigail thought he looked tired—as indeed would any man, who had been given the chore of enforcing the King's Law in a town that would have none of it. It was a commonplace in hundreds of pamphlets—including the one Harry Knox had been printing on the night of the murder—to accuse the British of being either knaves or brutes, but in fact Abigail was well aware that Alexander Leslie, second son of the Earl of Leven, was neither.

And while he would certainly have welcomed the opportunity to put a suspected Son of Liberty to the choice of death on the gallows or turning King's Evidence, she didn't think he looked the kind of man to relish going into court against clear evidence of conspiracy with nothing more than a jealous father's trumped-up story about scarves and faces seen providentially by moonlight.

"And this Mrs. Sandhayes—"

A knock sounded on the office door, and a young midshipman put his head through. "Colonel Leslie, sir, Captain asks, with his compliments, will there in fact be a prisoner to transport to Halifax? If we're to be in open water before the tide turns, sir, Captain says, it must be soon."

Leslie held up a finger. "Thank you, Mr. Purfoy, just one moment more—This Mrs. Sandhayes simply asked Sir Jonathan to tea and he went? Drinking tea with a complete stranger in a strange house? And then she admitted as much to you?"

"I had made her angry, sir," replied Abigail. "And as she was holding a pistol on me—by which means she meant to persuade me to drink tea, which I believe I can prove to be poisoned—I suspect she was confident of my later discretion. I am here in your quarters, sir—having never been introduced before—drinking tea, without thought that it contains anything but tea."

"I think you'll find, sir," put in Coldstone, "that the undated letter I found in Sir Jonathan's room concerning questionable title of lands in the Kennebec Grant is written on paper identical to that to be found in the Fluckner household, where Mrs. Sandhayes was staying as a guest."

"Circumstantial evidence."

"As a scarf," inquired Abigail, "claimed found by an employee of a man who would like to see Harry Knox shipped away to Canada, is not?"

"I myself can vouch for the authenticity of the tea in question, Colonel," added Coldstone. "I entered the house and sealed the pot with my signet ring, and am confident that its contents are in fact lethal."

One corner of Colonel Leslie's mouth turned sharply down; he glanced over at the midshipman, still standing in the doorway. "My compliments to Captain Dashwood," he said. "Please let him know that he is free to make sail at his earliest convenience. There will be no further passengers at this time."

Abigail was heartily glad that she was the only American present. The Colonel of the Sixty-Fourth would not have taken kindly to the war-whoop of joy that would have greeted these words had any of the contingent still on the *Magpie* been privileged to hear them.

"And I have spoken to Lieutenant Dowling," added Coldstone, when the middy had gone. "Upon my request, he has just reexamined Sir Jonathan's body—which has been kept preserved in one of the post stores-depots, as the ground has been too frozen for burial. He says that the torso is certainly bruised beneath the arms, as if a thickly padded rope or line had been passed around it, to hold it suspended. Likewise, he attests that the discoloration of the extremities, which he took to be the result of cold, is consonant with *livor mortis*, in a body so suspended, and that the abrasions on the corpse's head and hands could easily have been produced as the result of convulsions caused by certain types of poison."

"She said," murmured Abigail, "that she did not wish Sir Jonathan to die swiftly. It appears that he did not."

It took another hour of arguing, however, to convince Colonel Leslie to release Harry Knox on a bond and let him return to Boston on the *Magpie* pending confirmation of Abigail's story. As Abigail emerged from the office, almost shaking with exhaustion, she heard behind her the Colonel's voice: "You will change your coat, Lieutenant, bullet-hole or no bullet-hole in your shoulder, and return to Boston this evening. And if you find the Sandhayes woman at the Fluckners' after all, so help me I shall have Mr. Knox and Mrs. Adams clapped in irons, and yourself as well!"

As the *Magpie* put to sea again—Charley and Tommy sleeping like tired puppies with their heads on Abigail's lap—Harry Knox dropped onto the bench beside her and whispered, "Thank you, Mrs. Adams." He looked like he'd lost a good ten pounds during his incarceration and had neither bathed nor shaved in that time, nor, Abigail guessed, slept much. "I cannot—there are no words. Thank you." He reached to clasp her hand, then drew back his own filthy one; from a pocket Abigail produced one of the several clean handkerchiefs that motherhood had taught her to always have upon her person, and draped it over her palm. Harry smiled—probably for the first time in two weeks—and gripped her fingers with a thankfulness that almost cracked the bones.

Dusk was gathering when Abigail finally reached her own kitchen again. Pattie, emerging from the cowhouse with a pail and a half of milk, cried, "Mrs. Adams!" and from the back door burst not only Johnny and Nabby, but John, Philomela, and, gorgeous as a peony among demure New England herbs, Lucy Fluckner.

"My God, Nab!" John cried, as the older children fell upon her, and Charley—just set on his feet by Paul Revere—said proudly, "We was in the mob!"

"Are you all right?"

"I'm well," she said, half crushed by his embrace, "I'm well—did you at least free Mrs. Teasel from jail?"

"I did indeed—having proved the murder on her husband's brother, who wanted to secure the property to himself before Teasel married again. The scoundrel cleared up his own tracks in the house but not those of his dog—"

"Mrs. Sandhayes has disappeared," cried Lucy, "and we found her walking-sticks here in Mr. Adams's parlor, and a *bullet* lodged in the paneling, and Pattie says there was shooting, and a fire, and a mob, and the British—" She broke off with a gasp, as the men who'd escorted Abigail back to the house moved aside, and Harry Knox stepped into the yard. "HARRY!!!"

Lucy flung herself into his arms, lice, jail-filth, and all, and buried her face in his shoulder. "Oh, Harry!" And was enfolded in a massive embrace and a blissful and reeking kiss.

"What happened, Nab?" asked John, taking her hand to lead her into the kitchen. "Miss Fluckner has been back and forth three times this afternoon, and Pattie was only able to tell me—and her—that Mrs. Sandhayes was here, waiting for you . . . and knows nothing further of what befell. But it appears that your Lieutenant Coldstone has put the teapot under seal . . ."

"I hope you left it so!"

"Good Lord, yes! The cups as well, which were set aside with a note from him to be left precisely *in situ*—"

"I knew I could trust my Lysander." Despite seasickness and fatigue so great she felt almost faint, Abigail managed a smile as John tucked a loose strand of her disordered hair behind her ear. "The Lieutenant—and he is not *my* Lieutenant—will undoubtedly arrive in the morning to impound pot, cups, tea, and all, and test them for poison. Lucy, dearest"—she turned back in the doorway—"perhaps you had best return home and inventory everything Mrs. Sandhayes left behind her before Lieutenant Coldstone gets there. I'm sure a look into her trunks will be instructive."

John's face, which had been smiling, turned suddenly sober as he loosened the arm which he'd put around her waist: "What's this?"

Abigail felt her side where his hand had been, just beneath her lowest rib. There was a short, straight gash in her bodice where Mrs. Sandhayes's bullet had passed, the edges of the cloth, and the sturdy corset beneath, charred with powder.

Charley turned to Johnny with reprehensible smugness and announced, "We had 'n *adventure*!"

Quietly, Abigail agreed, "To be sure we did."

Morning brought a note from Lieutenant Coldstone, by the hand of Sergeant Muldoon, begging her pardon for the inconvenience and requesting that the sealed teapot be turned over to the bearer, along with the contents of each teacup, placed in separate clean jars and labeled, as well as she could recall, as to which cup had been Mrs. Sandhayes's and which Abigail's guest had poured out for her.

I fear I cannot call myself, as I will spend the great part of the day dragging the marshes for the bodies of Palmer and Bathsheba, as you suggested. Be assured that I will wait upon you at my earliest convenience.

Abigail—who knew quite well which teacup was her own because it had for years been slightly discolored—obeyed the instructions with care, and sealed up the clean herb-jars, with labels signed by herself, John, and Sergeant Muldoon as witnesses. John remarked, "'Tis the act of a man who knows he has a case."

Calling that afternoon on Lucy Fluckner, she was greeted by Mr. Barnaby's stilted assurance that, *Miss Fluckner is unable to receive callers, m'am*, and was intercepted in half a block by Philomela, wrapped hastily in her mistress's red cloak. "I doubt you'll ever be welcome in the house again, m'am, begging your pardon," panted the servant. "Mr. Fluckner is in a fearful taking, to the point that I'm actually worried—I've never seen a white man turn that color! Mr. Knox has asked for Miss Lucy's hand in marriage, and Miss Lucy says she'll have him or none."

"Hardly the best time to make the request, of course."

Philomela half smiled. "M'am, meaning no disrespect, there will be no best time for that, not if everyone were to wait 'til Judgment Day. Miss Lucy said to tell you that we went through Mrs. Sandhayes's luggage and room last night, and found her trunk had a false bottom. Beneath it were a man's things—boots, coat, waistcoat, wig—and nearly five hundred pounds in sovereigns, all of it British, such as we found in Sheba's room. There were bottles and packets there, too, of what Miss Lucy said was probably poison. And there was this."

She held out a slim roll of drawing-paper, which, unfastened, displayed the image of an extremely pretty girl of about Lucy Fluckner's age. The sketch was a rough one, only shadowy suggestions marking the cloud of hair and the lace of her chemise, but the vividness of her smile was captured there for all time, the dancing light in her eyes. Around her throat was Margaret Sandhayes's Medusa cameo. On another part of the page the artist—whoever it had been—had sketched a blocky little church-spire and part of a churchyard, labeled St. Onesimus's. A scribbled note in one corner marked the date: June 1765.

Margaret's only weakness, Coldstone had said. For one instant, Abigail seemed to hear the giggles of two irrepressible sisters, over the parson's mispronunciation of *concupiscence.*

And a little of her rage at the woman turned to sadness, as she understood.

If Mrs. Sandhayes followed Sir Jonathan across the whole of the ocean on purpose to kill him," asked Pattie later, as she was clearing up after dinner, "why did she come *here* to do it? Could she not have done so just as easy in Barbados?"

Abigail, gathering up the remains of the pork pie, glanced across at John and raised her eyebrows. She guessed what the answer might be but was curious as to how he would see the matter.

"Bridgetown isn't much of a place," said John. "I suspect she thought society too small on the island, and herself too noticeable. Perhaps the opportunity simply did not present itself. By the time she reached the island, Cottrell may have already had orders to go on to Boston, and Margaret Seaford thought her chances for not only killing him, but getting clean away, were better in a larger city, with all the continent to flee to if need be. Does that sound right to you, Portia?"

"It does," said Abigail. "But I had thought also, that while she was forming plans to accomplish her vengeance in Bridgetown, word reached them both of the dumping of the tea. She had acquired Palmer as a tool by that time—a means of duplicating Cottrell's appearance so as to tamper with the apparent time of her victim's death—but whether she knew at that time that New England winters get cold enough to preserve a man's body, I don't know. She certainly could have," she added thoughtfully. "Heaven knows we're known for it. And while she couldn't have known she would find a house with a well in its cellar, that isn't the only fashion in which a body could be frozen, by any means."

"Yes." Pattie frowned, and spread towels on the table to do the dishes. "But she couldn't have known Sir Jonathan was going to Maine, or that he'd get engaged to Miss Fluckner."

"She didn't," Abigail agreed. "Thank you, John—" She stepped back as he settled the basin, then drew near the rag and the gourd of soft-soap. "But even a moderately intelligent woman could have figured out that given Cottrell's mission here—and the fact that Boston is known to be crawling with men who hate the King—'twould be surprising if the man weren't murdered, and the Sons of Liberty could take the blame. As indeed one did."

"And she'd have let an innocent man die." Pattie shook her head wonderingly. She was, Abigail reflected, really very young.

"That is the Mark of the Beast, Pattie," said John, "that

the Reverend Cooper spoke of: the conviction that one's own cause is sufficiently righteous to justify crimes against the innocent. Once a man, or a woman, takes that mark on the forehead—their thought—and their right hand with which a person acts, their hearts are altered, and it becomes very hard for them to go back to what they were. As I think our friend Mrs. Sandhayes will learn."

Abigail had not thought to see the Lieutenant—nor hear the results of his search of the Mill-Pond and the river—for several days, but as she and Nabby were drying the last of the dishes, a knock sounded on the front door. As Pattie hurried out into the hall, John said, only half in jest, "And if that's a squad from Colonel Leslie come to arrest you after all—"

"Lieutenant Coldstone, m'am."

"You may let Mr. Knox know," he told her, "that he need have no further concern for his position vis-à-vis the law, in the matter of Sir Jonathan Cottrell's death. Thurlow Apthorp has identified the coat and waistcoat that Miss Fluckner found hidden in Margaret Sandhayes's luggage as belonging to the so-called Toby Elkins, and in the pocket of the coat we found Sir Jonathan's missing memorandum-book. The final entry was dated the twenty-first of February, the day before his intended departure for Maine. Moreover, when we brought up the body of Androcles Palmer from the Mill-Pond, Sir Jonathan's signet ring was in his waistcoat pocket." In the chilly pallor of the spring evening—lingering bright in the parlor window—he looked tired to death, and haggard, as if his strapped and bandaged arm was paining him. Though it was clear to Abigail he'd cleaned his boots (or had Sergeant Muldoon clean them) before appearing on her doorstep, flecks of marsh-mud clung to his snow-white trousers in places, and to the sleeve of his crimson coat.

"And did you find Bathsheba's body?" asked John. It was the first time John had come to join one of Abigail's conferences with Coldstone in the parlor: generally, since the dumping of the tea, when the British officer came to the house, it was the signal for John to disappear. If the Lieutenant had any instructions regarding John's arrest for sedition, he didn't mention them. Perhaps Colonel Leslie knew no redcoat with a prisoner would make it back to the wharves, particularly after Harry's arrest had caught the Sons off-guard on a Sunday morning. Perhaps, after a long, cold day on the marshes, Coldstone was simply too tired to try.

"We did," said Coldstone, and by the way he said *we*, Abigail guessed he and Muldoon had had plenty of help from the Sons of Liberty. "Because iced water is in fact somewhat colder than ice itself, the body, though waterlogged, is not decomposed at all; there was no question of her identity. She bore no mark of violence, so we must assume her to have been lured to Pear Tree House and poisoned as well."

"That would have been on the day she disappeared, would it not?" asked Abigail. "That was the day that Miss Fluckner slipped away from her guardian to meet Mr. Knox."

"Given her father's anger over that," mused John, "no wonder nobody asked Mrs. Sandhayes's whereabouts." He glanced across at Coldstone, sipping the coffee that Pattie had quietly brought in on a tray. "Was Palmer poisoned as well?"

"Mr. Palmer," said Coldstone, "had been shot through the body, at so close a range as to burn his clothing." For a time he was silent, gazing at the last of the spring sunlight in the parlor window, his good hand stretched to the warmth of the fire.

"Was he as like Sir Jonathan Cottrell as all that?" asked Abigail curiously. "Or is it no longer possible to tell?"

"That I do not know. I suppose the only ones who saw both of them in life were Cottrell's valet Fenton and Bathsheba. And Margaret Sandhayes herself, of course."

"So what will happen now?" asked Abigail at length. "Who handles a murder done in the colonies, if the murderess flees to Britain? Can a letter be sent—?"

"What happens now?" There was a chill note of anger in the young officer's voice, and his features had the look of a Praxiteles statue that has bitten into a lemon. "Nothing, Mrs. Adams. 'Tis not only Colonel Leslie who has learned to distrust Boston witnesses. Were I to send the depositions from you, and Mr. Adams, and Mssrs. Brown and Miller, and all the others to a British Court, do you really think any English magistrate would so much as read them? A barrister's clerk could tear them to pieces in minutes."

Abigail stared. "But it wasn't only Cottrell she killed! The woman murdered Fenton, and Bathsheba, and Palmer in cold blood—"

"An actor and two servants." Coldstone shook his head. "Colonel Leslie will write to Whitehall, and I shall send the facts of the case to my friends in Bow Street, for all the good it is likely to do. But if Margaret Sandhayes is taken at all, I doubt she will even be tried. And for that," he added bitterly, "you may thank the politics of this country, and the late actions of defiance that your townsmen have chosen to pursue."

"May we thank those actions, Lieutenant?" John leaned his shoulder against the chimney breast. "Or the *re*action of your government *to* those actions? My experience—and my studies in the histories of empires—lead me to conclude that it takes two to make a quarrel. Justice is justice, and does not—or should not—read the political newspapers."

Coldstone sighed and looked aside. "You are right, sir. And I speak in anger that a woman who caused so much harm—not to speak of putting a bullet through my shoulder—should escape in the smoke and confusion of a general insurrection."

"I doubt she will escape." John bent to the fire and tonged up a coal for his pipe. "Like Hamlet's mother, her punishment must be left to Heaven . . . as indeed the Queen of Denmark's was, and was speedily accomplished nevertheless." Red reflection flickered deep in his eyes. "I suspect in time Margaret Sandhayes will bring other punishment upon herself, through acquiring the habit of thinking that she can kill with impunity . . . even as the man she pursued had come to feel that he could rape without penalty. Rather than sacrificing all for vengeance, she took a great deal of trouble to make sure that she could return to England unprosecuted, but I doubt she will find it quite so simple as she thinks, to return to her old life, with the Mark of the Beast on her forehead and her hand."

"What does one do, I wonder," murmured Abigail, "when one has lived for something for eight years, striven toward it without thought of anything else . . . and then achieved it. She was a brilliant strategist, but it seems to me that she turned the whole of her life into a psalm of vengeance for her sister. Where does one go from there?"

"I have often wondered the same," replied the officer, "about your patriots, Mrs. Adams." He turned his pale blue eyes to John's face, rubbed unconsciously at his aching arm. "Have you, Mr. Adams, or your cousin, or Mr. Knox, or Mr. Revere, or any of those others, even thought about what sort of world you would create, or *can* create, if you teach your followers—and yourselves—that violence is the best answer to a political question? Can those who learn this lesson do other than continue to perpetuate it by force rather than law?"

John said nothing. From the kitchen, Abigail heard the friendly rumble of Sergeant Muldoon's voice and the laughter of Pattie and the children.

"I suppose," she replied after a moment, "that is something we shall all soon see."

Author's Note

Harry Knox and Lucy Fluckner were married in June of 1774. In April of 1775, a British regiment attempted to seize a colonial powder-store hidden at Concord, Massachusetts, some seventeen miles from Boston, an event that triggered the American Revolution. In the wake of the battles of Lexington and Concord, the British retreated to Boston and were besieged by a makeshift force of colonists camped on the mainland. Harry and Lucy Knox sneaked across the British lines to join the American forces, Lucy concealing Harry's military sword, the story goes, in the lining of her cloak.

Thomas and Hannah Fluckner remained in Boston, still under siege by the colonial army, until March of the following year. In the dead of winter, Harry Knox led a small force of men to bring sixty British cannon three hundred miles through the snow from the captured British forts at Crown Point and Ticonderoga in the Hudson Valley—guns that comprised the colonial army's first artillery, without which

General Washington could never have driven the British from Boston. With the British evacuation of Boston, on March 17, 1776, the Fluckner family—along with hundreds of other Americans who remained loyal to the Crown—were passengers on the British ships that carried the British Army out of Boston. This ended the New England phase of the conflict. Lucy's parents subsequently crossed to England and never saw their daughter again.

Harry Knox was promoted to Major General, and Lucy—cheerfully bearing an ever-increasing brood of babies—followed him from camp to camp for eight years of war, "fat, lively, and somewhat interfering," renowned for dancing even that inveterate rug-cutter George Washington to a breathless standstill. After the war, as the only member of the Fluckner family not deemed a "traitor," Lucy was awarded the whole of her father's Maine lands—several million acres—where she and Harry built an enormous mansion and lived with their many children in baronial splendor. Harry Knox, who during the war founded the United States' first officer-training school at the age of twenty-eight, went on to become George Washington's first Secretary of War. Fort Knox and the city of Knoxville, Tennessee, are named after this extraordinary man. He died of peritonitis resulting from a swallowed chicken bone in 1806 at the age of fifty-six.